Readers Love I

An Earlier Heaven

"I really loved *An Earlier Heaven* and I think you guys will too! The pace is slow and steady, indicative of the day to day domesticity of their family. Yet, the plot with Cory is wonderful and heartbreaking, and I found myself growing to love him just as I had William, David, and Jerry. If you love family stories, be sure to pick this up. It is a treat!"
—Reviews by Jessewave

"I loved this book…. Mr. Marchwell develops such wonderful characters you just don't want to leave them behind when a book ends."
—Mrs. Condit & Friends Read Books

"While some parts of this story will have you close to tears, there are even more times when you will have to keep from laughing out loud. An Earlier Heaven is a wonderful story and one not to be missed."
—Top 2 Bottom Reviews

When Memory Falls

"I think this story has a bit of everything in it to make it worth your while to read and most of all it has a Happy Ever After."
—MM Good Book Reviews

Roots and Wings

"Reading a book like this reminds us that life is meant to be lived and that there are bumps in the road. We see that love helps us get through. I enjoyed this because it made my own problems seem unimportant."
—Reviews by Amos Lassen

By D.W. MARCHWELL

NOVELS

Falling
Pictures on Silence
Sins of the Father
A Still, Small Voice
When Memory Falls

GOOD TO KNOW SERIES
Good to Know
An Earlier Heaven
Roots and Wings

Published by DREAMSPINNER PRESS
http://www.dreamspinnerpress.com

Pictures
on
Silence

D.W. Marchwell

Dreamspinner Press

Published by
Dreamspinner Press
5032 Capital Circle SW
Suite 2, PMB# 279
Tallahassee, FL 32305-7886
USA
http://www.dreamspinnerpress.com/

Pictures on Silence
© 2013 D.W. Marchwell.

Cover Art
© 2013 Maria Fanning.
Cover content is for illustrative purposes only and any person depicted on the cover is a model.

ISBN: 978-1-62798-386-0
Digital ISBN: 978-1-62798-385-3

Printed in the United States of America
First Edition
December 2013

For Diane Berger,
who taught me how to do seventeen
things at once!

Chapter 1

"A painter paints his pictures on canvas.
But musicians paint their pictures on silence."
(Leopold Stokowski)

BARKLEY REINHARDT stood at the foot of his parents' graves in Mount Pleasant Cemetery, his hand absentmindedly petting the fur and ruffling the left ear of Mozart, the three-legged dog at his side. The other mutt, Salieri, was on lookout duty. He was sitting on his haunches, his ears perked, his head swiveling in the direction of all the sounds he'd spent so many years running away from. "It's okay, Salieri," Barkley soothed again and again. "You're safe. I've got you."

He'd been visiting these graves once a week since his parents died within a year of each other. First his father, four years ago, and then his mother. Well, he tried to visit them, but his career took him away from Toronto and to just about every corner of the globe on a very regular basis. Barkley had tried to make at least a monthly visit during those busy times when he'd been booked months and even years in advance by some of the most well-known opera houses in the world. But he had not always managed it. It was always a relief to come home to Toronto, to his condo on Merton Street, near the cemetery where'd he laid his parents to rest. He wished, even now all these years later, that he'd be able to bury his guilt one day, but he knew it wouldn't be any time soon.

Barkley Reinhardt was the only child of two parents who were dedicated and loving people. They were also music teachers in the public school system of Toronto. They'd sacrificed many things to provide everything for their son: piano and violin lessons when he'd been in school and then voice lessons when he'd been "discovered" by one of his professors at the university. He'd enrolled in the University of Toronto as a piano major, never having really enjoyed playing the violin, but eventually changed his major to voice when Professor Berger had contacted his parents, explaining that a voice like their son's came along only once in a generation.

That had been ten years ago. Barkley was now almost thirty years old and had been receiving mixed reviews for his performances and his recordings for the last two years. He was still fulfilling all of his contracts, some signed years before, but was not accepting any new engagements. A few of his contracts had actually been cancelled by the houses that had booked him, the same houses that had once seemed so eager to have him perform one of his many signature roles. Barkley hadn't cared, though, since they had had to pay him anyway. When his then-agent, the premier agent for classical artists, had questioned those directors seeking to opt out of having Barkley perform, the answer was always the same: There were fewer and fewer conductors willing to work with Barkley Reinhardt.

And so, at the age of twenty-nine, Barkley figured his career was over. As he looked down at the names on the stone markers he'd paid a hefty price to commemorate the parents who'd given so freely and unselfishly, he found that he wasn't disappointed that his singing career was over. The condo was paid for—in fact, on the advice of his manager, he'd bought the entire building when it had come up for sale—he had enough money to last at least his lifetime, and his life would no longer consist of obeying flight schedules and rehearsal calls; nor would it involve having to tolerate the overbearing and dominating personalities of conductors or tenors or sopranos who felt that they were the real reason the seats would be filled during each of the performances. Besides, he'd found a much more important calling for his life now. He looked down at his two precious babies and smiled. "Not really babies, are you, boys?" He smiled at Mozart and Salieri, the two rescue dogs he'd saved from being euthanized at the local shelter.

On the day after a benefit performance for the newly elected mayor of Toronto, Barkley had been on vocal rest and, out of sheer boredom, was surfing the internet, mindlessly clicking from one image to another as he'd done a million times before. But this day, unlike all of those other attempts to alleviate boredom, Barkley had ended up clicking on a story about the funeral of a courageous soldier killed during an enemy bombing in Afghanistan. The use of only the soldier's last name, without anything to signify rank, in the title of the article had, at first, struck Barkley as incredibly disrespectful. But when he clicked through, he discovered that while the article did feature the brave soldier and all he'd done for his country, the article's title, "Hunter says goodbye," referred to the sergeant's loyal dog of eleven years. And within moments of seeing pictures of the beautiful black-and-white Siberian Husky sitting at attention beside his dead master's casket and reading about how the sergeant had rescued Hunter from a sad and lonely life on the streets, Barkley was sobbing uncontrollably.

There were, of course, links to the stories about other animals on that same webpage. Some of the stories were inspirational and some of them featured pleas from the public to help animals that had been beaten, tortured, abused, neglected, or lost. With each new article Barkley became more and more saddened and enraged, feeling helpless, confused, and angry with himself; he'd been so focused on himself that he'd never bothered to notice all of this needless suffering. The feelings of helplessness turned over and over in his brain as a plan had started to form. He had the money, he had the time, and now he had the motivation. He knew what he had to do. He had a new purpose in his life.

"That's when I met you two beautiful babies, isn't it?" Barkley asked of the two mutts. Mozart sat up and licked Barkley's hand while Salieri barked once, probably sounding the all clear, Barkley assumed. Barkley felt his knees protest as he stood up. "And Tinkerbell and Princess and Marco and Butter." Mozart barked once and Barkley laughed, bending to plant a kiss on the dog's snout and then leaning over to plant one on Salieri's. They were one big, crazy, temporary family now. Barkley, three mutts, including Mozart and Salieri and a six-month-old diabetic puppy named Butter, a two-month-old blind cat named Tinkerbell, a nine-year-old Flemish Giant named Princess, and a three-month-old Abyssinian guinea pig called Marco. "Time for lunch and then naps, huh? Should we go see if Princess and Tinkerbell are still getting along?"

Barkley found himself laughing as he thought of Princess, the twenty-pound rabbit who did not like her personal space invaded unless she invited you to do so, and Tinkerbell, the blind eight-pound Tortie who had the worst case of ADHD Barkley had ever seen. He shook his head as he thought back to those first few weeks when he had had to spend almost every moment playing mediator to his blended family. Mozart and Salieri were never a problem, but Princess and Tinkerbell required quite a bit of supervision. And sweet little Butter, with her beautiful eyes of two different colors, would just bounce back and forth between Princess and Tinkerbell wondering why all of the commotion wasn't leading to playtime. Barkley shook his head again, suddenly missing his precious brood of misfits.

Barkley said goodbye to his parents, promising to return again next week, and made his way down the winding paths to Yonge Street, his two loyal companions at his side. He spoke softly, reassuring Mozart and Salieri that the noises of the street weren't anything to fear anymore, but he kept himself between them and the street anyway. He led the two mutts on the short trip north one block to his condo on Merton Street, always conscious of what was around or near the dogs, still fearful that one of them would get spooked and try to run away. It hadn't happened in the two months since he'd rescued them, but he still didn't want to take any chances.

He'd bought the building on Merton several years before his parents died, thinking at the time that it seemed like a good investment decision: why not buy a condo building in one of the hottest neighborhoods in Toronto? It had seemed like a bad omen at the time to buy a building so near a cemetery, but now he was glad. He was together with his parents again, just as he should have been, instead of jetting around the world. *No*, he said to himself as he turned onto the street he'd called home now for more than eight years, *I won't mistake fame for something worthwhile ever again. And I certainly won't miss it.* He was reminded why while he waited at the crosswalk, two young teenagers, each with a skateboard, a few feet behind him. Barkley was on his haunches, petting and congratulating Mozart and Salieri for being such well-behaved pooches. He turned when he heard the teenagers get closer and offered a smile.

Barkley was a tall, well-built man and didn't worry about people around him—or even behind him—but years of having photographers and fans accosting him, anywhere they wanted, had made him keep track of his surroundings. It was a precaution he'd adopted. And now that he was responsible for these two beautiful mutts, he was even more on guard than usual.

"That's that singer that lost it," one of the boys said. Barkley smiled, the sardonic and patient smile he'd learned long ago when listening to people who didn't have all the facts and didn't care if they ever did. Barkley ignored the comment and stood, still bending over to pet the dogs. For boys like the ones behind him, accuracy of information was no more important than possessing manners that prevented them from speaking about someone behind his back.

"Who?" his friend asked, not even bothering to whisper.

"You know, dude, that singer who lost it and pushed that chick into the band pit."

Band pit? He wondered what students learned these days. Was every collection of instruments a "band"? Barkley resisted the urge to turn around and point out, yet again, that he had actually been nowhere near the soprano when she'd tripped over her ridiculously long scarf and fallen into the pit. But the news organizations hadn't bothered to mention that, preferring instead to sensationalize the whole affair as some sort of rivalry between two of the biggest stars of opera finally coming to blows. Even the conductor had been quoted as saying that Barkley and Nikki Barnett, the lyric soprano du jour, were utmost professionals, and that the whole situation had been blown all out of proportion. Then again, who listened to conductors these days? Certainly not the same media who would wait for hours for a compromising photograph of some teenage movie star who probably was drinking to forget about how her life wasn't her own anymore or of some too-young pop sensation who'd come to realize—too late—that fame really wasn't anything worthwhile.

Mozart and Salieri lifted themselves from their sitting positions, ready for the last few yards before they would be home. The light changed to green and the two teenagers skated past Barkley on their boards, the taller of the two turning around, laughing, and pointing. "Dude, look at the fucking dog, man. He's a tripod!"

Barkley smiled and thought of pointing out, quickly, that the young man's board would probably catch on the lip of the sidewalk, but continued walking instead. When the young man did fall like a sack of potatoes and his buddy did nothing but laugh, Barkley took the opportunity to point out, "See? Sometimes people fall with*out* being pushed."

The young man said nothing in return except to cuss and swear at his friend for just standing there. If anything more was said, Barkley did not hear it; he was busy planning out the rest of his week. He had to visit Whispering Pines as well as check in with the local shelters for any more high-needs animals that might need saving. "Okay, boys," Barkley said to Mozart and Salieri as he unhooked their leads. "You've got a couple of minutes before lunch. Who wants to play fetch?" The dogs barked in unison, their stances rigid and waiting as Barkley pulled a thick piece of rope out of his pocket. As he always did, he feigned throwing to the right and watched Salieri take off. Barkley then threw the rope to the left, allowing Mozart one of his few chances at actually being able to get the rope before his brother. "Go on, Motzie, get it before your brother figures it out." Barkley smiled to himself as he watched the two run free on the lawn.

DUNCAN SPENCER hated his boss with a passion. Actually, to say that he hated him would imply that he thought enough of him to summon up some sort of emotion. And Duncan liked to think that he had better things to do than to waste any kind of emotion on a complete and total fool like Thomas Middleton. Perhaps Thomas had been a good editor in his day, and perhaps he'd even had the respect of the journalism community, but not for the past ten years at least. Duncan found him to be overweight, overbearing, and overextended in terms of his ability to assign stories.

Another goddamn fluff piece about some singer who travelled first class and had never lost a night's sleep over what real life is actually like. Duncan's thoughts, as usual, were on his latest "assignment" and not on what his editor was saying. These were the worst moments of Duncan's job. When he was actually writing or when he was doing the research and making contacts—contacts he hoped would one day lead to his reentry into the world of serious journalism—Duncan was much happier than sitting here and listening to some pompous half-wit telling him how to write a story. A story about some opera singer who'd squandered away the opportunities mingling with the wealthy elites of every major city in the world would have brought his way. No, Duncan was not really in any kind of mood to hear how he should treat the guy with kid gloves and make him look as good as possible.

"Didn't this guy just announce his retirement?" Duncan knew asking the question would mean sitting here longer, but he wanted to get a good idea of how seriously he should take this assignment. With any luck, he could be at home and working his way through a fifth of bourbon before dinnertime.

"Last week," Thomas said, the look on his face daring Duncan to interrupt him again. "His last public performance won't be for another eight months."

"How the hell do you retire after only nine years?" Duncan flipped his spiral notebook closed, not having written anything down since he'd not bothered to listen to his editor. "Guy must be fuckin' loaded if he sings for nine years and then retires." Duncan sat there, shaking his head for a moment. "I sure as shit picked the wrong line of work," he muttered to himself.

"Anyway," the half-wit said. Duncan recognized that one word; it meant that Thomas was getting tired of being interrupted. And if Duncan had had any respect for the loser, he would have shut his mouth and started listening.

"So why are we doing this piece now? I mean, if the guy isn't retiring for another year...." Duncan tossed the folder back on Thomas's desk and shrugged, hoping his editor wouldn't press this point. It had never worked so far, but that didn't mean that Duncan should give up.

Thomas picked up the folder and tossed it back at Duncan, fixing him with a very tired expression. "Because I'm telling you to do it now." Thomas sat back down in his chair and folded his hands over his ample belly. "Of course, if you're not interested, I'll be happy to accept your resignation."

Fuck, yeah, you'd love that wouldn't you, you prick? Duncan was under no illusions. If he ever wanted another shot at getting back into serious journalism, like he'd had before his fall from grace, he knew he would have to keep taking these crappy assignments until the one moment, that single moment he needed to get back to the real reporting. But the salt in this particular wound was sitting right in front of him. Thomas knew that Duncan would keep taking his shit, not to mention these ridiculous assignments, as long as he needed the money.

"He's agreed to meeting at his place, but had a clause added to the contract." Thomas fixed Duncan with that stare—the one that Duncan always figured a constipated pit bull would have. "No photos and no references to where his condo is."

"Fuck," Duncan spat. "Half the city knows who this guy is, knows where he lives."

"Then we'll just make sure the other half doesn't find out. Okay?" Thomas's smirk made Duncan want to jump over the desk and shove the folder down his throat.

Duncan put the folder and his notebook in his messenger bag and stood up, smiling for his editor. Maybe he didn't have any power in this particular situation, but he wasn't about to let the half-wit know that he'd put Duncan Spencer in his place. As he reached the door, Duncan turned back to look at Thomas.

"Deadline?"

"I want to see it before the deadline," Thomas said icily. "I want your outline by next Friday."

Outline? What is this, high school? Duncan offered his editor a thank you and opened the door, leaving it open behind him on purpose. Fucking blimp could use the exercise anyway, Duncan thought as he looked at his watch and decided the bourbon couldn't wait any longer. Of course, it was Duncan who couldn't wait any longer, but those were the kinds of distinctions that Duncan never really paid much attention to. *And the kind that got your ass in this mess to begin with*, the nagging voice in his head said. He tried to ignore that voice—and succeeded most of the time—but it did have a way of creeping up on him.

He was halfway to the subway station when he realized that if he went to meet this guy tonight, he could spend twenty minutes with him, start on the story, and have plenty of time to go back to his crappy apartment to get a few shots of bourbon *and* still be on time to pick up some hot young thing who didn't have a problem with getting fucked by a daddy with an attitude.

Duncan dismissed that little voice in his head that told him he wouldn't like himself in the morning and ran to the other platform to head north to see if he could charm the has-been singer into meeting with him tonight. Duncan could worry about not liking himself tomorrow, or Sunday, even.

WITH THE two mutts in tow, Barkley walked into his building after having made a pit stop at the little mom-and-pop grocery store across the street to buy some ice cream. He'd returned from the last performance of his recital series two nights ago and had been a very good boy by avoiding all dairy and caffeine products, just as his voice teacher, Diane, had always told him. It hadn't been hard to forego the ice cream; he'd been in too much of a rush to head out to the various shelters to pick up his little brood of animals. But this evening he had nothing to do but curl up with a good book or finally watch a few of the movies he had recorded on PVR while he was away and eat the pint of mocha almond he bought that would be soft enough to eat in about ten minutes' time. His little menagerie would be sleeping or sitting quietly while Barkley enjoyed some time alone. He would fill up the bowls with a little midnight snack and water for his babies, then go have a shower and read until he was too tired to keep his eyes open anymore. And as he nodded to the doorman, Charles, Barkley figured he might just do the whole routine again tomorrow, except maybe tomorrow he would try a different flavor of ice cream. Maybe something with caramel or fudge. Charles nodded and squatted down to say "hi" to the mutts, and Barkley beamed with pride at how well behaved his two boys were.

Barkley herded Mozart and Salieri into the elevator and they ascended to his condo on the twentieth floor. He was pleased he had the elevator to himself, and when the doors opened, he turned left and stopped right in his tracks, not ten feet from his condo and the perfect evening alone with his new, if temporary, family.

"Mr. Reinhardt?"

Barkley saw the man advancing. By instinct, Barkley leaned over and, with his left hand, grabbed Salieri's collar; he was the barker, the one who wasn't always fond of strangers. He had to give the stranger credit; he didn't let Salieri's posture scare him. The good-looking—in a disheveled, rebellious sort of way—man had a smile on his face. Barkley was used to seeing that kind of smile on some of the other singers he'd worked with over the years. It was a smile that said *I'm better than you and we both know it* and *I'm only doing this for my image* all at the same time. Barkley was very well acquainted with the look.

"Yes. And you are?"

"Duncan Spencer," the man said, giving Barkley's hand a vigorous shake. "I'm with *The Communiqué?*"

Barkley pulled his hand back and motioned to his door, the one that Duncan had been waiting beside. Barkley suddenly found himself wondering how Duncan had managed to get past Charles. "Of course," he said, without smiling. "I thought someone would call to warn me about this appointment."

"Yeah, look, I'm sorry about that, but my editor just dropped this on me, and he wants some sort of first draft by next Friday, so…."

"I repeat, I thought someone would call." Barkley herded his boys toward the door and shoved the key in the lock and wondered if this man was hard of hearing. *Your editor inconveniences you and that means you can show up unannounced?* "How long were you planning on staying?"

"I was hoping to get enough information to figure out my slant," Duncan said as he wiped his hands on his jeans. "Maybe twenty minutes?"

"Slant?"

"How I'm going to approach the story, you know. What kind of point of view I'll present in the piece."

"Do you have a copy of the contract with you?" Barkley opened the door, shooed the dogs inside, and stood at the threshold, waiting while Duncan searched through his messenger bag. Barkley glanced inside as he put the bag with the ice cream on the small entrance table. He was prepared for Tinkerbell's one hundredth escape attempt. He caught movement out of the corner of his eye and squatted quickly to catch the blind cat under the ribs, hoisting her up for a quick kiss or two. He smiled as Tinkerbell protested yet another capture. "It's okay, sweetie, we'll be going to see John on the weekend, and then you can run around all you want." Losing his smile, Barkley turned to the reporter. "Well, you might as well come in so I don't have everyone running into the hallway." Barkley stood aside as he let the reporter pass, then leaned over to let Tinkerbell run amok within the safe haven of the condo. Barkley closed the door and turned back to the handsome, flustered man who was still searching for a copy of the contract.

Duncan seemed to be losing his patience, and that would have been fine with Barkley; he'd never wanted to do this interview anyway. It had been his former agent's idea. *It will humanize you, help you show that everyone has the wrong idea.* Barkley had asked what the hell everyone's idea of him had to do with opening his mouth to sing, but his agent had just dismissed his concerns. That was one of the reasons that Christopher had quickly become his ex-agent.

Duncan took out a yellow folder and searched through the jumble of papers, finally finding and holding out the requested contract. Barkley perused it, found the appropriate page, and held it out for the journalist.

"The contract is quite specific about the *slant* the story is to take," Barkley said, still not smiling. "This is just an interview piece."

"Yes, but...," Duncan said, smiling, obviously trying to dazzle with his rugged good looks and his sparkling green eyes. Barkley wondered if it actually worked on anyone this man interviewed. "We could always do something a little different, make this a special piece since you'll be... retiring soon."

"Right," Barkley drawled, unconvinced. "So, twenty minutes you said?"

"Twenty and then I'll be gone," Duncan said, flashing that smile again.

Barkley motioned for the reporter to have a seat, wondering whether he should even offer a beverage.

Chapter 2

"WOULD YOU like anything to drink?"

Duncan glanced up from the mess that was his messenger bag and saw the singer standing there, grocery bag once again in his hand. "Uh, water?" Duncan saw him nod and head into the kitchen, heard him mutter something to some thing named Princess, and then heard the sounds of food being poured into bowls and the familiar sound of dogs' toenails on tile flooring.

Turning his attention back to his messenger bag, Duncan pulled out the folder and his laptop, one of the few things he'd not been forced to sell in order to pay his rent or keep food in his belly or Zeus's or Neptune's. His equipment was set up and he sat in the fancy chair, looking through his bag for the small file of biographical information, momentarily shocked when the little cat with no eyes hopped onto his bag, mewing loudly. He petted the cat a few times and then glanced up to see if he was being watched. Realizing he was not, he picked up the cat and put it back on the hardwood floor. He pulled the thin folder of biographical information out of his bag and dropped it on the coffee table, relief washing over him that he'd not been kicked back to the curb. He shifted farther back on the chair, his hand almost sliding off the shiny, slippery fabric. The fabric reminded Duncan of the curtains his mother had had in the living room for twenty years.

He looked around the huge condo as Barkley puttered in the kitchen, Duncan guessed putting his groceries away and getting a glass of water. He wondered what kind of booze this kind of money would buy and whether he should ask for a bourbon the next time as the singer came back into the well-appointed living room carrying two glasses of water with ice.

"Thank you," Duncan said, accepting the glass and pushing the power button on his laptop. "I always like to record the interviews I do," Duncan announced. "That way we're both protected."

"No problem," Barkley said, sitting on the overstuffed sofa that Duncan found to be more to his liking than most of the other furniture in the room.

"Okay, then," Duncan said, typing in his password and then opening the program that he had that would record every word. "The mic is built-in, so just speak in a normal voice and it will pick up everything."

Barkley nodded and stood, then sat back down so his right foot was under his left leg. The cat reappeared and hopped into Barkley's lap. It drew Duncan's attention to the long, lean legs, and he found himself feeling a little flushed and flustered. He cleared his throat.

"Duncan Spencer, Barkley Reinhardt interview, part one, Friday, June 29." Duncan picked up a piece of paper containing some biographical information and then decided to try a little test. "Why don't we start with the basics? Name, place of birth, birthday, schooling…." He looked over and smiled as Barkley took a long drink from his own glass of water, his other hand absentmindedly stroking the purring cat.

"Barkley Arthur Reinhardt… Toronto, Ontario, Canada… October 8, 1982… Sunny Haven for kindergarten to grade 8 and then West Central Composite for grades 9 to 12 and then University of Toronto where I graduated in 2002 with a major in Voice and a minor in Piano pedagogy."

Duncan looked up from his paper, the smile still plastered on his face, expecting something else. When he realized that there was to be nothing more, Duncan chuckled to himself. "That was… very efficient."

"I've learned not to expound too much since those pieces of information are already very well publicized." Barkley leaned forward and put his glass on the coffee table and then sat back, giving belly rubs to the cat that had now turned on its back.

Duncan lost his train of thought when he saw a beautiful little puppy stroll into the living room. It was a pale yellow color and had the saddest blue eyes half covered by droopy eyelids. "Right," Duncan said, willing himself not to grit his teeth or lose his temper at how distracted he was becoming. "What made you realize you could sing? *And,*" he was quick to add, "could you please tell me a little about your training. Was it *actual* training or is it just a matter of singing scales. As a nonsinger, I've always wondered what's involved in training a voice." *There,* Duncan thought as he sat back and sipped his water, *try and get by with point form answers on that one, you smug bastard.*

"Training the voice is much like training anything else. It's a matter of repetition... of scales, as you mentioned, but also of technique." Barkley leaned forward and took the glass back into his hand, seeming to have noticed the puppy that had wandered over to his feet. Duncan found himself focusing on the strong hand and wondered if Barkley was actually *only* a singer; he seemed like he was in pretty good shape. "Technique involves perfecting everything from tongue position to breath control. It can be a very daunting task at first, but most singers learn very quickly what *feels* right when they're singing." Duncan smiled as he watched Barkley bend over and pick up the puppy, placing a few quick kisses on its neck and then placing it on the sofa beside him. Without too much more fanfare, the puppy fell fast asleep.

"And when did you realize you had the talent for singing opera?"

"I was nineteen and I was earning extra money working for some voice majors as an accompanist. One of those singers was having some difficulty with a particular combination of notes, so I sang it for her, trying to let her hear what the precise timing was," Barkley explained. "She made note of the fact that I had a very nice *timbre* and told me I should consider singing. So I auditioned, as a joke really, for one of the voice teachers at the university and she took me on as a private student."

"And the rest is history?"

"Very well-documented history," Barkley said with a smile. Duncan wondered if that was a jab at the need for these questions but chose to ignore it. "One year later, I won the famed Respighi Prize in New York."

"And trampled the competition, from what I understand. And making it even more incredible, yours was the first *ever* win by a baritone."

"Second," Barkley corrected. "Giuseppe Di Giordano also won the prize in 1948."

"I stand corrected," Duncan said with a nod to Barkley. "But impressive nonetheless." And Duncan was impressed. Barkley could have just as easily let him go on believing that his win was a first, but he didn't. Didn't even wait two seconds before giving credit to the baritone who'd won the prize before him. Duncan made a mental note to see if that particular win, in 1948, would be easily discovered. If so, then Barkley was probably covering his own ass. If that piece of information was difficult to find, then perhaps Barkley wasn't the pampered asshole Duncan had assumed; after all, who didn't try to get away with a little white lie from time to time?

"And your parents were both music teachers, I see," Duncan said, noticing almost instantly the change in Barkley's expression. "I'm sorry," he said quickly as he reached for his messenger bag and the list of questions Barkley was not willing to discuss, "is that one of the off-limit questions?"

"No," Barkley said immediately. "Yes, my parents were both music teachers, here in Toronto."

"Um, is… uh," Duncan stammered. *Fuck me, I can't let him see I'm flustered.* "And when did you give your first paid performance and where was it?"

"I was twenty years old, had just turned twenty, and I was engaged by the Canadian Opera Company to perform in an avant-garde production of *Orfeo* by Gluck," Barkley explained, and Duncan noticed he seemed to be a little less… sad; that was the only word that Duncan could think of to describe that look.

"Sorry, I don't really know much about opera," Duncan said, smile turning to an embarrassed grimace.

"Orfeo is a man who has lost his wife. She is taken to the underworld, and with the help of Cupid, he tries to get her back. Cupid gives him warnings, one of which is not to look or speak to his wife when she is on her way out of Hades. He does this, but his wife fears he does not love her anymore and wishes for her own death, again. He turns to look at her, and she dies… again. Cupid, however, takes pity on Orfeo because he is so devoted to his wife and brings her back to life." Barkley's eyebrows flew up as he quipped, "Cheery stuff, huh?"

"Is it a very… common opera?" Duncan asked, uncertain of his words now. Opera was completely out of his realm of expertise. He didn't know half of the words he probably should.

"I wouldn't think so," Barkley said, setting his empty glass on the coffee table. "And it's not a standard role for baritones, the role of Orfeo. The role is usually sung by a mezzo or contralto." Duncan shrugged again. "The lowest of female voices," Barkley explained with a chuckle. Duncan was about to open his mouth to ask his next question, but he noticed the singer take another breath. "But as I said, it was an avant-garde production."

"Avant-garde because of the casting?" Duncan didn't really understand why that choice would be considered avant-garde, especially in this day and age.

"And because the soprano and I were half-naked for almost two hours," he said. Duncan noticed the slight blush coming to the pale skin and made a mental note to try and find pictures, or better yet, video.

"Is that what started the trend of you having open shirts or no shirts during performances?"

"There were only ever two other performances where I was shirtless," Barkley said quickly. "I was fully clothed for the other nine hundred performances I gave."

"Sorry," Duncan said. "Research must have missed that." He cursed his editor, imagining the fat prick sitting somewhere right now laughing his ass off at the misinformation he'd given to Duncan.

BARKLEY SAT there in his own home, forcing a smile. *Another eight months and all of this will be behind me forever.* He'd agreed to this interview over six months ago, knowing full well that the shirtless thing and the soprano falling into the pit would be mentioned, but it still bothered him that they were *always* mentioned. During his ten years as a performer, he'd helped raise money for six or seven worthy charities, he'd visited hospitals and long-term care homes, he'd done national ad campaigns against bullying and homophobia, and he'd even donated almost one million dollars out of his own bank account to educational foundations meant to teach music to low-income or disadvantaged youths. Barkley supposed that the journalist's *research* must have missed that as well. Barkley glanced down as Tinkerbell's ears perked up, and she was off. *Probably just realized I put food out for her about ten minutes ago,* Barkley thought as he watched her saunter off toward the kitchen.

"Is physical fitness important to you? As a singer, I mean. There seem to be so many... heavier... singers and I've often wondered if that is harmful to their careers."

Barkley found the question interesting. He'd never heard anyone ask that question of him before, and he wondered if there was some sort of angle to it. He took a deep breath and sighed, his brow knitted in thought. "I've always kept myself in shape because I find it easier to deal with the physical demands of traveling so much and, of course, the hours-long rehearsal process." He looked down and saw his glass was empty and remembered draining it moments ago. "As far as excess weight affecting a singing career, I don't know if it would or not. There have been many, many great singers who were heavier and had very long successful careers."

"I once read that Barbra Streisand did not want her nose fixed because she thought it would change her voice in some way," Duncan said, glancing down at the sheet of paper in his hand.

"Just as with other professions, there are plenty of superstitions among singers." Barkley shifted his weight so he was leaning against the back cushion of the sofa. "Many critics truly believed that Maria Callas's voice was never the same after she lost so much weight."

"And what do you believe?"

"I think there's a difference between weight loss affecting a voice and overuse or misuse affecting a voice."

"Misuse?"

"When a singer, say for example, a coloratura soprano, insists on singing repertoire that takes her voice out of where it naturally sits." Barkley leaned forward again, becoming a little restless. "Maria Callas was very fond of reviving forgotten or lost works and would sing these roles or arias for recordings, if you will. What she didn't realize—or perhaps did realize and just didn't care—is that *forcing* the voice to do something that is not in its nature can be very detrimental to overall vocal health and the length of one's career."

"Wow," Duncan said, his voice low and quiet. "So, did you ever accept a role that you shouldn't have?"

"Once or twice," Barkley admitted, nodding his head. "But only if two or three performances were all that were asked. To sing such a role for an extended period of time, say a week or two, could *set* your voice and compromise your technique."

"How so?"

"Before it was possible to record interviews, for example, the journalist had to try and devise some way of getting all of the information, as accurately as possible, by writing on a piece of paper." He noted Duncan nodding, a look of concentration on the face. Barkley had not noticed until now the square jaw or the day's worth of beard or the way the sunkissed lines at the corners of the journalist's eyes were tinged with white. Barkley imagined that Duncan probably spent a lot of time at the beach with his wife or girlfriend. "Once the typewriter was invented, it was possible to type faster than you write, even using some sort of shorthand." He put his right hand on his thigh and turned it palm upward. "Now imagine that I ask you to use a typewriter for a week or two and then go back to writing out your notes. It would take you a while to make the adjustment, in either direction." He saw the journalist nodding.

He looked at the ornate grandfather clock his father had brought over from Austria that was built almost one hundred years ago and wondered if he should tell Duncan that his twenty minutes were up. He took a deep breath and grabbed his empty water glass.

"Would you like some more water?"

"No," Duncan said, his eyes still on the sheet of paper in his hand. "I'm fine, thank you."

"I'll be right back," Barkley said and headed to the kitchen to refill his glass. "I'm just going to check on their food."

"So," Duncan said from the living room. "When you do retire next year, what will you do?"

Barkley didn't feel like yelling from the kitchen, so he checked that everyone was eating, that Tinkerbell wasn't sitting in Princess's food bowl, dropped a few more ice cubes in his glass, poured the water, and then strolled back to the living room. "I haven't really thought much about it at this point." He knew exactly what his plans were, but he didn't really feel like sharing those with this man he'd only met less than thirty minutes ago. "I guess I'll figure that out when I've fulfilled all of my remaining commitments."

"One last question, then," Duncan said with a smile, "and then I'll leave you to your plans." Barkley returned to his spot on the sofa and waited. "Were there any roles you wanted to sing, but never got the chance?"

Barkley made a show of looking up at the ceiling. If he'd come right out and said "No", then the journalist might have found it defensive, or at least a little too rehearsed. "I don't think there was any one in particular," Barkley said finally, shaking his head. "I think I would have loved to try to sing a Verdi role or two, but my voice is far too light."

Duncan folded the piece of paper in his hand and reached for his messenger bag. He stuffed the paper into the bag and reached for his laptop. "Okay, then," he said, clicking a few buttons on his computer and then closing it. "I thank you very much for seeing me without an official appointment, and I'll get in touch with your agent to set up the final interview next week. How's Mon—"

"I'm no longer represented by an agent," Barkley said, cool as could be, leaning over the arm of the sofa to reach the side table. He wrote his landline number on a piece of paper by the phone and handed it to Duncan. "You can call me directly and leave a message on the machine. We can set something up then."

"Okay," Duncan repeated. "How does Monday or Tuesday sound?"

"Fine," Barkley replied and headed for the door. "Let me know what time you'd prefer when you call with the precise day, and I'll be sure to alert the doorman." Barkley opened the door to his condo and smiled as Duncan passed to the other side. "Which reminds me. How did you get in without the doorman seeing you?"

"I didn't," Duncan said, and Barkley couldn't help seeing the heat of embarrassment creep into the journalist's cheeks. Barkley made a mental note to do some checking on the internet about Duncan Spencer, Journalist. "I explained who I was, showed him my ID, and he called the paper to confirm. He told me that I could come up here to wait for you, that you'd be home in about fifteen minutes."

"Fair enough," Barkley said as he offered his hand. When Duncan took it, Barkley found himself even more intrigued by this tall, handsome reporter. He couldn't help but wonder what this guy's story was. He seemed like a fairly intelligent person; why was he working for some rag like *The Communiqué*?

When the door was closed, Barkley turned the deadbolt and fastened the chain, letting out a slow breath. He laughed out loud when he saw Tinkerbell make a run for the door. "You little stinker," Barkley chastised as he scooped her up in his arms again, sparing a moment to find her favorite little stuffed bear. "You're too late." He kissed her a few times, ignoring her protests, and then headed to the kitchen to pull the ice cream out of the freezer. He would grab a quick shower while the Mocha Almond defrosted and then be enjoying a movie within ten minutes.

He turned the television on, opened the trunk that sat beside the television, and pulled out the faux fur throw he'd picked up the last time he was in London. He tossed it on the sofa, wondering how many of the animals he'd have to kick off it when he returned. Truthfully, he didn't mind sharing the throw; it was just one of the many creature comforts most of these animals had never known. A soft blanket, a warm bed, a full belly. Barkley was prepared to give them anything.

As he stripped in the bedroom, he found himself thinking about that journalist. Duncan Spencer was a very attractive man, in an unkempt kind of way. Barkley had been with a few of the tuxedo and witty repartee crowd and had never really felt like he belonged with them. And then, of course, Barkley had also been with a few blue-collar boyfriends; he'd never really felt like he belonged there either.

As he stepped into the shower, Barkley reminded himself to do some research of his own, just to see who this reporter was and why he was working for that quasi-tabloid anyway. He stood under the scalding hot water for as long as he could before turning the cold-water faucet. Soaping his hair and then his body, he stood under the spray, moving his head in a very slow circle, his arms out to the side while he let the water rinse him clean.

After a couple of minutes to ensure that all the soap was gone, Barkley reached out to the side and hit the button that would activate all ten showerheads. The hot water would hit him from all sides, beating him into relaxation.

He was definitely going to sleep well tonight.

Chapter 3

DUNCAN POUNDED back his second bourbon since arriving at Woody's. He'd almost made it all the way back to his studio apartment, but then he'd realized he wasn't really interested in being alone. He wasn't really interested in spending a couple of hours in a gay bar, either, but it was a necessary sacrifice if he didn't want to be by himself. So, he was sitting on a stool, turning the little shot glass around and around on the stained and scarred surface of the bar, thinking about the day when it would all turn around for him, the day he could tell Thomas—and the rest of the world—to kiss his ass because he'd paid for his crime.

The word still stuck in his throat: *crime*. He'd hear the word *criminal* or *felon*, and it would always take him a minute or two to realize that those words applied to him too. Duncan had been so relieved to be released from jail after only twenty-eight days, so pleased that he was going to be able to return to his regular life, that he'd not even considered the possibility that the paper would fire him. Maybe his former editor-in-chief was right and it was *standard practice*, in order to protect the reputation of the paper, but there had always been one very significant problem: Duncan hadn't committed any crime.

"I can tell you want to buy me a drink."

Duncan heard the sultry voice near his ear. He hadn't realized that he'd been so lost in thought. "'Scuse me?"

"You've been staring at me."

"Have I?" Duncan studied the tall, skinny blond twink who had now taken a seat beside him. The blond's hand was resting on Duncan's thigh. "Sorry," he said without any sincerity.

"Don't be sorry," the blond said, batting his eyelashes for all he was worth. "Just make it up to me."

"Sammy," Duncan called to the bartender, the same bartender who'd been working at Woody's for the last fifteen years. "Another shot of bourbon and…." Duncan turned to his new friend.

"Lemon Drop, please."

"Are you even old enough to drink?" Duncan leaned back in his chair, wondering if this was going anywhere or if he'd just wasted nine bucks on a cocktail.

By way of answering, the twink pulled out his wallet, although from the snugness of the jeans, Duncan couldn't imagine how he fit it in any of the pockets. He pulled out his driver's license and held it up for Duncan's inspection. "I just turned twenty-two."

Duncan looked wide-eyed at the license and nodded. "Looks like it, doesn't it?" Sammy dropped off the drinks and Duncan passed him a twenty. Duncan hoped he could seal this deal soon; his own wallet was now empty. "Keep the change," he said, wondering what he would use to pay for this week's groceries. He had more than enough food for Zeus and Neptune, but he didn't really have anything other than cans of tuna and soup. He figured he would spend another week trying to ignore the growling in his stomach and downed his third bourbon in one gulp.

"Thank you for the drink, Bourbon."

Duncan looked back at the blond and frowned, noticing a smile on his new friend. "Duncan," he said, offering his hand.

"Jamez," the twink said, taking his hand. "With a 'z'."

He felt the limp handshake and wanted to run out of the bar. He remembered the lessons his father had taught him about firm handshakes. Duncan could actually hear his boss's voice telling him not to trust a man who didn't grip your hand. *Real men, important men, can tell what kind of man* you *are by your handshake.* Duncan had lived by that rule and had only been disappointed twice. "Pleasure," Duncan said and nodded.

"Eventually, if you want," the blond said and winked.

Duncan started to feel like he was speaking in code; everything that came out of the little twink's mouth was either well rehearsed or this kid was really hard up for a quick fuck. "So, you're twenty-two,"

Duncan sighed, leaning on the bar as he swiveled his stool to look the blond in the face. "Care to guess how old I am?"

"I'm not very good at guessing games, papi," the twink said, sucking his plump bottom lip in between his teeth. "Not as good as I am at other games."

Duncan was mildly annoyed at the *papi* comment. He'd always dreaded that day when some young thing would call him *Daddy*. "I'm old enough to know that ID is a fake."

"Ah," the twink cooed. "Come on, Duncan. Does it really matter how old you are?" Duncan felt the hand on his thigh travel between his legs and offer a slow squeeze. "I'm just looking for a good time tonight."

Duncan thought about it for all of five seconds before spreading his thighs a little more. He leaned forward even more so that his lips were right on the shell of the little blond's ear. "There's no doubt I can give you that," Duncan said as he felt himself harden. "But I have a boyfriend at home, so…." He lied, not because he didn't want the possible strings that came with this offer, but because he didn't want them with this particular piece of ass.

"I don't have a roommate," the blond said with what Duncan figured was unadulterated availability.

Duncan winked and looked at the blond's martini. "Drink up, Jamez with a 'z'."

Twenty minutes later, Duncan found himself flat on his back, his jeans and boxers around his ankles, while the little twink was showing him what he meant by a good time. Jamez had been on him the moment they'd stepped into the very nice two-bedroom apartment on Dundonald Street. And if Jamez didn't have such a talented mouth and smooth touch, Duncan figured he would have spent more time trying to figure out how he rated a studio, but some supposed twenty-two-year-old managed a sweet apartment like this one.

BARKLEY AWOKE with a start, the book on his lap falling shut and hitting the floor. He looked over at his alarm clock; it was only two o'clock in the morning. "Fuck," he cursed out loud before rolling over onto his side, finding a cooler spot on the pillow inches from a sleeping

Tinkerbell. He closed his eyes, trying to imagine nothing, a blank screen inside his brain, so that he could get back to sleep and hopefully stay that way until a less inconvenient hour. Barkley knew that if he let his mind begin to contemplate why he'd woken up, he'd be awake and wandering around his condo until he collapsed on the sofa sometime tomorrow afternoon, and then the cycle would begin again.

The first time the cycle had started, Barkley was preparing for a new role, a difficult role. He had been engaged to sing *Don Giovanni* at La Scala in Milan. Barkley had never had any problems singing Mozart, although he did wonder about the dramatic tone of the final act. He would be singing in the lower area of his range for almost the entire act, not something that frightened him necessarily, but he had worried about pushing his voice too hard. He'd only been twenty-four when he had accepted the contract, eager to impress and craving the applause and adulation more and more.

Those had been the hardest drugs for Barkley to resist; there was nothing more intoxicating than standing in front of a huge crowd, all of them applauding *him,* all of them telling him that he had not disappointed them, that he had proven worthy of their praise. It wasn't something he'd lacked as an only child, and Barkley found himself trying to pinpoint where and when in his childhood this need had taken control. Or perhaps, Barkley thought as he rolled on his back, *control* wasn't the right word. Maybe *precedence* was a more accurate way of describing the feeling that was becoming more and more insistent.

Regardless of the right word, however, Barkley couldn't seem to figure out when it had all started, when the *Bravos* and the six-figure contracts had begun to mean more to him than everything else. He'd had a wonderful childhood; everything that two loving parents could provide had been given freely, even if it meant that his mother and father had to sacrifice something that they would have enjoyed. Free time and family vacations were spent taking day trips or perhaps two-day trips to visit museums or attending some concert so that Barkley was exposed to as much culture and as many opportunities as his parents could afford. There were many times since his rise to fame when Barkley had mistakenly thought that it was the money that he'd found so alluring, so enticing. But as he lay in bed, still unable to sleep, Barkley recognized—and not for the first time—that it had never been about the money.

At just after three in the morning, Barkley accepted defeat and threw off the duvet and soft cotton sheets before sitting on the side of his king-size bed and wiping his hand over his face. "You coming?" he asked as he saw Tinkerbell's ears perk up. With a heavy sigh, he pushed himself to his feet and headed for his office located in the spare bedroom, Tinkerbell following close behind. He studied Butter for a moment; she was asleep in her little bed that Barkley kept separate from the others. Right now, Butter's diabetes was controlled through proper diet, complete with high-fiber intake, and she was really good about eating her own food. He'd caught her a few times sniffing the other dogs' food, but she'd not seemed terribly interested in anything but her own.

He plopped into the chair, patting his lap, glad for the company when Tinkerbell took her usual place. He would surf the internet for an hour or so and then try to fall asleep again. And if that didn't work, he would fix himself a mug of tea, camp out on the sofa, and watch some more recorded programming until his eyes grew heavy with sleep or weariness or both.

He punched the power button on his laptop and relaxed back into the soft leather. He leaned back and stretched out, like a cat, and let go of a long, slow yawn. When the screen showed the ubiquitous little box requesting a username and password, Barkley punched all of the necessary keys and watched the parade of images and sounds that followed a successful login. He opened a browser window and then, after checking his e-mails—nothing but spam and e-mails from fans— he went straight to Google to enter in *Duncan Spencer*.

He would soon learn what had happened to the journalist and began hitting the keys to spell out the name of the reporter who'd left a lasting impression on him. At first Barkley had thought the journalist a little disorganized and—despite that character flaw—quite arrogant. But throughout the entire thirty-five minute exchange, Barkley had begun to see a commanding type of frailty to Duncan's demeanor; he'd tried to show that he was a professional but then made a few rather major blunders.

It had always been Barkley's experience that journalists and talk-show hosts came completely and annoyingly prepared. Yet, Duncan had not known certain facts about Barkley that even his most ardent critics would have known. Even the people who loathed Barkley Reinhardt—for whatever reason—could recite chapter and verse about his education and early career. But Duncan hadn't known any of it, and Barkley found himself wanting to know why. Of course, he was also more than willing to admit that he didn't know anything about the journalist. "But then he'd not been a public figure," Barkley said out loud as he scanned the screen, catching not only Duncan's name but also various other words like *prison, jailed,* and *indictment*.

As he opened the first article, Barkley found it all rather amusing that he was visiting the site of the paper that had once employed Duncan Spencer and reading an article written about the lax moral judgment shown by one of the paper's best and brightest. *Loyalty.* Barkley would be laughing right now, but he was all too familiar with the concept of lack of loyalty—especially his own. There were some people who saw it as nothing more than another opportunity to move ahead. For the last five years, Barkley had often watched this little game play out and had always suppressed the urge to explain to the greedy idiots that the fame and the money had not yet made anybody *truly* happy. But then, it was like his father always said: *There are people who will learn their lesson the first time, and then there are those who will have to sit through the same lesson five, ten, or twenty times.*

Reading about what Duncan had *allegedly* done, Barkley was somewhat impressed at the disheveled journalist and his willingness to take a stand, albeit a very unpopular one. He couldn't imagine what it must have been like to write an article calling into question the ethics of a prime minister who was seen as "pulling strings" for a constituent—and a very rich one who'd always given heavily to every campaign. Duncan was ordered to reveal his source, but would not, preferring to spend thirty days in jail on a contempt charge. It had been on day seventeen—if Barkley chose to believe the timeline presented by this other journalist—that the confidential source had committed suicide, citing Duncan Spencer as one of the many reasons his life was no longer worth living.

Barkley read the tearful testimony of the informant who had accused Duncan of having been relentless in pursuing the story with an endless assault of e-mails, phone calls, and visits to his office. Of course, all available records showed that this informant did not have many e-mails or phone calls, and his office was in a secure government building with a receptionist and security detail. Duncan had been blamed for the suicide on page one. And when the documents that showed it was the informant who'd been calling incessantly, that Duncan had never once signed the security log—or been visible on any surveillance—and that the informant's e-mail accounts were free of even one single e-mail from Duncan had finally come to light, Barkley was not surprised that they'd been relegated to a blurb on some back page near the bottom.

There had been many times Barkley had wanted to strap a camera around his neck and stand outside a few of the reporters' houses, snapping pictures and yelling questions. He wasn't really sure it would have made any difference at all, but he did find himself wondering if the reversal of roles—and fortune—had taught the down-on-his-luck journalist anything of value. Duncan had seemed nice enough last night; he'd even worried, very briefly, that a question might have been on *the list*. Although Barkley had not seen the need for the list in almost four years, he'd felt an odd sense of comfort that Duncan hadn't wanted to offend. Barkley's previous experience with the media had been contrary to the events of last night.

As he scrolled down the article, Barkley's attention was drawn to a photograph of Duncan. There was a twinge of desire that almost overwhelmed him while he studied the rugged and handsome face, the navy suit that was obviously too small for his broad shoulders and the long, muscular legs that certainly lay beneath the dress slacks. The man who'd shown up at his condo the day before seemed thinner.

Barkley zoomed in on the photograph, his desire quickly replaced with a sense of compassion for the look on the journalist's face. *Yes,* Barkley thought as he studied the square jaw and the high cheekbones, *this man had definitely lost some weight during his ordeal.* There was no sun evident in the picture, no shadows to tell of its presence, yet Duncan's eyes were squinted as if the sun shone right in his face. Barkley knew that squint all too well; it was the look of someone who'd had one too many cameras thrust into his face. Barkley felt somewhat guilty at his previous thoughts of Duncan needing to learn a lesson about what it was like to be hounded by the press.

With a deep sigh, Barkley promised himself that he would be a little less… *bitchy* when the journalist showed up again. After all, they had something in common now. They both knew what it felt like to be misjudged and cast aside by the very people who once put you on a pedestal.

DUNCAN PUSHED the twink's arm off his chest and slid out of bed, pressing his feet on the cold hardwood and feeling a little more awake after only a few hours of sleep. He bent to pick up his boxers and pull them on, then his socks and his jeans. He picked up his T-shirt and padded to the bathroom so he could empty his bourbon-filled bladder. As he pressed one hand to the wall above the toilet tank, he let his muscles relax and soon felt the sweet feeling of relief, trying to ignore the voice saying *I told you so.*

As he'd anticipated, Duncan was regretting allowing himself to end up in another trick's bed and cursing himself for having spent most of his grocery money for the week. His only consolation was that the little twink had not been lying about his abilities. Duncan had found himself coaxed and sucked and rimmed to fill three condoms during his five hours in this apartment. But it was small consolation, the comfort as cold as the tiles beneath his feet in yet another stranger's bathroom.

After finding his messenger bag and his sneakers, Duncan headed to the door, not bothering to say goodbye or leave a phone number, and started the thirty-minute walk ahead of him. The subway wouldn't be running at this time of night and he certainly didn't have the money for a cab; of course, there was the all-night bus routes, but even with a monthly pass, Duncan would rather walk than take one of those busses. He'd only ever used one once, but it had been one time too many. Filled with drunks and reeking of something foul and noxious, it had been a ten-minute ride he wasn't in any hurry to repeat, even if it would reduce his walking time by a third.

He shoved his hands in his pockets, his right hand wrapped tightly around his wallet, and made his way down Eglinton to Yonge, turning right and then making the journey straight south to St. Clair. He would be back at his little studio apartment on St. Clair East with just enough time to scrub himself clean under the hottest water possible, given the age of his building, before sitting down to a nice cup of instant coffee. He'd use his unexpected extra time this morning to go through his notes and come up with some more interesting questions for Barkley. And with any luck, it might make him tired enough so he could have a nap in the afternoon.

As he passed Davisville, he glanced down Merton Street, his mind still replaying his meeting with the operatic baritone. Of course,

Duncan had heard of the singer long before he'd been reduced to working at *The Communiqué*, but he'd never given much thought to what the guy would be like. Despite Barkley's heavy distrust of the media, Duncan's imagination was still wondering what his chances were with the incredibly attractive baritone.

As Duncan turned around one last time to look at the building where Barkley was probably fast asleep right at that moment, that well-photographed chest and belly lifting and falling slowly, he found himself smiling. *Who'd have ever thought I'd be turned on by some opera singer?*

Chapter 4

DUNCAN WASN'T exactly sure why he'd suddenly gotten the urge to organize and clean his small apartment, but he was done by five thirty in the morning, standing back near the small door that led to the equally small balcony and appreciating his work. With his dogs, Zeus and Neptune, having eaten and been taken out for a quick tour of the park across the street, Duncan found himself dreaming, again, of the day he'd be able to not only get a bigger place, but also fill it with nice furniture. To pass the days sometimes, when he was between assignments, he would spend an hour or two visiting the websites of some of the more upscale furniture stores in Toronto. He'd not done it for quite a while however, since it seemed like he was never actually getting out of this apartment.

Duncan checked his alarm clock. Six in the morning. The laundry room would be open now. He threw some loonies into his pocket and then stripped his bed, tossed his sheets and towels and soiled clothing into the well-used plastic laundry basket, and grabbed his keys and detergent. He headed out of the apartment and walked down the four flights of stairs.

The laundry room was filthy, as usual, and before he stuffed the three washing machines with the basket's contents, he picked up the anti-static dryer sheets that littered the floor and deposited them in the trash. He left the empty detergent bottles beside the dented and rusted trash can and then turned his attention back to his laundry, filling the ancient machines and using just enough detergent to get the job done, and then headed back up to his apartment.

He'd started to do some research on Barkley Reinhardt shortly after arriving home earlier, but then he'd found himself distracted by just how dusty and depressing his little kitchen table had become. And as he cleaned, for almost an hour, he promised himself a little treat once the job was done: he could do some research for anything interesting while listening to the little bit of an interview he'd done yesterday. He thought maybe even listening to whatever he could find on YouTube might help him in developing his next series of questions.

Sitting down at the clean and well-appointed table that served as both kitchen table and desk, Duncan opened up his laptop again and went to his favorites menu, clicking on YouTube. Once he'd located a playlist of Barkley's performances, Duncan placed the earbuds in his ears and clicked the first video in the series.

It was done by an ardent fan of the singer, the video nothing more than a slideshow of photographs that featured a shirtless or bare-chested Barkley Reinhardt. Duncan glanced quickly at the time bar to see that this particular video would last almost ten minutes. So he propped his chin on his hand and waited, listening to the orchestra play the introduction to some piece by Bach. Duncan wasn't really sure what a cantata was, apart from a type of musical arrangement, and didn't much care at that point in time. He was listening to an incredibly powerful combination of notes and phrasing. The violins seemed to be pleading, begging even.

Then he was hearing the voice, the voice that had been lauded by many and criticized by a few. Duncan didn't know anything about classical music, other than the semi-classical pieces he'd learned to play on the guitar, but he knew that the voice he was hearing was warm and rich and soothing, like the best cup of coffee he could imagine. He clicked on the title bar to see the lyrics, but they were written in German. Duncan didn't understand German, so he copied the words and then searched for a free online translation service, finding one almost instantly and pasting the copied words into the little white box at the top of the site.

When the translation appeared only seconds later, Duncan repeated the process; there were maybe thirty words in total. There must have been some sort of glitch with the site, Duncan figured. If there hadn't, how would a song last more than seven minutes with only thirty words? He repeated the process a third time and then tried a different plan, searching for a translation that already existed. When

Duncan found that four different sites all gave him the same translation, he figured he'd find out soon enough how to make thirty words last seven minutes and read while the pleasing sounds of Barkley's voice washed through his tired brain.

Contented peace, beloved delight of the soul, you cannot be found among the sins of hell, but only where there is heavenly harmony. You alone strengthen the weak breast.

Duncan found it odd, the juxtaposition of the risqué photos to the meaning of the song, and opened his Word program to write down his first question. At about the midway point, Duncan decided to improve his vocabulary, entering more search terms to discover the right words for what he was researching. An *aria* was the name for what Barkley was singing now, but Duncan soon learned that there were different types of arias: the lyrics to an operatic piece or *libretto*, and an operatic-type of aria dealing with religious themes—an *oratorio*.

Duncan researched the term *cantata* and wondered what the precise difference between an oratorio and a cantata was, apart from the duration. He checked the time on his alarm clock again and made a mental note to ask Barkley about some of these things. It might not necessarily make it into the interview, but Duncan figured that engaging in a little small talk about Barkley's world might be a way to earn some respect and trust.

He grabbed the laundry basket, checked his pocket to ensure that his last two loonies were still there, and took the stairs back down to the laundry room. To save himself some money each week, Duncan put the towels and sheets together into one dryer, using the other for his T-shirts, underwear, and socks. He popped the coins into the appropriate slots and, after pressing the silver *start* buttons, headed back to his apartment. He had a full hour before he needed to take his things from the laundry, which would give him enough time to come up with a few more questions. Then he would try to take a nap after taking Zeus and Neptune for their afternoon tour around the park. Maybe he'd even call Barkley to see if they could meet again tomorrow.

BARKLEY WAS napping on the sofa when he heard the shrill ring of the telephone. He saw it was just before noon, closed his eyes again, knowing that the machine would pick up, and tried to get some more sleep. It wasn't until he heard Duncan's voice, deep, loud, clear, and a little on the raspy side, that he suddenly felt a little bit of regret at not getting up to take the call himself. With his eyes still closed, Barkley listened to the husky bass of the journalist's voice as it thanked him again for being so accommodating and asked if it would be possible to meet tomorrow, Sunday, for the final part of the interview.

I've done my homework this time, Duncan was saying, *and I'll be better prepared. I've consulted many of the online tabloids and am really anxious to ask you about the alien abduction.*

Tinkerbell and Princess were obviously in one of their loving phases, the two of them parked near his feet sleeping soundly. Barkley found himself laughing as he shifted to be on his side and curled up to finish his nap. But after another few moments of lying there and smiling, he lifted himself off the sofa and sat there staring into the fireplace, his hand reaching out on its own to caress Princess and Tinkerbell.

Duncan had not mentioned a specific time, and Barkley found himself contemplating calling him back to suggest a lunchtime meeting; he could go out today and find some nice sandwiches and salads. They could eat out on the spacious balcony that faced south, enjoying the view of the green trees and landmarks that dotted the Toronto skyline while having a nice lunch. Of course, he realized as he turned to look over near the balcony doors where Mozart and Salieri were napping peacefully, it would mean they wouldn't be able to go out and see John until Monday, but Barkley didn't think his menagerie would mind too much.

He flopped back down on the sofa as it registered that he was planning for a date instead of an interview. Barkley figured he must be lonelier than he'd thought. Duncan was a very handsome man and probably could have his pick of any man or woman. Closing his eyes at the realization that he didn't even know whether the journalist was gay or straight, Barkley scolded himself for allowing his brain to run away with planning a lunch date with some man who could very well be married with children. Recognizing that he was falling into bad habits—habits that he'd corrected four years ago—Barkley felt suitably cowed and guilty. He would not make that mistake again.

Barkley reached for the universal remote, thinking he might finish the movie he'd started watching at five o'clock this morning, and punched the power button for the television and then turned on his PVR. He scrolled down to find the movie, and the screen came to life with pirates and open ocean and a roaring score that was as beautiful as it was inspiring. He stretched himself out on the sofa, careful not to disturb the rabbit and the cat, and bunched the pillow beneath his head, trying to remember what he'd seen this morning.

He didn't bother going back to bed when he felt himself growing drowsy again while watching the movie, preferring to remain on the sofa. It was warm and cozy, and he didn't feel the need to move. He fell asleep surrounded by his new family. He wondered about calling Duncan back before he fell asleep again, but decided to make himself wait. It was the same reason he hadn't jumped up to answer the call when he heard the gravelly voice: he didn't want to seem overeager or too compliant. His career may be coming to an end, but he still had a reputation as an enigmatic man to protect.

As he drifted off to sleep, Barkley's mind was focused on what kind of opinion history would have of him. Would he be remembered as the artist who was always meticulously prepared or would he become a blip on the radar? Regardless of the answer, Barkley knew only one choice was certain: Barkley Reinhardt was a name that would rank among the great operatic artists or he'd become a media joke, known only for the supposed tantrums. As he continued to relax, the sunlight from the balcony warming his forehead and cheeks, Barkley wasn't sure whether that would be a good thing or not. He'd loved the idea when he first began to receive notoriety, but now, after ten years in the public spotlight, Barkley found himself wondering whether he would have been happier working in an office all day long and then returning home to a man who would have loved him for something other than his fame.

DUNCAN DISCONNECTED his call confirming their interview time, more excited than he could remember being in a very long time. While he'd been leaving the message on Barkley's machine, he'd had an idea, one that could see him wealthy and respected. He'd have to approach the subject very slowly and with great delicacy, but he was pretty sure he could convince the world-famous baritone to allow him to author a biography of his life and career. The hours he'd spent this morning pouring over every piece of information he could find on the singer had yielded some incredibly fascinating ideas. Duncan had not known much about Barkley Reinhardt when he was handed the assignment yesterday—other than the fact that the man was talented and gorgeous—but now he could see the story forming inside his tired brain.

A gifted and talented pianist, Barkley had been an only child, his days spent practicing scales and studying music theory with his equally talented parents. The young Barkley had been a stellar student at Ashworth Academy for Gifted Students, excelling not only in his academic studies but also in his enriched program of music. It was at the Academy that he'd also learned to play the violin, although, as Duncan noted with some amusement, Barkley himself had always classified himself as being a virtuoso on the piano but a *virtual-no-show* when it came to the violin.

Duncan had also noticed throughout his research that the sense of humor Barkley had shown in several of his earlier interviews was sorely lacking in the subsequent media releases. He wasn't sure if that was just poor editing or if something had changed in Barkley's life. *Was that when he realized he didn't want this life anymore? Was it around four or five years ago Barkley had chosen to give up the fame and fat six-figure fees?* Duncan was just itching to ask why, but he wasn't sure if that wouldn't get him shown the door all the faster. It would suffice to get this interview done, and hopefully, during their meeting tomorrow, Duncan would be able to sense if Barkley was amenable to the idea of more time together, or even collaborating on that biography.

There was no doubt Barkley was gay. It was common knowledge in the media and the press since Barkley had never denied it and had chosen to work with or represent one or two charities that dealt with the LGBT community in one way or another. His previous evening aside, Duncan was not always the most comfortable nowadays when it came to putting himself out there and flirting with someone he found as attractive as Barkley. The man was gorgeous, rich, and lived in a beautiful condo. Duncan, on the other hand, had very little self-confidence left after his brush with humiliation, always imagining there weren't too many men who wanted anything from him but a quick roll in the hay.

Out of all the aftershocks that had come with his fall from grace, his lack of self-esteem was one of the hardest things to deal with.

Before being jailed and getting fired, Duncan had had no difficulties in approaching any man he wanted; he was self-assured, confident, and he knew he had more than enough sex appeal. He went to the gym regularly, watched what he ate, and did everything possible to make sure no man could resist him. But the interesting side effect of his experience had been his social exile, self-imposed though it may be. Even after two years, he didn't trust himself enough to hit on any man he wanted. He'd lost weight, most of it muscle, because he usually couldn't afford to eat anything more than canned soup and Kraft dinner. Anything other than the occasional can of tuna or pizza had been a luxury for so long, he didn't remember what they tasted like anymore.

The days following his release had been the hardest. He'd spent many sleepless nights trying to figure out the most convenient way to kill himself. The only thing that had stopped him, other than the thought Zeus and Neptune might never find another home, was the realization it would make him look guilty, cowardly, and spineless. He had no family to concern himself with. His mother was long dead and he'd never known his father. He'd struggled through so much to achieve success; he knew he could do it again. Determination and self-loathing combined with the overwhelming desire to prove that he was right in protecting his source, that he hadn't had anything to do with the man's suicide, had ensured Duncan's survival for the first year. The next year was nothing more than a roller coaster ride of surviving the lows, knowing that there was another climb to another high somewhere around the next bend.

Duncan hoped that Barkley could be one of those highs. He knew he was being ridiculous, if not completely delusional. If nothing else came of their working together, at least Duncan could hope he'd found someone who would be willing to help him produce something that would contribute to his long hoped-for return to mainstream journalism. Of course, if he could sweet talk Barkley into agreeing to the biography, his return would be even closer. As he headed back to the table to review the questions he'd already written and to think of even more, he felt a certain level of excitement he hadn't experienced in years.

He lowered himself into the rickety chair in front of his laptop and woke it up, trying to think of other questions as he waited. Part of his research this afternoon after he'd woken up from his hour-long nap had focused on the roles that Barkley had played throughout his career. Of course, there had been the womanizing roles such as *Don Giovanni, Don Escamillo,* even *Macheath,* but there had also been some of the more endearing roles such as *Papageno, Ezio,* and *Dr. Malatesta.*

Then he had happened upon a few pages detailing Barkley's extensive work in oratorio. Duncan had even managed to find several YouTube videos that featured the baritone singing the role of Elijah in the oratorio of the same name. As he did with too many of his videos while researching, Duncan had scanned ahead, stopping on a particular duet entitled *What Have I to Do With Thee.* The beauty and magnitude of Barkley's beautiful voice had left Duncan almost in tears.

There had been several other videos on YouTube that featured Barkley singing other songs that were not precisely operatic in nature; everything from his interpretation of "Music of the Night" to "Razzle Dazzle" could be found somewhere on YouTube. Duncan had found himself quite mesmerized by all of them, especially the ones where the singer could showcase his tremendous range. Listening to the swoops up and down, the machine-gun fire of the runs and scales, Duncan had found himself staring at the screen, holding his breath, afraid that he wouldn't hear everything.

One of the many articles he'd read mentioned something about Barkley's enviable breath control, how he could do so much for so long on one lungful of air. Duncan thought he remembered Barkley saying something about how vocal training helped with breath control. As a lark, he quickly jotted down a question that he would ask. *Just how long can you sing on one gulp of air?*

Duncan giggled to himself, looking around his tiny apartment and feeling foolish for doing so, as he took as much air into his lungs as he could and began to hum one note, his eyes tracking the second hand of his watch. He hummed until he ran out of breath completely: twenty seconds. Duncan took in another lungful of air, wondering how opera singers could stand that head rush feeling and not pass out from lack of oxygen. He clicked on the YouTube video of the duet from *Elijah,* finding that one specific spot where it seemed like Barkley sang for at least one minute without taking a breath.

Forty-five seconds of continuous, beautiful music was flowing through the apartment and Duncan leaned back in his chair, fearing the creaking sound from the old chair as much as he ever did. *Simply astonishing*, Duncan thought as he picked up his pen. *I have to ask him if that's something anyone can learn.*

Noticing that the clock on the wall was showing eight, Duncan padded off to the bathroom to brush his teeth and pop a few Nytol; he wanted to make sure he was well rested for his appointment with Barkley Reinhardt. He was prepared for the interview, but now he had to prepare himself for being back in front of a man he found more and more fascinating by the minute. He filled Zeus's and Neptune's bowls again and sat quietly for a moment, petting them and apologizing yet again for having to leave them.

Just don't let me do anything stupid, Duncan thought as he kissed both of his dogs and then headed to the sofa. *And I'll never ask for anything again.* Not that he had ever asked God; Duncan didn't believe in God, being able to pinpoint the exact moment when he knew it was a lie. Those people, such as Duncan, who'd done the right thing and found themselves abandoned could never forget the moment they'd realized the same thing.

Chapter 5

BARKLEY HAD managed to get himself to bed before midnight, waking just after eight on Sunday morning. The deli on Davisville would not open for another hour, so he decided to take his time and treat himself to the long version of his morning ritual. After setting out more food for his kids and taking some time to love on them a little and then brushing his teeth and shaving, he let the tub fill with hot water and the bathroom with steam, trying to plan the menu for his lunch with Duncan. He poured some bath salts into the water and stepped into the claw-foot tub, descending slowly into the hot water. Barkley let the hot, scented water relax his mind and his body, his back coming to rest against the plain white enamel of the tub. He closed his eyes and let his arms fall limp at his side. As usual, he only had to wait a few moments before he felt the familiar raspy licking against his fingers. "Hey, Stinkerbell," he cooed after opening his eyes and seeing the precious little face hovering near the edge of the tub. "You wanna come in?" He knew it would only take her a second or two to realize the room she'd wandered into, and sure enough, within a few moments, the licking stopped and Tinkerbell beat a hasty retreat out of the bathroom.

After several minutes of lying there and imagining every possible combination of lunch menu, Barkley sat up, grabbed the loofa, and brushed it over his heated skin. He pulled the drain stopper, standing to rinse himself off with the handheld shower attachment as the water drained away. He dried himself and headed to his bedroom, pulling on a pair of shorts and a polo shirt before heading to the kitchen to fix himself some tea and breakfast. He sat on the floor with his cereal, feeling like Saint Francis among the animals, and double-checked that everyone had had some of their breakfast as well.

This routine of having a hot bath and then sitting with the kids was not something he did very often in the morning, but this ritual was the one thing that would always bring him down from a performance. Most people didn't think twice about falling asleep after a tough day of working and then taking care of children or loved ones. But an opera singer's day didn't start until five or six in the afternoon, just when most other people were planning dinner or getting home from work.

But even Barkley, single as he was, still had to perform those routine tasks like grocery shopping and waiting in line at the ATM during the same hours as everyone else. And now that he had his animals, Barkley was glad that he was leaving the business. There was nothing more difficult in an opera singer's life than ensuring there was a balance between getting enough sleep and waking in time to run all the errands on the list. This was the one aspect of a *normal* life that Barkley envied. He'd always imagined it must be incredibly reassuring to know that you would go to bed at the same time every night and wake up at the same time every morning; and if you were lucky enough to find someone who would do that beside you, in the same bed? Barkley couldn't imagine needing anything else besides that.

He was always amused when people talked about the glamorous life of a celebrity or about how great it must be to be admired and fawned over, everything being done for you and having nothing but the best. And he supposed that there were those individuals, unaccustomed to relying on their own sense of self, who could be easily swayed into thinking all the attention meant something. But these were usually the same people, Barkley had discovered early on in his career, who would never be happy with any amount of attention, with anything other than having their egos stroked twenty-four hours a day, as if going one minute without it would mean that they were worth nothing.

It had taken Barkley only a few years to realize that being famous, despite its occasional perks, was really just an illusion, a severely distorted one, filled with its own problems. It's why Barkley had fired his agent, his manager, and his publicist. They had all been interested in doing what was best for Barkley Reinhardt, the singer, not Barkley Reinhardt, the frustrated and lonely man. Barkley had no delusions about their individual jobs. He knew that it was not their responsibility to keep him happy or to ensure that he had anything but a stellar image and enough contracts that would make them all wealthy and independent. But he had hoped that each of them would be interested in sharing more than just a desire to keep making more and more money.

His agent had been the first to go. Christopher had made the unfortunate mistake, on more than one occasion, of booking Barkley for roles that neither interested him nor suited his voice. *But you can sing anything you put your mind to, Barkley.* That had been his agent's rationale for just about every decision, as if keeping promises Christopher had made without consulting him first was only a matter of Barkley working harder, concentrating even more. *I've told you before that I will not damage my voice singing these heavier roles on stage.* Singing a Verdi role for a recording was one thing, but to sing the same role on stage, where projection and diction would be scrutinized by the critics, could mean irreparable damage to the one thing that kept them all employed. So without any fanfare, Barkley had dismissed his agent and wished him luck in all of his future endeavors.

The publicist and manager had been next to go. Within a few hours, Barkley had gone from a commodity to something he'd been long before any of the three had entered his life: independent. Regardless of where Barkley's career went—if anywhere at all—he would remain independent and in control of any and all decisions that affected his life. The advantages or perks of being famous had actually stripped him of any kind of autonomy; being famous had actually made him dependent on far too many people. And Barkley knew, all too well, that people would eventually let you down. It wasn't that Barkley wasn't willing to give people second, or even third or fourth, chances; it was the realization that no one could be counted on to do what was right.

With all of his kids napping except for Tinkerbell, Barkley had spent what time he could trying to find as much information on Duncan's time in jail and what had caused it. He'd consulted articles written at the time and had even read the ridiculous comments posted by every moron with a keyboard. The only thing that Barkley could state without equivocation was that Duncan had gone to jail instead of revealing the name of a confidential informant, a source that worked for the prime minister's office. The subsequent suicide of this informant had been widely blamed on Duncan, although Barkley didn't understand the reasoning. How could the suicide of a confidential informant be blamed on the man who'd gone to jail to protect the informant's identity?

Of course, there had always been those extremists who could make anything seem like it had never happened or like it was the responsibility of some covert government department gone rogue. Those explanations were easy to dismiss. What wasn't so easy to dismiss were those arguments that the confidential informant had been misled, wrongly convinced that his identity would never be revealed. Or the theory that the identity of the informant wasn't as confidential as it might have appeared. There were only a half dozen individuals who would have had access to the information revealed in Duncan's article, but only three of them would have had access so early in the campaign for re-election.

Barkley wondered how anyone would have been able to identify the informant, even if the possibilities had been narrowed down to three people. Each one of them would have been nervous, denying his or her culpability, something that would put them all at an equal level of suspicion. *No*, Barkley thought to himself as he saw Princess making her way to his bedroom, *no one who wasn't trying to sell an even more sensational story could blame Duncan for the man's suicide.* And as he grabbed his keys to head to the deli, Barkley quickly surmised that, if the man hadn't killed himself, the truth would have remained buried in governmental bureaucracy and red tape.

He whistled for Mozart and Salieri and grabbed a trash bag from the wicker basket underneath the hall table. "Hey, boys, come on, time for poops." Salieri was the first to arrive at the door, his tongue licking Barkley's face, as if they hadn't seen each other in days. Mozart hopped around the corner and waited for his turn, closing his eyes so that Barkley could rub and stroke his chin.

The phone rang and Barkley thought about letting it go to voice mail. *What if it's Duncan?* He reached over to the hall table and picked up the handset. "Hello?"

"Barkley?"

He recognized Duncan's voice almost immediately. "Yes, this is Barkley. Duncan?"

"Hi, yes, it's me." Barkley couldn't help but notice that there was a certain hesitation. "I'm just calling to make sure we're still okay for the interview." Barkley was about to answer when he heard barking in the background followed by Duncan's voice; it sounded distant, as if he'd cupped a hand over the receiver but not completely. "Yes, Neptune, we'll go to the park as soon as I get off the phone." Barkley smiled; he was a dog lover too. "Sorry," Duncan said with a chuckle. "They're not good at waiting."

Barkley looked down at his two angels, using his free hand to stroke and ruffle fur absentmindedly. "I'm still available, yes." Barkley heard more barking and wondered what kind of dogs they were. "Listen, since we'll be working over lunch and there's plenty of room, why don't you bring your dogs with you? I'm sure they'd love to get out for the day."

"Oh, I don't think—"

"I insist," Barkley said with a certain finality. "Oh, by the way, is there anything you don't like to eat?"

"Ah, no," Duncan said, his voice betraying a little confusion. "Not really."

"Okay, we'll see you in a couple of hours then."

They said their goodbyes and Barkley turned back to the two mutts. "How about that, guys? You're going to make some new friends today."

Barkley took the elevator to the lobby, dogs quiet and obedient as always, and wondered again if Duncan had ever had anyone with whom he could discuss all that he'd been through, or if he'd simply been abandoned by those once close to him, those people finding it more convenient to distance themselves. Barkley knew all too well that abandonment could eat away at a person until he felt like nothing more than a ghost.

DUNCAN WAS back from his trip to the park, his dogs seeming less rambunctious. He'd purposely tried to tire them out so he wouldn't have any embarrassing moments in the posh condo of Barkley Reinhardt. The last thing he needed was to have to pay for something his dogs chewed or broke. They weren't ill-behaved dogs, in fact, Duncan thought they were perfectly well behaved, but he wasn't going to take any chances. If he knew Zeus at all, he knew that he could be somewhat unpredictable. He leaned over to rub under Zeus's chin, smiling at his furry friend. "You drink out of Barkley's toilet or chase his kitten, and I will be very disappointed." Duncan tried to look stern, but failed miserably when the two-year-old Lab just cocked his head to one side and opened his big brown eyes really wide. "Yeah, don't give me that look. You know what I'm talking about." Unlike his brother Neptune, Zeus had a penchant for chasing smaller animals, especially squirrels. Duncan had learned the hard way that Zeus saw everything small and furry as a squirrel.

Duncan finished lacing up his desert boots and then turned to the small mirror that hung near the door to his apartment. For the first time in a very long time, Duncan was impressed by what he saw. His pants still showed a great ass, one of the many assets that had gotten him plenty of action before his fall from grace. And his shirt, with the first few buttons left unfastened, still showed his well-toned torso, thinner but more defined. He'd taken special care this morning to use one of the new razors that he saved for times such as this. Razors cost money, but using the electric trimmer he'd had for many years meant using something that was already bought and paid for. He'd learned to think that way, to never waste what he couldn't spare.

He was wearing a clean and pressed white button-down shirt, his dress pants were ironed, and he actually found himself feeling like a member of the human race again. He didn't eat any breakfast, but with any luck, Duncan figured he might be able to scrounge around later and find enough change to be able to buy some more Kraft dinner. He'd gotten to the stage where he despised the stuff, but ignoring that fact had allowed him to eat most days.

Duncan ushered the three of them out of the apartment, the two leads firmly in his grip, and pocketed his keys after locking the door to his apartment. He headed down the four flights of stairs, shrugging his messenger bag higher onto his shoulder. Once out of the building, he felt the heat of the afternoon, already somewhat more oppressive than it had been this morning. He had about half an hour to get to Barkley's condo on Merton, so he decided to walk slowly, allowing himself and his two companions to enjoy the bright colors and the fresh air. He walked by the banks and the specialty shops, imagining he would soon be able to enter because he had the money to do so.

He passed the Baptist church that had always put him in mind of those medieval stories of princesses locked in towers and their handsome and charming princes coming to rescue them and then living happily ever after. Lost in those kinds of thoughts, he found himself walking alongside the cemetery he'd passed last night, the cemetery he'd often thought of entering and wandering around, just to see how many famous names he could recognize. He knew of Glenn Gould, but that was about it.

With Zeus and Neptune pulling only occasionally against their leads, Duncan walked under the overpass, the one that had been covered in those weather-beaten tarps for what seemed like years, and then he turned east onto Merton. He glanced down at his watch and stopped in his tracks, both Zeus and Neptune looking back as if to ask whether they'd get to explore this new territory. He was about ten minutes ahead of schedule. Ten minutes wouldn't necessarily have bothered him before, but he didn't want to seem too eager. He saw the Ethan Allen store on the corner, its bright blue signs enticing him to come in and dream about the kind of life he'd had and would have again. Instead of entering the store, however, he just stood outside gazing through the huge windows with Zeus and Neptune lounging on the ground, seemingly content to just rest and soak up the sun. He thought of Barkley's furniture and wondered if this was the store where he'd purchased some of the beautiful furnishings that gave the condo so much warmth.

He respected Barkley's style of having just the right amount of tastefully elegant, yet functional, furniture. Duncan wasn't necessarily one of those gay guys who felt the need to spend time and money making sure his apartment, or his body for that matter, was always dressed in the latest finery, but he did have an appreciation for those men who always managed to look their best.

Checking his watch again, he decided that he could live with being five minutes early and walked to the building he'd left last night. Duncan crossed the street and walked the short distance to the quaint semicircular driveway and the double doors, hoping that the same doorman would be on duty. If not, he would have to hope that Barkley was around to answer the phone when the new doorman called up to his condo.

As he entered into the elegant lobby of the building, the same doorman waved to him and told him that Mr. Reinhardt was expecting him. *Hmm,* Duncan thought as he made his way to the bank of elevators, *it's a nice feeling not to have to worry about waiting, to just be waved in.*

As the ping of the elevator sounded just before the doors opened, he made a mental note to thank Barkley for planning ahead like that. It was an encouraging thought to have someone thinking about him.

Before the elevator doors opened on the twentieth floor, Duncan checked his appearance one last time and reminded Zeus and Neptune about their behavior. He turned left out of the elevator and headed to Barkley's door, surprised when it opened before he even had a chance to knock.

"Welcome, Duncan," Barkley said and squatted immediately to be closer to the two dogs. "And welcome to you beautiful pups as well." Duncan smiled when Barkley held out a hand to Zeus and then to Neptune, both of them eager to shake.

"Thank you, Barkley. This is Zeus and this is Neptune." Duncan said as he pointed to each dog. "They're brothers. I rescued them about ten years ago when they were just puppies." Duncan felt a little warm all of a sudden and didn't know whether it was the long walk or the beautiful smile that Barkley flashed him during the introductions.

"Please," Barkley said as he stepped aside. "I have mine in the bedroom for now. We can make the introductions slowly."

Duncan took a minute while he removed his boots to notice that Barkley was dressed much more casually than he was. The summer shorts rode low on the singer's hips so that only his moderately hairy and muscled calves were visible. He noticed that Barkley was wearing flip-flops, the sandals showing the distended veins of the perfectly proportioned feet. He guessed the man's shoe size to be about the same as his own. "I'm sorry," Duncan said quickly. "If I'd known that, I would have left them at home."

"Nonsense," Barkley remarked as he bent down and unhooked the leads of both dogs. "It won't be any problem. They're absolutely perfect so far." Barkley wound the leads around his hand and waited for Duncan to let go of them. Duncan did so and he watched as they were placed on the entryway table. "I took the liberty of laying out some lunch for us on the balcony," Barkley said as he locked his door and moved to the center of the living room. "I hope you're hungry."

"Starved, thank you," Duncan said with a huge grin, trying to remember why he'd not wanted this assignment. "But you didn't have to go to all of that trouble."

"It's no trouble," Barkley said as he led Duncan to the balcony. "It's not too hot out there right now. And it beats feeling like an ice cube in here." Duncan watched Barkley pet Zeus and Neptune again and asked, "I bet you two are thirsty, huh? Who wants some nice cold water and something to eat?" Barkley led the dogs, who'd turned briefly back to Duncan as if asking for permission, into the kitchen where he'd already placed two big bowls of water and two big bowls of wet dog food on the floor near the other bowls for his own animals. Counting a total of five bowls, Duncan followed and felt the coolness of the tiles through his thin socks. Duncan could live with feeling like an ice cube right about now. The walk had made him quite warm, and his own apartment had no air conditioning at all.

"It doesn't seem fair keeping your animals locked up while mine are enjoying water and food."

"I made sure they all ate so there wouldn't be any squabbles over food if you brought yours." Barkley motioned to the balcony.

"I see five bowls," Duncan said after clearing his throat and checking Zeus and Neptune one more time. "How many cats and how many dogs?"

"I have three dogs. You saw all three of them already. And, of course, my escape artist, Tinkerbell the Tortie. Then there's Princess, the giant rabbit—she's a Flemish Giant. And there's also Marco, a guinea pig." Barkley turned and headed out on the balcony.

"Wow," Duncan stated after a low whistle. "And I thought I was an animal lover." He followed the singer out to a patio that was maybe eight feet by four feet and sat down in one of the wooden chairs, his eyes feasting on the assortment of sandwiches and salads. To keep his mind, and stomach, away from the most delicious-looking meal he'd seen in many months, he began riffling through his bag for his laptop and his notebook full of questions. He perched them near the edge of the small rectangular stool beside him and looked up when Barkley spoke again.

"I wasn't sure what you'd enjoy, so I just got two of everything," the man said, suddenly holding up his hand. "In terms of drinks, I have lemonade, water, beer, or iced tea."

Duncan felt his shoulders slump and a sigh escaped his lips. "If it wouldn't get me in trouble, I'd love a beer. But I'll just have water."

"I won't tell anyone," Barkley said, his smile making Duncan think this seemingly straight-laced musician could probably be hell on wheels if presented with the right motivation. "I'll bring out a couple of beers. Okay?"

Duncan nodded, focusing first on the calves as he watched the man retreat through the open French doors. He found his gaze traveling upward, taking in the smooth cotton fabric that clung to the finest ass he'd seen in a very long time. Duncan felt himself growing a little sweaty at the thought of peeling away the man's clothes slowly in order to explore, as equally slowly, the perfectly proportioned body hidden under the light summer clothes. He continued to watch, his eyes focusing on the hairy, muscled forearms, as Barkley twisted off the caps of two bottles and headed back outside.

"I hope Heineken is okay," Barkley said, his brow knitted with concern and apprehension.

"Perfect," Duncan said, reminding himself to go slowly with the beer. The last thing he needed was to get drunk and give his editor a valid reason to fire him. The bottles began to sweat as Duncan held his up. "Salut," he said with a smile.

"Absolutely," Barkley said, and Duncan found himself transfixed by the little pucker of those full lips.

Duncan brought his bottle to his lips, the feel of the green glass and the aroma of the barley and hops and malt making his head spin just a little. He tilted the bottle back and counted to two, then forced himself to pull the bottle away and set it on the little teak table.

"Okay," Duncan announced, proud of himself for showing some restraint. "Did you want to eat first, or should we do both at the same time, or...." He held his hands to the side, waiting and hoping that Barkley would want to eat without discussing business.

"Eat, then work," Barkley said, laughing, and unfolded his napkin. When the napkin was firmly in his lap, he held up the platter of sandwiches. "These are Italian sausage and Havarti on cheese and onion ciabatta bread." He gave the platter a quarter turn. "These are turkey, cranberry, and brie paninis." Barkley turned the platter one last time. "And these are my favorite: Bell peppers, Provolone, and spinach on cheese buns."

"Wow! Thank you, Barkley," Duncan said, embarrassed that he'd not thought to bring anything at all, as he reached for the cheese sandwich. "Since it's your favorite, how can I go wrong?" He took his own napkin and unfolded it, laying it across his dress pants.

"Please feel free to start with a salad," Barkley said with a smile, enjoying the fact that he'd managed to impress Duncan. "I usually eat mine at the end of the meal. My parents were very European that way." Barkley picked up his fork and held it over the first salad, still in its transparent plastic container. "This is an arugula salad." He pointed to the next container. "This is a cucumber and dill salad." Barkley let his fork hover over the last container. "And this is just a plain green salad."

"This is…." Duncan shrugged his shoulders and shook his head. "Of course, you realize now I'm going to have to take you out sometime to return the favor." He noticed the bashful look on Barkley's face and wondered if he knew Duncan had just asked him out on a date. He wasn't terribly sure he'd be able to take Barkley to any place he was used to, but Duncan was feeling confident that he would find some out-of-the-way place that wouldn't break his budget while he showed Barkley just how grateful he was. And Duncan was grateful, very grateful in fact, for being treated with such kindness.

"That's not necessary," Barkley said as he picked up his sandwich. "It was just a gesture…. That's all." Barkley smiled, and Duncan wondered what Barkley wasn't saying.

Chapter 6

DUNCAN SAW the flush across Barkley's cheeks and wondered if the singer was lying or not admitting something.

"Well, I don't know how to thank you," Duncan said, picking up his sandwich and reminding himself not to inhale the whole thing at once. *Try to show some class,* he kept saying to himself. *Try to act like this isn't the best meal you've seen in months.* "Do you have any other gigs coming up soon?"

Barkley looked at him with the strangest smile on his face, leaving Duncan to wonder if he'd misspoken. "At the end of the month, in about four weeks," Barkley said and then took a bite of his sandwich.

Duncan nodded and took a bite of his own sandwich, the aroma and flavors all assaulting him at once. He chewed slowly, enjoying the taste and textures in his mouth. After the bite had been reduced to near-liquid state, Duncan put down his sandwich and reached for his beer, wanting to let his eyes roll back in his head from the mix of beer and provolone and spinach. He pushed his tongue over his teeth quickly before opening his mouth again to speak. "Are your parents originally from Europe?"

"Yes," Barkley said around a mouthful of sandwich. Duncan wanted to reach across the table and kiss the man, he was so down-to-earth. He found himself wondering why he'd ever thought this man, from humble beginnings himself, would never speak with his mouth full. "They were both born in Austria but moved here when they were teenagers… with their parents, of course."

"So you speak German, then?" Duncan asked as he reached for his beer and took another tiny sip.

Barkley nodded as he swallowed and reached for his own beer. "Yes. German, French, English, and Spanish."

Duncan heard his own laughter. He didn't find it funny. It was more the laugh of a man who was watching himself fall farther and farther out of Barkley's league. "I can barely manage English," Duncan said, shaking his head and picking up his sandwich to take another bite. He noticed that Zeus and Neptune had approached the balcony, both of them sprawled out on the floor soaking up the sunshine but obviously preferring to stay where it was cooler.

"I don't know that I'd ever be mistaken for *being* German or French or Spanish, but I can get by just enough to learn the score quickly and not have too many people correcting my diction."

Duncan held up a finger while he finished chewing. "That was something I was quite surprised to find while I was doing some research yesterday." He swallowed and continued. "Most opera singers don't necessarily speak the languages they sing in, so how do you learn how to say all those words?"

"Most singers have some sort of a connection with either a vocal coach or a colleague that does speak that language." Barkley took a sip of his beer before continuing. "For example, when I speak Spanish, I'm sure there are a lot of native Spanish-speaking people who cringe and want to put pencils in their ears," Barkley said, laughing. "But I have a friend who is from Barcelona who is also a singer, so if I'm learning a piece, I call him and he gives me tips and tricks."

"So most singers have to hear the words over and over before they can actually perform the song?"

"Exactly," Barkley said as he continued eating his sandwich.

Neither man spoke again for a few minutes, each of them seeming to prefer to finish his sandwich.

"So you would call him, and then the two of you would meet somewhere to go over diction?"

"Yes," Barkley said, and Duncan tried not to show his disappointment. "Well, I usually just call him since he lives in Florida. But yes, then he would help me pronounce the words correctly or give me pointers on what vowel to sing on... stuff like that."

"Oh, I see," Duncan said as he felt the butterflies in his stomach. "It must be difficult to maintain friendships and relationships. How do opera singers maintain a marriage when they're traveling so often?"

Barkley leaned back in his chair and seemed to be pondering this question. "I don't know," he finally admitted. "Although, I do know of quite a few singers who travel frequently with their spouses, so maybe the trick is to hire your spouse as your agent or assistant or...."

Duncan noticed the slight shrug, another question coming to him almost immediately. "What do you mean *what vowel to sing on?*" Duncan had the urge to reach for his laptop and start recording again, but he didn't want the atmosphere to become formal. He wondered, too, as Barkley started to explain, whether he would actually use any of this in the article. Duncan figured the odds were slim and tuned back in to listen to the singer's explanation of vowels.

"So since there are only five pure vowels, singing is a matter of choosing the most appropriate vowel and singing with an open mouth on the vowel. When a consonant comes along, you articulate it very quickly and move on to the next vowel." Barkley popped the last bit of his sandwich into his mouth and chewed slowly.

"So," Duncan began, reaching for his beer and noticing that he still had half of it left. "Pop and jazz singers who sing with a closed mouth, are they risking damage to their instrument?"

"Not necessarily," Barkley said and then drained his beer. "But singing on a consonant or with a closed mouth limits projection and makes the words much harder to understand." Duncan watched as Barkley lifted himself out of his chair and held up his bottle. "Another?"

"Perhaps later?"

Barkley smiled and excused himself to go into the kitchen for another Heineken. While he was by himself on the balcony, Duncan found himself wondering what it would be like to have this kind of Sunday every week. A shared walk to the deli followed by a lazy afternoon of good food, good conversation, and moments of companionable silence. Perhaps a nap together on the sofa.

"The truly great singers in jazz and pop seem to understand, instinctually, that their voices carry much more power, much more beauty if the mouth is relaxed and if they sing only on vowels," Barkley said as he took his seat again.

"Do you think everyone has the ability to sing?"

"I don't know," Barkley said slowly. "I think it's possible there are some people who can't perceive rhythm or differences in pitch, just as there are people who can't perceive the various changes in hue when it comes to color." Barkley picked up the platter and held it out in front of Duncan again.

Duncan reached out and took another sandwich and then wiped his hands on the napkin in his lap. "Thank you," he said. He took one long swig of his beer and then replaced it on the table.

"That's a very interesting question," Barkley was saying, taking one of the sandwiches and cutting it in half. "Have you ever done any singing?"

"Me?" Duncan felt his eyes go wide and tried not to show his amusement at the question. "God, no. I play guitar, but that's about it." Duncan finished his beer and before he could put it down on the table again, Barkley was up and taking it from his hand. He disappeared only to come back seconds later with another Heineken for Duncan. "Thank you. I think two will have to be my limit, otherwise I might embarrass myself." He laughed as he felt the intense amber eyes on him. "Um, right, singing. No, I don't think anyone would ever want to hear me sing."

"That's what I used to say about my voice," Barkley said, his eyes still focused on Duncan's face. "Everyone is always his or her worst critic."

"True enough," Duncan said as he picked up his second sandwich and bit into it, the cranberry and turkey combination making his tongue so very happy. He chewed until he was able to speak. "Honestly, Barkley, I can't thank you enough for going to all this trouble. It was a really classy thing for you to do." Duncan watched the man's intense smile fade just a little.

"I'm sorry, Duncan. I've never been very good at being coy… or keeping secrets… or keeping my mouth shut," Barkley said as he leaned forward, bracing his forearms on the small table. "But I just wanted to tell you that I respect, very much, what you did all those years ago. And I'm sorry you were wrongly blamed for that man's death."

If Duncan had had anything in his mouth, he probably would have done a spit-take. Luckily, the only thing in his mouth had been saliva, and that seemed to be drying up far too quickly. Duncan looked across at the handsome face, noticing the pink cheeks and the warm and sincere smile. He nodded his head, just once, and said, "Thank you, Barkley. I appreciate that."

"I'M SORRY, again," Barkley said, noticing how surprised Duncan had been at his statement. "I know it's none of my business, but… I just wanted to tell you that."

"Only fair, I guess," Duncan said with a shrug. "I mean, after all, I'm butting into your life, so…. It's okay. Actually, I'm glad you know that about me." Barkley knew his confusion was plain on his face. "I want to make sure this article is… really great. Not just for me, but also for you." Duncan leaned his arms against the table. "I mean, if you're actually going to retire, this article could show everyone the real you, clear up all the misunderstandings."

Barkley thought about that, and while he appreciated the sentiment, he also knew that the misunderstandings would persist. It seemed that no matter what anyone ever said or did, the vast majority of people kept telling the same stories and lies over and over again as if they were some newborn who'd imprinted on a lie instead of the truth. Barkley had learned a long time ago that a lie was too entertaining to be disregarded for something as mundane as the truth. "Well, there's no doubt about the retirement, and I'd love to see this article help you regain some of the respect you lost, but I'm afraid most people don't really care about some opera singer." Barkley laughed self-deprecatingly and picked up his beer. "Here's to a great article."

"And to mutual respect," Duncan said, lifting his own glass.

Barkley decided that he liked this Duncan much better than the one he'd met Friday evening. He wondered about the change and what had prompted it. A strange kind of paternal feeling came over Barkley as he sat and watched the man plough through a second sandwich. The Duncan sitting in front of him on the balcony was the same Duncan he'd seen in most of the photos and press coverage, but there could also be no doubt that this man was thinner, perhaps more wary of life. The Duncan in the photos had seemed cocky, arrogant even, but this man with whom he was sharing lunch was less so, perhaps not entirely beaten into humility, but aware of the need to pretend as much.

"I don't understand how you managed to pick a favorite among these sandwiches," Duncan said, chewing his last bite. He leaned back, patting his belly and reaching for his beer. "That was excellent. Thank you, Barkley."

"You're very welcome," Barkley said, imagining what it would feel like to come home to this every day. No more round-the-world recital tours, no more waking up in hotel rooms and not having any clue what city he was in, and no more snooty society people thinking they'd hired him personally. *Society people*, he thought with some derision, although he chastised himself for the thought since it was the society people and their bank accounts that were responsible for the museums and the opera houses.

With the swiftness of a coloratura's cadenza, Barkley felt an idea forming inside his brain. He'd turned down a request from Mrs. Green, one of the grande dames of Toronto's elite, just last month. And Mrs. Green—or rather her husband, Edward—was in a perfect position to help Duncan. Barkley would have to think about it a little more, but he definitely thought he'd stumbled onto something. A little bargain, perhaps, that would see Barkley performing at a charity ball and Duncan working, again, as a serious journalist.

"Did you want to get started?" Barkley asked as he pointed to the laptop that was perched on the stool. "We can stay out here, or we can move inside if you're feeling warm."

"Here's fine," Duncan said, reaching for his laptop and notebook.

"Great," Barkley said with a smile. "I'm just going to wrap these up to keep the flies away, and I'll be right back." Barkley picked up a tray behind one of the French doors and put everything on it except the beers. "Would you like another beer? Oh," Barkley said quickly, "two is your limit, right? Sorry. Can I get you some water, then?"

"Water sounds great," Duncan said as he opened his laptop and flipped through his notes.

Barkley wrapped up the remaining three sandwiches and put them and the untouched salads in a plastic shopping bag, hoping that Duncan would not be insulted when he handed them over at the end of the interview. *You'll be doing me a favor*, Barkley would say. *I won't eat them all and they'll just go to waste. And besides, that's all I've been doing since I got home last week. Eating.* He figured if he did it as nonchalantly as possible and with his best charismatic smile that there would be no way for Duncan to refuse. And if Duncan didn't buy any of that, Barkley could point out that most of the sandwiches contained meat, and that he was a vegetarian. And Barkley was pretty sure that Duncan wasn't, not with the way he'd practically inhaled the turkey sandwich.

After filling a glass with ice, he poured some water from the filtered pitcher he kept in the fridge and returned to his guest. "Okay," Barkley said as he sat down. "Shoot."

"Right," Duncan said with a little chuckle. "Okay." Duncan punched a few keys on his laptop and then rubbed his hands together. "For the record, I didn't know too much about opera, but I've spent a couple of days poring over videos and previous interviews. So my first question for you is.... I noticed that when you sing oratorio... say *Elijah*, for example, that your face is almost glowing and your expression serene. But when you sing opera, even in concert footage, your face is a little harder, sharper. Is there a difference between singing the two genres? And if so, is it a technique thing or more a psychological approach?"

Barkley heard the question, but didn't know how to respond. He shook his head for a moment and brought a hand up to shoo away a fly.

"Sorry, was that a stupid question? Should I just move on?"

"No, absolutely not," Barkley said, perhaps a little too forcefully. "I... uh... don't think I've ever given that any thought." Barkley looked at Duncan and shrugged, a smile on both of their faces. "That's a very interesting question. Let me think for a moment." Barkley leaned back in his chair and took a couple of long pulls on his beer. After a moment or two, he leaned forward again, closer to the microphone. "I guess I'd have to say that it's both, really. When I'm singing oratorio, I'm always conscious of the fact that those are sacred texts. And regardless of my own beliefs, there are people out there for whom those words are the very words of God. Then there's the reality that I'm not necessarily playing a character as I would be in an opera, that the audience has come to see *me* and not my portrayal of *Figaro*, for example. So when I'm singing oratorio, there's no real *scene* that I'm playing. It's just me singing words and not the character singing words." Barkley felt a little pleased with his answer and leaned back again, draining his second beer. "If that makes any sense."

"Perfect sense," Duncan said, nodding his head. "And speaking of oratorio, would you say you prepare differently for an oratorio than for an opera? By prepare, I mean in terms of learning the libretto and planning the delivery, so to speak."

"Wow," Barkley said with a chuckle. "You really did do your research, didn't you?" He was caught off-guard by the way Duncan's cheeks pinked at the compliment. The man was beautiful, Barkley had to admit. "For me, I think the only difference would be that there isn't necessarily any blocking to memorize. I mean, when I'm singing an operatic role, I know I have to be upstage or stage right at this word, or I should have my hand pulled back ready to slap someone at this high note... that kind of thing. But in terms of warming up and preparing the instrument, there's no discernible difference for me."

"Would you say that you have a favorite oratorio you would like to perform? One that you will miss when you retire?"

Barkley found himself frowning when he thought about the question. He would miss all of his roles and all of the music he wouldn't be singing again, at least not in public anyway. He opened his mouth to give Duncan an answer, but then closed it again just as quickly. After thinking for another few seconds, he decided to be truthful. "I don't think I'll miss any of the music when I retire because I can just as easily sing it around the condo while I'm doing Saturday cleaning. I think what I'll miss when I retire is the *feeling* after I've gone out there and given a particularly good performance." Barkley picked up his empty beer bottle and stood up. "I'm going to get another. Can I get you anything else?"

Duncan shook his head and Barkley took another beer out of the fridge and returned, speaking before he'd even sat down again. "What I guess I mean by that is that there's a certain satisfaction in knowing that you've prepared yourself and know every nuance of the performance you'd *like* to give that evening, be it oratorio or opera. But then going out and having it actually happen... that's what I'll miss." Barkley noticed Duncan nodding. "But to answer your question, more often than not, I usually find myself singing selected arias from *Elijah* or *Saint Matthew Passion.*"

"That's actually my next question," Duncan said as he flipped to the next page of his notebook. "When they use your recording in a movie or in a television commercial, do they have to ask your permission or do they just approach the record company?"

"If it's a particular piece from a recording I was contracted to do through a record company, the producers must have their permission and not mine, since I'm not the owner of the recording. But they would also need the permission of the music's copyright owner. And that's the trickiest part."

"How so?"

"Most classical music wasn't written by the composer for his own use. Most composers, like Mozart or Bach or Verdi or Mendelssohn, were commissioned to write those pieces of music by kings, queens, counts, nobles, the Pope, or other religious organizations. So, not only would it be next to impossible to track where those copyrights landed, but most of that music is so old that the copyright laws of most countries no longer apply."

"So you make no money if one of your recordings is used in a film?"

"Not always, no," Barkley said, wondering why this particular topic was so fascinating to Duncan. "Sometimes, there will be consideration for the artist who made the recording—especially if it's written into the contract before he or she even makes the recording— but generally, if you don't think of it ahead of time, the record company owns the rights to that recording and can do whatever they want with it."

"That doesn't seem fair, does it?"

"That's why you need a good agent and a good lawyer," Barkley said, lifting his beer bottle in a silent toast.

"Do you ever listen to your own recordings?"

"No," Barkley said, somewhat flatly. "Never." Duncan seemed rather shocked at the answer, so Barkley elaborated. "I'm just like almost everyone else on the planet who hears his or her recorded voice and can't stand to listen to it. I remember hearing myself on some sort of recording when I was in school still, and I was… horrified, to say the least. Ever since then, if I can get out of hearing my recordings, I will. I guess it would be like finding out that Santa isn't real; it changes my perspective and I find myself compensating." Barkley noticed the wide-eyed expression on Duncan's face and he stopped talking. "Are you… is something wrong?"

"Santa's not real?"

IT WAS a cheap ploy for a quick laugh and Duncan knew it, but he still delighted in the beautiful smile and the wonderfully warm laughter wrapping around him. He tried not to smile or laugh at his own joke, but he couldn't help but smile at those happy amber eyes. "Sorry," Duncan said as he looked back down at his laptop. "I have a weird sense of humor sometimes."

"That," Barkley said emphatically. "That was funny."

Duncan nodded and looked over at Zeus and Neptune, who'd perked right up at Barkley's laughter. "I'm sorry to keep harping on this, but I'm feeling really guilty that your animals are all locked up still."

"Well," Barkley said as he got up and headed over to the dogs. "I don't let Princess or Marco or Tinkerbell outside, but we can take the dogs out, maybe let them run around and get to know each other?"

"Sounds great."

"Okay then," Barkley stated as he slapped his own knee. "I'll go and get the dogs, and we can make the introductions."

"Actually," Duncan said as he closed his laptop and raised himself off the chair. "Why don't I take the boys outside first, and then we can introduce them slowly?" Duncan saw Barkley's eyebrows come together in what he assumed was a moment of confusion. "Oh, no, Zeus and Neptune are great around other dogs and they love all animals, but I just think it might be better outside of a confined space." He wasn't sure he'd explained himself too well, but he didn't want anything to go wrong now; the afternoon was going so well.

"Okay," Barkley said with a smile. "We'll be down in a moment then."

Duncan smiled in return, wiping his palms across the front of his trousers, and nodded before calling his boys over to the entryway table so he could put the leashes back on. "Come on, boys, we're going out for a little play date." He looked over to Barkley, who was standing in front of a closed door. He watched as Barkley pushed open the door.

No sooner had the door opened than Duncan saw the same little kitten dart out toward freedom. "I got her," Duncan said with a laugh as the kitten made a beeline for the front door. He squatted down quickly and put his hands gently under the rib cage of the little kitten and pulled her against his chest, letting her smell the dogs on him first. "Hey, precious, do you remember me?" Duncan looked down at the sweet face and noticed for the first time that the little kitten had no eyes at all; for some reason, he'd assumed that the kitten had just had her eyes closed when he was here last. But then, he wasn't really watching her yesterday; he'd been too busy studying Barkley. "Do you wanna meet my boys?"

Duncan squatted on his haunches, keeping his palm up toward both of his dogs. "Zeus? Neptune? This is...." Duncan looked over at Barkley, who was holding a gigantic rabbit in his arms.

"Tinkerbell."

"This is Tinkerbell." Duncan moved a little closer with Tinkerbell still nestled against his chest. "Tinkerbell, this is Zeus and this one is Neptune." He watched for a moment, expecting barking and hissing, but after a few sniffs, the dogs just looked at him as if to say, *So what, it's a cat!* "Stay," he commanded before getting back up and walking Tinkerbell over to Barkley. "She's darling and so well behaved."

"Did you hear that, Stinkerbell?" Barkley put Princess back on the floor of the bedroom and took Tinkerbell from Duncan's arms, a jolt of electricity passing through him as his hands encountered rock-hard pecs. "He thinks you're well behaved, but he'll learn soon enough what a little stinker you are."

Tinkerbell mewed, in protest, Duncan assumed, and after planting a few kisses on her head, Barkley put her on a cat tree that was just inside the bedroom door. "Wow," Duncan exclaimed as he saw the cluttered bedroom. "That is quite the menagerie."

"Yeah," Barkley sighed. Duncan thought he could hear a little sadness in that one word. "It was either take them in or let them be killed." Barkley kept his hands on the cat tree; Duncan assumed to stop any further escape attempts. "I couldn't let them kill these animals."

"It's hard, I know," Duncan said in commiseration. Silence fell over them for a moment before Duncan reached out and touched Barkley's elbow. "Okay, I'll take the boys and meet you outside."

Barkley just nodded and picked up two leashes off the doorknob of the bedroom.

Duncan attached the leads to Zeus and Neptune and then headed out, his hand reflexively patting his pockets to make sure he had his keys, and pressed the button for the elevator. *Maybe the guy's not such a spoiled, rich brat after all. Seems to have a big heart.*

As he rode down in the elevator, Duncan wondered what other surprises were in store for him today.

Chapter 7

GETTING TO sleep Sunday night had been an exercise in futility, so Barkley had stayed up, drinking tea and sitting out on his balcony until after three in the morning. He was out there for hours, trying to think of how to proceed with the idea he'd had during his lunch with Duncan, the plan that—if it worked—could see the journalist back in mainstream media.

And then, of course, there were the thoughts of Duncan himself; they were random, disconnected thoughts about his eyes, his lips, his clean-shaven face, the way his muscles flexed and shifted underneath the thin cotton of his dress shirt. During the play date with the dogs, Barkley had found himself transfixed by the sight of Duncan's muscled ass underneath the thin fabric of those dress pants. It was such a beautiful ass, and Barkley couldn't keep his mind focused on anything but the way it would feel beneath his hands, what pleasures the snapping of those hips and those muscled thighs could bring. He'd had to readjust himself, as unobtrusively as possible, when he'd imagined himself positioned before it, looking down on it as he claimed it, their bodies sweaty and yearning for each other. He'd had to take himself in hand later that evening to find some release from the images, from the frustration of having done without for so long.

He'd finally fallen asleep on the overstuffed sofa, but couldn't remember at what time, precisely. Barkley only remembered waking up just after five and then heading back out to the balcony and letting the cool morning breeze soothe his tired brain. Since Duncan had entered his life, Barkley had not been sleeping as well as he usually did, which might prove to be a minor obstacle if he was serious about singing this weekend in exchange for the favor he would ask of Edward Green.

Barkley spent several hours early Monday morning puttering around his condo, completing little odd jobs that he'd left undone due to his hectic schedule, thoughts of Duncan never far from his mind. When he saw that the large clock on the kitchen wall was showing half-past eight, Barkley picked up the phone and dialed the number that he had memorized.

"Edward? It's Barkley Reinhardt." Barkley was putting his plan into motion. If he wasn't so nervous about how all of this would work out, he would have come up with some catchy name for this particular operation. As it was, however, Barkley was just hoping he wouldn't make a complete fool out of himself.

"Barkley, my boy, how are you?"

"I'm fine, sir, thank you for asking." Barkley took a deep breath and continued. "Listen, I was wondering if you would still like me to perform at your charity event this weekend." He looked over at Tinkerbell and Butter, the two of them arguing over a little stuffed mouse.

"Of course," Edward Green said, his voice as loud and grating as ever. "We've already had the posters and the programs printed up, but we can toss you in there as a nice last-minute surprise."

"That's fine," Barkley said, closing his eyes and using all of his years of technique to keep his voice from shaking. "Would I be able to ask one favor in return?"

"Well played, Barkley, well played," Edward said, his tone teasing and playful.

"I would be very grateful if you could give a friend of mine an interview," Barkley began, uncertain of how much of the story to tell. "He's a very experienced journalist, used to print media, but something tells me he would do very well with your enterprise." He took a deep breath. "Just an interview. If nothing comes of it, I'll still be the last-minute surprise at the charity event this weekend." Barkley closed his eyes and hoped that this would all turn out the way he wanted.

"I'll have my assistant set something up for later today," Edward said and then quickly added, "Of course, now I'll have to call my wife and have her call you so you'll know which songs you'll be performing on Saturday."

"Well played, Edward," Barkley said into the phone, his smile growing. "He's very… unique."

"Uh-huh," Edward commented. "And what would this unique man's name be?"

"Duncan Spencer."

"I'll have my assistant take care of the details."

"Thank you, Edward," Barkley said as he fell into the armchair nearby. "I'll see you on Saturday."

"Yes, you will," Edward promised.

Barkley heard the line go dead, not really being surprised that Edward Green, the sole owner of Teleglobal Media Incorporated, did not waste time on trivial things like saying *goodbye*. Teleglobal Media Incorporated had been built from one lonely radio station almost forty years ago by a very young and a very ambitious Edward Green. That ambition had seen one radio station expand into a media conglomerate that put Edward Green in the top five of the Fortune 500.

Barkley had met him through the man's wife many, many years ago after Barkley had agreed to perform at another charity event. The two men had hit it off right away, having much in common besides humble beginnings and a work ethic that saw them give little thought to working twenty-hour days. Barkley just knew that if anyone could see past the bullshit that had been heaped on Duncan, it would be Edward. He wanted to call Duncan and tell him, explain it to him, but he figured that that would just make the poor man even more nervous. All Barkley could do was hope that Duncan would go and be just as honest and charming as he'd been during their few times together.

The next call Barkley had to make was to find out whether Mrs. Green already had an accompanist picked out for him or whether he would have to arrange for his own.

DUNCAN POPPED the last bite of sandwich into his mouth and smiled. He shook his head at the memory of Barkley presenting him with a grocery bag full of sandwiches and salads after they'd spent most of yesterday afternoon together. Duncan's first reaction had been to refuse, feeling as if he were some sort of homeless man who needed charity. But then he'd looked up to see how much the gesture had meant to Barkley; how could he refuse an act of such generosity? It didn't feel like charity coming from Barkley, and Duncan had been completely undone by the smile that had spread across the flushed and handsome face when he'd taken the bag.

They'd worked together for almost six hours yesterday afternoon, sitting on the balcony or playing with the animals. Duncan was going over the recordings, chastising himself when he found himself listening to the voice but not the words; if he didn't get this attraction under control, it would take him forever to finish this article. He remembered every moment of their time together yesterday in vivid detail, from the way Barkley would compliment him on his unique and thought-provoking questions to the way the man's body looked and moved in those baggy shorts. Duncan was even sure that Barkley had been flirting with him once or twice, but he was also willing to admit that could have been wishful thinking. And the way Zeus and Neptune took to Barkley and his two mutts? There was nothing more attractive to Duncan than a fellow dog-lover.

He found himself daydreaming again when the phone rang. He leaned over and picked it up, hoping it would be Barkley.

"Hello?"

"Duncan Spencer?"

"Yes," Duncan said, wondering who this man was on the other end of the line.

"My name is William Ford, and I am the personal assistant to Edward Green." Duncan's heart began to race, his thoughts muddled and confused. He thought for a moment he might be in trouble, that he'd done something wrong, but Edward Green was in broadcasting, not in print news, so how could Duncan have done something to piss off Edward Green? "Mr. Green would like to know if you are available to meet with him, for an interview of sorts, at four this afternoon."

Duncan's mouth opened, and then he realized that this must be a joke; someone was playing him for a fool. Maybe it was his editor, Thomas. He felt like telling whoever this was to go fuck himself, but then realized that, even if this was a joke, and even if Duncan did tell this guy where to go, he could be screwing himself out of the job he already had.

"Hello? Mr. Spencer?"

"Yes, I'm still here." Duncan's brain was working furiously, trying to figure out what to do. "I'm sorry. I don't understand. I'm in print news, not broadcasting."

"News is news, Mr. Spencer. Are you interested in attending the interview?"

"Of course," Duncan said, still not totally trusting this wasn't all some elaborate hoax. "I'll be there at four. The building on King Street?"

"Yes," the disembodied voice agreed. "If you have a portfolio, please bring it."

"Yes, I will… thank you," Duncan said, but then realized that the voice had already disconnected from his end.

What the fuck? Duncan sat at his tiny kitchen table and stared at his phone. He didn't really understand what was happening. Why would Edward Green, the media mogul, be calling him out of the blue for an interview? It certainly couldn't have been for the piece-of-shit fluff assignments he was doing for *The Communiqué*. Duncan doubted very much that his articles on the pseudocelebrities and the wannabes of southern Ontario would catch the eye of the most powerful man in Canada.

When the screen of his phone went black, Duncan realized he would need to wash his shirt again, the only good dress shirt he owned. It was still sitting in his laundry basket from yesterday. He pushed himself away from the table and started riffling through drawers and coats and even behind the sofa cushions looking for two loonies. He found them at the bottom of his winter coat, grabbed the detergent bottle, his shirt, and headed down to the laundry room, checking his watch on the way. He had two hours to wash and iron his shirt, steam the creases out of his dress pants and head over to the interview. He didn't even dare think about the interview itself.

As he fussed and fidgeted with the machines and the bottle of detergent, his hands shaky and uncooperative, he told himself to take all of this one task at a time. Just like he would take each of Edward Green's questions one at a time. He would answer honestly and try to convince the mogul that he would not be sorry for hiring him. He would somehow convince Edward Green that Duncan Spencer had grown up and recognized what an empire like Teleglobal Media needed from its reporters.

Duncan just hoped that between now and the interview, he would figure out what that was, exactly.

DUNCAN LEFT the Human Resources offices, copies of his new contract and his personnel papers in the envelope he was stuffing into his messenger bag. As he exited the huge building and stepped onto King Street, he replayed the interview over and over in his head.

What can you bring to my enterprise that no one else can?

The question was pretty standard as far as interviews go, and Duncan had already anticipated his answer. *I'll bring the same dedication to truth and honesty as I do with any story, but with an increased awareness of what the story actually means for the people, for the community, for how that one story can touch so many lives.*

What would you do differently if you could go back to before your incarceration?

Duncan had anticipated that one, as well. *I don't think it would really matter right now, since the legislation now tells us that there can be no such entity as a confidential informant. But if that legislation didn't exist, I know I wouldn't do anything differently. The informant came to me. I explained the risks, the dangers, and he chose to go ahead with the story. There's nothing I could have done to prevent the outcome.*

It was after that answer that Edward Green had punched a button on his telephone and asked his assistant, William, to come into the office. Duncan had squared his shoulders and looked directly at Edward Green. If the interview was over and he was to be escorted out of the building—after only a five-minute interview— then he would do it with dignity.

William, Mr. Green had said to his assistant, *would you please show Mr. Spencer to the HR offices.* Duncan had watched Mr. Green pass some papers to his assistant. *Give Judy these papers and make sure that Mr. Spencer gets a pass card.* The assistant merely nodded and motioned to the door. *Welcome, Duncan. Oh, and tell Barkley that my wife won't be calling him until Wednesday; she's off on some shopping trip in New York for another two days.*

Duncan had turned around, wondering what Barkley had to do with any of this, or even how Mr. Green knew that he knew Barkley at all.

Sorry? Duncan had said to the media mogul. *How did you—?* Duncan stopped talking, choosing to follow the assistant instead. Duncan had read everything he could find about the baritone; if he had a scheduled performance this weekend, Duncan would have known about it, would have read about it online or seen a poster. No, there was something odd about these two pieces of information.

Listen, Mr. Ford, Duncan had said in the elevator, turning to regard the assistant. *Why would Mr. Green tell me to pass that message on to Barkley Reinhardt? How does he know I even know the man?*

The assistant's reaction had been nothing more than a knowing glance before the doors opened and Duncan was escorted into the very large office of one Judy Knowles. *Director of Human Resources* was spread out across the door just beyond which the redhead in the elegant suit sat behind a desk easily four times her size. Very quickly, and with great efficiency, Duncan found himself immersed in signing paper after paper, his brain inundated with facts and figures and schedules and all sorts of other information he'd not thought much of since his fall from grace.

But that's all over now, he thought to himself as he made his way out of the building, contracts and security key card in his front pocket. He took the security card out and studied it, laughing when he saw his stunned expression staring back at him. He wasn't sure, precisely, what Barkley had to do with this, but he decided he had to go and see him. Not to find out, but to let him know that he knew. Barkley had had something to do with this bright new horizon in front of Duncan. He steered himself toward the subway station and prayed Barkley would be home. And after he thanked the man, he'd be heading to the subway to buy three juicy steaks: one for him and one each for Zeus and Neptune.

Duncan was soon in the elevator of Barkley's building, tapping his fingers nervously against his thigh, the thought of what he was about to do overwhelming him a little more than he'd anticipated.

He'd taken the subway located near Edward Green's downtown office, had received a smile from the doorman, and was waiting to be let out on the twentieth floor. His life had been turned upside down more times than he cared to remember since his thirty days in jail, but he'd never had so much change before he'd met Barkley Reinhardt.

The doors made the heavy clanging sound as they opened, and Duncan found himself moving quickly, his messenger bag dangling and swinging at his side, to the door that had Barkley on the other side. He reached out and knocked three times in rapid succession.

"Coming!" Barkley's voice, so familiar to Duncan now, got louder as it approached the door.

Finally, just when Duncan didn't think he could wait any longer without chickening out, the door opened and Barkley stood there right in front of him. Duncan didn't waste any time by admiring the view. He stepped inside, let the bag fall to the floor, not even caring that his laptop was in there, and wrapped his arms around the beautiful man standing in front of him. There, with the door to the condo wide open and his desire to consume this man on total display, Duncan wrapped one arm around Barkley's trim waist and let the other hand find its way up to rest at the base of the warm neck.

He looked into those breathtaking amber eyes before he took the soft and slightly parted lips. Duncan's eyes closed on instinct, and he felt himself growing hard inside of his dress pants. It had been so long since he'd felt anything even remotely close to the wave of complete abandon that flowed through him as he stood there, Barkley safe in his arms, his hands and lips devouring the man who had single-handedly changed his life.

When his lungs screamed for oxygen, Duncan pulled his lips away but kept his hands and his body pressed to Barkley's. He didn't want to open his eyes. A lifetime of lazy Sundays lying in bed with this man flashed before his eyes, and he didn't want to see anything else at that moment. He could feel an accelerated heartbeat, but didn't know if it was his or not. He pressed his forehead to the slightly shorter man's. That thought made him smile. *It'll be nice to be able to kiss someone while standing up without straining my neck.* He caressed and kneaded the warm flesh of the singer's neck.

Finally, he opened his eyes and looked down to see Barkley's kiss-swollen lips.

"I know I should apologize, but...." Duncan closed his eyes, willing with all his might Barkley's next words.

"Do I seem like I'm upset?" Barkley moved his hands down to Duncan's waist and began tugging on his dress shirt.

"Thank you," Duncan whispered, his lips ghosting over Barkley's. Both of them seemed out of breath. "Just.... Thank you."

Barkley didn't say anything for a moment or two, and it was during this wait that Duncan realized Barkley's hands were stroking up and down his back, always stopping just before moving underneath the waistband of his pants. "Did you get the job?"

Duncan nodded, his forehead still pressed to Barkley's.

"I only got you the interview," Barkley sighed as Duncan's lips moved softly, purposefully, over his. "If you got the job, it was because of you and not me."

"I don't know what to do, what to say," Duncan said with a little tremor in his hands. "I've never met anyone like you before."

"Do whatever you want, say whatever you want."

Duncan closed his eyes as he felt Barkley's hands glide over his torso, his fingers beginning to undo the buttons of Duncan's shirt. "Wanna taste you," Duncan sighed, his lips finding Barkley's again. "Wanna be inside you, feel you around me."

"God, yes." Barkley's answer was nothing more than a puff of air across Duncan's lips. Duncan felt a hand caress and knead his stiff cock through the dress pants. "Please?"

"Jesus," Duncan hissed as he felt both of Barkley's hands working to free his erection. "Bedroom?"

Duncan smiled, for only a moment, when he heard Barkley's soft laughter, felt his heated breath against his lips. Barkley pulled away, shutting the door and locking it before leading Duncan to the master bedroom, closing the door behind them. Duncan barely noticed that all of the clutter had disappeared before they were on each other, hands moving slowly, discovering and exploring.

There was a huge bed in the center of the wall opposite the door. It was neat and orderly, just like everything else in Barkley's life. Before reaching the bed, Duncan turned Barkley around and returned his hands to the small of the singer's back and the base of his neck. He ducked his head slightly and began to kiss Barkley's neck, rejoicing in the insistent sighs and repeated approval for what he was doing. Duncan continued to back up until they were at the foot of the bed. He placed his feet on either side of Barkley's and began to lower him to the surface of the bed, one hand coming out to brace himself while the other stayed at Barkley's lower back.

Barkley's hands came out and held on to Duncan's shoulders, their bodies descending slowly until the two of them were kissing again on the cool softness of the duvet. As he kept himself suspended a few inches above Barkley, Duncan moved to undo the button of the cargo shorts the singer was wearing. He had it undone in no time and then felt his own erection twitch at the sound of the zipper as it mingled with the soft, insistent words of encouragement from the voice he would recognize anywhere.

"You must be my very own angel," Duncan sighed against the singer's lips. "You sing like one, and you did that for me. You don't even know me."

"Please," Barkley said, and Duncan claimed his lips again, reaching with his hand under the waistband of the cargo shorts. He hissed his approval when he found no underwear and an impressive erection already leaking and straining against his touch. Barkley pulled his head back slightly and stared into Duncan's eyes. "Want you."

It was all Duncan needed to hear. He pulled himself off the shorter man and reached down, pulling off the cargo shorts in one swift movement while Barkley removed his polo shirt and tossed it on the floor. Duncan returned his attentions to the fully naked man beneath him, kissing and caressing and licking whatever skin he could reach.

"Naked, please," Barkley gasped as Duncan took one of the man's nipples in his mouth. "Want to see you."

Duncan pulled off the writhing body beneath him once more and stood, unbuttoning his own shirt before removing it and tossing it behind him. The muscles on his chest and in his arms flexed as he undid his dress pants, letting them fall to the floor. He kicked off his only decent pair of dress shoes and then reached down to pull off his socks. He stood there looking over the flushed skin of a man he'd only met three days ago, pulling on his own cock and watching Barkley's reach out for him.

Positioning himself at the edge of the bed, Duncan dropped to his knees and hooked his arms underneath Barkley's muscular thighs, moving his hands up to stroke and pinch Barkley's nipples while his mouth took the singer all the way to the base. He closed his eyes as his senses were overloaded with the scent of this man's musk, the feel of the smooth skin beneath his fingers, and the taste of his throbbing erection.

"Duncan, please, fuck me," Barkley whispered, his hands moving over the hands that were squeezing and pinching his nipples. Duncan felt those hands wrap around his wrists, pulling him up with an urgent sense of need.

"You got it." Duncan said as he positioned himself on top of the singer's needy body. "Condoms? Lube?"

"Fucking hell," Barkley grunted. "Forgot about those," he said as he flipped himself onto his stomach and crawled across the bed to open the drawer of the nightstand. "Here," he said, handing Duncan a tube of lube and a chain of five condoms. "Please, Duncan, hurry."

"Jesus," Duncan hissed as he watched the man squirm and wiggle underneath him again. He lubed two fingers and reached down, inserting them inside of Barkley, the muscles clamping down almost immediately. The heat of that hole sent shock waves through Duncan as he pushed his fingers in even farther, finding the bundle of nerves that made Barkley cry out. "God, you're beautiful," Duncan said and tapped against Barkley's prostate again.

"I'm ready, Duncan," Barkley moaned. "Now, Duncan."

Duncan looked down at the writhing body, felt the man's hands skimming over his body until they found his erection. While Barkley pulled and massaged his aching cock, Duncan worked to free the condom of its wrapper. He slipped two fingers back inside of Barkley and pushed the hands out of his way, working to put the condom on with one hand. "So impatient, Barkley," he teased as he thumped a finger against his prostate. "Gonna make you feel so good, baby."

He positioned his dick at Barkley's hole and moved his hands, bracing them on either side of the flushed face, looking down between their bodies. Duncan felt the hands moving up and down his straining arms, felt Barkley's wet tongue licking up and down his forearms, the smaller man's teeth nipping and teasing his overheated flesh. "Touch yourself, baby," Duncan demanded, sucking in a quick breath as the man did as he was told.

Duncan pushed inside, breaching the ring of muscle and feeling the exquisite pressure as it pulled him inside, all the way. "Fuck, yeah," he grunted as he pulled out against the suction. "Hold on, baby," he said as he moved his arms, hooking each of Barkley's legs over an elbow. "Oh, oh, fuck, yeah, baby," he panted as he pegged the prostate, making the ring of muscle contract. "Squeeze me, Barkley."

"Duncan," Barkley whispered, nipping and sucking at the muscled forearms with his teeth and lips. "Yes, yes," he panted, finally opening his eyes.

"Jesus, baby," Duncan said again as he began to pump in and out of the heat, his movements picking up speed and his hips snapping, his balls slapping against the tight ass he'd fantasized about. "Wanna watch you come, Barkley."

As he lowered his body to kiss the swollen lips, Duncan knew he wouldn't last too much longer, not with the pressure and the heat driving him to pump faster and faster. He couldn't remember the last time he'd felt so totally turned on, so completely aroused he felt as if his body were on fire. He looked down into Barkley's amber eyes as he pulled away from that mouth, that tongue. "Come for me, Barkley. Wanna feel you squeeze me when you come."

Duncan saw Barkley's eyes close again, his head thrashing from side to side, his fist moving over the head of his swollen prick. With a look of total abandon on his handsome face, Barkley sucked in a breath, and then Duncan saw the heat spray up and hit both of them. He felt the contractions around his engorged cock as Barkley rode out his orgasm, his hand slowing.

"Jesus, Lord, Barkley," he said as he felt his balls pull up, his lungs aching for more oxygen. Duncan felt himself growing closer and closer to the edge, to the moment he'd been dreading; he didn't want these sensations to end. He wanted to stay inside of this man forever, feel this connection every minute of every day.

Duncan's spine began to tingle, his toes began to curl, and he quickly lowered himself to take Barkley's lips in a scorching kiss. With three final thrusts, each one ending with him squeezing his ass to thrust farther and farther inside the heat, Duncan felt himself fall over the edge, his entire body thrumming with the intensity of his own orgasm.

As he rode it out, Barkley murmuring sweet words against his hair, Duncan felt the man's arms wrap around him and hold him close.

Chapter 8

THE TWO men lay there, spent and exhilarated at the same time. Duncan couldn't believe how his life had changed in only three days. He held an amazingly generous man in his arms, would be starting a new job on Wednesday, and he couldn't remember feeling so happy in a very long time. Barkley was fast asleep, his head and hand resting against Duncan's hairy chest. He looked down at the sleeping man and traced lazy circles over the smooth skin of his lover's well-defined back and arms. He heard the birds singing outside in the dying sunlight of the evening and felt as if he'd just awoken from a bad dream, a nightmare that had all ended when he'd met the man lying safely in his arms.

Duncan looked over at the green numbers of the digital clock, hearing Barkley snuffle and feeling him shift against his body. He sighed contentedly when the head came off his chest and the sleepy eyes focused on him. "Hey," he said, wanting to shake his head at such a lame greeting.

"Hey yourself," Barkley said, his lips pressing lightly, repeatedly, against Duncan's chest and shoulder. "Hungry?"

"I'm good," Duncan said, grinning. "Don't feel like moving right now."

"Okay," Barkley said with a smile.

Duncan saw the mischievous smile and watched as Barkley wiggled his way down the bed, his hands and mouth leaving trails of electricity on Duncan's warm skin. He reached out to caress Barkley's cheeks, wondering what this adorable man was up to. "But I have to go see to Zeus and Neptune," he said and then felt the heat of Barkley's breath on the head of his cock. "Come here," he whispered, pulling Barkley up to lie next to him. When he had the singer settled next to him, he rolled onto his side and pressed his lips to Barkley's, the kisses soft and slow, their tongues moving toward each other.

Barkley was on his back, so Duncan used this time to spread his hand out over the wide expanse of chest, moving it slowly, back and forth, from chest to belly. He felt Barkley roll onto his side and press against him, their lips never parting. Duncan broke the kiss and put his hands on either side of Barkley's face, his eyes focused on Barkley's. "That was a very generous thing you did for me."

"I thought you might be pissed at me," Barkley admitted, his eyes darting away as he said it.

Duncan just smiled and shook his head. "I don't know what it is about you... yet... but when he mentioned your name, I remember thinking, *Of course, who else?* It's been a long time since someone believed in me." He laughed and shook his head. "And you haven't even seen the article yet."

"Doesn't matter."

"I'd love to be able to walk into Thomas's office and tell him to go fuck himself," Duncan admitted with a heavy sigh. "But I don't want to give him the satisfaction."

"He can't do anything if you quit without notice, can he?"

"I doubt it," Duncan admitted. "I'll finish the article on you and then tell him I won't be able to accept any more assignments. I doubt he'll pursue legal action."

"Well, if he does, I know a couple of really great lawyers," Barkley said and leaned forward, brushing his lips against Duncan's.

Duncan kissed his lips gently. "The sandwiches... the interview," he said, smiling at the blush creeping up his lover's neck and cheeks. "You're a very kind man, Barkley Reinhardt."

"The more I read about you, the more I realized how unfairly you'd been treated."

"It's all in the past now," Duncan whispered, "thanks to you."

"I just made a phone call and got you the interview," Barkley said, his hands trailing up and down Duncan's back. "You were the one who must have impressed him enough to offer you a position."

"You don't mind if I keep thinking of you as my own personal angel, do you?"

By way of an answer, Barkley leaned forward and kissed Duncan softly on the lips. After a few moments, Duncan felt the man shiver. He reached behind himself and pulled up the duvet, wrapping both of them up in the silky fabric. A few moments later, Barkley rolled onto his back, reaching out to pull up the other half of the duvet. Duncan took advantage of the moment to roll on top of the smaller man, working his legs between Barkley's, loving the feel of their heated bodies pressed together.

"He only spoke to me for ten minutes, asked me a couple of questions, and then called his assistant," Duncan confessed as he lay atop Barkley. "I thought I'd fucked it all up, but then he offered me a job."

"Tell me about it?"

"The job?" Duncan saw Barkley nod, the singer moving and pressing his lips to the skin of his shoulder and neck. "He told me that I'll start out as a researcher and that, *if I play my cards right*, I could be producing by Christmas."

"I'm so happy for you," Barkley said before pressing their lips together again.

Duncan looked into the amber eyes and said, "Now I really do have to do something wonderful for you, and not just because of the lunch."

"I have a suggestion," Barkley said, his eyebrows raised.

"And what would that be?"

"Stay with me tonight? We can go and get Zeus and Neptune, and you can stay here tonight."

"Try and keep me away," Duncan said with a huge grin, then brought his lips to Barkley's neck, kissing and nipping at the sensitive skin. "Oh, I almost forgot. Mr. Green told me to tell you that his wife is out of town, in New York I think he said, and won't call you until Wednesday." Duncan raised his eyebrows, as if he was asking Barkley to confirm that message made sense.

"Got it," Barkley said as he moved his hands to cup Duncan's ass. "I should tell you right now that I have a thing for hairy men, especially hairy men who don't trim or shave the aforementioned body hair."

Duncan laughed, his body shaking on top of Barkley's. "Tried that once. Itched like hell when it grew back in." Duncan left a trail of kisses from his lover's collarbone to his ear. "So, are you going to tell me what you had to promise in exchange for this favor?"

Barkley's shoulders moved and Duncan assumed he was trying to shrug, as if to say it was no big deal. "Edward Green is a very big patron... or I should say his wife is a very big patron of the arts. I met them years ago and have often agreed to sing at charity events. Since I announced my retirement, I've declined any such invitations. I called Edward and told him I'd sing at the scheduled event this weekend if he'd agree to meet with you."

Duncan nodded and stole a kiss. "What I don't get is why you would do that for someone you barely know."

"It's a long story," Barkley said softly. "I'll explain it all to you someday."

"Okay," Duncan said as he rolled off the smaller man and threw aside the duvet. "I would like to take a shower with you. And then we can go and get Zeus and Neptune." He laughed as Barkley literally jumped over him, landing on his feet, and bent over to pick up Duncan's discarded clothing.

"If these are too wrinkled, you can borrow something of mine. I think we're about the same size." Barkley folded the pants and shook out the dress shirt, placing both of them over the back of the armchair Duncan had just noticed.

"Oh, man," Duncan cooed as he raised himself off the bed to stand next to Barkley. "Do you have any idea how much that idea turns me on? Wearing the same clothes that you've worn."

Barkley regarded him for a moment and then shrugged. "You're kinda kinky... but in a good way. I like that."

"Baby," Duncan sighed, "you have no idea."

DUNCAN WOKE up, Barkley's skin warm against his own, and thought he'd died and gone to heaven, escorted by his very own angel. He and his pups were with an incredibly thoughtful and generous man who was sensual and hot; they were in a beautiful condo that seemed to isolate them almost from the world twenty stories below; and they had nothing to do for the next thirty-six hours. Duncan dismissed the thoughts he was having, the ones that reminded him that he would have to leave the peace and quiet of this condo in order to go back to his own studio apartment.

He tried to console himself with the thought that there would be other nights like the one they'd spent together, other nights where the only worry would be how many hours of sleep they could manage to get because they did not seem to be able to keep their hands off of each other. Duncan felt Barkley stir beside him, and he pressed himself against the warm flesh of the broad back, feeling as if he were nothing more than a magnet, drawn by his attraction for the singer.

But Barkley was so much more than just a singer. Duncan had come to realize this more and more since he'd first met him. He had a head full of questions now, and not just because of the article, but because he wanted to know everything about the man he very well could be falling in love with. He'd dismissed the notion late last night, when he lay awake with Barkley snuggled up against him, as nothing more than hero worship; Barkley had done something kind and good for him, something no one had done in a very long time. *Even if it was hero worship*, Duncan had realized, *who says he can't fall in love with his hero?*

Duncan felt himself growing aroused, pressed up against the unassuming man. His chest was pressed to Barkley's back, and his hand was skimming lightly over the silky flesh of hips and ass and belly while his lips scattered kisses along the man's shoulder and neck. He smiled as he felt Barkley stir, his hand catching Duncan's as it moved around his waist and pulled him even closer.

"I'm sorry for waking you," Duncan said. "I promise we'll have a nap after lunch."

"Deal," Barkley said, shifting to lie on his back. He looked up at his lover, a slow smile parting his full lips. Duncan's heart rate increased, his hand stilling itself on the firm belly. "Good morning, Duncan. Sleep well?"

Duncan nodded, a small smile on his own lips. "Good morning, Barkley," he said before kissing Barkley gently, the singer's hands in Duncan's hair. He shivered slightly at the touch, wondering if he would ever get used to the idea that this man wanted him. Duncan leaned over the broad chest and kissed it, just once, and then rested his head against it, luxuriating in the feel of Barkley's hands sweeping over his head, neck, and back.

"Did you need to go back to your apartment for anything?" Barkley's voice sounded hesitant, cautious.

Duncan looked up and saw that the luminous smile was gone. "I was planning on doing some work on the article," he said with a slight shrug. "Why?"

"I thought we could make a day out of it," Barkley said, still stroking and caressing Duncan as he turned his head to look at the alarm clock. "It's only eight. We can shower and get ready, be at your place by nine to get whatever you need, do some grocery shopping, and then come back here." Barkley's hands stilled. "You don't start at Teleglobal until Wednesday, so we have a couple of days to do… stuff." Duncan looked down and waggled his eyebrows. It wasn't too hard to read his mind. "I didn't mean that kind of stuff. Well, I did, but I also meant exercising the pups or watching movies or you working on your article while I read or take care of the menagerie."

"Sounds like heaven," Duncan said finally. "I was gonna go out and buy some steaks for me and the pups, to celebrate this new direction." He ducked his head again and pressed his ear to the muscular chest, not really sure if it was his heart or Barkley's that was beating faster. "Speaking of the charity event," Duncan began and then stopped to place some more kisses over the pale flesh of Barkley's torso. "Is this a private affair, or do you get to invite a friend?"

"Would you come?"

Duncan heard the surprise and shock in the question and lifted his head, fixing his lover with a stare. "Are you kidding? A chance to see you sing live?" Duncan turned his body so that he was lying on his stomach, his face mere inches away from Barkley's. "I've watched all sorts of videos, and I kept wondering what it would be like to hear you sing live."

"Well, then, you're in luck," Barkley said, pushing himself down the bed a little and kissing Duncan's mouth. "Because I can bring whomever I'd like."

"What would I have to do to move to the front of the line?" Duncan suddenly felt playful.

"Nothing," Barkley said as he moved his body so that he was lying facedown on Duncan's back, his erection pressing between the cheeks of his lover's ass. "Because you're the only one in line." He ground his hips. "You've got the most incredible ass," he said as he lifted off it and settled himself between Duncan's legs.

Duncan could feel Barkley moving his legs, spreading them, before he felt the strong hands kneading and touching and caressing the globes of his ass. "Jesus, Barkley," Duncan sighed. "You keep doing that and I'm going to fall asleep again."

"Got all day, Duncan," he said, leaning down to kiss and nibble at the moderately hairy ass. He pulled himself up so that he could whisper in Duncan's ear. "But I'll stop if you want me to."

"No," Duncan said with a chuckle. "Feels good."

"We can stop off at the deli on the way back and pick up a couple of those sandwiches you like so much and get those steaks for your beautiful pups."

"You know, I still have one of those sandwiches sitting in my fridge," Duncan said as he moved his hands to his sides, teasing and petting Barkley's knees. "Still can't believe you've done all of this for me."

"Just wait until I like you a lot," Barkley said, moving his fingers up to Duncan's neck and kneading gently. "Then you'll be really impressed."

"Can't wait for that day," Duncan said as he began to turn over, forcing Barkley off his body. Duncan sat in the middle of the huge bed, his legs out in front of him, and pulled the smaller man onto his lap, Barkley's legs wrapping around his waist. "But I find it hard to believe," he said as his hands began to explore, "that I could be any more impressed with you than I already am."

Barkley sank in between Duncan's thighs, squirming as the hands continued to move all over his back and shoulders, and pressed his chest against Duncan's. "You're a very tactile person, aren't you?"

Before answering, Duncan covered his lover's lips with his own, his tongue finding its partner almost immediately. He moved his left hand up to the base of Barkley's skull, and he tilted his head a little bit more to the right, their hungry and eager mouths devouring each other. After a few moments, and because he was breathless, Duncan pulled away and slipped a hand between them, taking up both of their cocks in his hand. "Not usually, but around you I don't seem to have any willpower."

Barkley pressed their foreheads together again as Duncan continued to stroke and pull gently on their erections. "I love your hands... how they feel on me," Barkley sighed, letting his head fall back and moaning as Duncan's lips found the sensitive skin near his collarbone.

"You have the most perfect skin I've ever seen," Duncan whispered against Barkley's neck, his tongue coming out to taste and lick a path back to his lover's mouth. "Should I keep going?" The question was almost lost inside of Barkley's mouth. "Or do you want something else?"

"Keep going," Barkley grunted.

Duncan could feel Barkley's writhing growing more and more insistent, lifting his knees so that he could align their cocks perfectly. He moved his feet farther apart and pushed gently on the magnificent chest until Barkley was on his back, their cocks still joined in Duncan's hand.

Their pricks lost contact for a moment as he struggled momentarily to get to his knees. Duncan wanted to hover over Barkley's body. "I wish you could see your face right now. So hot the way you open up for me." He used his free hand to caress and stroke over the flushed skin of that chest and belly and sensitive inner thighs and took both of their cocks into his hand again.

Duncan spread his thighs so that their balls touched and moved against each other. He continued to stroke and pull on their dicks, his eyes never leaving Barkley's face. He felt the man begin to move against him, their cocks moving contrary to one another. "Oh fuck, yeah, baby," Duncan hissed as he stilled his hand. "Feels so good, Barkley. Love the way you move," he said as he snapped his hips and heard Barkley call out his name.

Duncan moved back to rest on his haunches, his other hand free to probe and caress and pinch. He slapped a hand gently against Barkley's chest and kneaded the hard muscle of one pec, the opposing movements of their dicks growing more and more frenzied. He felt his sensitive balls moving against Barkley's and closed his eyes, his hips seeming to have a mind of their own as they moved up and down and side to side.

The friction was incredible, his spine tingling in anticipation of the orgasm that was building in his toes and zipping its way through every nerve and fiber of his body.

"Close, Duncan," Barkley said, reaching up and pinching Duncan's nipples.

"Yeah, baby, me too."

As he arched his back and leaned forward, once again using his free hand to brace himself, Duncan looked at his lover's amber eyes. "Stick out your tongue," he commanded, and when Barkley complied, Duncan drew it between his lips, sucking it and grazing it with his teeth. He heard the whimpering coming from beneath him and felt like he was some sort of god, as if he were imbued with some sort of power to reduce this sexy, irresistible man to moans and whimpers.

Barkley began to thrust quickly against Duncan, their cocks and balls finding even more friction. The hands at his nipples stilled and then Duncan felt his lover's release spill between them. He snapped his hips one last time, and Barkley called out his name again, his arms flung out to the sides, his hands fisting the sheets and duvet.

Seeing what he'd been able to do to Barkley sent Duncan over the edge, and he let go, pressing his balls against Barkley's as the thick ropy jets of cum shot out, over and over, from his rock-hard dick. He brought his right hand to his mouth, licking and cleaning. He thought for a moment that he would be able to come again right away when he saw Barkley grab the same hand by the wrist and take each of his fingers into his mouth one at a time, licking and laving and teasing.

Completely sated, the two of them lay pressed together, Duncan on top, as they kissed and tasted each other. Duncan finally rolled off to the side, his head finding its way to the smooth, muscular chest. He thought about the biography he wanted to write about this man for a while, writing the first few lines in his mind before erasing them and starting over, before he finally let sleep claim him.

Chapter 9

IT WAS just after six in the evening on Wednesday, and Duncan was sitting in his little cubicle in the huge glass and steel skyscraper on King Street. He still had three phone calls to make before he was free to leave. His first day as a researcher had gone well, but mainly because he'd been kept so busy that he didn't have time for anything but ensuring that he did every task to the best of his ability. He'd arranged for interviews for upcoming story ideas, read hundreds of pages of text to check facts, and even spent a few hours booking transportation for the guests that would be part of the studio's week-long feature on contemporary trends in men's fashion.

The work, Duncan knew, would be mind-numbingly boring at times, but it was also a relief to be away from the oppressive environment of that tabloid and the incompetence that used to be his editor. Instead, he was working for a major player in the field of journalism and had been sent off this morning by a man he'd just spent almost two full days with. Two days that had been filled with everything and anything; they'd gone on long walks around Barkley's neighborhood with the pups, had stayed home to watch movies, and had passed more than a few hours making love.

Barkley had even woken him up this morning to serve him a great breakfast and then, when Duncan was on his way out the door, handed him a little brown bag containing one of his favorite deli sandwiches along with an apple and a pudding pop. Duncan hadn't been able to find even a moment to himself until two or three this afternoon, but he'd managed to eat most of the sandwich while doing some fact-checking. It was when he was returning the uneaten portion into the bag that Duncan had discovered the note that Barkley had written him. He'd smiled to himself as he read it. *Whether or not it's a good first day, we'll be here waiting for you.* The *we* was not only Barkley, but also their combined brood of animals. Barkley had insisted that since Duncan would be spending time away from his own studio apartment, it seemed cruel not to leave the dogs with Barkley. How could Duncan say "no" to that? Duncan wasn't sure if it was a good day or not since he'd been far too occupied to think about it, but he did know that he would have an incredible evening.

He picked up the phone, to make his final phone call, and wondered if his lucky streak would continue. He'd been able to do nothing more than leave messages for the first two people, and if this held true for this final call, Duncan would be with Barkley in less than twenty minutes. He smiled to himself as he heard the click of the voice mail announcement and then the monotone voice of the lady he'd already spoken to three times today. He left a quick message about needing to make yet another transport arrangement for a guest on the early morning show next week and hung up the phone.

Pulling out his cell phone, he dialed Barkley's number and gathered all of his things and stuffed them into his messenger bag. He heard the sweet sound of his lover's voice as the elevator dinged and the doors opened.

"Hey, handsome," Duncan said, feeling like such a goof for the huge grin on his face. "I'm just heading your way now."

"I'll be here," Barkley said, his voice soft and inviting. "I'll leave the door open for you."

"Sounds good. I should be there in about fifteen minutes."

"Okay," Barkley responded. "Did you have a good first day at school?"

"Tell you all about it when I get there," Duncan promised. "But I will have to get that article done tonight."

"No problem. That will give me time to do some rehearsing. Mrs. Green called me this afternoon and gave me the list of songs she wants me to sing on Saturday."

"I get a free concert?"

"Absolutely not," Barkley scolded. "There will be a fee, of course."

Duncan felt his pants stir as he headed out of the elevator and through the lobby. "Really? Well, I hope I have enough to… uh… pay… this fee."

"More than anyone I've ever met."

"I'll see you soon."

"I hope you're hungry," Barkley said, and Duncan felt his pants stir again.

"You keep up this innuendo, and I'm going to be very embarrassed on the subway train." Duncan smiled when he heard the laughter on the other end of the line. "I'm just heading into the station now. I'm practically at your place already."

"Oh, sorry," Barkley said, his tone sounding serious. "One thing I forgot to mention."

"What's that?"

"I'm naked right now."

Duncan closed his eyes as he swiped his metro pass and tried not to imagine a naked Barkley spread out on the huge bed. He walked to the platform and sighed. "You're really evil, you know that?"

"I'm sorry. I couldn't resist." Barkley's laughter subsided somewhat, and then Duncan could hear a more serious tone. "I'll see you soon, Duncan."

"You bet you will," Duncan said, his tone just as serious as his lover's. He closed his phone just as the next train was pulling into the station. He stood aside to let a few people out and entered the car to find a seat. Duncan tapped his foot nervously for the next fifteen minutes, the train speeding up and slowing down as it passed through the next eight stations.

At the Davisville station, he exited the car and walked toward the stairs that would have him on Merton Street in a matter of seconds. He found himself picking up the pace as his mind pictured Barkley in a pair of shorts and one of his usual polo shirts. Duncan hadn't been in high school in almost thirteen years, but he was pretty sure that Barkley was what he would have called a *preppy* boy back then. As for Duncan, he was most definitely *not* preppy when he'd been in high school.

Making his way down Merton Street, Duncan found himself laughing and shaking his head at the memory of how his hair was long with no discernible part, sweeping down and into his eyes. He'd often been referred to as goth—something that drove him crazy—but he'd always seen himself more as a nonconformist. Whatever he had been, he was quite sure that he would have never imagined himself being with someone like Barkley. In fact, he was pretty sure that he'd probably bullied a few kids who had been like Barkley; *preppy and perfect*, he'd always called them.

After a nod to the doorman, Duncan was in the elevator, along with Mrs. Pavlic, the nice woman who walked her dogs twice a day every day. He made idle chitchat about her two schnauzers—Dante and Inferno—and couldn't help but think about what was becoming Zeus's and Neptune's new group of siblings. The elevator slowed at the third floor, and he nodded and wished Mrs. Pavlic a good day, taking a second to bend down and scratch the puppies behind the ears before the doors closed.

Leaning against the back wall of the elevator, Duncan grinned again when he realized that, regardless of how tired he was, he didn't care at all. It was a good kind of tired, the kind that came from being determined not to screw up this second chance he'd been given. He was already at the elevator doors before he heard the bell and was out of the elevator before the doors were even half-open.

He opened the door to Barkley's apartment slowly and removed his shoes and put down his messenger bag on the bench by the front door; he knew it would only be a matter of seconds before he saw a flash of fur bounding for yet another escape attempt. He was wondering where Barkley was when he saw Tinkerbell's little head around the corner and then run for the door. He was a little taken aback when Tinkerbell stopped in front of him and mewed softly, rubbing her cheek against his leg. "Hi, Tink, how was your day?" He kissed the little kitty a couple of times and then nuzzled his nose against her neck. "Where's your dad?" Duncan wanted to sneak up on the gorgeous man and do a little loving on him before anything else got done. He was hoping that he'd find him in the kitchen so he could surprise him from behind, wrap his arms around him and do a little groping, but Barkley wasn't there. Nor was he in the bedroom or on the balcony. He was about to check the spare bedroom when he smelled the scent of vanilla coming from the bathroom. Duncan knocked on the door and was anticipating hearing Barkley's voice telling him to come in, but instead, the door was pulled open and Barkley stood there, a towel around his hips.

"What's...? How...? I...," Duncan stuttered before Barkley reached out his arms and wrapped them around Duncan's shoulders.

Duncan looked around the bathroom, at the steam and the bubble bath in the huge bathtub, the half-dozen candles placed around the room, and the two glasses sitting beside the bottle of wine.

"I know you're probably hungry, but I wanted to do something special for you," Barkley said, unbuttoning Duncan's shirt, then moving underneath the fabric to push it off his torso and arms. Letting the shirt drop to the floor, Barkley then focused his attentions on removing Duncan's dress pants, boxers, and socks. "In honor of your first day at your new job. The dogs are walked, the animals fed, and we have as much time as you'd like before you work on your article."

Duncan was about to protest, feeling a little overwhelmed by all of this consideration, but Barkley was kissing him quite thoroughly. Duncan wasn't about to do anything that would part their lips, so he decided to shut up and enjoy all the attention this man was willing to give him.

BARKLEY DUNKED the sponge back into the hot water and let it hover over Duncan's beautiful chest, squeezing it and watching the dark hairs glisten as the water cascaded down the defined muscles. Barkley was leaning against the back of the tub, Duncan's broad back resting against his chest. They'd been in the tub for almost fifteen minutes and had done nothing more than kiss while their hands and mouths explored. They would have another ten minutes before dinner was ready. Barkley had planned everything down to the last detail, wanting to make this evening special for his lover.

"How's the water for you?" Barkley asked as he continued to run the sponge over Duncan's chest and shoulders.

"I'm so relaxed right now, you have no idea," Duncan said, sliding his hands up and down Barkley's calves and thighs.

Barkley decided to be playful and dropped the sponge into the water, freeing his hand to move over Duncan's chest and belly. He stopped his hand when it encountered his lover's burgeoning erection. "I think I have a good idea," Barkley said, giving Duncan's thick cock a squeeze. "But this doesn't seem relaxed," he joked as he let his tongue circle Duncan's ear. "In fact, it seems quite… rigid."

"That's because some evil man told me he was naked just as I was getting on the subway," Duncan growled. "I had to hold my messenger bag in front of me the entire time."

Barkley felt the cool air against his own chest as Duncan pulled himself away and got to his feet, turning himself around before sitting back down in the water. He pulled Barkley to him, guiding his legs over the top of his own, their bodies and pricks aligned perfectly.

"Do we have time?" Duncan's eyes were hooded, his voice husky and low.

Barkley nodded, his eyes closing as Duncan wrapped his hand around both of their cocks, pulling torturously slowly a few times before leaning forward for a kiss. Barkley obliged him, opening his mouth almost immediately, darting his tongue out to find its partner. He moved his hands up and down Duncan's arms, starting at the forearms and then stroking and squeezing the biceps and triceps. Barkley had always had a thing for forearms, and Duncan's were the best he'd ever seen.

"Play with my balls," Duncan said seductively. "And I'll play with yours."

"God," Barkley sighed, putting one hand under Duncan's ball sac while the other covered the hand that was jacking the two of them, the movements becoming more and more excited as Barkley felt his balls cupped by the strong hand; he deepened the kiss, unable to get enough of Duncan's tongue.

"I got your note," Duncan panted when they separated for air. "And I have a feeling that every day with you is going to be perfect."

Barkley looked at Duncan's beautiful eyes, heavy with want and need. He listened to that deep, husky voice saying words that, at any other time, would have been met with a *Thank you*. But Barkley was so aroused, so turned on by Duncan saying them in this intimate moment, that he felt the frenzy of emotion creep slowly up his spine. He pushed his mouth against Duncan's one more time, trying to breathe through his nose so that he would still have Duncan's tongue in his mouth when they came.

Barkley heard the whimper escape his own mouth as his orgasm hit him, slowly at first, and then more powerfully when he heard Duncan say his name over and over. He'd seen Duncan come many times in the last couple of days, but he had yet to be in a position to see only his face, to see the mixture of desire and protectiveness. Barkley moved his hands over the broad back and pulled Duncan closer as his lover rode out his own orgasm.

Duncan released their cocks and brought his arms around Barkley's shoulders, still trembling with the occasional aftershock. "Best day of my whole life," Duncan said, nipping and kissing at Barkley's neck.

Barkley watched Duncan pull back slightly and felt the big hands move up and down his back. They looked into each other's eyes for a moment, Barkley wanting to say that he was falling in love with Duncan but knowing it was that kind of impetuousness that had gotten him in trouble before, had prompted him into decisions he regretted later on. "You deserve it," Barkley said instead. After another five minutes of kissing, the need to go anywhere with it all but gone, Barkley rinsed both of their bodies thoroughly. He dried Duncan and then quickly moved the towel over his own body. "Dinner should be ready," he said as he led his lover into the bedroom so they could both get dressed. "I've made salmon."

"So, you're a pescetarian as opposed to a vegetarian?"

"Sometimes," Barkley said, pushing Duncan to the bedroom door.

Sitting on the balcony enjoying the maple-glazed salmon served with green beans almandine, long grain rice, and a mango salsa, Barkley took a great deal of pride in the contented look on Duncan's face. Neither of the men did much besides eating and smiling at each other. He got up after seeing Duncan had finished his first Heineken and walked to the kitchen, taking their empty plates with him.

"Would I frighten you away if I told you I think about you all day?" Duncan looked up as he took the bottle of beer.

"No," Barkley said, the smile coming to his lips automatically. "You wouldn't."

"I've never met anyone like you," Duncan said as he reached across the table to take hold of Barkley's hand. "It's hard to believe that we've lived in the same city all of our lives, and we're just finding each other now."

"I, uh," Barkley said, the sense of dread coming over him quickly. "I thought about you all day too." Barkley looked down at their joined hands.

"Why do I feel like there's a *but* at the end of that sentence?"

Barkley looked up to see the concerned expression on Duncan's face. "There are some things I've done that... well, I'm not proud of... and...."

"You mean that stuff that the tabloids always used to report?"

"No," Barkley said, shaking his head. "That's the crap they usually get wrong. I'm talking about things that I've never told anyone, things that... might make you think that I'm not...."

"So, you're telling me you're a bank robber or something? Or you're like that singing group that didn't actually do their own singing?"

In spite of himself, Barkley smiled, shaking his head. "It's part of the reason I wanted to help you, why I called Edward Green... and why I decided to stop singing."

"Well," Duncan said, the confusion obvious on his face, "it can't be anything too serious. I mean, you're one of the most generous people I've ever met."

"But I wasn't always like that," Barkley said, pulling his hand back and leaning back in his chair. "My parents are buried in that cemetery right there," he said as he pointed over the railing of the balcony. "I was on tour when I got a phone call from my mother; my father was sick and...." Barkley looked over the railing at the exact spot he knew to be the final resting place of his parents. He'd been there this afternoon, asking again for forgiveness. Barkley had known since their first evening together that he was falling for Duncan, but he also knew that he would have to be honest with his new lover if they had any chance of building a life with one another. "I didn't even take her phone call. Didn't want anything to disrupt my concentration."

"Oh, Barkley," Duncan whispered and then pulled his chair alongside his lover's. "You had no way of knowing how things would turn out."

"No," he agreed, relief flooding him at Duncan's reaction thus far to something that Barkley had never been able to forgive himself for. "But I did nothing." Barkley looked away from Duncan's compassionate eyes, the truth of what he had yet to admit filling him with shame all over again. "My mother eventually had to call my agent... and that's how I found out. While I wasn't calling my mother back, my father died."

"I'm so sorry," Duncan said, one hand resting reassuringly on Barkley's leg while the other stroked up and down his back. "It wasn't your fault."

Barkley took a deep breath and let it go slowly. "Thank you," he said after a few moments.

Duncan leaned forward and placed a gentle kiss on Barkley's lips. "We don't have to talk about this right now."

"I think I need to… finally," Barkley whispered and looked up into Duncan's understanding eyes. "I need to know that you won't…." Barkley didn't know how to finish that sentence. *Hate me? Think I'm a selfish prick? Turn me away?*

"We all have baggage, Barkley," Duncan said while he caressed his lover's forearm. "If I let something like that, something that's over and done, change my mind about you, then that would make me the asshole." He offered another chaste kiss and Barkley took it gladly. "Besides, you didn't let my past stop you from throwing yourself at me so shamelessly."

Barkley laughed and didn't bother to remind Duncan that it had been he who had thrown himself into Barkley's more-than-willing arms only two days ago. "Less than a year after my father died, my mother just… wasted away, really. I was in Europe and cancelled some performances so I could be with her, but…." Barkley was surprised that he wasn't crying; he'd done nothing but cry for months after finding his mother in the home they'd all shared as a family. "I tried to… be a good son, but I… the attention was like a drug."

"It's not your fault, Barkley," Duncan said, his hands still warm and soothing on Barkley's skin. Neither of them spoke for a moment. Then Duncan took his hand and led him to the living room. They sat on the overstuffed sofa, Barkley safe in Duncan's arms. "They knew you loved them, knew that you would have been there if you'd been able."

Barkley curled up against his lover, not really any more convinced that he hadn't abandoned his parents, but relieved that he'd finally confessed the truth of what he felt. And that relief was made all the more welcome because Duncan did not blame him for what he'd thought was the worst thing a child could do to his parents.

Chapter 10

BARKLEY LIFTED his fingers off the piano keys and turned when he heard Tinkerbell express her disapproval that he'd stopped playing and singing. He'd discovered her penchant for classical music quite by accident when he'd brought her home from the shelter that first night. She'd been very timid, remaining inside her carrier for the first several hours; he'd placed treats and a bowl of water just outside the carrier hoping that she would discover that she was safe, that she was home. But despite several tentative approaches for a few quick sniffs, Tinkerbell did not move. Barkley thought he would lose it completely when he looked in from time to time to see her shaking; at least, that's what it looked like to him.

At the time, he'd only had Mozart and Salieri, and he'd done enough reading to know that he shouldn't introduce them all too quickly. So, frustrated that first evening with his failure to connect with the frightened and blind kitten, Barkley had gone to check on them. He'd put them in one of the spare bedrooms. While he was in there, playing and giving the two of them some attention, he heard his cell phone ringing. It was new. He'd been in a playful mood when he'd chosen Wagner's "Ride of the Valkyries" because he couldn't help singing along, "Kill the wabbit, kill the wabbit."

He hadn't been in time to find out who had been calling, but he had been in time to see Tinkerbell far outside of her cage, ears on alert and searching for the sound that was coming from the cell phone. Since he'd missed the call anyway, he decided to try and make Tinkerbell feel a little bit more at home. That's when he picked up the home phone and dialed his own cell phone number, finding it almost impossible to keep himself from laughing every time the tune would play and he would sing, "Kill the wabbit, kill the wabbit"; Tinkerbell not only found the phone, but eventually made her way over to him, meowing to beat the band.

It didn't seem to matter what Barkley would sing or play; Tinkerbell was a fan of it all. So he could understand her disappointment when he had stopped practicing his songs for the charity benefit. He'd sung all of the requested songs so many times that he could probably do them in his sleep. In fact, he wasn't so sure he hadn't sung them in his sleep. He made a mental note to ask Duncan when he got home from work, a sly smile coming quickly to his lips when he thought about Duncan.

"Okay," Barkley said, relenting when Tinkerbell hopped up onto the piano bench and started kneading his thigh, her mews getting louder with each passing second that she didn't hear music. "*Schwanengesang* just once more, and then I have to start dinner."

He shook his head as she stopped mewing and sat down beside him as soon as the words were out of his mouth. "I always knew there was something extra special about you."

Tinkerbell offered a single meow.

"You're welcome," Barkley said, laughing out loud and opening the bound volume of Schubert songs. "Okay, I'd like to dedicate this one to a special young lady who is my biggest fan."

Barkley placed his fingers gently on the keys, closing his eyes and imagining that it was the dark of night. He is alone but he is not lonely; he is in love and will ask his lover to come to him. He will sing of his love and let his message be carried on the trees, the wind; his message is so pure that even the nightingales will surely help deliver it to his one true love.

He began with the opening chord, quickly tapping out the five dotted eighth notes. He'd always imagined someone, breathless with anticipation, their heartbeat so loud in their ears. The next chord, the next five dotted eighth notes. The feelings of wanting and hoping. Another three bars before he would begin to sing softly into the distance, certain his song would be carried to his love. *My songs beckon softly through the night to you; below in the quiet grove, come to me, beloved! The rustle of slender leaf tips whispers in the moonlight; do not fear the evil spying of the betrayer, my dear.*

Barkley glanced down at Tinkerbell when he felt her paw pushing against his thigh again. She wouldn't know that this part was a rest for the singer, so he hummed to placate her. The few bars without singing were among the most beautiful to Barkley, not solely because he got to rest, but rather because they were musical echoes of what he had been singing. They put him in mind of the song to his beloved floating on the wind, his words of eternal devotion being whispered among the tallest branches on every tree. It was some of the most sublime music he'd ever heard.

Do you hear the nightingale's call? Ah, they beckon to you; with the sweet sound of their singing they beckon to you for me. They understand the heart's longing, know the pain of love; they calm each tender heart with their silver tones.

DUNCAN HEARD Barkley say something to Tinkerbell. He'd almost gotten his key in the door when he heard the music, heard the soft, quick tapping of the keys and felt an overwhelming sense of anticipation. Even before hearing the beautiful voice of the man who'd given him a second chance at life, he could feel his heart begin to race, could hear an urgency he'd never before felt while listening to any piece of music.

Duncan was in no way what anyone would call a fan of classical music. Whenever he even heard the term, it would do nothing but conjure up images of stuffy musicians dressed like penguins playing music written by people who'd died hundreds of years ago. He didn't have anything against the people who liked it, but it had just never done for him what it obviously did for others. Others like Barkley. He couldn't imagine the dedication involved in learning all of those other languages, learning to play an instrument, all for the sake of being one more person in the world who could "interpret" these ancient songs.

But at that moment, he stood, his eyes closed and his ear pressed against the door, not understanding any of the words Barkley was singing but understanding everything else. He shook his head as he realized that he may be guilty of a little transference; perhaps he was so captivated by this piece of music because it was being sung by the first man he'd ever met who was more haunted than he was. This quiet and beautiful man who had so far not asked for anything; thus far, he'd only given. At that moment, Duncan realized he was standing on the other side of the door, voluntarily keeping himself from being with this man.

He turned the key as quietly as he could and stepped inside, not wanting to distract Barkley. There was no chance of Barkley seeing him; the piano was in the corner, and Barkley would have his back to the door. But he still moved slowly, methodically, setting down his bag and pushing his keys into his pocket, trying to make no noise at all. He smiled as he saw Barkley's broad back, the light fabric of his short-sleeve shirt blowing gently with the wind coming in from the open French doors. He almost laughed out loud when he saw Barkley look over to Tinkerbell every now and then, singing directly to her. Tinkerbell was kneading Barkley's thigh, her nose pushing forward every so often to nuzzle against the soft cotton fabric of Barkley's cargo shorts. In all the years he'd been chasing men, trying to find the one, he'd never imagined that his most serious competition would come from an adorable blind kitten with ADHD.

He listened as he moved closer, one step at a time. He'd almost made it to the coffee table when Tinkerbell turned and jumped off the bench, heading right for him. He squatted on his haunches and scooped her up, nuzzling her neck.

"May I remind you, young lady, that I dedicated this—" Duncan heard Barkley's beautiful voice, saw him turn on the bench, looking down to see where Tinkerbell had run off to.

"Sorry," Duncan said, trying not to laugh. "My fault. I stole your audience."

"She was cooped up in here all day with me," Barkley said, his hands outstretched as if to show his complete surrender. "How can I compete with someone new and infinitely more cuddleable."

"Cuddleable?" Duncan was speaking to Tinkerbell. "I don't think that's a word, Stinkerbell. Do you think that's a real word?" Tinkerbell mewed once and licked at Duncan's hand. "I didn't think so either." Duncan leaned over as Barkley approached, offering a kiss. "But I thank you for the thought."

"You're welcome," Barkley said as he scooped up Tinkerbell and put her on the floor with her jingle-bell toys. Duncan opened his arms and wrapped them around Barkley. "And how was your day?"

"Very… busyable." He felt Barkley trying to pull away. He tried to hide his smile as he looked into Barkley's amber eyes.

"Okay, Mr. Thesaurus," Barkley scolded as he reached down to slap Duncan's ass.

"What was that song you were playing?"

"It's a serenade, German, from 1829," Barkley explained as he settled against Duncan's body. "Written by an incredibly prolific and talented composer who did not live to see his thirty-second birthday."

"Ah," Duncan said, thinking he knew this one. "Mozart." He leaned in for the congratulatory kiss.

"Wrong century," Barkley said, providing a kiss even though Duncan's guess was incorrect. "Franz Schubert."

"Never heard of him," Duncan said with a shrug. "Where are the pups?"

"Spare bedroom," Barkley said. "Along with the rest of the menagerie."

"So, you're all set for the concert?" Duncan began to unbutton his shirt, but found his hands quickly pushed out of the way by Barkley's long, slim fingers.

"I am," Barkley stated matter-of-factly as he finished with the buttons and ran his hands along Duncan's chest, then over his shoulders, pushing the shirt off completely. Duncan grew hard as he saw Barkley lean forward for a kiss. While Duncan got lost in the soft, yet firm, pressure of that mouth, Barkley reached down and began to unbuckle his belt for him, then unbuttoned his pants and ran his hands underneath the plain white boxer shorts. As Duncan felt the hands settle on his ass, he found himself struck by the thought that those fingers had just played a beautiful song on a very expensive piano, and Duncan found himself very aroused when he thought of himself as one of Barkley's instruments. "I missed you."

Duncan opened his eyes to see Barkley's half-lidded expression. He was licking his lips as he lowered himself to his knees, his hands working to free Duncan's legs from the trousers, socks, and shoes. "Missed… you… too." Duncan's head was filling with images that he'd imagined a thousand times before. But this time, everything seemed different and he didn't know why. Was it because he'd found someone who seemed to know exactly what he needed when he needed it? Or was it because he was with a man who didn't seem to want anything from him but to please him?

Duncan wasn't really happy with either of those thoughts, so he pushed them aside, content to focus on the matter at hand: giving back, even if Barkley wasn't asking for anything. He reached down as Barkley began to tug at the hem of his boxers. "Come here," Duncan said huskily. "I've wanted to do this all day long."

Barkley didn't resist; he went willingly to the bedroom and to the side of the bed. He stood while Duncan removed first his shirt, kissing and nipping his way over the muscled torso. The only sound in the room was the occasional sigh or hiss as Duncan found a sensitive piece of flesh. "Do you have any idea what you do to me?" Duncan stood up briefly and took Barkley's lips roughly, licking and biting playfully with his teeth.

"I think I do," Barkley teased as he caught Duncan's bottom lip between his teeth and his engorged endowment in his left hand.

"HOW'S THE article coming along?" Barkley deposited another beer on the small balcony table, then sat opposite Duncan. He held Marco, the guinea pig, against his chest. "I think she likes you," he said, a big smile on his face as he saw Tinkerbell sleeping soundly on Duncan's lap.

"I guess I'm done," Duncan sighed, reaching for the beer bottle with his right hand while he continued stroking the kitten with his left. "Keep meaning to ask you how you ended up with such an odd mix of pets."

"They're not pets," Barkley stated quickly as he brought Marco up to his face and nuzzled his neck. "Well, I adopted Mozart and Tinkerbell. The rest are just here temporarily until I can get them to John and Lori's."

"They run some sort of shelter or something?" Duncan leaned back in his chair.

"Or something," Barkley said without taking his eyes off Marco's pink little nose. "They run a sanctuary for homeless or abused animals or animals that have special needs."

"Like this little gal?" Barkley smiled as he watched Duncan pick up Tinkerbell and cuddle her against his chest, distracted momentarily when Duncan teased her with her favorite little bear. The kitten mewed briefly then settled herself against Duncan, falling asleep again without too much effort.

"Yes, like Stinkerbell," Barkley admitted. "My former agent thought it would be a good idea for me to have a Facebook page and a Twitter account and all that crap. Didn't last very long because I found it all pretty boring and trivial, but the one good thing to come out of it was discovering just how many animals were being murdered because no one wanted them. I discovered John and Lori's place through Facebook and sent them a message offering to help. I'll be taking them out there this Saturday. You're welcome to come if you'd like."

"Murdered?"

Barkley heard the dismissive tone in Duncan's question, but didn't want to ruin the evening by reciting all of the statistics for someone who probably never thought twice about the millions of animals that were killed each day because of lazy and careless owners. He kissed the guinea pig's little nose one more time and then got up, looking over at Duncan. "I'll let you get back to work." He walked into the kitchen, suddenly angry at Duncan and not really knowing why. Just that one word, in the form of a question, had gotten his back up and he didn't like Duncan's tone. He set Marco down by his bowl, and while the guinea pig lapped at the water, Barkley opened the fridge and took out a few julienned carrots and a couple of lettuce leaves and crouched down to put them into the food bowl.

"What's wrong?" Duncan was standing up, framed by the French doors to the balcony, still cradling Tinkerbell in his arms. "Did I do something? Say something?"

"Nothing is wrong, Duncan," Barkley said as he stood up and wiped the moisture from his hands. "I forget sometimes that some people don't care as much about animals as I do."

"Stay right there," Duncan ordered, and Barkley watched him walk away into the condo, only to come back a few moments later without the kitten. "What, exactly, have I done to make you think I don't care about animals?"

Barkley began to pick up each of the bowls one by one and empty them into the sink. As he began refilling each bowl with fresh, filtered water, he looked over at Duncan. "That's not what I said."

"It sure as hell is!" Duncan stood with his hands on his hips, his gaze boring holes into Barkley. "You said that you forget that some people—"

"Did I say you? Did I use your name?"

"Don't be coy, Barkley."

Barkley placed the last bowl on the floor and stood, his hands going immediately to his temples. "Look," he said, softly but firmly. "I'm sorry if I said anything to offend you, Duncan, but there's something you should know about me right from the beginning." Duncan cocked his head to the side and raised both eyebrows as if beckoning Barkley to continue. "I will talk about anything you'd like, but I'm not going to yell or be yelled at. You want to discuss this, we'll do so as two grown men."

"That's what you call grown? Grouping me in with a bunch of other people because I questioned your word choice and then walking away?"

Barkley turned toward the opposite end of the kitchen, then turned back suddenly. "I'm taking the dogs out. Are you coming?"

"Yes," Duncan said, and Barkley realized he'd been holding his breath. He turned away from Duncan and closed his eyes. Barkley didn't have much experience with fighting and arguments; he was an only child with two parents who adored him and each other. They'd always discussed things as a family. In fact, Barkley didn't ever remember hearing either of his parents raise their voice even once.

They gathered the dogs, attached leads, and got in the elevator heading downstairs. They both nodded to James, the nighttime doorman, and headed outside to the large patch of grass that surrounded the condo complex. Barkley stood, watching Duncan throw balls and frisbees, the guilt eating away at him more and more for what he'd started. Mozart came running over to Barkley, the loss of a leg not seeming to slow him down any, and Barkley couldn't help but think back to how close this poor mutt had come to being euthanized. If Barkley had been held up in traffic or if he'd put off the trip to that particular pound until the next day, Mozart would not be here now.

"Hey, boy," Barkley said as he sat down on the grass, taking the ball out of Mozart's mouth. "Did you come over to see me? You tired of playing with your brothers already?" Barkley petted and stroked the mutt's head and ears, kissing the snout over and over. "You're a beautiful boy, aren't you?" Mozart barked once and nudged the ball by Barkley's knee. "Okay, boy," Barkley said excitedly, picking up the ball and holding it out for Mozart to see. "Go get it." He threw the ball off to his right, far enough away from the other dogs so that Mozart would have a fighting chance at getting there first, and laughed as he watched the mutt turn and run after the ball.

Barkley leaned back on his hands and looked over at Duncan, marveling at how attentive he was to all of the dogs, not just his own. Even the way Duncan held and cared for the other animals in the condo, like he'd done with Tinkerbell while trying to finish his article, should have been enough to prove that Barkley had been wrong in judging Duncan so harshly. Barkley had even caught him wrestling with Princess. Barkley laughed as he remembered finding both of them on the bedroom floor; he'd just come out of the bathroom after his morning shower to find Duncan had not yet left for work. *She stole my lunch*, Duncan had tried to explain as both sets of eyes turned when they noticed Barkley enter the room. *I set it down to put on my shoes, and when I turned back around, I saw her beating a hasty retreat.*

"What's so funny?" Duncan was settling himself down on the ground beside Barkley. Barkley looked over to see the other dogs were amusing themselves with the frisbees and the tug-o-war ropes. It was as if they'd known each other for years.

Barkley leaned over, their shoulders touching, and kissed Duncan's cheek. He pulled back slightly and stared into his lover's eyes. "I'm sorry, Duncan. I'm sorry if I was rude. I won't do it again." Just then, Mozart came back with his ball. Barkley scooped it up and threw it again, leaning back on his hands once more.

Barkley was relieved to feel one of Duncan's strong arms come out and wrap around his shoulders. He was even more relieved to feel the lingering kiss on his temple. "I'm sorry too, Barkley. I'm still learning that not everything is a personal attack on me. I've been kind of defensive ever since… well, for a while now."

"I was actually laughing just now because I remembered how you were fighting with Princess. When she stole your lunch?" Barkley heard Duncan's deep bass voice and watched as he tilted his head back and laughed. *God, this man's voice never fails to give me goose bumps,* Barkley thought as he saw the twinkle in his lover's blue eyes. *Too bad he can't carry a tune in a bucket.*

"I do remember that," Duncan scolded as leaned over and deposited another kiss on Barkley's temple. "And if I remember correctly, you took her side."

"I did not take her side," Barkley said, laughing again. "I just offered to pay for her attorney." Barkley smiled for Duncan and leaned forward for another kiss. "I'm sorry. I never even asked. You're okay with me kissing you in public like this?"

Duncan closed his eyes and pressed his lips to Barkley's and brought one hand up to cradle his neck. After a brief and very tender kiss, Duncan pulled back and looked at Barkley. "I should be asking you that."

"Trust me," Barkley said, trying to keep the derision from his voice. Mozart came back with the ball, but would not let it drop; he placed the ball behind him, out of Barkley's reach, and lay down, resting his legs across his master's lap. "A picture of me in the tabloids kissing a handsome man? I'll take that over some of those other god-awful pictures they like to print."

"Well, thank you, but I didn't mean the handsome part, more the jailbird, disgraced journalist part."

Barkley did not respond right away. There was something in Duncan's voice, something in the way his eyes looked down as he finished the question. "I don't see any of that when I look at you, Duncan. And I told you before that I think that whole situation was completely mishandled." Barkley brought a hand up and caressed Duncan's cheek. "I could ask you the same thing about a failed singer?"

"Failed? I don't think so," Duncan said and pushed himself up onto his feet, reaching out a hand to pull Barkley up as well. "So it's settled: You're nuts about me… and me? I'm still weighing my options."

Barkley laughed and bent over to pick up Mozart's ball. He threw it at Duncan and crossed his arms as he watched Mozart run after Duncan to get the ball. Barkley wasn't sure if Duncan was just a pathetically slow runner or if he let Mozart attack him, but Mozart had him down on the ground soon enough, ball forgotten, licking his face. "Get him, Motzie!"

Barkley was still shaking his head in wonder and complete amazement as he pulled the leads out of his pocket and started rounding up the dogs.

Chapter 11

AS HE put the receiver into its cradle, Duncan took a deep breath and realized he had an entire weekend with Barkley in front of him. He'd faxed over the article to his former boss, Thomas, and was now officially free and clear of *The Communiqué*. He would never have to deal with that pompous, self-righteous prick ever again. He'd already said his goodbyes to most of his colleagues that occupied the other cubicles; they'd left more than an hour ago, but Duncan was still there getting caught up. *Once I've been at this particular job for a while like the rest of them,* Duncan thought to himself as he double-checked that he had everything in his messenger bag, *I'll eventually be able to leave early on Fridays as well.*

Finding that thought comforting, he smiled as he headed to the elevator. Another fifteen minutes or so and he'd be in Barkley's apartment with an ice-cold beer in one hand, and if he played his cards right, he'd have a soapy loofa sponge in the other and would be running it up and down a very wet Barkley.

He heard the opening bars of Beethoven's Sixth and reached for his phone. His previous ringtone had been just a simple old-fashioned ringing telephone, but ever since he'd met Barkley he'd been keen to try new things. He was listening to different music and even eating different foods. He flipped it open and saw Barkley's name.

"Duncan's escorts," Duncan said, barely able to keep a straight face. "If you're in a pinch, we'll give a lot more than an inch." Duncan delighted in the laughter he heard over the phone.

"That's funny," Barkley sighed, but Duncan could tell he was smiling. "Listen, I completely forgot about your outfit for tomorrow night. It'll be black-tie. Do you have a tuxedo?"

"Of course," Duncan said. He waited for a beat. "I'll just get Armando, you know him, the pilot I keep at the summer house, to fly in and deliver it to me."

"A simple *no* would have sufficed."

Duncan closed his eyes when he heard the laughter over the other end of the phone. The bell rang and he exited the elevator. "Sorry, couldn't resist." Duncan pushed his back into the gargantuan glass door and stepped out into the evening breeze. "No way I can get away with just a suit?"

"None whatsoever," Barkley said almost immediately. "It's okay. We'll see what we can do with one of mine. I think we can make it work."

"Fair enough," Duncan said as he found himself at the top of the steps that led to the subway. "I'm heading into the subway, so I might lose you."

"Okay," Barkley said. "I'll see you in a bit."

"You bet," Duncan answered and looked at the screen one last time before shutting his phone.

Duncan had never really thought of himself as someone who would settle for this kind of life, a life of getting home to the same someone every night, of walking dogs in the evening and having the highlight of his week being a rousing discussion on whether or not Barkley should become completely vegan.

All Duncan had ever thought about while he was growing up with his alcoholic mother was adventure. He remembered hearing about astronauts and cowboys and marines and pirates; he'd wanted to be all of those things. When he'd earned enough money from delivering papers in the wee hours of each morning, he'd run to the store and buy comic books, and every once in a while, Mr. Turner would give him some old paperback books about sailing the high seas or swashbuckling adventures complete with damsels in distress.

He smiled to himself as he remembered Mr. Turner, the owner of the bookstore just down at the end of the street where Duncan had lived with his mother in a dilapidated two-bedroom bungalow. Duncan had never known his father and had been taking care of himself for as long as he could remember. If there'd ever been someone even close to being a father to Duncan, it was Mr. Turner. The elderly gentleman had never said anything when Duncan would turn out to be a few cents short of the real price; he would just wink and hold a finger up to his lips. *Our secret,* he would whisper.

Eventually, Duncan started letting his imagination run wild and he would write his own stories. He would use the lined workbooks he should have been using for math or science. Duncan was like a sponge, soaking up any and all information he could find that would fuel his stories. It didn't matter what the subject was, Duncan would find inspiration anywhere. Writing these stories was his salvation.

The familiar yellow and tan subway tiles began to flash by the windows of the train car and Duncan knew he was home. *Home,* he thought. He wondered what that said about him that he'd begun to think of Barkley's condo as *home.* In all the years that he'd been writing those stories of the brave and heroic men risking life and limb for adventure, he'd never once imagined that his very own story would end with a gorgeous man who had seen more of the world than he had, nor with a condo full of animals. Life certainly had a way of throwing you curve balls when you least expected it.

Duncan took the steps two at a time and was at the intersection of Yonge and Davisville in a matter of seconds. He waited for the line of cars to thin and watched the lights, anxious to get home and see how long it would take him and Barkley to end up naked and panting on the king-size bed.

One week, Duncan thought to himself as he crossed the street and made a last-minute decision to head over to the flower shop on the corner. He had no idea what was appropriate for a one-week anniversary, but he would just get a bunch of different ones. He reached into his pocket and pulled out a twenty-dollar bill, telling the young woman to keep the change as he scooped up the flowers and headed for the corner. He chastised himself momentarily that he'd not had the foresight to think of a more special gift, but then he rationalized that it wasn't an important anniversary or anything. *Doesn't matter anyway*, Duncan thought as he took out his keys and let himself into the lobby, *we'll laugh about it just as much tonight as we will on our fiftieth anniversary.*

Duncan smiled and nodded to James and rolled his eyes as he waited for the elevator. *When the hell did you become such a romantic? Fifty years with the same man?* Duncan shook his head when he realized that he would be eighty-two on that particular anniversary. Still, he wasn't as freaked out by the idea, not as much as he'd been only a couple of years ago. After the past couple of years of starving and having to take all of Thomas's crap, Duncan wasn't surprised to find that his priorities had shifted. "How many nights did you lie awake wishing for someone to believe in you? To give you a second chance?" Duncan said out loud as he looked at the flowers, remembering the promise he'd made to the ceiling of his rundown studio apartment. "And what did you promise to whoever would do that for you?"

He practically ran down the hallway and rang the bell, holding the flowers behind his back. He heard Mozart bark once and that familiar baritone voice telling Tinkerbell to calm down and get away from the door. And then, Duncan saw that face.

"HI. FORGET your key?" Barkley looked at the big grin on Duncan's handsome face and wondered what sort of trick he might be playing. "Did he accept the article?"

"Don't know, don't care," Duncan said and bent slightly at the waist. Barkley was suddenly staring at a beautiful bouquet of flowers. "Happy one-week anniversary."

"What?" Barkley took the flowers as Tinkerbell made her escape into the hallway, Duncan in hot pursuit. "You mean of our meeting for the first time?"

"Sure," Duncan shrugged as he caught Tinkerbell around the tummy and lifted her to his chest. "I know, what a mean daddy you have. Making you stay inside the apartment all the time." Duncan made his way back to the apartment door and leaned in for a kiss. Barkley stood to the side, revealing Zeus and Neptune waiting patiently. "He's such a meanie. I know what we'll do: I'll write a letter to the Toronto Humane Society and you can affix your paw in testament to the abominable conditions. You'll be an overnight celebrity."

"You didn't have to do this," Barkley said as he closed the door behind himself. "But that's very sweet of you. Thank you, Duncan." Barkley approached and leaned in for another kiss.

"You're welcome, Barkley." Duncan kissed Barkley one more time and then nuzzled Tinkerbell's neck before letting her down in the hallway. He crouched to pet his dogs for a moment.

"I didn't get you anything," Barkley said as he walked toward the kitchen. "I feel horrible now."

Duncan started laughing and pulled the messenger bag over his head, tossing it on the floor beside the umbrella stand. He toed off his shoes and followed Barkley into the kitchen. "You are the only person I can think of who would think that giving me food, getting me an interview, and looking after my dogs all day long is nothing." Duncan pushed himself against Barkley's back and wrapped his arms around the trim waist. "I do have one other surprise for you, though."

"Oh," Barkley said as he placed the flowers in a vase, turning his head to look behind him. "Does it involve less or more clothing than I've got on right now?"

"Definitely less," Duncan said as he spun Barkley around to face him. "You might say that if I get my way, there won't be any clothes on your incredible body until you have to put on that tuxedo tomorrow night."

"Really?" Barkley wrapped his arms around Duncan's neck and stole a quick kiss. "I wonder what John and Lori will say to that."

Duncan let his forehead come to rest on Barkley's broad shoulder. "Fuck," he muttered to himself. Barkley laughed. "I'm sorry, baby," Duncan said as he brought his head back up. "My bad. I completely forgot about tomorrow morning." Duncan extricated himself and stood back a few inches. "Okay, so change of plans. You and me up early tomorrow morning, we get the animals settled in their new home and then we're back here doing things that will freak out Tinkerbell and the pups."

"It's a good thing I know you're kidding about Tinkerbell and the pups," Barkley said as he turned back to arranging his flowers and pouring some water into the vase. "But," he said as he turned around to face Duncan before setting the vase on the kitchen table. "I'm with you on all the rest of it."

"Now," Duncan said as he took Barkley by the hands and brought their bodies together. "What would you say to spending some time soaking in a nice, hot bath?"

Barkley laughed and brought his arms up to wrap around Duncan's neck. "That is, quite possibly, the stupidest question in the history of the world." Barkley brought their lips together for a brief moment and then pulled back slightly. "I'll make sure everyone has new water and snacks while you get the bath going." He leaned in for another kiss, but Duncan had somehow managed to get free and was already halfway to the bathroom before Barkley even realized his arms were empty.

"SO, DO I need etiquette lessons or something?" Duncan leaned back in the bath and reached down to the floor for his beer. He took a swig of the cold liquid and closed his eyes at how good it felt. The problem of the tuxedo was now solved. Duncan would have never guessed he and Barkley were almost the same size. He was a little taller than Barkley, but if he pulled the pants down a little past his waist, no one would ever know it wasn't his tuxedo.

"Etiquette lessons? For what?"

"For the benefit tomorrow night," Duncan explained. "That's not my usual social circle, so is there anything I need to know about how to behave around the super-rich?"

Barkley leaned forward with the loofa and trailed it slowly down Duncan's chest. He moved himself toward his lover, his legs finding a place behind Duncan's back. Their erections touched as Barkley took the beer bottle out of Duncan's hand, placing it on the tiled floor. "Why would you think you have to behave any differently?"

"Well, you know," Duncan said, shrugging his shoulders as he brought his torso forward so that his hands could caress Barkley's smooth skin. "I don't want to do anything that might embarrass you or…." He shrugged again. "You know, whatever."

"I appreciate the thoughtfulness, but you don't have to be anybody but yourself."

"I know, but—"

Barkley smiled and kissed Duncan softly. He threw the loofa behind his body and brought both of his hands to rest on his lover's pecs, moving them south ever so slowly. He looked into Duncan's blue eyes, continuing to kiss and skim over lips and cheeks and neck. "Would you shut up while I'm trying to seduce you?"

Duncan closed his eyes when he felt Barkley grasp him. Barkley had both of their erections lined up and wrapped within his two hands, his movements over the sensitive flesh as maddeningly slow as the movement of his lips over Duncan's. "Sorry," Duncan said as he placed one hand over Barkley's, brushing his thumb over each cock's head again and again. "Do you want to take the edge off, or should we get dried off so I can make love to you in bed?" Duncan felt the increased pressure of Barkley's hands around their cocks and figured that was his answer. "Jesus, Barkley," Duncan sighed as he ran his hands over Barkley's, then up and down the solid arms. "You are so beautiful."

Barkley brought his lips to Duncan's right ear and took the earlobe between his teeth. He sucked it into his mouth for a moment while he let go of his own cock and held Duncan's in his hand, his thumb pressing and stroking the frenulum. "So are you, baby." Barkley moved back slightly and cupped Duncan's balls with his other hand. "I love that you're uncut," Barkley said as Duncan closed his eyes. "Love that your huge mushroom head is so sensitive when I do this." On the downward stroke, Barkley could feel the foreskin recede to expose the head of Duncan's sizeable cock. He brought his hand up from Duncan's sac and used it to hold the base of the rock-hard cock, while with the other, he formed a ring between his thumb and index finger, moving it up and down the head of Duncan's cock.

"Fuck, Barkley," Duncan hissed, his eyes still closed.

"Look at me, Duncan."

Duncan opened his eyes and saw those half-lidded amber eyes boring holes into his soul. He let his hands find their way to rest behind Barkley's neck.

"You're absolutely perfect the way you are."

Duncan exerted slight pressure against Barkley's neck and brought their mouths together. Duncan felt the need and desire rise inside of himself like a palpable thing. He crushed his lips against Barkley's, his tongue demanding entrance almost immediately. Barkley obliged and Duncan heard small moans coming from somewhere deep inside. His entire body was on fire, his senses overloaded. His tongue flicked and licked, poked and prodded, while his hands caressed every inch he could reach. "Close," he whispered into Barkley's mouth.

"Jesus," Duncan sighed as he felt his hips involuntarily push up to meet Barkley's hand.

"Me too," Barkley said, and Duncan wondered how he could be close. Neither of them had Barkley's cock in his hand. "Those eyes, your lips, the feel of your gorgeous cock…. They're enough to make me…"

Duncan moved one hand down and began to stroke Barkley's impressive cock. "Love your belly and your mouth. Think about these lips all day long. And I think about your face when you're turned on, just like now."

"I'm ready," Barkley announced as he let his head fall back, eyes closed. "I'm ready, I'm ready."

Duncan continued to thrust his hips up, the pace of Barkley's movements speeding up with him. "Fucking hell, Barkley, I'm gonna come."

Duncan was the first to come, his hands on top of his lover's. Barkley followed only a few seconds later, both men breathing heavily, their foreheads resting against each other. Duncan brought both of his hands up and let them rest on the squared-off jaw, tilting Barkley's head up so that he could kiss lips and cheeks and ears.

"You're amazing, Barkley," Duncan said as his breathing slowed. "Amazing, amazing, fucking amazing."

Barkley just smiled and pulled him closer, his arms caressing the strong back while his head rested on a well-muscled shoulder. "I wish I'd met you years ago," he said, his voice a mere whisper against Duncan's skin.

Duncan wondered if they would have been attracted to each other years ago. There's no doubt that Duncan would have found Barkley impressive as a physical specimen, but he was pretty sure that he wouldn't have had the emotional maturity to see Barkley as kind and giving instead of weak or fragile. After having survived the last couple of years, Duncan knew that what he'd found in Barkley was unimaginable strength and conviction, but back before his fall from the top, Duncan was almost certain he would have interpreted the same qualities as indecision or vulnerability.

He was perceptive enough to realize that there was something deeper happening within Barkley's psyche, and he wasn't convinced it was that he'd simply become tired of singing or fame or both. Duncan could tell that this 180-degree change from world-famous, million-dollar fee artist to unemployed animal advocate had been brought on by some sort of watershed moment in Barkley's life. The only thing he wasn't sure of was whether or not Barkley knew it. If he did know it, would he ever see it for what it was: a reason to change his life and not just throw it away.

Duncan squeezed Barkley and kissed the side of his neck. "Okay, sleepyhead, time to get to bed so we can get out to John and Lori's bright and early." He released Barkley and stood up, reaching for the handheld showerhead. He waited for Barkley to stand up as well before rinsing him off and then turning the spray on himself.

"Thank you for coming with me," Barkley said as he stepped onto the bath mat and reached for a towel. "It's a really magical place."

"Can't wait," Duncan said as he raised his arms and let Barkley dry him off. "From what you've told me about the place, I may end up tagging along quite often." Duncan heard his own words and panicked. *Did that just sound like me making myself part of his future?* "I mean, if you want me to." Duncan took the towel from Barkley, not making any eye contact, suddenly aware of a feeling of loss for something he wasn't sure he ever had. *It's only been a week.* He began to dry off Barkley's hair.

"Of course I want you to come, as often as you'd like." Duncan finished drying Barkley's hair and put his hands on his shoulders to spin him around so he could dry off the wide back. But Barkley didn't budge, not even an inch. "Why would I not want you to come?"

Fuck, Duncan cursed to himself. "I've already taken so much from you, and I mean, I was hoping that this is the start of something. I mean, I know it is for me, but I just wasn't sure if you.... I mean, you didn't have to do any of that stuff for me... and I'm so very grateful that you did, but... well... I did sort of throw myself at you, and—"

"Duncan?"

He stopped rambling and looked up into Barkley's eyes. He saw the smile on the handsome face and wondered why Barkley seemed so amused all of a sudden. "Sorry," he said and let his eyes dart to the door and back to those hypnotic amber eyes.

"I did those things because you're a man of integrity and conviction, something that I've found to be lacking in certain other members of your profession. I did those things because I thought you'd more than paid the price, and you hadn't even done anything wrong." Barkley stepped closer and reached down to take hold of Duncan's hands. "If this ends with the two of us just being friends, I'm certainly not going to be stupid enough to turn that down. God knows, I don't have a lot of friends, but believe me when I tell you that I've been growing more and more attracted to you with each passing second."

"Yeah?"

Barkley laughed and leaned forward to kiss him. "I can't believe this is the same man who came into my apartment and kissed me—like I've never been kissed before, by the way—just because I called in a favor to get him an interview."

"Nicest thing anyone's ever done for me, Barkley," Duncan said as he squeezed his lover's hands.

"Sad, isn't it?" Barkley was shaking his head. "I make a twenty-second phone call to get you a ten-minute interview and it's so… rare that…." Barkley looked at Duncan and smiled. "My parents and I did things like that for each other all the time. It's what I grew up with. Something people should be doing more often."

Duncan noticed the slight sadness that clouded over Barkley's expression and wondered if he'd wanted to say more. Duncan chose to leave it alone, for now.

"Amen," Duncan said before taking the towel and hanging it on the rod. "Okay, then, now that I can call you my *boyfriend*, I would like to go to bed and do some serious spooning." He ran his fingers through Barkley's hair, pushing it away from the handsome face, and kissed him softly, just once more.

They made their way to the king-size bed, finding Tinkerbell waiting just outside the bathroom door. Barkley called to her as they entered the bedroom, and as she'd done every night since Duncan began spending the night, she ran into the bedroom and hopped up onto the bed, kneading and finally settling herself onto the pillow that she liked to share with Barkley.

Duncan pulled himself close to Barkley's back, aligning his body perfectly with his lover's, kissing and grazing across the smooth, silky flesh of Barkley's neck and shoulders. "Barkley?"

"Hmm?"

Duncan let his hand stroke the defined chest and the flat belly. *I don't think you'll ever truly understand what you did for me that day. But I do. And for that, I will love you forever.* He couldn't bring himself to say the words; he wanted to, but it wasn't the right time or place. "You *are* an incredibly amazing man."

"Thank you, Duncan." Barkley rested his hand on top of Duncan's. "You're very special to me too."

Duncan closed his eyes, stealing one more kiss from his lover's skin. *I don't know how or when, but I will be there to help you when you need it the most. Whether we're just friends or whether we're old and still sleeping in the same bed, I'll do anything I can not to disappoint you.*

Chapter 12

"COME ON, little Butter, come on, we're going to your new home," Barkley said to the little pup who was squirming and trying to get back down to finish playing his game of tug-o-war with Zeus. Zeus and Neptune had adopted the little diabetic pup almost from the minute they'd met him. At first Barkley had been nervous and tried to keep Butter away from the larger pups, but then quickly realized that Zeus and Neptune were two of the most gentle dogs he'd ever come across. Barkley finally succeeded in wrestling the little guy into his arms. "I feel like such a shit for taking him away from Neptune and Zeus."

"Then keep him," Duncan said with a shrug of his shoulders.

"I can't," Barkley sighed. "By-laws state that I can only have three dogs at this residence, and with Zeus and Neptune and Mozart, we're full up."

"What?" Duncan seemed surprised, and Barkley couldn't help but wonder if he'd ever done any research into city by-laws before getting his two pups. "How the hell will they ever know?"

"If I want to keep fostering, I have to tell the truth," Barkley responded, perhaps a little too indignantly. "If I can't foster, it'd be like killing those homeless dogs myself."

"Okay," Duncan said, raising his hands in surrender. "Do you want me to leave my dogs at my place?"

"No," Barkley stated emphatically, shaking his head. "I offered to look after them. I couldn't stand the thought of them being cooped up in that tiny apartment all day when I have more than enough space." Barkley sighed with resignation. "I'll just have to figure something out.

I might have to find another place where there is no such by-law, or at the very least, a by-law that will permit more animals."

"And give up this place?" Duncan said as he put leads on Mozart, Salieri, Zeus, and Neptune. Tinkerbell had decided she would try to hide in the leg pocket of Duncan's cargo shorts, but he found her and held her close to his chest.

"No," Barkley said as he put Butter into the basket with Princess and Marco. "Why would I have to give up this place?"

"Jesus," Duncan said with a whistle. "How much money do you *have*?"

"Money in the bank or money on a balance sheet?" Barkley laughed when he saw Duncan's jaw drop. "Come on, we've got to get these little beauties out to their new home on a big, wonderful farm."

Ten minutes later, they were in Barkley's SUV and heading to the Tim Horton's on Chaplin Crescent so Duncan could get his morning fix of caffeine and processed sugar in the form of a box of Timbits. Barkley waited in the car while Duncan, who'd managed to free himself of Tinkerbell for a moment or two, ran in to get his travel mug filled with black coffee and order some Timbits and doughnuts for John and Lori. Barkley had explained it wasn't necessary, but Duncan had insisted: *I'm going to show up for the first time with only mouths for them to feed?* Barkley had laughed and acknowledged that the gesture would certainly be welcomed. Gestures like that and the flowers last night were two of the many reasons why Barkley was sure he was falling in love with this beautiful man. "Now, if I can only get him to stop drinking coffee and stop eating meat," Barkley said to Tinkerbell as she started kneading his lap. She looked up and mewed loudly. "I am *not* picking on him, Stinkerbell," Barkley said as he picked her up and nuzzled her pink nose.

The passenger door opened and Duncan placed the bag of pastries at his feet, the mug going almost immediately to his lips. "Okay, where's my little lap blanket?" Barkley rolled his eyes when Tinkerbell practically scratched through his denim shorts jumping off his lap and onto Duncan's. He looked over at the sheer delight on Duncan's face. "You just wait," he warned as he put the SUV into reverse and backed up. "She'll lose interest in you for whatever reason, and then you'll be discarded, just like me."

"Never," Duncan said as he brought his hand down to Tinkerbell, who had just rolled onto her back looking for tummy rubs. "Stinky and I have an unbreakable connection. Don't we, Stinkers?"

"And what would that be?" Barkley asked as he steered the vehicle toward Highway 400. "You both have hairy ears?"

"Oh, ho ho ho," Duncan howled. "Nice. So, Stinky chooses me and you become a four-year-old, huh?" Duncan shook his head and rubbed Tinkerbell's furry tummy. "You said that didn't matter. You said I was stupid for getting them waxed for the last guy I dated."

"Oh, calm down, you big girl," Barkley said as his own laughter subsided. "I was just teasing you." He reached across to squeeze Duncan's bicep. "Besides, they're vellus hairs and completely white. It's like you have down on your ears."

"Great," Duncan said after sipping from his mug. "Now I'm a duck."

"Only the ears," Barkley said consolingly. "The rest of you is like a racehorse. Muscled, sleek, sexy, and really well-hu—"

"Barkley!" Duncan raised his voice, but Barkley could tell he was playing, covering Tinkerbell's ears and looking behind him. "Not in front of the children."

Barkley laughed, tears coming to his eyes. He reached for his sunglasses on the top of his head and fixed them in place. "Okay, we're coming to the 400, and highways make me nervous with the goddamned Mach 3 speed limits, so don't bug me."

"You want me to drive?"

"No, I'm good. You can drive on the way back." Barkley pulled the vehicle to a stop at the last set of lights before the highway and looked over. "Besides, if you drive, she'll be in my lap, and since I'm not you, I'll be nothing but strips of flesh by the time we get there."

"Oh no, my, my, Stinkerbell," Duncan said as he reached for the bag on the floor and fished out a plain Timbit. He broke off a piece and let Tinkerbell sniff at it before grabbing it between her paws and nibbling at it. "You wouldn't do that to the man who saved you, would you? You love him, don't you?"

DUNCAN LOOKED down at the little furry angel in his lap. "Yes, you do, don't you?" He rubbed her tummy one more time and then picked off another piece of the Timbit and held it out for her to sniff. "Yes, Stinkerbell loves Barkley." *Who wouldn't?* Duncan thought to himself as he looked over at the stern concentration on that breathtaking face. He'd wanted to say something last night, but he ended up being a coward and playing it safe. *Who doesn't want to hear that? What made you so sure you'd scare him away?*

Duncan returned his eyes to the road, his hand petting Tinkerbell's tummy, her tongue coming out occasionally to lick at the sugar on his fingertips. He'd pull himself out of his daydream when she did that and pull off another little morsel of pastry for her to nibble on. After three little morsels for her, he popped the rest in his mouth so that he wouldn't make her sick or overdo it with the human food.

"So, tell me about John and Lori," Duncan said when he grew tired of berating himself for letting fear make his decisions for him.

"Well, where to begin?" Barkley lifted the sunglasses back on top of his head and turned briefly to look at Duncan. "They're my heroes. They were living in Aurora, and through a different series of events, began caring for two orphaned baby goats. Cut to two years later and they receive a notice from the by-law officer that they'll have to get rid of the goats."

"They obviously didn't."

"No," Barkley laughed. "A month later, they were living on a farm in Tottenham, and within months, they had goats and donkeys and llamas and pigs and horses and dogs and cats and were even raising a baby raccoon until she grew up and they released her back into the wild."

"Wow," Duncan said with a whistle. "Now that's dedication."

"Lori has always had a special way with all animals." Barkley said, glancing at Duncan again. "She takes it really hard when they don't make it."

"So, is it strictly abused and neglected animals, or...."

"No, she takes in lots of different animals for whatever reason and even manages to find good homes for some of them away from Whispering Pines, but her priority is providing an abuse-free home for all the animals for however long they have left."

"She sounds like an amazing woman," Duncan observed as he finished off his coffee and placed the travel mug in the cup holder in between the two front seats. His hand moved, all on its own, it seemed, over to Barkley's seat and shoved in between his lover's thigh and the seat. "She must have thought you were an angel when you called and offered to help."

"Oh, it's not just her. John is pretty passionate about what they're doing for the animals as well." Barkley dropped his right hand from the steering wheel. It came to rest on Duncan's forearm and stroked it lightly a few times. "And Lori didn't even know who I was when I called. She just figured I was another do-gooder who would volunteer until the work got too boring or too hard and then quit like some of her other volunteers." Barkley laughed, more to himself, it seemed to Duncan. "If you tell her you want to help, she'll make sure you get more than enough work to do."

"Bring it on," Duncan said with a smirk. "So, does she know who you are now?"

"Of course," Barkley said, glancing at Duncan. "One of the first things I did was give her and John a big, fat check to help out with some repairs that were desperately needed, and the second thing was to line up some publicity so she could tell her story and get even more money coming in."

"*Then* did she think you were an angel?" They both laughed and Duncan pulled his hand out and brought it up to squeeze Barkley's shoulder. "Although I have to tell you, I'm going to miss these little monsters back here." Duncan turned in his seat and saw that Princess, Butter, and Marco were all sleeping in the basket; Mozart and Salieri were chewing bones on the floor behind him and Barkley. And his own pups? Duncan wasn't surprised to find them doing what they were doing. Each of them was licking furiously at the windows at the very back of the SUV. Barkley had cracked them open a little to let some air in, so now, Duncan supposed, Zeus and Neptune were taking their usual approach to problem solving: Keep licking it until something happens.

"One of these days I'll have a huge spread, and I'll take in every animal so that none will have to be killed," Barkley said with a sigh. "But for now, I'm saving the ones who've outstayed their welcome or aren't cute enough or young enough to find a loving home."

"Well, they'll have one now. Thanks to you... and Lori and John."

"Amen," Barkley whispered.

Duncan sat back and looked over at his lover, wondering yet again what Barkley had experienced to make him so passionate about helping and saving other living souls. *Was it the loss of his career? Was this something to focus on until he figured out what he wanted to do? Was it because he was alone, with no family in his life? Or was it because he was just an incredible soul who'd learned lessons that were still unknown to Duncan?*

"Another ten minutes and we'll be there," Barkley announced.

And what about that, Duncan thought to himself. *Who were these unselfish people who spent their entire lives giving and sacrificing for other people or animals or stricter laws or better working conditions? Why were there so few people like this in the world that stories of selfless people could go viral within hours? What was lacking in so much of the population that stories of unselfish sacrifice were so hard to come by? Why was so much of the news about cheating politicians, school boards who could no longer educate their students, more gun massacres because of frightened morons who thought their right to own a gun was more important than a four-year-old's right to live? Why did the media cover so many stories about the upper elite who would spend millions of dollars on clothes and jewels while homeless people died on the streets?*

It made Duncan wonder sometimes why he'd never noticed all of this before, why he'd allowed himself to become so distracted by all the trappings and glamour that he'd been blind for so long to the difference one human being could truly make in this world. He suddenly felt disgusted with himself and, for the first time, thanked all the powers that be for his having survived his fall from grace. If he'd killed himself, like he'd wanted to several times, he never would have made it to this moment. He never would have met Barkley, and he never would have realized that he could continue to sit by and watch the suffering or he could do something about it.

"Okay," Barkley announced suddenly as he slowed the van. "You don't need to worry about the pups or Stinkerbell. They just run free all day and do their thing, introducing themselves to the other animals and playing." Barkley pulled up the long driveway and parked beside the barn. "Lori and John will put out a good spread for lunch—all vegan, sorry." Barkley cringed and shrugged. "Okay. Are you ready to work until your arms fall off?"

"You don't scare me. Bring it on, baby." As Duncan exited the vehicle, he sincerely hoped and prayed to whoever was listening that he would be able to keep up. *Just don't let me make a fool of myself.*

"If you're lucky, you'll get to meet Ro-Ro and she won't head-butt you." Barkley said as he came around to the same side of the vehicle as Duncan. "She's a little goat, about sixteen months old, who took a liking to me the first time I came out to the sanctuary." Barkley looked around for a moment and then back at Duncan. "Lori raised Ro-Ro and her sister Jo-Jo in the house just after their momma died." Barkley's smile got very big and Duncan could tell he was trying not to laugh. "You should have seen the two of them jumping around the house in their diapers."

"Diapers?"

"Yeah," Barkley said, his laughter becoming infectious. "Lori would put them in diapers so she wouldn't have to keep cleaning up their accidents." Barkley's laughter died down and he exhaled. "Oh, man, they were so cute."

"And Jo-Jo?" Duncan wondered if he should be asking. Barkley hadn't mentioned the possibility of meeting her, and he wasn't sure if she might still be around. "Is she…. Will I maybe meet her too?"

Barkley shook his head slowly, his smile disappearing completely. He pointed to the long lane they had just traversed before parking. "She's one of the whispering pines now." Duncan looked at the long driveway, his brow furrowed. "When an animal passes on, Lori and John lay them to rest and plant a sapling with a little plaque so everyone will know that these animals were special… were important to someone."

"I'm sorry," Duncan said, placing an arm around Barkley's shoulders.

"It's how Lori and John named this place," Barkley said, forcing a smile back on his face. "Whispering Pines Animal Sanctuary."

On impulse, Duncan leaned forward and placed a brief, chaste kiss on Barkley's lips, delighted by the surprised smile it caused. "Come on, time to show you how completely useless I am around a farm." Duncan felt Barkley's move to encircle his waist and give it a quick squeeze, realizing for the first time that he would have at least a couple of hours to work out the perfect way to begin the biography of this extraordinary man.

And if he managed to do that much, he promised he'd find some time, perhaps while Barkley was sleeping tonight, to get some of it onto his laptop.

BARKLEY LOOKED over at Duncan, trapped as he was in amongst the llamas. They were honking at him—although none had spit so far—and sniffing. Barkley tried not to laugh, but he couldn't help it. This was Lori's usual initiation for the... uninitiated. After she'd put Barkley through it during his first visit to the sanctuary, she'd explained that she recognized the "keepers" right away from their response to the llamas. If they didn't run screaming, Lori was pretty sure they weren't just here for the cute and cuddly babies.

"Got a new female coming over later," Lori announced as she came to stand beside Barkley. "Owner said she lost her cria and her mate all within a two-month period." Barkley frowned and tilted his head to the side. "Said she's not eating or sleeping and has lost too much weight. They don't wanna give her up, but they don't want to watch her die, either." Lori pulled off her gloves and shoved them down the front of her overalls. "Called me to see if I might be able to bring her back around."

"Poor little love," Barkley sighed.

"How's he doin'?" Lori wiped the back of her hand across her forehead and looked over at Duncan. "He complained yet?"

"No," Barkley said with a laugh. "I may get an earful later on, but he's passing with flying colors so far."

"Seems like a hard worker," Lori acknowledged and slapped Barkley on the back. She began to walk away and then turned. "Not too hard on the eyes, either." She winked and Barkley wondered just how hot his skin would get.

Barkley had never discussed his sexuality with Lori, but then he'd never hidden it from anyone either. So all Lori would have to do is look him up—which Barkley was sure she'd done after getting a check for more than three hundred thousand dollars—to discover that he was a homosexual. And if Lori did know, and if she had a problem with it, she'd never said one word in front of Barkley. Of course, considering what she'd just observed about Duncan, Barkley was willing to bet she wouldn't have a problem with people who loved animals loving each other.

Barkley looked over at Duncan again and smiled, deciding to put him out of his misery. He'd passed the test with flying colors. Duncan was now among the initiated.

"Hey, you!" Barkley called out as he passed through the gate to the llama pen.

"What?" Duncan stood up, took his shirt out of his back pocket, and wiped his forehead. "Am I doing it wrong?"

Barkley approached and raised an eyebrow. "You don't do anything wrong."

Duncan's jaw dropped momentarily, and then he was laughing out loud. "Throwing yourself at me in front of the llamas? Do you have no shame?"

"If I did," Barkley said as he removed his own shirt and pressed himself against Duncan's sweaty torso. "I wouldn't be doing this." Barkley shoved his hands inside of Duncan's back pockets and squeezed the hard globes of his ass while he brought their lips together, his tongue invading Duncan's mouth almost immediately. They kissed until they were both out of breath. "God, you have no idea what seeing you all hairy and sweaty does to me."

"I think I'm getting the picture, sweet cheeks."

"Make me a promise?"

"What's that?"

"When you're fucking me after the benefit tonight, call me *sweet cheeks*?"

"I think I can do that for you," Duncan said as he brought his hands up to caress Barkley's back. "Do me a favor?"

"Anything."

"When I'm fucking you into the mattress tonight, call me *Beethoven*?"

Barkley stopped his exploration and looked at Duncan, who could not hold back the smile on his face. "Jesus H. Christ, Duncan," Barkley said, trying to be heard over Duncan's laughter.

"Hey, I owed you one for the hairy ears comment."

"Prick," Barkley said as he pulled Duncan closer by his belt loops and surreptitiously placed one foot behind his leg. Barkley kissed Duncan quickly and then shoved against his shoulders, watching Duncan land in an expansive pile of llama dung. He blew him a kiss and turned to walk away, annoyed that Duncan chose to lie there and laugh at his own joke. *I wonder what he'd do if I did call him Beethoven tonight?*

Barkley made his way to the garden hose just as John came out to call everyone to the picnic table for lunch. *Oh, this is gonna be good,* Barkley thought to himself as he realized this would be Duncan's first lunch surrounded by farm animals. Barkley quickly rinsed himself off and washed his hands using the little dispenser of soap that Lori and John put out every morning.

"Hey, sweet cheeks," Duncan said as he came up behind Barkley and slapped his ass. "Wanna hose me down?"

"You got it," Barkley said as he turned the hose on his lover.

"Oh fuck me," Duncan hissed as the cold water hit his overheated skin. "That's cold."

"Give it a minute there, Beethoven, you'll get used to it." Barkley grabbed the soap and tossed it to him. "Make sure you wash your hair too."

"No. Spare. Clothes," Duncan snorted between gasps.

"Taken care of," Barkley said as he pointed to his backpack. "Do you honestly think I'd bring you out here and not take care of you?" Barkley rinsed out the remaining suds from Duncan's hair and turned off the hose. He pulled the towel off the peg by the hose and held it open for his lover.

"I think my balls are up around my heart somewhere," Duncan said as he shivered into the open towel.

"Don't say that around here," Barkley cautioned. "You might get a stampede of jealous geldings trying to get back what was stolen from them." Barkley wrapped the towel around Duncan's strong body and began to rub up and down the well-muscled back. He turned Duncan around and dried the front, their eyes meeting when Barkley was almost done. Barkley's smile faded a little when he noticed the intensity of Duncan's blue eyes. Neither of them spoke for what seemed like hours, until Barkley finally looked away and leaned over to get the extra pair of shorts out of his backpack.

"Here," Barkley said as he glanced up at Duncan. "I'm pretty sure these will fit. And Lori will be more than happy to wash the ones you've got on." Barkley looked down and turned to walk away, but Duncan stopped him with a gentle hand to his chest.

"Barkley?" Duncan's hand was still on his bare chest, directly over his heart as it threatened to beat right out of his chest. "I… I want you to know that this has been the most incredible… happiest week of my entire life."

Barkley didn't know what to say or do, so he placed his hand over Duncan's and smiled up at those earnest blue eyes. After a moment, he saw Duncan visibly relax and leaned forward and placed a soft, chaste kiss on his lover's lips. He nodded off to his left, indicating the picnic table. "We'll wait for you to get changed."

"SEEMS LIKE a good man," John said as he took a seat beside Lori.

"Yes," Barkley said. He could feel himself blushing. "He is a very good man."

"Serious?" Lori took the cellophane off the large bowl of potato salad

"Lori!" John stopped arranging plates to glare at his wife.

"I hope so," Barkley whispered and offered a shrug. "It is for me."

"I'm glad," Lori said with a smile. "I won't lie and tell you I haven't worried about you a time or two."

"Lori!"

Barkley laughed at the two of them. "John, in all the time I've been coming out here, has doing that ever stopped her from speaking her mind?"

"Yeah, John," Lori said with a halfhearted attempt at indignation. "Quit trying to be the alpha here."

"I'm starving." All three turned at Duncan's arrival.

"Well, dig in, hon," Lori said as she deposited the last spoon into the last bowl, making sure to point the handles toward the guests.

"Don't normally have meat, but your fella here told us you weren't vegan."

"You didn't have to do that for me," Duncan said as he picked up the spoon in the potato salad and started loading up his plate. "I've been thinking about giving up meat anyway, so it would have been a nice introduction."

"Really?" Barkley looked over at Duncan. He could feel their legs pressing together. "Why didn't I know that?"

"Saw a video on your Facebook page about how farm animals are treated before they're slaughtered," Duncan said, looking over into Barkley's eyes. "Horrible stuff."

Barkley was at a loss for words. He'd always wondered if posting those videos ever did any good, and now here he was sitting beside someone who'd not only taken the time to visit the page, but to think about something he'd seen there.

"Oh," Lori said, raising herself out of her seat. "Almost forgot something." She disappeared into the house and came back a few moments later with Tinkerbell in her arms. "She was in the house playing with some of the other kits, and I was gonna let her eat with them, but Barkley told me she's kinda sweet on you." Lori deposited the blind kitten on one of the remaining chairs beside Duncan. Lori put a little bowl of water and a plate with a few pieces of meat in front of Tinkerbell.

Barkley felt Duncan's hand caress his thigh a few times and then offer a quick squeeze. "Figures," Barkley sighed. "She's my cat and the little stinker goes and falls for Duncan."

"Doesn't seem like she's any different than you."

"Lori!"

Chapter 13

BARKLEY CLOSED his eyes and inhaled deeply, remembering to relax his shoulders and to imagine his ribcage spreading out in all directions. He exhaled through pursed lips, the rushing air making them vibrate just as his vocal chords vibrated with one continuous note. His lips stopped vibrating as he ran out of air, the familiar tingling feeling spreading across his lips. He ignored the tickling sensation underneath his nose as he inhaled deeply yet again and blew out the air slowly, repeating the movements over and over while he added one more note each time.

He heard something crash in the living room. The momentary distraction led to his losing focus, and his lips ceased to vibrate with the rush of the air out of his lungs. *Dammit,* he thought to himself and reached for the doorknob to the third bedroom, his rehearsal space. Barkley had only another two hours to finish warming up and change into his tuxedo.

"Sorry," Duncan called out as he came out of the kitchen holding the lid for a covered saucepot in one hand and Tinkerbell in the other. "I put her down on the counter for a moment, and she got away from me."

Barkley couldn't help but smile. He shook his head as he continued toward Duncan and Tinkerbell. "No biggie," Barkley said as he leaned over and stole a kiss from the kitten. "How can I be mad at someone so adorable?" Barkley looked up at Duncan and puckered his lips; he was asking for a kiss. "Thank you," Barkley said after Duncan obliged him.

"Okay, go practice," Duncan said as he put Tinkerbell back on the floor. "I'll get her fed and then take Mozart, Zeus, and Neptune outside so we won't have to worry about them while we're out."

Barkley smiled and went back to his warm-up. To say his mind wasn't really focused on his performance—as it usually was—would have been an understatement. He was worried about not being able to take any other shelter animals with three dogs now in his condo; he was worried about Mozart not being as agile and quick as his two new playmates; he was worried about reentering a world of privilege and snobbery he'd thought he'd be done with by now; and, most importantly, he couldn't stop thinking about Duncan.

He closed his eyes and let his mind focus only on his warm-up routine: breathing, rib cage expanding, maintaining the vibration of his lips, adding one more note each time. After ten minutes, he proceeded to the next step. He would sing scales, imagining a staircase; all of the notes would ascend the staircase, even if the scale was actually descending. It was his way of imagining the consistent energy of a phrase, of maintaining the strength of the arc of that phrase.

After another twenty minutes, Barkley stood, looking down at his keyboard, as he plunked the first chord of the first selection that Mrs. Green had asked him to sing. It wasn't necessarily procedure to allow the patron to choose the repertoire, but since this would be one of the final public appearances for Barkley Reinhardt, he had been feeling magnanimous. Of course, it was one of the original reasons he'd declined Mrs. Green's invitation to sing at her charity benefit. Barkley did not always respond well to other people telling him what to do or what to sing or who to associate with. But for Duncan, Barkley had been willing to make an exception. Barkley still wasn't sure if that one act of generosity made him altruistic or naïve.

"Votre Toast" from *Carmen*. It was not a difficult aria by any stretch of imagination, but did require a presence and an attitude that could sap Barkley's strength pretty quickly. *Escamillo*, the bullfighter, enters a tavern and sings a toast full of the exciting imagery of the life of the toreador, both inside and outside the ring. It was an aria sung by a braggart, a man who knew that all eyes were on him, especially the dark eyes of women. Barkley could relate to everything about the aria, except, of course, the bulls and the women.

With a rousing beginning guaranteed by "Votre Toast," Barkley would then perform "O du mein holder Abendstern" from Wagner's

Tannhäuser. It was Wolfram's aria: he is in love with Elizabeth, but she is in love with Tannhäuser, who is off on a pilgrimage to beg forgiveness for his many sins. When Tannhäuser takes too long to return, Elizabeth asks the Virgin Mary to take her to heaven. Wolfram prays to the evening star to protect and guide the woman he loves on her way to heaven. It would be almost six minutes of incredibly heavy music, both in terms of theme and the sheer weight of the performance.

But then he would end with one of Mrs. Green's favorites. An incredibly depressing piece—or so Barkley had always found it to be—by Schubert. He could remember loving it at one time, but he had found himself disliking it more and more each time he performed it. It was a serenade, one song contained within a cycle of many songs. The cycle was *Schwanengesang* and this particular song, "Ständchen." The song was not difficult, but it was deceptive in its simplicity. Though the accompaniment would be at times staccato and at other times legato and flowing, Barkley would need to express his love to the trees and the winds and beseech them to deliver the message to his beloved. And he would need to do all this with a seemingly effortless, flowing grace.

DUNCAN SAT on the hardwood floor outside the door to Barkley's rehearsal room, still holding the three leads in his hand. He'd come back in time to hear that same song that he'd heard Barkley practicing just yesterday. He sat with his eyes closed, wondering what the words meant. Even if he spoke German, he wondered if he would be able to distinguish one word from the other. It was a problem for him in any language, trying to decipher what words the singer was actually singing. There were some artists who seemed to be better at it than others, but for the most part, Duncan always found himself singing words and combinations of words that made absolutely no sense.

But even without knowing what Barkley was actually saying, Duncan felt his heart race as he listened; he felt out of breath, speechless even. The melody and the harmony made him feel such an odd mixture of emotions. He felt hope one moment and then despair. He felt excited, yet restrained, eager, yet cautious. It was as if the composer had been suffering some sort of schizophrenic episode when he wrote this song, unable to decide whether the song should ultimately inspire or discourage.

Raising himself off the floor, Duncan decided that he could barely wait to finally see the song instead of just hearing it. He couldn't wait to see Barkley's face as he sang about whatever the song was about. He thought back to all of those YouTube videos he'd watched after meeting Barkley and how he'd felt completely captivated by how Barkley used his entire body to pull the audience into the song, deep into his world.

He made his way back to the living room and took a seat on the overstuffed sofa, patting his lap a couple of times in quick succession. He smiled as Tinkerbell came around the corner from the kitchen, her tongue stroking the sides of her mouth. "Hey, girl, you all done eating?" Duncan patted his legs one more time, and Tinkerbell jumped up. "How do you do that, huh, sweetie? How do you know exactly where to land?" Duncan reached out beside him and found her favorite little bear, letting her swat at it while he teased her with it.

Duncan figured it had something to do with almost satellite-like ears, or perhaps it was the combination of smell and hearing that told Tinkerbell exactly where his lap was. Regardless, Duncan found himself, as he always did, smiling down at her while he scratched her tummy. "Who's a perfect kitty, huh? Who's the best little kitty in the whole world?"

"Give her a minute and she'll answer you by peeing on you or running out in front of you when your arms are full of groceries or laundry." Barkley was leaning against the corner that joined the hallway and the living room.

Duncan patted the sofa beside him and quickly glanced at the clock. "So, we have just under an hour to go." Duncan looked back up at Barkley as he approached and sat down on the sofa, his hand coming out to rub Tinkerbell's tummy. "Nervous?"

"Always," Barkley admitted. "Any singer who tells you they're not nervous before a performance is either lying or is about to give a really good example of apathy."

"I don't know how you do it," Duncan said, shaking his head. "I mean, not you specifically, but performers. Going out there when you're already nervous and then trying to remember all the words, *and* in the right order."

Barkley laughed and leaned against Duncan. "I'll let you in on a little secret. Only the truly die-hard fans know when a singer has made a mistake or has forgotten the words." Duncan must have looked puzzled because Barkley continued: "We hardly ever sing in English, so that means the other person will need to understand the language we're singing in. And since we sing on the vowels, it's pretty easy to get away with mistakes."

"Okay, but what about forgetting the words?"

Barkley shrugged and smiled. "Just make something up."

"Have you ever had to?"

"No," Barkley admitted. "But then again, the more you sing it, the more it becomes like an automatic reflex." Barkley shifted so he could rest his forearm on Duncan's shoulder. "For example, name one of your favorite groups."

Duncan looked up at the ceiling and squinted. "Ah, Pink Floyd."

Barkley cleared his throat and began to hum, introducing words after a moment. "We don't need no education," Barkley began to sing and then looked at Duncan.

"We don't need no thought control," they sang together. "No dark sarcasm in the classroom." Zeus and Neptune, who'd been lying quietly near the French doors to the balcony suddenly began to howl in time to the song. Barkley and Duncan both stopped, looked at each other, then the dogs, then back at each other before dissolving into a brief fit of laughter.

"There," Barkley said after they stopped. "You see, you know that song so well you can remember the lyrics after all these years. It's the same for us. We sing it and practice it so often, I don't think I could ever forget the words."

Duncan nodded and looked back down at Tinkerbell. "So," Duncan began and looked back up at Barkley. "I don't want you to laugh or anything, but is it possible for you to teach me about opera or about classical music?"

"Sure, although there's really nothing to teach." Barkley pushed himself off the sofa and ran his hand through his hair. "If you like Pink Floyd, you already have an appreciation for music. The rest is just finding what you like."

"So, you don't like every piece of classical music you've ever heard?"

"No," Barkley laughed. "Just like I don't like every country song I've ever heard."

"You like country?" Duncan raised his eyebrows and studied Barkley's expression.

"I like music," Barkley stated almost immediately. "If I like a song, it doesn't matter whether it's country or pop or jazz or blues or hip-hop. If I like the song, it's the song I like. There are a lot of classical music pieces I don't like, and that goes for all other genres as well."

"Kinda like when someone asks me whether I'm a fan of a particular author," Duncan said, nodding. "There are some books I love, but then others from the same author I couldn't stand."

"Exactly," Barkley said with a smile and turned toward the hallway. "I'll get changed and then it'll be your turn."

Duncan looked down at Tinkerbell; she'd apparently not received enough attention while he and Barkley had been discussing music because she was biting and nibbling on his fingers. "He's a very interesting man, isn't he, Stinky?"

Her response was to knead his thigh and then to curl up into a little ball of fur.

"BARKLEY, DARLING!" Mrs. Green was one of those upper-echelon society hostesses who, despite not having done any of the actual organizing for this particular event, seemed to enjoy portraying herself as harried and stretched too thin.

"Mrs. Green," Barkley said as he accepted a kiss on each cheek. "May I present Duncan Spencer?" Barkley turned to Duncan. "Mrs. Rosemary Green."

"Mrs. Green," Duncan said as he extended a hand. "Enchanté."

Mrs. Green, Barkley noticed, offered a sincere smile to Duncan and then turned back to him. "I'm so thrilled that you could help us this evening. It has been an absolute triumph keeping you a secret for the past couple of days. And I *am* sorry to do this to you, but I simply *must* go and see what that caterer is doing."

"She seems nice," Duncan said as he shoved his hands deep into his pockets. "What's this event for?"

"Fundraising to send children to music camp," Barkley answered, turning slightly to study his date. "Are you going to be okay? You look really nervous."

"Sure, yeah, uh huh," Duncan said almost immediately.

Barkley couldn't help but smile, wondering why Duncan could be so nervous. "You don't have to schmooze or anything, but I'll tell you, there are a quite a few big-time media moguls here."

"Please, I'm not about to look a gift horse in the mouth, Barkley." Duncan brought his hands out of his pockets and began to wring his hands together. "I'm going to start looking to further my career when you've gone to all this trouble for me?"

Barkley put his hands in his pockets and stepped closer to Duncan. "Well, then, I'll tell you what. When this is all done, I'll have a nice surprise for you." Barkley smiled as Duncan raised an eyebrow. "And yes, it will involve being naked."

"Barkley, my boy!" Edward Green stepped up to the two men and presented each with a glass of champagne. "You have no idea how much easier you've made my life. I didn't even mind having the programs reprinted, at my own expense."

"Good evening, Edward," Barkley said with a smile. "Thank you," he said as he accepted the glass of champagne. He would not drink any of it, but he was certainly not about to offend the man who'd given Duncan a job. "You know Duncan Spencer, of course."

"Of course," Edward said as he extended a hand, shaking Duncan's hand and then Barkley's. "Not only did you make my wife very happy by finally agreeing to sing for the benefit, but I've also been hearing great things about our latest addition here."

Barkley smiled and looked over at Duncan, who seemed to be blushing as he sipped his champagne. "It is really I who should be thanking you."

"I've been hearing about the fireball of energy and efficiency from the producers," Edward said, looking at Barkley and then at Duncan. "It would seem that you're making quite an impression after only three days, Duncan."

"Well, thank you, sir," Duncan said, almost in a whisper. "We're all part of the same team, right? If they don't look good, I don't look good."

"Well, you two young men enjoy yourselves this evening," Edward said as he shook their hands again. "And, Barkley, you'd make my life even easier if you promised my wife you won't be retiring."

Barkley laughed and watched Edward retreat into the crowd. He turned to Duncan almost immediately after. "I have to go soon and get ready," he explained. "You gonna be okay out here?"

"Sure, yeah, uh huh," Duncan said again, and Barkley had to force himself not to laugh.

"When you begin to feel intimidated or out of place, just remember: Most of the people here will love you because they're good and kind human beings. And the others? They have no clue their toothbrushes are used to clean their toilets by their overworked and underpaid maids."

DUNCAN WAS still laughing at that particular mental image when he felt a hand land on his shoulder. He turned to see the sneering face of the owner of the newspaper, the owner who had thrown him under the bus and sent his life into absolute chaos.

"Well, Mr. Spencer," he oozed, the sneer so firmly affixed to the man's reptilian face that Duncan always had to fight the urge to ask whether it was his mother or father who had been descended from geckos. "Would you be a good boy and bring me another champagne?"

It took Duncan a moment to realize that Mr. Paul Black seemed to be under the impression that he was a waiter at this particular event. Duncan drained his glass of champagne and smiled, pressing the empty flute into the ample belly of the print media mogul. He didn't bother waiting until Paul had ahold of the glass before he walked away without saying a word.

Duncan moved to the area where the chairs were arranged in tidy rows, each of the chairs decorated with ornate gold brocade fabric on the seats and backs. Duncan couldn't help but wonder just how much each of these chairs would cost.

"I hear you've managed to land on your feet."

Duncan rolled his eyes and didn't bother turning around. From what he remembered of Paul Black, the man didn't like to be shown up. He was a regular op-ed contributor to his own papers, touting the decline of the Western civilization's values. As far as Duncan could tell, the man could barely string two sentences together, but he fancied himself as witty and urbane, the voice of the everyman even though he'd already relinquished his Canadian citizenship in what turned out to be a fruitless bid for a British knighthood.

"Writing fiction now, as I hear it."

Duncan heard the laughter of other voices behind him and affixed a smile to his face before turning around. "Interesting," Duncan said as he quickly scanned what was supposed to pass for the society "elite" who obviously had more money than education since they couldn't tell the man they currently found so amusing was, by all accounts, a thief and a swindler of the first order. "Isn't that what Canada Revenue has said about your last ten years' worth of tax returns?" Duncan's smile grew as the media magnate's fell. "Excuse me," Duncan said after a moment and moved to the other side of the room, finding a seat and sitting down.

He wasn't worried about Paul chasing after him; even *he* wasn't that stupid. He pulled the beautiful program from his pocket and studied the photo on the front. It showed a group of children playing various instruments, and the inside cover gave a lengthy explanation on what the foundation did to help the underprivileged children of the city receive education in the arts.

The remaining pages were dedicated to the three artists who would be performing this evening: a young violinist, only seventeen years of age, but already being groomed to be the next virtuoso of his generation and, Duncan noted with some appreciation, a recipient of funds from this particular charitable trust; a wind quartet, each member also a recipient and the eldest of which was only eleven years old; and finally there was Barkley. Duncan smiled as he studied the picture—probably a stock photo—showing the perfectly coiffed blond hair, the strong jaw, and the sparkling amber eyes. He traced the photo with a finger, wondering again at how this man had single-handedly changed his professional and personal lives.

As the throng of benefactors began to take their own seats, Duncan skimmed the lengthy writing beside Barkley's photograph. Duncan's eyes grew wide when he read of how Barkley's parents had been instrumental in the founding of this particular charity, how they'd given so freely of their time and talents—both inside and outside the classroom—to ensure that all students, regardless of the family's income, could pursue a love of music.

That's where he gets it from, Duncan thought to himself as the seats filled and Mrs. Green stood before the microphone to begin the evening. Suddenly, Duncan could not wait for the benefit to be over. For some strange reason, he wanted to have Barkley in his arms right then. The desire to be close to him, to kiss him, was more powerful than it had ever been before.

Chapter 14

DUNCAN OPENED his eyes, his entire body feeling more relaxed than it had ever felt before. Duncan was leaning against that magnificent chest of Barkley's. The benefit had ended several hours ago, and since then he and Barkley had returned home to change clothes and walk the dogs. They played with Tinkerbell while having a quick snack and then explored each other's bodies and made love for over an hour before ending up in the hot tub on the roof of the building. "Won't we get in trouble for being naked in the hot tub?"

"We wore bathing suits up here," Barkley said as he caressed Duncan's chest. "We only took them off once we were in. Besides, I'm on very good terms with the owner of the building. That's why I have the keys and know how to turn off the video cameras." Barkley reached down and smoothed his hands over the flat belly.

Duncan sighed and sat up, turning so he could pull Barkley toward him. He hooked his hands under Barkley's knees and grinned as the beautiful blond floated effortlessly toward him. When Barkley was straddling his thighs, Duncan took his lips softly at first and then increased the pressure, his left hand encircling both of their cocks while Barkley's hands played through his hair. "Would you get yourself in trouble with the owner if he found out I couldn't control myself and had to have you right now, in this hot tub?"

"No," Barkley said as he accepted one kiss after the other. "Besides, the owner of the building really, really likes you."

Duncan stopped kissing Barkley and pulled his head back, his eyebrows coming together almost immediately. "I've met the owner?" Barkley nodded and Duncan wondered out loud, "Edward?"

"No," Barkley said as he continued to kiss Duncan's lips and face and neck. "Not Edward."

"Then who?"

"You're the investigative reporter," Barkley said as he brought his hand down to join Duncan's, both men pinching and fondling and stroking. "But I do know that he thinks you're the most incredible lover he's ever had."

Duncan wondered which one of his past lovers could have.... Duncan opened his eyes wide and looked at Barkley. It wasn't hard to figure out whom Barkley meant, considering all of his past lovers had been barely able to afford the drinks that Duncan had always ended up paying for. "You?" Duncan noticed the smile on Barkley's face. "You own this building?"

"Actually," Barkley said, his lips coming off Duncan's earlobe. "I own all three of the buildings in this complex."

Duncan looked into Barkley's eyes. "Holy fuck," he said as he found himself shaking his head. "The only thing I own is my motorcycle." He continued to shake his head as he imagined the kind of discipline that must have taken. Sure, Barkley commanded astronomical fees for his singing, but after all the deductions for taxes, agents, publicists, wardrobe, and all the other stuff, Duncan found it hard to believe that a singer could make millions of dollars in only a few short years.

"I hope that doesn't bother you," Barkley said as he finally stopped kissing Duncan's neck.

"God, no," Duncan protested, somewhat loudly. "I just don't want you to think that.... Well, I mean I appreciate everything that you've done for me, but I... damn."

Barkley huffed a little laugh and leaned back. "It's the recordings," he explained. "I've done quite a number of recordings and have usually managed to negotiate a higher-than-normal percentage of sales."

"I guess that's possible when you can do what you did tonight, huh?" Duncan accepted a kiss as thanks for the compliment. "That was absolutely... mesmerizing," Duncan said as he slowly moved his hands up and down Barkley's back. "I've watched who knows how many videos on YouTube, but they don't even come close to hearing you sing live."

"Thank you," Barkley said, his hands coming out to pet at the hairy, muscular chest. "I heard you even managed to piss someone off tonight."

"Just the one? I must be losing my touch."

"For what it's worth," Barkley said with an air of commiseration, "I've never liked Paul Black. He always seems to find what he says funnier than everyone else around him does."

"I'm wondering," Duncan said, his eyebrows furrowed and his hands beginning to explore Barkley's body in earnest. "Why is it that we're talking about that prick when we could be talking about this one." Barkley laughed as Duncan took his hand and guided it between their bodies. Duncan brought their lips together, tongues finding each other, nostrils flaring as they tried to take in as much air as possible. When he couldn't get enough air, Duncan pulled off. "I can never seem to get enough of you, Barkley Reinhardt."

"Know the feeling," Barkley whispered.

"YOU REALIZE," Barkley said, after they'd finished. "Now I'll have to drain and clean the hot tub."

"I'll help," Duncan said, gathering Barkley into his arms. "Small price to pay."

Barkley snuggled into Duncan, delighting in the feel of the soft hair against his back. "Deal." After a few minutes, when each of the men were breathing a little more evenly, Barkley turned sideways, so that his right arm was behind Duncan's head while his left caressed the defined, hairy chest. "May I ask you a question? A personal question?"

"Sure," Duncan said, leaning in to kiss Barkley's lips.

"You don't have to talk about it if you don't want," Barkley said cautiously.

"You want to know why I didn't reveal my source," Duncan said with a heavy sigh.

"No, no," Barkley said, raising his hand quickly.

"No? Then sure, ask away," Duncan said with a smile. Barkley noticed the look of relief on Duncan's face and wondered if it would still be there after he asked the question he really wanted to ask.

"I was just wondering about your childhood." Barkley's hand went back to caressing his lover's chest. "I mean, everyone knows about the trial and you not wanting to compromise your ethics and reveal your source, but I kept on trying to find information about Duncan Spencer *before* all of that happened."

"Well," Duncan said, pulling Barkley a little closer. "I was born and raised in Mississauga. I managed to get through school, barely, although I did love English classes and reading and writing. But I just figured I'd be one of those people who gets a job he doesn't particularly like to pay the bills all while hoping I could actually make my dream come true of being a writer."

"Did you go to university or college?"

"No, no money for that," Duncan said, pushing some hair off Barkley's forehead.

"How did you end up becoming a journalist, then?"

"That's three questions, by the way," Duncan said, teasing.

"I'm sorry," Barkley said, moving to the side of the hot tub. "I was just curious."

"Hey, hey," Duncan responded, grabbing hold of Barkley's wrist and pulling him back. "Where do you think you're going?" Once Barkley was once again leaning against him, Duncan took a deep breath. "I had a few good friends all the way through high school, but when they went off to university, I ended up working at various odd jobs, never really holding any of them for more than a couple of months. I would get bored or would end up clashing with my boss.

"This one friend, Jimmy, went off to Ryerson. We kept in touch and called each other to go out for drinks or to a game, you know, that kind of thing. Anyway, he called me up one day and invited me out for drinks with his new girlfriend. He said he had something important to ask me." Duncan laughed at something and pulled himself closer to Barkley. "I figured it had something to do with the new girlfriend. But, long story short, he told me that he was working in the mailroom of the *Star* and that there was a position open. So, he gave me the details, I went in for an interview thinking it could possibly lead to other things." Duncan smiled when Barkley looked up at him. "And it did."

"You worked your way up from the bottom, then," Barkley said, pulling himself onto Duncan's lap. "I am very impressed."

"I think there were probably a few colleagues who resented the fact that I didn't have a degree, but…."

"Jealousy can be a real bitch, can't it?" Barkley leaned forward and kissed Duncan's ear, nibbling a little before leaning back and studying him.

Duncan just looked at him and winked, the two of them dissolving into laughter.

"HEY, STINKERBELL," Duncan said as he and Barkley came back into the condo. Tinkerbell was there on the couch with her favorite little bear, pawing it toward Duncan's voice. "You wanna play?" Duncan picked up the bear and threw it a few feet away, the little bell inside ringing out to the kitten that Duncan was willing to play.

Duncan watched as Tinkerbell not only found the little bear, but pounced on it and began to swat at it. She grasped it between her front paws and then began to pummel it with her hind legs, the little bell noisily confirming the poor bear's defeat. Duncan wondered how the bear still had any of its fake fur left. Barkley had already sewn one eye back on and had had to completely remove the little ribbon that had been tied around the bear's neck, but regardless, there was no question that this was Tinkerbell's favorite toy.

He stood in the middle of the living room, fascinated by this blind kitten's indomitable spirit, and felt two arms snake around his midsection. "I'll get up early tomorrow morning and go refill the tub," Duncan said without turning around. "And I'll try to control myself better the next time so you won't be cleaning at…." Duncan looked around at the grandfather clock. "Seventeen minutes after midnight."

"Do you hear me complaining?"

Duncan turned in Barkley's arms, bringing his own arms around the shorter man's neck. "No, but then you never complain about anything."

"Well, that's not true," Barkley said, goosing Duncan's ass. "In fact, I'm thinking of complaining right now."

"About?"

"You."

"Me?"

"Yes," Barkley said, trying to avoid the kiss that Duncan was offering. "Why are we out here and not in bed? I have a very busy day tomorrow, and I need my beauty rest."

Duncan finally grabbed on to Barkley's cheeks, forcing his lips to jut out, and kissed him firmly on the lips. "Okay, then let me just get our little pillow warmer, and I'll be right there." Duncan kneeled down on the hardwood floor and picked up Tinkerbell's favorite bear, shaking it to get the kitten's attention. "Come on, sweetie, it's bedtime." He began to make his way to the bedroom and suddenly realized that he had not yet seen Zeus or Neptune or Mozart since coming back from the hot tub. "Hey, Barkley? Where are the pups?"

He didn't hear an answer, but did hear laughter. He looked over to see Barkley standing in the doorway to the master bedroom, shaking his head.

"Oh, don't tell me," Duncan moaned and bent over to pick up Tinkerbell. "Have they taken over the entire bed?"

"Pretty much," Barkley said with a certain resignation.

Duncan kissed Tinkerbell on the top of her head and peeked into the room. Zeus and Neptune were sprawled out vertically on the bed, almost as if they were spooning, and Mozart was lying on his back with his head hanging over the side of the king-size bed, his three legs bent, but otherwise sticking straight up in the air. "I'm so sorry," Duncan said as he handed the kitten to Barkley. "They're not normally like this. I've never let them get away with this at home."

"It's not a problem, Duncan, really." Barkley kissed the kitten and cradled her in the crook of his elbow, stroking her belly as he watched Duncan make short work of getting the dogs off the bed. "I was actually going to tell you that most mornings, I would wake up to find Mozart and Stinkerbell here, in or on the bed with me." Barkley kissed Tinkerbell one last time before depositing her on her pillow—or at least the pillow she obviously thought was hers. "All of those years that I was singing and spending so many nights away from home, I dreamed of the day when I would have a house full of pets, wake up with them lying all over me, come home and be bowled over by the charge of slobbering animals happy to see me."

"I know, but they have to know who's alpha. Otherwise, they'll take over the whole place." Duncan finished brushing dog hair off the duvet and quickly stripped out of his swimming trunks. "So, what's so busy about tomorrow?" Duncan asked, changing the subject.

"Tomorrow is shelter day," Barkley responded, stripping out of his own trunks and climbing between the sheets. "I go to the various shelters around the city and take the most at-risk animals or the ones who've never had a home or even the ones who might never get adopted."

"And then take them to Lori and John's sanctuary?"

"Not all of them," Barkley sighed, scooting closer to Duncan's side and making sure he didn't disturb Tinkerbell. "Some of them find homes with loving families, some go to specialty rescue missions, and others I might keep."

"I never realized there were so many kill shelters in Toronto," Duncan said as he moved his right arm above his head and then lowered it as soon as Barkley was nestled in beside him. He exhaled as he put his arm around the strong shoulders and closed his eyes as he felt Barkley's long fingers come to rest on his chest.

"There aren't, but some of them do eventually have to make room for other animals." Barkley raised his head briefly and looked into Duncan's eyes. "I make a point of getting there first so they won't have to kill any of the animals."

Duncan lifted his head before Barkley could lower his own and planted a tender kiss on the singer's forehead. "You're a good man, Barkley Reinhardt. I wonder if people really know that about you." Duncan felt Barkley shrug.

Duncan let his mind wander for a moment, as it had since meeting Barkley, to thoughts of writing the biography. He was still in search of the perfect opening sentence.

"I DON'T know what people think of me, but I think they'd be surprised at how much charitable work most of us do." Barkley wondered if he sounded self-important and egotistical. For anyone who might be interested, his public service and volunteer efforts were a matter of public record, but then not everyone knew who he was or followed his every move.

"What else have you done?"

"Whatever needed doing," Barkley said, starting to fidget with Duncan's chest hair. He forced himself to still his fingers.

"Like the five or ten appearances you've made on behalf of the LGBT community to stop homophobia and bullying or the PSAs you've made in the States about marriage equality and how it didn't destroy Canada." Duncan chuckled and squeezed Barkley's shoulders. "Those ones are some of my favorites."

Barkley raised his head again. "Well, if you knew, why did you ask me?"

"Or," Duncan went on as if Barkley had not just spoken. "Those black and white, very tongue-in-cheek, adverts you did warning the public about how allowing heterosexuals to marry and breed would ruin property values and infect our neighborhoods with polyester track suits and children who had been deprived of good, traditional values like sewing a simple tablecloth or baking a low-calorie flan."

Barkley found himself laughing at the memory of making those satirical PSAs. The originators of those PSAs had only ever intended them to be an in-joke amongst the gay community, showcasing them during Pride Week or showing them before gay-themed movies, but all of the videos had quickly gone viral and Barkley had found himself the target of some of the most vitriolic feedback he'd ever received during his entire career. Of course, he'd also found himself with a completely new fan base. Whether it was a gym bunny on Yonge Street or a middle-aged man near Church Street, Barkley had found himself unable to go out in public for many, many months without being stopped just about everywhere he went. "So, I repeat: Why did you just ask what else I'd done if you already knew?"

"I was just curious to see if you'd list everything or if you'd downplay it," Duncan said, kissing the top of Barkley's head. "And I was right. You downplayed it."

"I promise I will be more pompous and self-congratulatory in the future."

"No, you won't," Duncan sighed as he settled himself again, pulling Barkley a little bit closer. "Because that's not who you are. And don't think I didn't notice how you blushed every time someone complimented you after the benefit." Duncan brought up one of his hands and rested it on the hand that Barkley was using to comb through his chest hair. "An egomaniac would never blush like that when he was getting exactly what he wanted."

Barkley didn't respond, just stretched out against Duncan's solid, warm body. He didn't know if that was the way egomaniacs actually behaved, but Duncan had gotten the rest of it right. Barkley had always known that he would have difficulty with the fame part of his chosen career. And he'd been right to be wary of it; it had not taken very long for the vultures to come swooping out of the sky. Even just a few years ago, Barkley had found it almost impossible to go anywhere at all without being accosted by fans and onlookers. And while most of the fans were very grateful for whatever brief period of time Barkley could spend with them, there were always those who would make rude remarks or pass judgment when Barkley could not spend the time to which they felt entitled.

Barkley felt the soft caresses over his scalp and neck, a sudden realization making him look up into Duncan's eyes. "What was your family like?"

"Nothing special," Duncan said, leaning forward to kiss Barkley's forehead. "Why?"

"Just curious. You know so much about me, but I don't know anything about you."

Duncan didn't offer any more details. Barkley found himself wide-awake, wondering if Duncan had secrets of his own he didn't feel like sharing. Duncan's breathing slowed, his caresses stopped, and when Barkley looked up, his face was so serene and at peace. *No, Barkley thought to himself, a man who sleeps that soundly is not burdened by the shame of his past.*

Barkley wasn't sure if he found that thought comforting or terrifying.

DUNCAN AWOKE slowly, reaching his hand out and over to pull himself closer to Barkley, only coming fully awake when he realized that Barkley had somehow sprouted a substantial amount of hair during the night. He pulled his hand back and raised his head off the pillow. No Barkley; Duncan was alone. Well, not completely alone, since the three pups had managed to find some room on Barkley's empty side of the bed. He leaned over, resting on one elbow while he kissed each of the pups, before noticing Tinkerbell had taken over Barkley's entire pillow. Duncan smiled to himself as he watched the kitten, stretched out on her back, her pink belly rising and falling. He kissed the pink nose and then made his way to the side of the bed, wondering where Barkley was and just how long he'd been gone.

As soon as he stood up beside the bed, he heard the familiar click of a mouse and the zipper-like noise of a scroll wheel. Duncan, scratching his head, made his way to the spare bedroom that served as both Barkley's study and rehearsal space. He stood in the doorway for a moment, watching his lover scroll through image after image of animals in need of a home. He remembered Barkley telling him that he would be going out later that day to rescue even more animals.

"Hey," Duncan said, stopping in his tracks when he saw Barkley jump at the sound of his voice. "Sorry, sweetie, didn't mean to scare you."

"'S okay," Barkley said as he reached up with his hands to stretch. "Did I wake you?"

"No," Duncan said through a yawn. "I reached over to cuddle and got a big handful of Zeus."

"Should I be jealous?" Barkley teased as he patted his lap.

Duncan chuckled as he sat in Barkley's lap and draped his arm over the solid shoulders. "You're getting a head start on your pickups tomorrow?" Duncan looked over at the screen, an almost involuntary smile coming to his lips as he saw a picture of seven tabby kittens, all in a box, looking up at the camera.

"Their mother was killed by a car and they were found by a nice lady out for a walk with her dog," Barkley explained as he rested his head against Duncan's chest. "I pick them up tomorrow for bottle feeding. They're only three weeks old." Barkley shook his head. "They were very hungry and very dehydrated and very scared."

"Wow," Duncan sighed as he turned back to kiss Barkley's forehead. "I wonder what Stinkerbell will think of them."

"I'll have to keep them isolated for a while anyway. I'll introduce them slowly."

"There's seven of them," Duncan said, a low whistle escaping his lips. "You are going to be one busy guy."

"I don't care about me."

"You should." Duncan looked down to see the knitted eyebrows. "If you don't take care of yourself, that's one less person to rescue these beautiful babies when they need someone the most."

"I know," Barkley said with a sigh.

"Hey?" Duncan put a finger under Barkley's chin and pulled it up until he was seeing those amber eyes. "You okay?"

Barkley nodded, but Duncan was not convinced. He got up off Barkley's lap and then took his hand before making his way to the door. He looked back to see the confusion on Barkley's face and smiled, almost running into the door jam on his way out of the spare room.

"What time do you head out tomorrow to pick up all the animals?" Duncan stopped pulling on Barkley's hand when they arrived in the living room.

"As early as possible. Maybe eight or nine. Most of the shelters know I'll be coming tomorrow, kind of a weekly thing. Why?"

"Because," Duncan announced as he motioned to the sofa. "I'll make sure you're up in time to rescue all the animals—and I'll even come with you if you'd like—but you need to get some sleep, and since I'll practically be sleeping on top of you, when you wake up, so will I."

"There's a perfectly good queen-size bed in the guest bedroom."

"Okay, so let's go there then," Duncan announced and began to move back toward the hallway.

"I'm fine, Duncan. I've sort of gotten used to functioning on minimal sleep."

"I don't care," Duncan said emphatically. "You need to take care of yourself. These animals are important to you, so you need to think of yourself too." Duncan pulled Barkley against his chest and kissed his lips. "And from a completely selfish point of view, I just found you and I'd like you to be around for a little while longer."

Duncan felt Barkley lean against his body, those amber eyes sparkling and that million-dollar smile making his heart feel as if it would beat out of his chest. Without another word, Duncan led Barkley to the spare bedroom and pulled down the sheets, first on Barkley's side of the bed and then on his own.

"We might have to use this bed every night," Duncan announced as he pulled himself closer to his lover. "It's smaller. Kinda like having to be so close to you all night."

"You're weird," Barkley said with a shake of his head.

"That's all a matter of perspective," Duncan answered and then kissed Barkley's temple. "Now go to sleep, or I'll sing to you until you do."

"You can't sing."

"I can't." Duncan closed his eyes, the arm across Barkley's chest bouncing a little as the laughter subsided.

Chapter 15

DUNCAN WALKED behind Barkley toward the back of the shelter. He couldn't help but look at all of the animals in cages. He understood why the cages were needed, but he didn't understand why almost all of them were full.

"These are all strays?" Duncan asked, more to himself than to Barkley.

"No," Barkley said, turning around to look at him briefly. "A lot of them are surrenders."

"Surrenders?" Duncan looked into one cage at a completely grey kitten that had obviously had a home at one point given its willingness to come over to him and be petted and its chubby appearance. "You mean, a lot of these animals are here because their owners *chose* to leave them here?" Barkley didn't say anything, only nodded before returning his attention to Cheryl, the shelter worker who had prepared the seven kittens for their departure today. "So what happens if they never find a home? If no one ever picks them?"

Cheryl came out of the back office with a cardboard box. Duncan couldn't see what was in the box, but he could certainly hear the mewing. "Thank God it doesn't happen often, but they stay here and we take care of them until they pass on." Turning back to Barkley, Cheryl added, "There are a couple of bottles already in there. I prepared them this morning."

"They spend the rest of their lives in a cage?"

"No," Cheryl said with a patient chortle. "We take them out for hours at a time so that they can play in the back rooms or so they can socialize with one another. But some of them go back in the cages at night; it's easier for us to ensure we don't have any problems between the animals."

"So you don't kill any of them when you run out of room?"

Cheryl crossed her fingers and sighed. "Every once in a while, I've had to euthanize an animal because of temperament or illness, but fortunately, it's because of people like Barkley here that we can keep taking more animals in."

Duncan looked over at Barkley and smiled. He was far too busy playing with the kittens. Duncan stood there, the feeling of helplessness and sadness at the thought of so many beautiful animals being killed because of disinterested owners quickly displaced by a feeling of joy. There were four of the kittens trying to climb up Barkley's arm, grabbing on to his shirtsleeve. "I can't imagine how you do it," Duncan said as he turned back to look at Cheryl. "I don't think I could ever...." Duncan heard the words in his head before he said them and quickly shut his mouth. "I'm *so* sorry. I didn't mean to make it sound like this is something you *want* to do."

Cheryl brought her hands up to fix her ponytail and smiled. "I don't think I've ever met anyone—worth knowing that is—who *wants* to kill animals simply because they're inconvenient, but I learned many, many years ago that the other option to not killing them is having an even greater number of homeless animals and therefore even more animals who would suffer and starve and be used as—" Cheryl shook her head and closed her eyes. "My point is... that I'd rather expend my energy every day trying to save as many as I can, rather than dwelling on the horrible decisions I sometimes have to make."

"If I had my way," Barkley said while still looking at and playing with the kittens. "I'd take them all, every day, and put them on a huge piece of land somewhere and adopt out only to those who could prove they'd not yet hurt or abandoned or mistreated an animal in *any* way."

"Amen," Cheryl said. "Okay, Barkley, I'll just get you to come and sign some papers and then you can get going."

"Hold on," Duncan said as he went to stand beside Barkley. "Are there any animals here who have been abused or mistreated or who've never had a home?" Duncan noticed Barkley and Cheryl share a look and then smile at each other. "What? Is that a stupid rookie question?"

"Told you," Barkley said to Cheryl before leaning over and kissing Duncan on the cheek.

"What? I don't get it."

"It's nothing," Cheryl said. "Barkley and I share this pet peeve. Neither one of us can stand it when people refer to animals as things. *Do you have animals* that *are this or that?*" Duncan assumed that he was still looking somewhat perplexed because Cheryl continued. "You said, any animals *who*.... As if the animals were people."

"Well, they are," Duncan said as he put his hand on the box of kittens and felt a tongue on his finger. "I've had my two pups for several years and they're my family. I could never give them up for anything." Duncan glanced quickly at Barkley, knowing he could understand how hard it must have been for him during all those lean years to keep his dogs happy and healthy. "So," Duncan said, retaking his original line of thought. "Are there any that need me?"

Cheryl smiled and pushed back a couple strands of hair that had escaped the ponytail prison. "There are quite a few who could use a good, permanent home." Cheryl made her way past Duncan, patting him on the bicep as she did so. "Come on, we'll see if there's any chemistry."

"I'm going to take these little ones out to the car and see if they're ready for a bottle." Barkley picked up the box of kittens and winked at Duncan.

"Duncan," Cheryl said as she stepped into a room at the back of the building and whistled. "I'd like you to meet Lumi and Rainbow. Lumi is a white shorthair and Rainbow is a calico." Duncan wasn't exactly sure he remembered what a calico looked like, but he was sure he could tell which one Rainbow was since she wouldn't be the white one.

Duncan looked into the room that was festooned with pretty pictures of cats and kittens and littered with cat trees and beds of all shapes and sizes. There were toys everywhere. But Duncan couldn't see any animals at all. "I don't see them." Suddenly, from the corner, Duncan thought he saw movement. There was a little nose surrounded by blindingly white fur inching its way out of the carpeted box of one of the cat condos. After a few moments, he noticed another little nose peeking out beside the first.

"It may take them a moment," Cheryl said, patting him on the shoulder. "And I have to get to work, or I'll be here all night again."

"Sorry, yeah," Duncan said, his eyes never leaving the two pink noses. "Of course. I'll just sit here for a while and see if they come out to investigate."

"Oh, they will," Cheryl said, laughing, as she turned and headed back into the front area of the shelter.

Duncan sat down cross-legged on the cool floor about five feet from the cat condo. He looked around on the floor, trying to decide which toy might bring the two cats out from hiding. He picked up a long stick with feathers on the end, and when he looked back, he saw that the pure white kitten had moved closer, completely outside of the box.

"Hello, beautiful," Duncan said, the smile on his face almost involuntary. "Did you want to come and play with me?" Duncan lifted the stick and the feathers began to bounce. To his surprise, it wasn't the beautiful white princess that lunged for the feathers; it was the calico, an adult female with almost perfectly symmetrical stripes of white, orange, and black across her back. "And hello to you too. What's your name, then, sweetheart?"

A sudden flash of memory hit Duncan like a physical force; he remembered, years ago, when he'd rescued Zeus and Neptune as puppies from the Humane Society. He'd not gone out that day looking to adopt dogs, but they'd been having some sort of event and he just happened to pass by close enough to see the two beautiful pups in side-by-side cages. He noticed Zeus's sad eyes first and then heard Neptune's little yelps, as if Neptune was complaining that he was just as cute and just as worthy of attention. It was at that moment that Duncan had understood the saying about the pets picking their owners. He'd been disappointed to be told there was a waiting period, and he'd been on pins and needles until the next day when he would be able to pick them up, but he'd known the moment he saw them that he would do anything to give them a good home. And he had and still was.

"Here," Cheryl said, from behind him, startling him. "Give them some of these and even Princess Lumi will be eating out of your hand." Cheryl held out a bag of cat treats, and Duncan took it, nodding to her. "These two beautiful girls have been here for almost a year. Each came to the shelter already pregnant and was an exceptionally attentive and caring momma." Duncan moved the feathers again and laughed when Rainbow couldn't seem to get to them fast enough. He shook them back and forth on the floor. "All of their kittens found homes right away, as soon as they were weaned, but these two gals? They're still waiting for their turn."

"These aren't the mommas of the kittens Barkley has?"

"No, poor thing. She was hit by a car, or so I was told. A kind lady was out walking her dog one morning when she saw a dead cat on the side of the road near the park at the end of her street. She used her doggy bag to wrap it up and she was planning on burying her in her backyard. She didn't get three steps when she saw her dog getting a little antsy. He started barking, and then she heard the cries of those little ones. She brought them to us hoping we could help them so they wouldn't die."

Duncan put the feather toy on the floor and picked up the bag of treats, shaking it to get their attention. He poured some of the soft treats into one palm and then divided them between his two hands, holding each of his hands out in front of his crossed legs, the back of each hand touching the floor. "Well, that won't do at all. Hey, mommas? Would you like to come home with me?" Rainbow was the first to approach and sniff at the treats. Not sensing any danger, or perhaps because she was guided by her stomach, she dug in and started to eat with gusto.

"Rainbow is our little food vacuum," Cheryl said. "She was in pretty bad shape when she arrived. She was so thin and her paws were scraped and cut and her fur wasn't as clean as it is now." Cheryl sat down on a bench just inside the door, and Duncan noticed Lumi head straight for her, sniffing at her hands. "And this one was no better. But they both got a warm place to have their kittens and regular meals and lots of love and attention. And they were the best moms any kitten could ask for."

"Why haven't you adopted them yet?"

"By-laws."

Duncan remembered Barkley mentioning something about fosters and a limit to the number of animals in a home. "You foster too?"

"Of course," Cheryl said as she used her hand to guide Lumi toward Duncan's open palm. "Most of our volunteers foster and vice-versa. Even some of the ones who live in apartments are allowed to have one or two small animals. We'd be sunk without our volunteers and all the people who donate."

Duncan opened his mouth to speak, but as he did so, Lumi ambled slowly over to his hand and began to nibble at the treats in his palm. "You are gorgeous, aren't you, Lumi?" Duncan looked up at Cheryl. "Unusual name."

"It's Finnish for *snow*."

Duncan tilted his head to one side. "Makes sense." Duncan let out a sigh and watched as Rainbow moved over to Lumi's treats and tried to nibble. Lumi wasn't too pleased with that idea, so Duncan used his now-empty hand to distract Rainbow by petting her. "Well, I think you know I won't be able to leave without them. Or do you have a waiting period?"

"Usually, twenty-four hours," Cheryl said as she stood and checked her ponytail one more time. "But since you're with Barkley, I'm comfortable letting them go home with you. Do you have carriers?"

"Carriers," Duncan huffed through a smile. "Blankets, food, water, old laundry baskets, towels, paper towels.... With Barkley picking up animals all the time, he's got everything we need in that SUV."

"Okay then. I'll go get the paperwork."

"Did you hear that, sweet girls? You've got a new home. It's your turn now."

BARKLEY WATCHED as the kittens slept in the cardboard box. He'd crawled into the backseat with them after leaving Duncan in the shelter and offered the bottle to all of them, but none seemed hungry at the time. He'd spent time trying not to laugh out loud at their tiny little voices or the ticklishness he felt every time they tried to crawl up his arm. These were the moments he lived for. Seven kittens, *seven*, who had no momma, would survive and thrive now because he'd decided to re-order the priorities in his life.

He gently stroked one little sleeping head after another as he thought about how Tinkerbell was going to react to having some serious competition for attention. Specifically, for Duncan's attention.

Barkley felt himself flush as he thought about this most recent change to his life. There was no denying that Duncan was ridiculously handsome and an incredible lover, but what attracted Barkley even more was how kind he was to other living beings. He was kind to Charles, the doorman, Najib, the owner of the little mom-and-pop store across the street from the condo, and he was certainly kind and compassionate to his own pups and all of Barkley's animals—whether they were temporary or not.

Barkley stifled a yawn as he thought of last night and how Duncan had come to rescue him. It wasn't that Barkley intended to get up every night and surf the internet looking at pictures of sweet faces he could never possibly save, but he found himself in these moods sometimes; he would feel overwhelmed at knowing that millions of animals were killed each year and there was nothing he could do about it. The rational part of his brain told him that there was, indeed, very little he could do, but the other part of his brain— the part he'd always relied on to tell him to push harder, reach farther—told him not to give up. And so, he would find himself staring at these precious animals wondering when the perfect idea would hit, the one that would help end all of the suffering.

Listening to the kittens' breathing, Barkley closed his eyes and thought about how happy he was right at that very moment. He'd not had a lot of happiness over the past several years, and although he'd never considered himself stupid, he thought about how long it had taken him to realize that he had not been happy because he'd always managed to convince himself that he was doing what he loved. And while it was true he loved music, he wasn't sure it had ever been true that he loved performing. Of course, he couldn't—and wouldn't—complain about it now; performing had allowed him to make some very smart investments that would allow him to continue this work for a very, very long time.

"Got room for two more stowaways?"

Barkley looked over and saw Duncan holding a beautiful white shorthair. Cheryl stood beside him with a knowing smirk, an equally beautiful calico in her own arms. "I see you've fallen victim to Cheryl's subtle charms."

"Hey, I just introduced them," Cheryl corrected. "He fell in love with them all by himself."

"I'm sorry, Barkley," Duncan said as he opened the rear door nearest the kittens in the box and reached for one of the carriers. He was about to say something else, Barkley noticed, but the cat in Duncan's arms became very restless. "You don't want a crate, Lumi?" Duncan spoke softly to her and put the crate back, reaching instead for a blanket. "How about if we let you have a seat to yourself, huh, sweetie?" Lumi seemed much more agreeable to that and settled onto her blanket without any further drama. Duncan turned to take the calico from Cheryl's arms. "And what about you, Rainbow, huh? Do you want to sit in the other one?"

Barkley watched as Duncan worked his magic and got Rainbow settled as well. But the most amazing thing of all was that none of that commotion woke the kittens. If Barkley played his cards right, he could make it to the other shelters, pick up the shy rabbit and the two beagles and be home within the hour. "You mind driving?" Barkley asked before Duncan closed the door. "I don't feel like moving."

"Yes, Mr. Reinhardt, sir," Duncan said as he gave a shallow bow. "And where would master like to go now?"

"Master," Barkley said as he leaned his head back against the headrest and closed his eyes again. "I like that. I think we'll keep that."

"I wouldn't bet on it," Duncan said as he pulled himself into the driver's seat and started the car. He turned in his seat and ran his hand up Barkley's inner thigh. "Thank you."

Barkley opened his eyes at the touch and the sincerity in the words. "For what?"

"For not freaking out that you'll have two more animals in the condo."

"They're not animals, they're family," Barkley said. He grabbed Duncan's hand and pulled it up to his lips.

Duncan smiled and Barkley felt as if he'd just hung the moon in the sky.

Forty-five minutes later, Barkley closed the hatch of the SUV, animals asleep in carriers. He wasn't sure how the shelter had made that happen, or even if they'd tried to make things work out so perfectly, but he couldn't imagine a more perfect arrangement. Now, they were heading back to the condo and then the long process of introductions and feeding and walking and playing and general mayhem could begin.

WITH THE box of kittens firmly in his arms, Barkley ran ahead to isolate Tinkerbell and the pups while the other two dogs, two cats, and bunny stayed in the SUV with Duncan. He greeted Charles, the doorman, once again acknowledging Charles's comments about how he had his very own zoo, and raced up to the condo. Upon entering the condo, he wasn't surprised to find Zeus, Neptune, and Mozart lounging on the king-size bed. But he was surprised to find Tinkerbell sleeping curled up in a ball against Neptune's neck. He shook his head in amazement at everything he was learning about animals and their love-hate relationships with each other and quickly deposited the sleeping kittens in his office, making sure to close the door quietly. If all went well, none of the animals would wake up until he and Duncan could make the introductions.

Barkley quickly went back down to the vehicle, and within another ten minutes, all the animals were safely in the spacious condo.

"And you normally do this by yourself?" Duncan stood at the door.

Barkley assumed Duncan would still be at the door, in part because Duncan knew there was a strong possibility that Tinkerbell would smell another opportunity to gain her freedom and partly because he'd said he wanted to walk the two beagles after they'd just woken up from their nap. He looked over and grinned. "Yeah, piece of cake."

"You want to come or are you gonna try and feed the kittens?"

"Kittens," Barkley answered as he walked over and wrapped his arms around Duncan's waist. "Thank you for helping me. It really means a lot to me."

"I think I'm just beginning to realize how much," Duncan said after accepting a quick kiss.

"Okay, go walk the pups and then I have a surprise for you."

"A surprise?" Duncan kissed the singer one more time and then grabbed a lead for each of the beagles, attaching them quickly. "What do you think it is, huh, boys?"

Barkley watched Duncan grab a ball, head out the door, and shut it behind him. He'd been wondering, since receiving the text message in the car, what Duncan would think about Barkley's news. He hoped it wouldn't put too much of a strain on their new relationship, but there wasn't much he could do to back out of the deal now. The text had been short and sweet: *Congrats, you now own a farm in Tottenham.*

Barkley ran a hand through his hair, willing the negative thoughts away, and headed for his office.

DUNCAN WALKED around the grounds of the condo complex. *He owns all of this,* Duncan thought as he watched the beagles' tentative exploration of their new surroundings. He tried not to let himself be distracted by these little surprises, but he was quickly realizing that Barkley was a man that could very well be out of his league. He was worth millions—and he wasn't even thirty years old—he was a successful singer known all over the world, he spent most of his days—and nights—helping give a voice to defenseless animals, and he was an incredibly giving and generous person to boot.

Definitely out of your league, he thought as he watched the beagles finally mark some territory. He pulled the ball out of his pocket and bent over to undo each of the leads, careful to throw the ball close so if he had to run after one of the sweet beagles he wouldn't be too far away from the other one. As both beagles bounded after the ball, Duncan realized that these two must also be surrenders. They seemed comfortable on leads and knew straight away that Duncan wanted to play fetch with them.

He'd tried not to dwell on all of the animals left behind at the three shelters they'd visited today, but he found himself thinking about them anyway. He was ashamed to admit he'd never really given those animals much thought when he'd been busy building his career, but coming face to face with these poor, abandoned animals, it was hard not to think about it. Like Barkley, he was enough of a realist to recognize that not every animal could be saved, but he could also hate the fact that it was a pointless waste of life.

Both of the beagles were trying to get the ball, sending it rolling farther down the slight hill. Duncan called to them and began to run over toward them, wondering all of a sudden why they were barking and why they'd stopped chasing the ball.

"Hey, fellas," Duncan asked as he caught up with them. "What'd you find?" Duncan stopped short when he noticed a frightened young woman sitting on the ground behind one of the bushes. "Don't worry," he said as he squatted down to reattach the leads to each of the beagles. "They won't bite." Duncan had no idea whether they would or not, but she looked so scared that he'd just blurted it out. "Are you okay?"

Duncan studied the young woman, not really sure if she was young or just small; the camouflage jacket she was wearing was clearly far too big for her. He stayed squatted, wanting to make himself appear as small as possible. He understood that look on her face; he'd seen that same look on his own face every day for the last two years. How many times he'd wanted someone to care about him, to ask him if he was okay, especially on those days when he'd been unable to chase away the overwhelming fear of not knowing whether he'd be able to eat that day or whether or not he'd lose Zeus and Neptune.

"I'm not going to hurt you," Duncan said, bringing the dogs to his side, the one farther away from the woman. He didn't see any bags or anything, but from her appearance and the dirt streaking her face, he guessed that she'd been out on the streets for at least a couple of weeks. "Can I get you anything? There's a store across the street. I can bring you some food and water, maybe enough to last a couple of days?"

No answer.

"Is there a shelter or somewhere you can stay?"

Still no answer.

"Okay, I'll tell you what," Duncan said, smiling at the scared woman. "I'm going to run across the street and get you some food, and I'll be right back. Okay?"

Still no answer.

With the beagles in tow, Duncan made his way to the little mom-and-pop store and greeted Najib as he entered. He made his way to the refrigerated section and picked out bottles of water and juice, filling his pockets when he realized he wouldn't be able to juggle all the food he wanted to buy. He picked out a half-dozen sandwiches and headed back up to the cash register, reaching out for a few chocolate bars at the same time.

"You must learn to cook, yes?"

"Yes," Duncan said, laughing at Najib. Even though Duncan had only been in the store fewer than a dozen times, it would seem that Najib could always be counted on for some words of wisdom about Duncan and Barkley's eating habits whenever they were in the store. "It's not all for me. There's a woman over in the bushes beside the condo complex. Have you ever seen her around here?"

"Maybe once or twice a week," Najib said as he punched up each of the items. "I usually see her with a gentleman. But I have not seen them yet this week."

Duncan shrugged and handed over a fifty-dollar bill, accepted his change, and threw it in the bag, just in case she needed money to get to a shelter or to buy extra for the gentleman she was usually with. He nodded and thanked Najib and then set off at a trot with the beagles to deliver the items to the scared young woman.

He approached slowly, not wanting to scare her, announcing his approach in a calm tone. He figured she wouldn't necessarily show herself to accept the food, but he would leave it near her and then return to the condo so she wouldn't feel uncomfortable with Duncan standing there gawking.

He peered around the bushes to see precisely how close he could get the bag near her and then stopped. She was gone. He continued around the bush in a complete circle, but she was not there. He looked up and down the street, but she was most definitely gone. He felt his shoulders slump and cursed himself for having frightened her away.

Feeling defeated, he walked the beagles back to the main door and headed for the elevator, chatting with Charles while he waited to go back up to Barkley. When the elevator arrived, he bid Charles good night and led the beagles inside the car. He couldn't help but wonder where she'd gone and whether or not she'd been frightened of the dogs or of him.

"Hey," Barkley said as Duncan reentered the condo. "Did you get the critters a treat?"

"No," Duncan said, feeling distracted. "Uh, while I was playing fetch with the beagles, they found this scared woman hiding in the bushes. She looked homeless and so I told her I'd go get her something to eat, but when I came back she was gone." Duncan held up the bag and showed Barkley. "I hope I didn't scare her away."

"If you leave it at the front desk, they'll make sure it gets handed out to the homeless in this area." Barkley came over and kissed Duncan's cheek. "It's one of the reasons I invested in this particular property. Charles actually started it all many years ago, letting some of the homeless use the lobby when it gets really cold in the winter." Barkley bent down and undid the leads, rubbing and scratching behind their ears. "And Najib is really good about giving away his day-old goods."

"I'll be right back," Duncan said as he opened the door again. He was still shaking his head as he exited the elevator and held out the bag to Charles. *Why am I not surprised?*

WITH THE two beagles, Mozart, Zeus, and Neptune safely in the master bedroom, Barkley had the box of kittens with him as he turned the corner into the living room, prepared for the first of many feedings to come until these kittens were stabilized, weaned, and able to eat on their own. He smiled as he set the kittens down on the floor, thinking of what it was going to be like with seven kittens running amok in the condo for the next five weeks.

"It's like your own little idea of utopia here," Duncan said as he came back into the condo. "No one goes hungry and no one complains about decreasing property values."

Barkley smiled, not really sure if Duncan was being facetious or complimentary. "It helps me sleep at night." Barkley was sitting cross-legged on the floor of the living room, on the expensive Persian area rug his parents had bought for him for his first apartment, and was feeding the kittens. He had a bottle in each hand and a kitten in the crook of each knee.

"Hey," Duncan said as he sat cross-legged opposite Barkley. "I didn't mean that as a slam or anything."

Barkley didn't say anything, just looked up when their knees touched, and smiled. He watched as Duncan took the three remaining kittens and positioned them, one right next to the other, across his lap. He picked up three bottles and held them so that each of the kittens could feed at the same time. "I let Stinkerbell out, but I haven't seen her yet. And I haven't seen Lumi or Rainbow either. I was hoping they'd come by and show some interest in their new family here."

"You're keeping all seven?"

Barkley couldn't help but notice that there was no surprise or incredulity in Duncan's voice. It was as if he was asking about the weather. "Well," he began as he felt his kittens squirm against his lap. He thought perhaps they were full and withdrew the bottles, but the immediate protests told him he'd been mistaken. He put the bottles back and the kittens continued to feed hungrily. "I was thinking about it… because my offer on the farm in Tottenham was accepted." He smiled as he searched Duncan's face for a reaction. He noticed Duncan look up for a moment and then redirect his gaze to his own three hungry kittens.

Duncan suddenly looked up again. "Accepted?" Duncan squinted and Barkley figured he was only half-listening and only heard part of the big announcement. "I didn't know you'd put in an offer. I thought you were still in the thinking stage."

"No, I'm done thinking," Barkley said, his heart not quite as excited as it had been mere moments before. "It's not far from Lori and John's, so we can take even more animals now."

"Well, that's great," Duncan said as a huge smile spread across his face. "So you'll need to find someone to run it or do you have someone already?"

"Yes," Barkley said. "I do." Barkley couldn't help but notice the smile on Duncan's handsome face dim slightly.

Chapter 16

DUNCAN WAS having a very difficult time sleeping. He had congratulated Barkley, of course, on this next step in his finding a new direction in his life. Duncan had not realized how important this new calling for Barkley was, but he was at that moment lying there feeling alone for the first time since meeting the man beside him. He was happy for Barkley and happy for all of the suffering animals, present and future, that would have a much better life because of his selfless devotion. Duncan was just having a hard time, so soon after the announcement, figuring out where he would fit into this new life of Barkley's. Of course, Barkley had reassured him that nothing would change between them, but with Barkley on a farm an hour north of the city, Duncan couldn't help but imagine the worst.

Duncan finally gave up trying to get to sleep and sat up, swinging his legs over the edge of the bed, careful not to disturb Barkley or Tinkerbell, who was in her usual spot on the pillow, purring away. After they'd finished feeding the kittens, they'd made sure to check on the rest of their menagerie, and with all of them fed, watered, and content, Duncan and Barkley had retired for the evening, exhausted. They shooed Zeus, Neptune, and Mozart from what they obviously considered their bed, each of the three dogs picking out a spot on the carpet near the two beagles. There were more than enough large dog beds scattered around the apartment, but the pups obviously didn't want to be too far from their humans.

Duncan looked to the foot of the bed and reached out. Mozart had somehow made it back onto the bed, and Duncan realized he'd not felt anything. He scratched behind the pup's left ear and wondered if he'd managed to fall asleep for a little bit or if he'd been so engrossed in his own thoughts that he'd not noticed Mozart make his way back to Barkley's side of the bed.

Duncan reached to the floor and scooped up his boxers, deciding he would go and check on the kittens in the next room. He didn't hear anything, but he knew their next feeding would be soon. He and Barkley had not made love, but they'd both stripped down, wanting as much skin-to-skin contact while they lay in bed caressing and exploring. He pushed himself off the bed and turned to look at his lover, pulling on the boxers as he studied the serene face. "My very own guardian angel," he whispered as he smiled and questioned, yet again, how he'd ever been fortunate enough to meet someone so completely altruistic. He thought of kissing the rosy cheek, but didn't want to disturb Barkley or Tinkerbell. He turned to go check on the kittens.

"I won't be selling the condo or the building, so you can move in here." Duncan turned, caught unawares. He thought Barkley had been sleeping. "If you want, that is."

Duncan watched as Barkley pushed himself up on his elbows, his eyes searching Duncan's face. He walked back to sit on the side of the bed, leaning over so that he could push the hair off Barkley's forehead. "Am I that transparent?"

"No," Barkley said as he took Duncan's hand in his own. "Just took a guess."

"You told me you wanted me at the farm whenever I could make it," Duncan said, feeling suddenly as if he were out of breath, as if he'd just finished a marathon. "I'm just not sure how much we'll see each other with you out there and me here."

"How about one day at a time?" Barkley let go of Duncan's hand and got on his hands and knees to go and sit behind him, wrapping himself around Duncan's strong back. "I'll need to be in the city a few days of the week to pick up the animals and if you're not too busy with work, we can spend the weekends out on the farm."

Duncan closed his eyes as he felt Barkley's hands caressing his chest and torso. He felt overwhelmed by this simple show of affection. He could feel himself relax into the touch, reassured that Barkley didn't want anything to change either. "A man could fall hard for someone like you." Duncan didn't wait for an answer, turning around quickly to study his lover's face. Duncan felt the smile transform his own face as he watched one spread across Barkley's.

"Charmer," Barkley teased as he straddled Duncan's lap.

Duncan pushed his face against the smooth, muscular chest and felt the rest of the tension leave his body. "I've never met anyone so kind and good and generous as you."

Barkley didn't answer, didn't say *Thank you*, even; he merely put his hands on either side of Duncan's face and brought their lips together. With those declarations out of the way and the feeling of invincibility Barkley's words had brought to Duncan's peace of mind, Duncan cupped his hands under Barkley's bare ass and pulled him even closer, wanting nothing more than to kiss the man senseless.

The music of the bedside Bose began softly. It was the alarm signaling the kittens' next regular bottle feeding; Barkley chose to use the music as the alarm so it wouldn't frighten the animals. Slowly, Duncan released Barkley and looked up at him. "I'm sleep-deprived, covered in cat and dog and rabbit hair, and I've never been happier than I am right now."

"Is that a challenge?" Barkley asked as he disengaged himself from Duncan's lap and walked over to the chair to retrieve his own boxers, pulling them on quickly while Duncan scrambled across the bed to turn off the music.

"No," Duncan said as he stood and rearranged himself in his boxers. "It's not your job to make me happy."

"I know," Barkley said, winking. "But it's important to have goals in life."

Duncan followed Barkley out of the bedroom and stood close to him as he pushed open the door where the kittens, along with Lumi and Rainbow, were sleeping. He peeked over Barkley's shoulder, noticing the towels Barkley had set out on top of the twin-size mattress protector that was on the floor, forming baffle-like rings. It was an impromptu solution to keeping all of the kittens contained within the circle and preparing for any nighttime accidents.

"Look at Lumi and Rainbow," Barkley whispered before entering the room.

Duncan looked over and saw the two kitten-less mommas sleeping, like sentinels, by the kittens. "They're protecting them, and they're not even their kittens." Duncan kissed the back of Barkley's neck and whispered, "Do we wake them—"

"Oops," Barkley said with a little giggle.

Duncan watched both Lumi and Rainbow wake up and crane their necks in the men's direction, as if they were about ready to scold them for making any noise that could disturb the kittens. Rainbow was the first to raise herself up and move inside the little ring of kittens, settling herself near the kitty pile. Lumi was not far behind, both of the girls on opposite sides, each of them beginning to lick the little bundles of fur. Slowly, the kittens started mewing, apparently having needed to be reminded that they should be hungry.

"I'll go and bring the bottles in here," Barkley said as he leaned up to kiss Duncan's cheek. "Something tells me your girls will be mighty pissed if we try to move them into the living room."

Duncan nodded and felt something soft rub against his ankle. He looked down beside him and saw the shy little rabbit that had spent most of the day hiding in the corner opposite the kittens. Duncan had brought her little bowl full of carrot pieces and lettuce in here when he'd noticed the rabbit seemed scared to leave the bedroom. He squatted and reached out a tentative hand, not wanting to scare her away. "Hey, fluffy one," Duncan said, smiling when he realized she wasn't going to run away again. He glanced over to her little bowl and noticed there were still some pieces of carrot and a few bits of lettuce left. "Are you hungry, huh? Do you want some new carrots? Maybe some water?" He scooped up the rabbit and kissed her little pink nose before walking over to the bookshelf that held bottles of water. He set the rabbit down for a moment and twisted the cap off the bottle, then took her back in his hand and sat cross-legged while he filled her bowl with some fresh water. "That was it, huh?" He watched as she inched closer to the bowl with each little gulp she took.

"She definitely likes you better than me," Barkley said as he came back into the room, his arms full of bottles and towels. "I filled up her bowl just before bedtime, but she wouldn't let me get anywhere near her."

"Don't take it personally," Duncan said with a chuckle. "She was probably so thirsty that she was willing to risk it, and I was closest at hand."

"I don't know," Barkley said as he plopped down to sit cross-legged near the kittens. "I might just have to start calling you *Dolittle*."

Duncan scooted over to sit beside his lover, laughing and shaking his head as he made his way. "Okay, same as last time?"

"Well," Barkley said, eyeing the situation before them. "Let's each take one that isn't being cleaned and we'll see if we can work with the two beautiful mommas and get some sort of assembly line going."

Duncan smiled and picked up a little grey kitty, putting it on its tummy and letting it begin to suckle so it could get suction on the nipple. Once he heard the now-familiar sucking sound, he used his free hand to caress and love on the little ball of fur, wondering if he was comforting it or if it was actually the other way around.

"You're getting good at that," Barkley said. He'd had to show Duncan how, exactly, to get the kittens to create the suction. Duncan had just assumed you stick the nipple in the kitten's mouth, but Barkley had explained that that action could cause formula to get into the lungs which could lead to pneumonia for the little babies.

"Not a lot of options, right? If I don't get this right, I could end up hurting one of these little guys." Duncan continued petting the fragile kitty as he spoke. "Which reminds me, how do we know which ones are girls and which ones are boys?"

"The vet showed me one time, and I know it's easier when they're, say, around eight weeks old, but in kittens this young, you can get a general idea by the distance between anus and genitalia." Duncan did his best to look like he understood that, but Barkley took pity on him. "The distance between the anus and the penis of the male will be greater than the distance between the anus and the vulva of the female." Barkley laughed as Duncan's eyebrows shot up. "Don't worry, when they get a little older, I'll show you."

Lumi let out a loud meow and Duncan looked down to see that his little kitty was trying to push away from the bottle. "Good girl, Lumi," Duncan said. "You're absolutely right. I should have been paying attention." Duncan picked up the little kitten and placed it quickly in front of Lumi, who immediately began bathing it. He noticed Barkley put his kitten in front of Rainbow, and he and Barkley reached for another. "Two down, five to go," Duncan said with a smile.

DUNCAN WAS having a very difficult time sleeping. This time, he wasn't agonizing over whether Barkley buying the farm had meant a change, or possibly an end, to their relationship. Nor was he wondering about whether he was moving too quickly. This time, he found himself trying to answer all sorts of questions he'd never anticipated. *Should I buy a car? What kind of car? Should it be something big so that I can help transport animals, or should it be something smaller and more fuel-efficient? What should I do with my few meager belongings at the apartment? Barkley didn't say whether he needed furniture at the farm, so should I volunteer my own?*

He looked down at the tousled blond hair and the rosy cheeks. Barkley had fallen asleep with his head on Duncan's chest and, even though Duncan was starting to get a crick in his neck from his awkward position against the headboard, he did not want to move and risk waking the man. They were due for one more feeding, and Duncan wanted Barkley to get as much sleep as possible. It didn't matter to Duncan that he'd probably be bone-weary at work all day; he figured he'd be able to do most of those things without giving them too much thought anyway.

In all the years he'd been working as a respected and admired journalist, Duncan had had to take care of every aspect of his stories, from interviews to phone calls to fact checking. There wasn't anything he'd been asked to do so far at the station that he'd not been able to figure out on his own. And his efforts had not gone unnoticed: there were plenty of the behind-the-scenes and on-air talent who'd already remarked about how much smoother things were running for their segments. Of course, Duncan knew he would not be happy doing this job forever; in fact, he gave himself maybe a year, tops, before he'd seriously have to start looking for some sort of promotion.

He'd never had any interest in doing on-air reporting. He didn't exactly have the kind of looks that would inspire much of anything other than suspicion. Duncan had always known he wasn't too bad looking, had always had more than his fair share of attention from both women and men. But Duncan's particular audience was comprised of those individuals who liked second-day scruffy as opposed to clean-cut and wholesome. Duncan had once heard one of his former coworkers describe his appeal as the *free-spirit-who-knows-how-to-fuck-but-couldn't-be-bothered-to-give-one* kind of man.

With far too many fights—both as a boy and as an adult—resulting in several breaks to his nose and a scar on his chin and one next to his left eye, and with an unquenchable desire to be out playing sports or doing anything but staying at home, Duncan did not have that pretty kind of face. He wasn't exactly *dangerous-looking*, but somewhere in between. With his less-than-perfect nose, his constant five-o'clock shadow, and his almost non-existent body fat, Duncan knew he would never stop traffic, not like the man whose breath was tickling his chest, but he knew what he had and how to use it to his advantage.

Duncan sighed as his thoughts turned toward his mother. He'd never known his father, and truth be told, he never really knew his mother, either. He'd lived with her until he managed to run away, for good, when he was seventeen, but she'd never really seemed interested in his life and he'd never really had too much of an interest in hers. So, he'd learned early on how to ask others for the things that he needed, whether it was help with his homework or how to drive a car. It was this kind of distance from his only living relative that made Duncan so fascinated by Barkley's story, the way Barkley spoke of his parents. He'd sat there, in this very condo, listening to Barkley tell of how his parents had sacrificed for him, worked so that their son could be successful and happy. Duncan really couldn't remember if his mother had done anything for him, other than the bare minimum like keeping peanut butter in the cupboard and a key under the planter on the top step so he could let himself in after school while she went to the bar after work each night. It was this stark contrast that had Duncan still thinking about doing a biography of Barkley's life. Duncan saw it as another chance to tell the story of Barkley's parents as well, of their immigration, their sacrifice, their love of music, and the love for their son. Duncan had not known anything even remotely close to that kind of attention and sacrifice. In fact, Duncan had always assumed that most children were left to fend for themselves.

He'd not learned that this was bad parenting until one of his friend's mothers had asked for his phone number to let his mother know he would be staying over for dinner. Duncan was only twelve years old then. Of course, he couldn't tell the truth and explain that his mother was never home, so Duncan had lied and said that their phone had been disconnected because they hadn't had enough money to pay the bill. He'd heard that excuse in a television show he'd watched one night at this same friend's house. There had never been a television at Duncan's house.

It was Duncan's paper route that had allowed him to save up enough money to buy the few treasures he'd always wanted, like his X-Men comics, his grunge music, and his first, albeit used, portable Discman. He'd carried that thing around with him every day, as proud of having one as he'd been of being able to pay for it himself. The batteries would wear out too quickly if he used it too much, but it was enough for him to have it on him, to feel it in his jacket pocket or in his backpack. It certainly had come in handy on those many, many nights when his mother would stumble through the door, drunk, with some man—who would mercifully be gone by the time Duncan had to get himself ready for school—after midnight.

Duncan never knew if any of the men were repeats, since he'd never bothered opening his door to any of them. And for the most part, Duncan had been okay with the arrangement. He didn't have to listen, not with his Discman readily available, and he knew his mother would never bring up the subject for any sort of discussion. It had become second nature to Duncan to get himself up the next morning and get ready to do his paper route, probably waking up the man so he could go back to his wife or his girlfriend or whatever. And most mornings, for five years, the men were gone by the time he returned to get ready for school, usually. The only time that one of them had decided to stick around, his mother had done nothing to discourage the man from doing whatever he wanted. That's when Duncan had decided to run away. He knew his mother would never come looking for him.

It had been a very ugly confrontation.

Duncan had just assumed the man had left that morning, but when he returned home from school, he found some guy named *Blake* sitting on the couch watching television. Duncan hadn't bothered to ask him where it had come from, mainly because he didn't care. He hadn't even introduced himself before the first words out of Blake's mouth were *Hey, kid, get me a beer, would ya?* Duncan had ignored him and gone straight to his room. And that was the extent of their relationship for the better part of a month. Blake would yell at Duncan to do this or do that, and Duncan would ignore him. Duncan thought he could live like that until he was old enough to leave that house. But then again, it had never even dawned on him that he would come home from school one day to find Blake half-baked out of his mind with some strange woman sucking him off on the couch and another strange woman going through his room.

He startled her when he announced from the doorway that he kept his money in the bank. She'd wiped her nose with the back of her hand and sauntered past him, looking up at him with an expression on her face that seemed to be one of disgust and one of beseeching at the same time. When she'd reached the living room, or thereabouts, he'd heard her yelling at Blake that there was *nothing in the brat's room.*

Duncan had started laughing uncontrollably and had had to shut the door quickly. He wasn't scared of any reprisals, especially since none of the three adults in the living room was able to do anything but teeter and stare vacantly. He'd been surprised to discover that he was laughing because the whole thing seemed so absurd and pathetic to him. He didn't spend too much time trying to analyze whether his mother had just never wanted him or whether she was making up for her lost youth or whether she was just one of those fucked-up people in the world who couldn't give two shits about anything. No, he'd shut the door so he could start packing his things and go somewhere else without waiting another minute. He didn't know what he would find, but anywhere else would be better than here. The only possible direction was most definitely up.

It may have been a bit of a roller coaster since that fateful day in 1992, but he had to admit, as he looked down at Barkley's peaceful expression, he wasn't really sure he would do anything different, even if he could go back and change anything. Not if changing anything meant not holding this man in his arms. It may not have been an easy journey, but Duncan was most definitely certain that it had been worth it.

The music from the Bose began to sound, Tinkerbell and the two beagles perking up at the symphony or concerto or whatever it was. *I'm going to have to get Barkley to teach me about that stuff,* Duncan thought as he felt the man stir against him.

"Hey, sunshine," Duncan said as he leaned over to kiss Barkley's forehead. "Sleep well?"

"God," Barkley said as he moved his hand over Duncan's chest, then pulled up the covers. "You're freezing." Barkley rubbed his hand vigorously over the duvet, trying to warm up Duncan's skin.

"Hey, hey," Duncan said, taking Barkley's hand in his and kissing it slowly. "Come on, don't worry about me." He brought his body forward, keeping his neck at that same angle until he could work out the kinks slowly. "Turn that music off and let's go feed the kits."

"I'm sorry, Duncan," Barkley said, leaning over and turning off the music. "I promise I'll make it up to you tonight."

"Don't tell me that," Duncan said as he brought a hand up to work at his trapezius. "I'll insist on those sleeping arrangements all the time then."

"Here," Barkley said with a laugh, moving his hands to massage gently and firmly. "Let me try…. There, how does that feel?"

"Jesus," Duncan sighed, loudly. "You have the best hands of anyone I've ever met."

"Okay, we'll feed the kitties; then I'll finish the massage, and then you're going to get some sleep before you need to be at work." Barkley held up a finger, a stern warning, Duncan assumed, not to argue.

"Yes, sir," Duncan responded with a salute. "Just one thing, though."

"What?"

"If I'm willing to go without sleep, can we fool around instead?"

Barkley laughed, his amber eyes shining and alive, and Duncan wrapped his arms around the smaller man and held on for a moment, his hand lost in the soft, blond hair while his lips kissed the warm skin of the strong jawline.

Yup, Duncan thought as he held on to the powerfully built body, *most definitely worth every moment if they all led me to him.*

Chapter 17

BARKLEY STOOD by the door, Tinkerbell at his feet sniffing and batting at the plastic bag in his hand. He reached out with his toes to tickle her belly, the little ball of fur quickly losing interest in the bag and focusing her attention to attacking and biting at the offending digits. Barkley was so engrossed in playing with the kitten that he didn't hear Duncan approaching from the bedroom, the only indication being that Tinkerbell stopped biting his toes and looked over in the direction of the hallway.

"Okay, so I'll be a little late after work so I can go to my place and pick up some things." Duncan wrapped his arms around Barkley and kissed him tenderly on the lips. He pulled back and looked at Barkley. "Maybe longer if I fall asleep on the subway."

"Roger that," Barkley said as he held up the plastic bag. "Your lunch, sir."

Duncan took the bag from Barkley and squatted down to give some belly rubs to Tinkerbell. "And you, you little Stinkerbell, you make sure you keep my spot warm until I get home." Duncan stood and offered one more kiss.

Barkley distracted the kitten with his toes again as Duncan headed out the door, taking a moment to admire the fine figure that was Duncan Spencer. *Nothing better than a perfect ass in a nice pair of dress slacks*, Barkley thought as he closed the door and immediately scooped up Tinkerbell. "Now, you get to play with your brothers and sisters while I take the puppies out for a walk," Barkley said as he turned to enter his study. Lumi and Rainbow were at their posts, guarding the tiny Russian blue kittens, while the shy rabbit had become bold enough to inch a little closer to them. He did a last-minute check of bowls and snacks before he left to retrieve the dogs in the master bedroom.

He stopped in the doorway and gazed upon the bed—the one he'd just made an hour ago—and sighed at how the dogs had quickly returned it to the way they obviously preferred it: duvet rumpled, forming waves of cozy down-filled softness, and pillows tossed onto the floor. He chuckled, feeling lighter and freer than he'd felt in some time, and walked to the chair to put on his shorts and T-shirt. The dogs, of course, did not move at all, sparing only the occasional glance at him, as if they were either challenging him to disturb their newfound comfort or letting him know how much they appreciated his choice in mattresses.

"Okay, you lazy pups," Barkley said, as he stood with his hands on his hips. "Who wants to come with me to the park?" Barkley wasn't going directly to the park, but he figured they didn't need to know that. He would be making his usual weekly stop to talk with his parents, and then he would take the pups to the park so they could get to know each other even better.

Mozart was the first to move, followed by a somewhat eager Zeus, then a near-comatose Neptune. The three of them made their way out of the bedroom, and the two beagles, who had been lying beside each other on the floor near the antique writing desk in the corner, perked up their ears but otherwise seemed confused—yet curious—at the sudden mass exit. Barkley got down on his hands and knees and made his way over to them.

With his face only inches from theirs, he had barely started to explain what they were doing when both pups began to lick his face. "I love you too," Barkley said, positioning himself cross-legged on the floor so he could pet and scratch the beagles. "Yes, I do. I love you too. And we're going to go out for a walk right now and then go play in the park." Barkley found himself wondering, again, what the story was behind these two brothers. There had been very little information at the shelter. They looked like they'd been cared for and seemed to be well behaved around—not to mention unafraid of—humans, but they didn't really react the way most dogs did when presented with a ball or a chew toy.

Figuring that they'd perhaps been companion dogs for an elderly person who hadn't been able to get out much, Barkley stood and patted his leg, beckoning for them to follow. They did, and within minutes, he had all five dogs on leads, and they were heading to the elevator.

He found he was excited to tell his parents about Duncan. He'd already explained to them about his change in career, about how he'd decided he'd not found any true happiness as a singer and how he'd managed to find it rescuing abused and abandoned animals, but he'd not yet met Duncan the last time he'd been to see his parents at the cemetery. Just that one thought made him second-guess himself again. *Am I moving too fast? Will this all turn out to be a big mistake when I come home and find Duncan has sold his story to some sleazy tabloid for a big, fat payday?*

As he made his way to the cemetery, amazed at how well behaved all of the dogs were, he chastised himself, forcing himself to remember that he'd made the decision not to over-think things this time. *It feels right; he's a good and compassionate human being. So, I'm going to keep going wherever this leads.* And the way Barkley was seeing this particular romance was that it would end one of two ways: Duncan would eventually get bored and leave, or Duncan really was falling in love with him and the two of them would be happy forevermore. Of course, Barkley knew which ending he would like, but only time would tell if Duncan wanted the same one.

As he reached his parents' grave markers, Barkley sat down beside his father's plot and got the dogs settled, congratulating and thanking them for having walked slowly enough that Mozart wasn't breathing too hard. He reached into his pocket and pulled out some treats for them to chew on while he carried on his imaginary conversation with his parents. It had only been the three of them, so they had known each other so well that each knew precisely how the other would react to any given piece of news, good or bad.

Barkley had always known that his parents loved him unconditionally. There had never been even one moment when they'd been disappointed in him or in his accomplishments. And he knew that they would never have reacted badly to his news of being homosexual. If anything, his mother probably would have been disappointed that he would never have children of his own. Of course, there wouldn't necessarily be any need for a music teacher to know about artificial insemination and surrogate mothers and all of the other fine print with which gay men and women were intimately acquainted, but Barkley was sure that no matter how he'd come to have his own children, his mother would have loved them as much as she loved him.

"You're my babies, aren't you?" He took a few moments with each dog, scratching bellies and ears and fishing out some more treats for each of them. Looking at the changes in these faces, even since he'd rescued them only yesterday, Barkley was always amazed at how much love and gratitude he saw in their eyes. It was as if each dog that was rescued knew that Barkley had saved his life, had saved him from being abused or tortured or killed on the street, or worse, led into that back room, the last sights to be seen—not the green grass or the setting sun, but the cold sterile walls of the building where he had been abandoned by thoughtless and selfish owners.

Barkley knew he would be doing this work for the rest of his life. It was why he'd purchased the farm, why he was trying to come up with a name for the sanctuary he wanted to create, and why he was already thinking of advertising and marketing and trying to educate the public to the horrors that went on in every city in the world every day.

And now he'd found a possible partner for his new life, hopefully one who would provide the balance that had so long been absent from his life, a life that had been spent in hotel rooms without any real sense or feeling of the home his parents had created for him.

"You'd really like him," he said out loud as he continued to give belly rubs to the pups. "He didn't really know anything about me when he met me." Barkley laughed at the memory of how Duncan had arrived, disheveled and looking like he would have rather been eating glass than doing an interview with some opera singer. At first, Barkley had barely been able to hide his irritation at the unexpected intrusion. *No one in the press had dared do anything so uncivilized as to show up unannounced days before the actual interview.* But Barkley had changed his mind about the man, especially upon hearing a few of the more intelligent questions he'd ever been asked.

Of course, if Barkley was going to be honest with himself, he'd never been interviewed by anyone quite so handsome as Duncan Spencer. He flushed as he remembered watching the strong hands and the chiseled jawline and the incredibly expressive blue eyes as Duncan fumbled through papers or pretended to understand the answers that Barkley gave him. But the real coup de grace had come long after Duncan's departure, when Barkley had finally put two and two together to realize that this was the same Duncan Spencer who had been treated so unfairly, not only in the courts but by his own colleagues. But then, Barkley was never surprised at the actions of the press. It seemed to him, sometimes, that their only goal was to stir up problems in order to bolster their profit margins.

He imagined hearing his father's warnings right then about jumping to conclusions, about making sure he had all of his facts before condemning an entire industry. "I know," Barkley said as he brushed off his hands and stood up, "there are good people in every industry, like Edward Green." Barkley had spent his fair share of downtime sitting, catatonic, in front of every television show imaginable, and he could honestly say that there weren't many media moguls who insisted on the impeccable standards that Edward Green set forth for his employees. While his media empire never shied away from presenting unflattering portrayals of newsmakers, Edward had always insisted on ensuring all facts and figures were thoroughly checked and accurate.

But it wasn't only that Edward Green was so insistent on integrity and honesty. Edward and Rosemary Green had been the only people who had called after each of his parents had died. And Edward had been kind enough to feature a brief story about their lives and their contributions to music within the newscasts; Barkley had been especially grateful that his name had not been mentioned even once. He was glad that Edward saw, as Barkley had always seen, that their accomplishments stood on their own. And if Barkley had thought that was more than enough, he'd been blindsided by the sizeable donation that Edward had made to the music funds, more than enough to continue his parents' work for many years to come.

No doubt about it, Barkley thought as he collected the leads and readied all the pups for the short walk to the park. *Duncan and his future in journalism are in very good hands indeed.*

He would play with the pups for another hour or so and arrive back home with plenty of time for the kittens' next feeding. He also reminded himself to call Lori with the good news, although if he knew his friend, she'd probably already heard about it and was already preparing lessons on how to care for goats, llamas, donkeys, and every other animal that would eventually show up at the farm.

The only thing Barkley had left to figure out about this whole situation was what name he would give his sanctuary.

DUNCAN ARRIVED home to chaos. Well, not exactly chaos, but a much more disorderly household than he'd left that morning. When he walked through the door to the condo, he heard Zeus and Neptune before he saw them. They were in the kitchen, each of them attached to a lead as taut as the expressions on their faces. The other end of each lead was inside of the locked dishwasher. Not far from them was Mozart, his expression one of complete calm and serenity. *What the hell is going on? Is it one of the animals?* It was only then that he realized he'd not had his usual welcoming committee at the door. *Stinkerbell!*

"Barkley?" Duncan dropped his messenger bag on the floor of the kitchen and ran toward the hallway, almost running into Barkley. The man looked like he was ready to throttle someone; his eyes were wide, his breathing was accelerated, and his brow showed a very thin sheen of perspiration. "What's wrong?"

"Nothing, really," Barkley said as he reached behind him to close the door to the master bedroom. "Tinkerbell was playing with the new kittens, and I guess Lumi and Rainbow thought she was playing too rough."

"Is everyone okay?"

"Of course, sure," Barkley said, his breathing returning to normal. He used the back of his hand to wipe his forehead. "Lumi chased Tinkerbell out of the bedroom and tackled her in the living room and that set the dogs off and then it was just damage control. I'm heading in to calm down the kitties right now."

"I'll help." Duncan wrapped his arms around his lover and kissed him softly on the lips, chuckling to himself as he pulled back to look at Barkley. "Hi, honey, I'm home. Did you have a good day?" They laughed and Barkley melted into Duncan's body. "I noticed Mozart wasn't banished to the dishwasher."

"I'm sorry about that—"

"No, no," Duncan said as he caressed the perfect skin. "I would have done the same thing. Those two can be very unpredictable sometimes." Duncan kissed Barkley's forehead again and smiled, mesmerized by those amber eyes. "Speaking of which, I'll go take them out and get them calmed down. Do you want me to take Mozart and the beagle twins too?"

"I'll let you decide if you have enough energy for five dogs. I took them out about an hour ago, so they shouldn't need to go yet, I don't think." Barkley let go of Duncan, but held his hands. "Thank you. Sorry that you had to come home to that."

Duncan leaned forward and stole one more kiss before pointing to the master bedroom. "Beagles in there?" Barkley nodded and then turned to go soothe the kittens. "We'll be back in about twenty minutes or so."

"I promise I'll have dinner ready by then."

"Nonsense," Duncan said. "How about I go buy us some sandwiches?"

"Sounds perfect."

Duncan entered the master bedroom and saw Tinkerbell scuttle between the pillows at the head of the bed. "Hey, sweetie, it's just me." Duncan closed the door behind him and made his way to the bed, noticing that the two beagles were as calm as Mozart, both of them lying on the little area rug near the end of the bed. He sat down on the bed and brushed his hand over the duvet, trying to make some noise to get Tinkerbell's attention. "It's okay, sweetie, it's just me. You don't need to be scared. Come on, Stinky."

Duncan was surprised to see her head pop out from between the pillows so quickly. She didn't look injured, and he was sure that Barkley would have told him if any of the animals had been hurt during the little skirmish, so he kept on encouraging her to come out. Slowly, she did, inching her way toward the noise his hand was making on the duvet. "There you go, baby." Duncan moved his hand more slowly so she could catch it. When she did, he let her bite his fingers for a moment or two before reaching over with his other hand to pet her.

He picked her up and couldn't help but notice that she was still shaking a little. He brought her soft neck to his lips and kissed her several times, telling her everything was okay. He tried to explain to her that she needed to be careful around the little kitties, that Lumi and Rainbow were as protective of the kittens as he and Barkley were of her. Of course, he knew she didn't understand a word, but he learned a long time ago that a familiar—and beloved—human voice could do wonders to calm down a skittish animal.

After another ten minutes, Duncan put Tinkerbell on her favorite part of Barkley's pillow and called to the beagles. The three of them left the master bedroom, Duncan noticing for the first time that he no longer heard Zeus and Neptune barking. Before heading to deal with the two of them, he peeked into the spare room to see Barkley lying on his side, his head propped up on one hand while tickling and playing with the kittens with the other. He couldn't help but notice that Lumi and Rainbow were very close by and keeping watch over Barkley.

"I had a little talk with her," Duncan said, his voice playful. "She says she's sorry and that she'll try harder from now on." Duncan smiled at Barkley's laugh and immediately got down on the floor to spoon Barkley, his own hand coming out to join his lover's. "She didn't cry, though. But she did ask if we were still going to let her go to the dance on Friday." He kissed Barkley's neck and brought his hand back from the kitties so he could stroke the smooth, flat belly.

"Thank you," Barkley said with a laugh. "You always manage to make me laugh."

"That's my second favorite sound you make," Duncan said as he slid his hand a little lower and slipped it between his lover's legs. "My favorite—"

"Duncan," Barkley chided. "Not in front of the kids."

Duncan kissed him one more time and got to his feet. "I'll be back in twenty or thirty."

He made his way with the beagles to the kitchen and freed his two dogs, promising them that the three of them would have a serious talk once they were outside. Zeus, for his part, had the decency to look chagrined, but Neptune gave Duncan that particular look that seemed to communicate, *None of this was my fault!* Duncan ignored it and held on to their leads while he stuffed a couple of balls into his pockets.

The leads for the beagle twins and Mozart were fetched, attached, and soon, the six of them were on their way to the little park beside the condo. Duncan sat in the grass, throwing the balls whenever they came back to him, and thought again about the pile of Post-It notes he'd been accumulating with various ideas about Barkley's biography. What kind of piece it would be, how he'd like the rest of the world to know how kind and compassionate and talented Barkley was. He felt like yelling it from the rooftops that he'd found the most perfect man on the face of the planet. *He's perfect, and he's falling in love with me! With* me!

When the next ball came back to him, Duncan made sure to throw it to the left so that Mozart could get his turn at fetch and wondered if he was right in his assessment of Barkley's willingness to cooperate with the biography. He'd already determined that he would make sure Barkley understood that all royalties could go to funding more rescue operations, or be used to fund education programs, or be provided to those shelters that were in dire need of additional funds.

The only thing he had to do now was get the courage to bring up the possibility of the biography.

After another twenty minutes of throwing the ball to the pups and after having his relatively one-sided conversation with Zeus and Neptune, Duncan pocketed the balls, left the pups with Charles, and ran across the street to get dinner. He picked up a few of the sandwiches, a couple of bottles of iced tea, and looked forward to a little one-on-one time with Barkley on the balcony. And if it led to touching and kissing, Duncan was never going to say *no* to that.

BARKLEY HEARD the phone ring and pushed himself away from the kittens so he could answer it. He was expecting it to be Lori and it was. But from the sound of her voice, it wasn't going to be the usual conversation.

"Those fucking bastards just keep pulling shit like this!"

"Lori? What's wrong?"

"At that fucking high-kill shelter in Aurora," Lori said. Barkley could hear the squeaking of the old floorboards in her farmhouse as she paced back and forth.

"What do you need me to do?"

"Fuck me," Lori sighed. Barkley could practically feel the weight lifting off her shoulders. "Owner surrendered a couple of days ago and they didn't even bother to fucking call me."

"It's okay," Barkley said as he heard the door open. He turned to see the pups come through the door with Duncan, his smile fading when he looked at Barkley. "It's okay, Lori. Where? Do I need to go now?"

"No," Lori said, her ire sounding renewed. "They closed an hour ago. She's on the kill list for tomorrow. She goes down at five if no one gets to her before then." Lori took a breath and let it out slowly. "I faxed them and e-mailed them, telling them that someone would be there first thing in the morning, and that if they put her down, I'll make sure those heartless fucking sons-of-bitches—"

"Lori," Barkley said, raising his voice slightly. "It'll be okay, but you have to tell me where."

Barkley watched Duncan come over to him and reach out a hand to smooth over his back. He hadn't realized how tense he was until he felt that now-familiar touch. He looked around for a pen and paper, spotting them on the counter. He missed Duncan's touch the moment he moved to write down the information that Lori was rattling off.

"I've got it," Barkley said, repeating the name and the address back to her. "I'll be there first thing tomorrow morning. Promise."

Lori thanked him again and again and they said their goodbyes. Barkley put down the pen and the phone and turned around so he could return to Duncan's side. Barkley let out a little yelp of surprise when he found Duncan standing right behind him.

"What is it?"

"Not sure," Barkley said as he took the bag of sandwiches from Duncan's hand. "I think it has something to do with an animal surrender and the shelter didn't call Lori in time for her to make the trip in or something. Anyway, I'm going to get the little one tomorrow."

"Poor thing," Duncan said as he helped, bringing out plates and glasses and napkins. "She must be so scared and frightened right now."

"I know," Barkley said, the anger and frustration mounting now that he didn't have anyone to calm down but himself. "Fucking pisses me off that you need a license to catch a fish, but any fuckwit can go into a shelter and get a pet and then just abandon it because they're tired of it or they're moving or—"

"I know, baby, I know." Duncan wrapped his arm around Barkley's shoulders. Barkley stopped setting out the sandwiches and took a deep breath. "But there are thousands of places like yours and Lori's that work so hard to save as many as you can."

"I'm sorry," Barkley said, leaning against the warm body and willing himself to relax. "This has not been a good night for you, has it?"

"I don't know that I'd agree with that," Duncan said, his lips finding Barkley's. "I'm with a gorgeous, talented, wonderful man who cares about me. I've got Zeus and Neptune with me, the two most insane and loyal friends I've ever had. I've become the proud papa of two aggressively protective cats. And I've become the surrogate father to a little kitten who waits for me to get home so she can try to escape... again and again and again." Duncan winked at Barkley. "I can't remember a better night."

Barkley smiled and reached out to place his hands on either side of the ruggedly handsome face. He looked deep into Duncan's blue eyes and let the smile slowly disappear from his face. "I do care about you... very, very much." Barkley didn't care if it was too soon or if Duncan didn't yet feel the same.

"Correction, then," Duncan said as he kissed Barkley's forehead. "I'm with a gorgeous, talented, wonderful man who cares about me very, very much *and* who has *excellent* taste."

Barkley laughed and swatted at the solid chest. Duncan grabbed Barkley's hands and held them under his own, against his chest. Barkley could feel how quickly Duncan's heart was beating. Barkley watched as each of his hands was brought up, in turn, Duncan placing a kiss on both palms. Barkley suddenly felt light-headed.

"I can't even begin to explain what I feel when I'm around you." Duncan placed Barkley's hands back on his chest, their eyes still focused on each other. "There's a very nice quote I came across when I was doing research, before I first met you. Something about painters painting pictures on canvas and musicians painting pictures on silence." Duncan let go of Barkley's hands and moved his hands to encircle the trim waist. "At the risk of being completely cloyingly saccharine, I just wanted you to know that you, just you, *only* you.... You are the reason I understand what that quote means now."

Barkley felt his knees go weak, and he quickly wrapped his arms around Duncan's neck. He closed his eyes as he saw Duncan begin to lower his head, and he welcomed the feel of the warm, full lips against his own.

Duncan pulled away again. Barkley felt the thumb caress his cheek and saw the small, serene smile on his lover's face. "I don't know what I ever did that makes you look at me that way, but I've never been one to question things like this too much."

"Odd line of work you've chosen, then, if you don't question things too much."

Duncan laughed and kissed the tip of Barkley's nose. "Things like *this*. I probably don't understand the human heart any better than anyone else, but I do know that I don't think I've ever felt like I belonged anywhere." Duncan wrapped his arms around Barkley a little tighter and sighed. "But I feel like I belong with you."

"I feel the same way, Duncan." Barkley kissed Duncan, caressing the strong jaw as the two men kissed passionately, their tongues finding each other, whimpers coming from both men as their hands explored and searched.

"Okay," Duncan said breathily as he pulled away from Barkley. "We have to eat, and by that I mean actual food." Duncan pushed Barkley away from his body, and Barkley couldn't help but laugh. "We've only got a half-hour or so before the kittens need to be refueled."

Barkley laughed at the choice of words and moved to the kitchen to check on food and water bowls, then reached into the fridge for a couple of bottles of beer, a thought coming to him from nowhere. "But surely...." Barkley realized that Duncan had never volunteered any information about his parents and stopped himself.

Duncan turned from the table and knitted his brow. "What?" he said and shrugged.

"It's not important," Barkley said, waving his hand dismissively.

"Yeah, like that'll work." Duncan laughed and took one of the beers. "But surely what?"

"You didn't feel you belonged with your parents?" Barkley felt himself flush a little. He'd been with this bewitching man for how many days and he'd always felt as if he'd be intruding if he asked more personal questions. Of course, Barkley knew about Duncan's fall from grace, but he now found himself wanting to know anything and everything.

Duncan looked down at his beer, studying it for a minute.

"I'm sorry," Barkley said after a moment of silence. "Please, forgive me. Let's eat and forget about my stupid question."

Duncan put his beer bottle on the table and took a step toward Barkley, reaching out and pulling their two bodies together. Barkley was a little stunned when he felt Duncan kiss his temple and sigh. Duncan pulled away after a moment or two and smiled at Barkley. "I don't ever want to hear you refer to anything you do as stupid, ever again." Barkley nodded. "And I want you to promise me that once I've told you about my family... you won't feel sorry for me." Duncan kissed him on the forehead. "You have an amazingly giving and caring soul, Barkley Reinhardt, and you had two wonderfully generous parents who obviously saw you as the precious gift you are." Barkley felt the heat forming behind his eyes when he heard those words, not sure if it was because Duncan had described his parents perfectly or if it was because Barkley had only seen his parents as a gift after he'd lost them. "But... not all children grow up knowing that they're wanted and loved."

Barkley didn't know what to say. "You mean...."

"I never knew who my father was, or is. I don't even know if he ever knew I existed." Duncan continued to stare into Barkley's eyes. "My mother never really cared about me, and if I hadn't had a couple of good friends when I was growing up, I don't think I would have ever figured out that I had any worth at all."

"Duncan," Barkley said, trying to keep from crying. "I'm so sorry."

"Hey," Duncan said softly, lowering his head to look at Barkley, to show him he was smiling. "Don't be. She may have been a rotten mother, but I didn't starve and I didn't grow up on the streets." Duncan shrugged his shoulders and winked. "It could have been a lot worse." After a few seconds, Duncan kissed Barkley's forehead and said, "*Now,* can we eat?"

Barkley laughed at the question and they both sat. "Thank you."

"For what?" Duncan asked before inhaling what seemed like half of his sandwich.

"For trying to make me feel better.... I should have been the one comforting you." Barkley picked up his knife, ready to dig into his salad, and felt Duncan's leg move against his.

"You're welcome," Duncan said around the mouthful of food, offering another wink. Duncan finished chewing. "You're a beautiful, generous, caring person, Barkley. Your parents must have been so proud of you."

Barkley didn't feel hungry anymore when he thought of his parents and what they would have thought of them had they ever known the truth. "I guess," he finally said with a nod.

"Modest, too!"

Barkley didn't say anything and forced himself to eat something.

"Listen," Duncan said after taking a swig of his beer. "I've been toying with an idea and I was going to work on it a bit before asking you, but…."

Barkley heard the hesitation in Duncan's voice and looked up. "What idea?"

"I was wondering if you'd ever given any thought to… a biography."

Barkley saw the look in Duncan's eyes. It was a look that seemed to be a combination of apprehension and desire. Barkley felt the disappointment run up his spine at the realization that he may have misjudged Duncan. Slowly, he put his fork down and leaned back in his chair. Without saying a word, he pushed his chair back and raised himself out of it.

"Barkley?"

He couldn't answer right at that moment. He felt so stupid and foolish that he hadn't seen it sooner. Duncan was like every other man who'd come into his life. Barkley wondered if he'd ever be seen as anything other than an opportunity. Duncan called his name again, and he finally stopped, turning to look at Duncan. "And if I say *no*?" Barkley tried to keep his voice calm, even. "Will that be the end of us?" He stood there, shaking, and when Duncan didn't answer right away, he turned back to the hallway. "I have to feed the kittens."

"Hey, hey," Duncan said as he advanced quickly to place a gentle hand on Barkley's arm. Barkley pulled it away. "I'm so sorry if I upset you, Barkley, and I'll never mention it again, but I think I've been very clear about my intentions here. I don't think I deserved any of that." Duncan moved closer to Barkley; he seemed almost afraid to touch him. "You don't want to do a biography, fine. I'll never mention it again."

Barkley looked up into Duncan's eyes. He felt suddenly even more foolish for his knee-jerk reaction. He brought his hands up and rubbed at his eyes. "No," he finally said. "I'm sorry. Of course you didn't deserve that. Please, forgive me."

"You don't even have to ask," Duncan said as he stepped even closer, his hands moving tentatively to Barkley's shoulders. "The kittens' next feeding is in another hour. Please, come back and eat?"

"I didn't mean to be ugly like that," Barkley began as he allowed himself to be led back to the table. "It's just...."

"Hey," Duncan said with a smile, kissing him on the forehead. "It's done, it's over. I should have realized someone as private as you wouldn't want something that public."

Barkley sat back down at the table and picked up his fork, trying to ignore that little voice at the back of his head that kept telling him he'd made a mistake in trusting Duncan.

Chapter 18

TINKERBELL WAS fast asleep in Barkley's study, along with a newly relocated, but still shy, bunny. Barkley had moved them there to avoid any further possible upset over the kittens, who had been fed and were now under the watchful eyes of Lumi and Rainbow, while the five pups were lounging in the living room with treats and toys to keep them amused.

Duncan headed back to the master bedroom and had his shirt unbuttoned and his socks off before he even reached for the doorknob. He could feel his pulse begin to race, his skin heat up just at the thought of having Barkley all to himself for the next couple of hours. He opened the door to find Barkley already stripped down to his boxers and bent over the nightstand, rummaging through a drawer. When Duncan closed the door, Barkley turned around, and Duncan could see that there was now a box of condoms and lube sitting ready beside the lamp.

"For future reference," Barkley said as he walked over to greet Duncan. "Undressing you is one of my favorite parts of foreplay."

Duncan heard the sigh as those hands came out to push the shirt from his shoulders, not really sure if it had come from him or Barkley. "Uh huh," Duncan said, bringing his hands to the back of Barkley's neck, his own head tilting back when he felt that warm tongue move across his collarbone and descend to his nipples. "God, you're amazing." He looked down when he felt the cool air replace Barkley's tongue and saw those amber eyes staring at him.

"I have to be to keep up with you," Barkley said, his eyes teasing, while he moved his hands to the front of Duncan's slacks. Duncan felt the hands move slowly, but deftly, followed by his pants falling to the floor. He felt Barkley's hands move underneath his boxers to cup each of his ass cheeks. "I've been thinking about this beautiful ass ever since I watched it walk away this morning." Barkley squeezed each cheek and moved his lips closer to Duncan's without making actual contact. Duncan could feel the hot, minty breath sweep across his face, the sight and the sounds and the sensations making him hard within seconds. Barkley moved his hands around to the front of Duncan's boxers, one hand encircling the engorged cock while the other cupped his low-hanging balls. Each hand squeezed slightly in turn as Barkley's lips finally made contact with Duncan's. Their tongues found their partners, and Duncan heard the growl coming from within himself.

His hands explored and searched the contoured back, the rounded deltoids, the slim waist, squeezing and petting, caressing and encouraging. Duncan pulled back and looked into Barkley's eyes, the need and the desire making his pulse race even faster. Duncan wasn't really sure where this Barkley had come from, but he had to admit that the way he was talking right now was incredibly arousing. "Please," Duncan whispered against Barkley's lips. "Need you... now."

Barkley's hands returned to cup his ass, and he felt himself being pulled toward the bed. The only sounds in the room were those of the two of them breathing heavily and the sounds of Duncan's belt buckle hitting the hardwood floor with each step. Barkley suddenly began to laugh and stopped moving. Duncan watched, still incredibly aroused, as Barkley bent over and helped free Duncan's feet from his trousers. After Barkley tossed them aside, he was back in front of Duncan, his hands returning to his ass.

"Want to take my time," Barkley said as he turned their bodies and lowered Duncan to the bed. "Want you to know what you do to me, Duncan." Barkley moved his left hand under the boxers, his fingers finding and squeezing Duncan's foreskin. "Want you to fuck me nice and slow until we both come harder than we've ever done before."

"Jesus," Duncan sighed as he felt the lips move to his nipples again. Barkley pulled his hand out of Duncan's boxers. "Barkley, baby, fucking hot." He sucked in a breath as he felt that tongue make its way down across his flat belly and then felt teeth pulling the waistband of his boxers. "Please, baby."

Duncan looked up when he felt the mattress move slightly. Barkley was off the bed and between his legs, his hands set to pull down the boxers. Duncan lifted his ass off the bed slightly and Barkley pulled slowly, tantalizingly slowly, until Duncan's erection sprang free. Barkley pulled the boxers off completely and tossed them aside, his lips and tongue moving back to take each of Duncan's balls into his mouth, laving, savoring, and licking each one until Duncan felt like the top of his head was going to shoot toward the headboard.

Barkley nuzzled that sensitive area between balls and asshole for a few minutes, and Duncan realized he hadn't taken a shower since he'd gotten home. As if reading his mind, Barkley whispered huskily, "God, you smell incredible." Before Barkley could get too much farther, Duncan reached for him and guided him up until Barkley's body was settled on top of his own, then wrapped his hands around the muscular torso.

"Your turn," Duncan said as he rolled over, leaving Barkley on his back. "I'm gonna get you ready, and then I'm going to do what you want. I'm going to fuck you nice and slow." Duncan crawled to the bedside table and retrieved a condom and the lube. "Jesus, Barkley, you make me so fucking hard."

"Tell me," Barkley whispered. "Tell me what you're going to do."

Duncan felt his prick leap at the words. "Fucking hell, baby, I do that and I'll shoot right now."

"Please," Barkley said as he reached out and stroked his hands over Duncan's flat belly. "How are you going to get me ready?"

Duncan took the lube and slicked some over his fingers. He pressed the finger against Barkley's entrance without penetrating it. "Gonna start with one finger," he said as he pushed it inside, pulling it out again almost as quickly. "Over and over again until you feel like you're going to come hard." Duncan used his other hand to relieve some pressure on his own cock as he watched Barkley writhing around, his arms over his head, his knees pulled up to that magnificent chest. "Gonna take my time looking for that sweet spot," Duncan said as he pushed his finger in slowly, flexing and bending it as he waited for that sign he'd found what he was looking for.

"Fuck!" Barkley's eyes opened and his back arched off the bed.

"There it is," Duncan said as he leaned over to kiss his way up Barkley's torso. "That's what I was looking for." He kept his finger moving in and out slowly as he positioned his body so Barkley could take his cock into his mouth. "And while I'm finding it again and again and again, want you to use that sweet mouth on my big dick. The one I'm gonna use to tap that sweet spot over and over until you scream my name." Duncan looked down and saw Barkley turn on his side, his mouth taking in the thick prick hungrily. "Fuck, yeah, Barkley, so sweet that mouth of yours." Duncan returned his attentions to Barkley's spread thighs, one finger still probing and tapping, kissing and teasing the slit of Barkley's cock with his mouth. He pulled the one finger out, slowly, and then pushed in again using two fingers, feeling only a momentary interruption in Barkley's attentions. "You like that, baby? You like having two fingers inside you? Just wait until my big dick is in there and I'm fucking you while I kiss those sweet lips."

Duncan heard nothing but moans from the other end of the bed as he tapped Barkley's prostate and swallowed the whole length of his cock, becoming more and more aroused at the sounds coming from Barkley. Duncan pulled off his lover's cock for a moment. "You ready for me to fuck you?" By way of an answer, Barkley simply kissed the head of Duncan's cock and then lay on his back, pulling his knees up to his chest. Duncan moved swiftly, positing himself at Barkley's entrance, his hands working quickly to sheath his prick in a condom.

He looked up and down Barkley's flushed skin, studied the heavy-lidded eyes, and delighted in the feel of those beautiful hands caressing his thighs and belly. Duncan took hold of Barkley's ankles and placed the man's legs against his shoulders, pressing his engorged cock to the tight hole. "Let me in, baby." Duncan looked down and saw Barkley open for him. "So pretty, Barkley." Duncan pushed against the opening and then pulled back, leaning forward so that their torsos were almost touching, their lips mere centimeters apart. "Tell me you want me to fuck you."

"Yes," Barkley sighed, closing his eyes.

"Say it for me."

"Please, baby, fuck me," Barkley said, his eyes opening, pleading, while his hands wrapped around Duncan's muscled neck. "Please, please, fuck me."

Duncan pushed in slowly, studying the kiss-swollen lips, the closed eyes. "Take me in, baby." Duncan felt himself being pulled in, the muscular contractions almost too much to bear. "Oh, fuck yeah, Barkley. So tight."

Barkley called out his name, and Duncan made sure to sweep over that spot again and again, then pull out momentarily only to repeat the same action over and over until Barkley was writhing underneath him, his hands fisting the sheets, the corded muscles of his neck and chest making Duncan want to speed up his thrusts. "Look at me, Barkley," Duncan demanded. Barkley did as ordered. Duncan balanced momentarily on one hand while he reached out for the lube, setting it on Barkley's belly. "Wanna see you jack off while I fuck this beautiful ass."

Barkley whimpered, but did as he was asked. Duncan watched as he took some lube in his hand and began to stroke his rock-hard cock. He honestly couldn't remember any moment, any night, any one second with any of the twinks that compared to what he was feeling at that moment. "Come for me, baby. Wanna see you come while I'm pumping inside you."

"Yes," Barkley sighed as he began to pump his cock faster and faster. "Feel so good inside me." Duncan shifted his hips and found that tender bundle of nerves. "Yes, please, there, there," Barkley shouted. Duncan clenched and released his ass muscles again and again, sending the engorged head of his prick across Barkley's prostate over and over. "Oh fuck, fuck, fuck." Duncan's eyes shifted between Barkley's hand and those amber eyes staring straight into his own.

When he couldn't take it anymore, Duncan increased the speed of his thrusts, punctuating each one with a brief pause while he pushed in as far as he could. He crushed his lips against Barkley's, pulling back only far enough so that he could mutter something to his lover. "So close, Barkley. Close. Squeeze me. Take me in."

Barkley used his free hand on Duncan's neck to bring their lips back together, silencing them both for a moment until the only sound in the room was Barkley's strangled cry. Duncan felt the wet heat spread between them, and it was more than enough to send him over the edge toward his own climax. His head fell to Barkley's sweat-soaked shoulder and his hands found their way underneath Barkley's back to hook onto each shoulder. Duncan used his position as leverage to thrust into Barkley deeper and deeper as he emptied himself into the condom. He felt Barkley's long legs and strong arms enfold him as he rode out the last waves of his release.

They lay there for a while, their limbs entwined, their bodies still sensitive to the slightest touch. Duncan caressed Barkley's neck and hair, while Barkley swept his hands lazily up and down Duncan's back, stopping occasionally to caress buttocks or thighs. Barkley was the first to speak. "I love you, Duncan Spencer."

Duncan pulled his lips away from Barkley's shoulder and looked down into those amber eyes. "I love you too, Barkley Reinhardt." Duncan shook his head and smiled when they heard a small mew outside the door, accompanied by scratching. "And I love every member of that crazy menagerie too. Well, before she tears the place apart, let's change the sheets and let her in."

Duncan rolled over to the side, accepted one final kiss from Barkley, and then got off the bed, still shaking his head at the thought that the rest of his life would be filled with this incredible man and about another couple thousand animals. He found himself wondering just how many of them he would end up adopting as Barkley threw the fresh pillowcases at him.

BARKLEY WAS up the next morning at his usual time and stood at the counter in the kitchen wrapping up one of the leftover deli sandwiches for Duncan's lunch when he heard footsteps on the hardwood floors. He smiled, remembering the evening they'd shared, realizing for perhaps the first time that there would be many more evenings like last night in their future. At least, he hoped Duncan would be the one to see past all of his idiosyncrasies and character flaws.

"Hey, handsome," Duncan said, clad only in his boxer briefs. He walked over to Barkley and wrapped his arms around the man from behind.

"Morning," Barkley said, turning around so he could feel the warmth from Duncan's body through his hands and on his cheek. "I'm going to be leaving in a couple of minutes to get the Lhasa apso puppy, but I'll be home in time for the kittens' next feeding and to have dinner ready for you when you get home."

"You know you don't have to do that, right?"

"But I want to," Barkley said as he leaned forward and kissed Duncan's warm lips. "It's one of my best memories. Helping momma make dinner and seeing how that one simple task would make papa so happy."

"Well, I'm just saying that I don't expect you to keep doing all these things for me." Duncan pushed his hands underneath Barkley's short-sleeve shirt and smiled when Barkley shivered. "I won't ever be as rich as you, but I'm hoping we'll be equals in this relationship."

"We are equals," Barkley responded. "If I choose to do these things for you because it makes me happy that doesn't mean you're a freeloader or don't pull your own weight."

"I know," Duncan sighed, stealing another kiss. "I just don't want you thinking you can't ask me to help or to do more so you're not running yourself ragged. And with the new sanctuary, you're going to need a big, strapping man to help you out."

Barkley moved his hands inside of Duncan's boxer shorts, caressing and squeezing the high-and-tight ass. "Big, strapping man?" Barkley released the ass cheeks and moved swiftly, pulling his hands out and turning his body a quarter-turn. With one hand under Duncan's right arm and the other behind his knees, he picked up a stunned and speechless Duncan and stood in the kitchen, grinning. "I hope you were joking."

"Jesus," Duncan said. "Yes, yes," Duncan said, his voice almost pleading. "I was joking! Now put me down."

Barkley obliged and pressed his chest against Duncan's again, cupping the magnificent ass with his hands. "You really do have an incredible ass."

"Says the man who looks like he's packing two bowling balls on top of his five-foot long legs," Duncan said with a laugh. "But thank you."

"You're welcome," Barkley said, releasing him and looking at his watch. "Okay, sorry to leave you like this, but kittens are fed, Tinkerbell is... well, she's probably still sleeping in our bed, the pups have been walked, and Penelope Shybunny seems to have been adopted by Lumi and Rainbow."

"Huh? When did that happen?"

"Must have just," Barkley answered, stuffing two bananas, an apple, the sandwich, and an iced tea inside of Duncan's reusable lunch bag. "I went in there this morning for the feeding and Rainbow was giving her a bath."

"Aww," Duncan said. "Good for her, poor little shy bunny." Duncan accepted the lunch bag and the kiss that was waiting for him as soon as he looked up. "I'll call you when I get a minute."

"Sure thing," Barkley said as he patted his pockets to ensure he had everything he needed and bent to retrieve the dog carrier at his feet. "I shouldn't be too long. I'll just be picking up the Lhasa apso, and then I'll be coming right home so the poor kittens don't starve."

"Okay," Duncan said, caressing the strong back. "Drive safe."

"Always do," Barkley said with a smile as he disappeared out the door.

Duncan headed back to the bedroom to sort his clothes and then hurried into the bathroom so that he could get ready for another very long day of phone calls, e-mails, and text messaging. It was mind-numbingly boring work sometimes, but he had to admit that he was actually enjoying it. It reminded him a lot of his early days hunting down stories, trying to fit all of the pieces together before finally sitting down to write the actual story itself.

"YES, I believe you're expecting me." Barkley deposited the dog carrier on the floor, leaned across the counter at the shelter, and gave the young girl his best, whitest smile. "I'm here to pick up the Lhasa apso that was left here last night."

"Oh, thank God," the young blonde girl said, her hand over her heart. "This is my week to help with the TBE list, and I just hate doing them."

"Well, there's one less now," Barkley said, empathizing immediately with the young girl who didn't seem old enough to be out of high school. "I'm here on behalf of Whispering Pines Animal Sanctuary in Tottenham." The young girl nodded and turned to face the door leading to the area where the animals were kept. "Sorry," Barkley said and waited for the girl to turn back around. "Are there any other animals that are scheduled out today?" It had always struck Barkley as far too polite a euphemism to say that the animals were "scheduled out" on a certain date, as if the animals were patients in a hospital or valued guests in some hotel.

"No, thank God," the young girl said. "There are two scheduled for tomorrow, but we have a bit of space right now, so hopefully they'll get adopted before they go down." The young girl smiled, crossing as many fingers as she could. "I'll be right back." With that, the young girl set off to find the Lhasa apso.

Barkley turned at the sound of the bell being hit by the front door. He hadn't even noticed the bell when he'd entered himself only moments ago. *Too many things going on in my head,* he thought as he nodded at the gentleman who entered, a lead in one hand that had a beautiful, older Labrador mix at the other end. The man did not bother nodding back, choosing instead to lean against the counter and hit the tiny bell two or three times.

"She'll be right back," Barkley explained with a smile. "She's just getting a rescue for me."

The man still did not smile, but Barkley thought he heard a grunt this time, so it was progress... of sorts.

The young girl came back through the door, carrying a beautiful Lhasa apso in her arms, a colorful lead in one hand attached to the happiest dog Barkley could have imagined. He wasn't sure why he was expecting a frightened and matted mess—although he'd seen his fair share of those—because this little dog was a writhing, licking bundle of joy. "I was telling her all about the wonderful man who is here to save her," the young girl said, looking up at Barkley. He wasn't sure, but he wondered if the girl was trying to keep from crying. "Okay, so I can tell you—"

"Miss, I'm in a hurry here."

Barkley turned when he heard a full sentence from the grunter and smiled at him. He turned back to the young girl who was blushing now and offered a much more sincere smile. "It's okay, darling," Barkley said. "You go and take care of him, and I'll introduce myself to the little lady while we wait."

The young girl smiled her thanks at Barkley and returned to her position behind the counter. Barkley was only half-listening as he tried to avoid the tongue of this little Lhasa apso. Barkley didn't like to dwell on dark thoughts if he could help it, but he wondered if this little girl knew that she was being given another chance at life, that her life wasn't over just yet. When he was in one of those darker moments, Barkley always managed to make himself feel a little better by reminding himself that the animals who did get rescued always knew it. The little Lhasa apso, whom Barkley had suddenly decided to call Honey because she was a dark golden color and was so sweet, licked Barkley once more when he heard the young girl's voice again. Up until that moment, he'd heard only the man's voice and, as Barkley had learned to do so long ago with ambient, irritating noises, had managed to ignore it. But he could hear the distress in the young girl's voice.

"But, sir," the girl was saying. "She's thirteen years old. There's very little hope of her being adopted and then she'll be put down."

"Yeah, I get that," the man was saying very loudly. "You're not listening to me. I don't care if you have to put her down. I can't keep her. I'm gone too much."

"Please, sir." The girl seemed almost in tears now. Barkley stood up from where he was crouched, wondering if he should intervene. "Won't you reconsider?"

"Look," the man said as he slammed his hand on the counter. "Do I need to ask for the manager, or are you going to do something other than cry?"

With that, Barkley stepped forward, a sympathetic smile on his face. "I don't mean to interrupt, but—"

"Then don't," the man barked without even turning his head. "Let me speak to your manager. Now!"

Barkley watched the girl jump back a little, unable to contain her tears anymore. She retreated into the back room, almost running. He turned back to stare at the older man, and Barkley was sure the contempt and disgust was plain on his face. *No problem,* he thought. *This guy will surrender the dog, and I'll take her with me. Problem solved. The pooch will obviously be better off with me than this hunk of shit anyway.*

The girl returned, obviously trying to compose herself. "She'll be right out," she said as she began to riffle through some folders on the desk. "We just need you to fill out these forms. And there will also be the fee, of course."

"Fee? For what?" The man's voice was getting louder and louder, and in Barkley's opinion, more and more irritating. All eyes swung to a middle-aged woman, probably in her late thirties or early forties, with a serene smile and piercing blue eyes. Barkley assumed this was the manager.

"There is always a fee when you surrender an animal," the woman said as she approached the counter and stood beside the young girl. "I understand you wanted to see the manager? Hello, my name is Anna."

"Yeah," the man said, his voice still loud and irritating. "Because this employee of yours is trying to make me keep my dog."

"Well, I certainly apologize for that." Anna's voice was calm and very beautiful. Barkley couldn't help but wonder if she did any singing. "We do care about all animals, sir, so it would be normal for Carla, here," the woman said while pointing to the young girl, "one of our most dedicated volunteers, to try to see if you might not consider providing a home for your beautiful dog. I mean, considering there's so little time left."

Barkley smiled to himself, a self-satisfied grin, and looked down at Honey. He didn't count the words that Anna had just uttered, but he was pretty sure that she had managed, in however many they were, to explain Carla's passionate plea, correct the ugly man's assumption that all people working at a shelter were paid to do so, *and* reinforce the idea that the man did have a lifelong responsibility to his dog.

"How much is this fee?"

"The fee for surrendering a dog," Anna started as she let her finger trail to the bottom of the form, "is fifty dollars." Barkley was already digging into his pocket, doing a silent countdown.

"Fifty bucks!"

"Perhaps I can help," Barkley said, smiling as Honey licked his face again. He set some bills on the counter and fished out a fifty-dollar bill. "I'll pay for the surrender, and I'll pay whatever the fees are for both pups."

"Who the hell are you?" The man, scowl permanently affixed to his face, was finally looking at Barkley.

"Does it matter?" Barkley asked, raising his eyebrows. "You don't want the dog anymore, so...." Barkley shrugged his shoulders and held out the money. He suppressed a grin as the man was finally at a loss for words, delighting in the smile that had come to Carla's flushed face.

"Sir?" Anna was looking at the man. "Is that acceptable to you?"

"Yeah, whatever," the man said, still glaring at Barkley. "So, how much then?" The man was leaning on the counter, studying Barkley.

It took a moment for Barkley to understand what the man was actually asking. He shifted Honey to his other side, farther away from the man, and glared right back. "Are you actually trying to sell me your dog? The one you couldn't be bothered to care for anymore?"

"You got fifty bucks to pay the fee; then you probably got more if you really want her."

"Look, buddy, the deal is I pay the surrender fee, and you don't need to worry about her anymore."

"Sir," Anna said, interrupting. "You did just agree to this gentleman paying the surrender fee. Are you now saying you no longer wish to surrender your dog?"

"What I'm saying is that if he wants her so badly, he can pay me for her."

Barkley had had enough of this douchebag; he squatted on his haunches and coaxed Honey into the dog carrier. He'd put a few dog treats in there earlier this morning in preparation for a shy and frightened dog. Now, they would be a reward for being such a loving and trusting pooch. "Thank you, Anna and Carla. If this… gentleman… does surrender the dog, please give me a call and let me know, and I'll come right down to pick her up." He scribbled his first name and his phone number on a piece of paper and handed it to Anna, catching Carla's eye and offering her a wink. He walked toward the front door, looking forward to getting away from this odious man. Barkley felt a pang of regret as he looked down into the beautiful brown eyes of the lab mix, but made her a silent promise that he would come back for her.

As he fished in his pockets for his keys, he caught movement out of the corner of his eye a second before he felt something hit his chest. He stopped in his tracks and looked down to see the dirty, greasy nails of the man's hand preventing him from moving any farther. He looked up slowly, trying hard to contain the anger that was building up inside.

"We ain't done here, buddy," the man said.

Now that Barkley was even closer to the man, could see the bloodshot eyes and smell the stench of alcohol on his breath, he had to fight the urge to knock the man flat on his ass and take the dog and run. "Not only are we done here, *buddy*, but unless you want to spend the night in jail, I'd suggest you get your hand off me."

"Or what?" Without moving his hand, the man stepped in front of Barkley and sneered. It did not escape Barkley's notice that the man was probably an inch or two taller than Barkley and had at least twenty pounds of muscle on him as well. Whether it was muscle or fat, Barkley didn't really feel like finding out. He had kittens to feed at home. "What's a little faggot like you gonna do?"

"Are you deaf? I just told you I'll have you arrested for assault."

"This ain't assault," the man said, his laugh even more irritating than his voice. "Assault would be if I take this hand, make a fist, and slam it into your face for reneging on a deal."

"What deal?" Barkley asked as he reached into his pocket for his cell phone. If this asshole didn't believe him about calling the police, Barkley would be more than happy to prove he was true to his word. "The deal was I pay for the surrender and then you surrender the dog." Barkley looked down as he flipped open his phone, momentarily stunned when the man had the gall to swat it out of his hand before he could dial any of the three digits.

"That's it," Anna said. Turning to Carla, she added, "Call the police."

Barkley had to give the guy credit. He was standing his ground, unfazed by the idea that the police would arrive and be able to arrest him for at least three or four different reasons. "You're digging yourself in here pretty deep, *buddy*." The man did not react.

"Barkley?" Anna was calling to him. He backed up, bent to retrieve his phone, and turned to face Anna. "Please come with me."

"I don't think so," Barkley said, turning back to the man. "I'll have a ring-side seat when the police arrive."

Barkley was now perhaps two or three feet from the man, but he noticed the lead was no longer in the man's hand. He began to return his gaze to the man's face, but he was almost caught off guard when he noticed the man take a couple of quick steps toward him, both fists clenched. Without really thinking about it, Barkley brought up his hand, palm open, and slapped the man across the windpipe when he was close enough to connect.

He wasn't sure if it was Carla or Anna that screamed, but they all looked up when a single police officer came through the front door.

It wouldn't be until later, when Barkley was sitting beside his lawyer at the police station, that he would wonder if the media would have yet *another* story. He could just picture Thomas making it a front-page story with god-awful photos to boot. And Barkley was surprised, but not altogether comfortable, when he found himself worrying about Duncan. If the tabloids did get hold of this story, would they drag Duncan's name through the mud? Would Duncan have to revisit his shame yet again? Barkley felt sick to his stomach at bringing this into Duncan's life. The only consoling thought he had was that he'd done nothing wrong.

Chapter 19

DUNCAN SET the last of the kittens into their makeshift pen, Lumi and Rainbow as watchful as ever. He had just finished feeding the last two, and now that he was done with that task, his mind wandered back to the phone call he'd received as soon as he'd arrived at his office. It had been some lawyer named Lawson Schmidt telling him that Barkley would be detained and that Duncan needed to get home to feed the kittens. Mr. Schmidt had been very vague on the details and had seemed in too much of a hurry to answer any of his questions. Duncan had fought the gnawing feeling in the pit of his stomach and had been, quite frankly, quite glad that the lawyer had kept everything very brief. Just hearing the smooth, unaffected tone in the lawyer's voice had brought back some very unpleasant and unwelcome memories of the last time Duncan had spoken with a lawyer.

He'd searched the internet in between the first and second feedings, searched for anything that might explain why a routine trip to the shelter had prevented Barkley from returning as he'd promised. Between the second and third feedings, Duncan had contacted a few of his former colleagues to see if anything had come across their desks, but none of them had heard anything. And now that he was between his third and fourth feedings, Duncan found himself reaching for his cell phone, wondering if he should begin contacting hospitals and police stations.

He finally decided that he needed some fresh air, and after setting out some food for the cats and the rabbit, he gathered the five dogs and the leads and started making his way to the elevator, attaching leads as he went. He would figure out his next move once he was outside and the dogs were getting some exercise.

With all five leads in one hand, he took a deep breath and tried to calm his mind, reassuring himself that the lawyer would have certainly told him if Barkley had been injured or had been taken to a hospital. Duncan had even tried to call Barkley's cell phone a couple of times while he was returning to the condo, but there had only been the voice mail greeting. Duncan had not left any messages.

He closed his eyes and rolled his head around, trying to loosen up the knots that had seemed to find a home there over the last several hours. He heard the ding of the elevator and the whoosh of the doors, looking down to ensure the dogs were far enough away from the heavy moving door. When he looked up, he saw Barkley standing in the elevator, and when Barkley saw him and the dogs, the look of frustration and anger that had been on the handsome face just moments before gave way to one of relief and contentment.

"Barkley!" Duncan laughed when he saw the dogs all lunge for the disheveled singer.

"Hey, babies," Barkley said as he got down on his knees and tried to wrap his arms around all of the animals. "I missed you too."

It wasn't until Barkley knelt down that Duncan noticed that he had not been alone in the elevator. There was the dog carrier that Barkley had left with that morning, and there was a beautiful chocolate Labrador waiting patiently beside the carrier. "Are you okay? I got a phone call from some lawyer, and he wouldn't tell me what was going on. Are you okay? Are you hurt?"

Barkley stood and reached out for Duncan, enfolding him in his arms while the dogs jostled for more attention from either man. Barkley kissed him on the lips and then placed a few quick kisses on Duncan's neck, finally releasing him. "I'm fine. I'm so sorry you had to miss work, but I'm here now, so you can go and get some work done and I can explain it all later."

"Bullshit," Duncan said, his hands still resting on Barkley's hips. "I brought it all home with me and told them I would be back tomorrow or whenever."

"I'm fine," Barkley repeated. "I don't want you getting in trouble because of me." Barkley leaned over for another kiss. "Please, go and do what you need to do."

"I'm not going anywhere until you tell me what the hell happened."

"Okay," Barkley said, finally relenting. "Just let me feed the kittens first and then—"

"Kittens are good for another hour and a half," Duncan said, checking his watch. "Spill."

Barkley moved back into the elevator, making room for Duncan and the dogs. It wasn't the best way to introduce new dogs to each other, but luckily Honey, the Lhasa apso, was still in the dog carrier and Liberty, which, Barkley explained, he had decided to call the senior Labrador surrendered by Mr. Asshole, was an incredibly affectionate and gentle dog. As they descended, Duncan watched as the existing brood introduced themselves to the two new dogs, and he listened while Barkley gave the highlights of the morning—and most of the afternoon. Duncan found himself growing more and more angry with each detail and each floor.

"I hope you got the fucker's name," Duncan said as he led his five dogs through the lobby.

"I did, but you're not getting it, so don't ask."

"Good thing, for him, that is."

"My knight in shining armor," Barkley teased. "Hello again, Charles." Barkley smiled at the doorman and Duncan turned and offered a good morning, as well. "Did you get the envelope I left for you?"

"Yes, sir, Mr. Reinhardt, I did. Thank you very much. My wife will be very happy."

"My pleasure, Charles," Barkley said, his smile growing. "I wish you both many, many more years of happiness."

"Thank you, sir. Thank you very much."

Duncan wondered what that was about, but kept leading the dogs through the front doors.

"It's their fifteenth wedding anniversary tomorrow, and Charles told me he'd tried to get tickets to the opera, but that he'd waited too long and he could only get nosebleed section."

"There's a nosebleed section in opera?" Duncan didn't know why he found this fact so amusing.

Barkley laughed as they both worked to free the dogs, all of them taking off almost immediately except for Honey and Liberty, who seemed to prefer to stay close to Barkley for the time being. "Of course, there's a nosebleed section," Barkley said, grunting a little as he let himself plop down on the grass. "Don't you know that that's what *le paradis* means in French?"

"You're so full of shit," Duncan laughed as he realized he'd forgotten the balls. He looked around and found a couple of small branches and threw one to his left and the other to his right. "I dated a guy once who loved opera…. He could never get me to go with him, but even I know that the *paradis* was called that because it means *heaven*."

BARKLEY LAUGHED again, feeling the frustration and anger at the day's unfortunate events disappearing faster now that he had Duncan and the animals all to himself again. "Ah, Mr. Spencer, you never cease to amaze me. Soon I'm going to learn that you're really some sort of secret weapon for the government, and you can kill me with just your little finger."

"Oh no, babies," Duncan said as he sat down and loved on Honey and Liberty as much as they would allow. "He's found out my secret." Duncan leaned over and stole a kiss. "Although, I think you already know that my little finger is good for *la petite mort*."

Barkley gasped and slapped playfully at Duncan's thigh. "How the hell do you know that?"

"Well, and I'm speaking on behalf of all the men like me, for whom men like you are way out of our league—"

"Stop," Barkley said, tilting his head.

"But I've found that knowing a few key phrases in another language *and* knowing a thing or two about romance," Duncan said, leaning a little closer to Barkley so he could kiss his earlobe. "And knowing a thing or two about"—Duncan put his lips against Barkley's ear—"sex and making love and pleasing a man…." Barkley shivered momentarily, regretting his decision to go without underwear this morning. "Can sometimes make someone like me more appealing to someone as gorgeous and sexy and perfect and—"

Barkley surprised even himself by grabbing the back of Duncan's head and pushing their lips together, his tongue probing inside of the mouth that had just about made him come inside his shorts. He kissed him, hard, invading every part of Duncan's mouth, until the burning in his lungs became more insistent. "You know how you told me you never wanted me to refer to anything I said as *stupid* ever again?" Barkley felt Duncan's forehead pressing against his.

"Yes," Duncan said, his voice a mere whisper.

"I don't ever want to hear you describe yourself as anything other than fucking perfect."

Duncan did not speak but only nodded, closing his eyes momentarily.

Barkley let go of Duncan's head. "I mean that."

"I believe you." Duncan cleared his throat as he reached out to pet Honey and Liberty. "And thank you." The other dogs were still bringing back the little branches, and Duncan would throw them. Mozart seemed to be getting tired, so he lay down in the grass, his head resting near Barkley's legs.

"You're welcome," Barkley whispered, letting his hand come to rest on Duncan's thigh momentarily before giving some attention to Mozart.

"So, how did this whole thing end?"

"Not well," Barkley said with a smile. "For the other guy. Lawson is a very good litigator… one of the reasons I called him when I went to the police station." Barkley held up his hand quickly. "I wasn't even arrested since the two women at the shelter were more than willing to come to my defense."

"Then why did you call a lawyer?"

"Because that halfwit was spouting off to the officer about how I'd assaulted him, and… I just figured it was best to go on the offense right away." Barkley brought his legs toward his body to sit cross-legged and reached out to scratch Honey and Liberty behind their ears. "And that's exactly what Lawson is good at. He met with the fuckwit, and they had a nice, long talk about how important eyewitnesses are to judges when they hear this kind of case, and… it would appear that the douchebag had second thoughts about trying to make me out to be some sort of celebrity gone bad." Barkley laughed as he remembered the final blow to the dipshit's ego. "*And* Lawson will even be sending me a check."

"Sending *you* a check?"

"Apparently, Mr. Temper Tantrum felt *so* bad about what he'd done—according to Lawson—that he insisted on writing him a check for the surrender fee." Barkley looked over and laughed at the expression on Duncan's face. "Lawson will be depositing it to his escrow account and then sending me the fifty dollars once the check clears."

"And you'll send him one that will end up being a hundred times that amount?"

"Actually, no," Barkley said as moved his hands so that Honey could climb onto his lap. "He heads up a local charity for underprivileged kids, and I've made a few hefty donations to him over the years, so…." Barkley leaned back on his hands and looked up at the sky. "Besides, Lawson is so good at his job that he's got more money than God."

"Wish I'd had Lawson as my lawyer…." Duncan did not finish his sentence.

"Me too," Barkley said quietly, returning his hand to rest on his lover's thigh again. "Me too." Barkley watched as Liberty moved slowly over to Duncan's side, settling herself on the ground so that she could rest her head on Duncan's other thigh. "You have another fan."

Duncan smiled and stroked the chocolate-colored fur on Liberty's head, stopping at the ears to scratch for a few moments before repeating the entire ritual again and again. "When do you move?"

Barkley was slightly confused by the question, and it took him a few moments to realize Duncan was referring to the farm out in Tottenham. "The farm is empty right now, so I guess I can move in whenever I want."

"Will you be taking all the animals with you right away, or…."

Barkley couldn't help but notice that Duncan was not looking at him. "Well, no, because they're not all mine to take." Barkley noticed the two beagles and Zeus and Neptune were growing somewhat bored with the game of fetch and had decided to join the rest of their adopted siblings.

"Not fair for me to keep them cooped up in the condo all day when they could be running around on the farm." Barkley said nothing. He could hear the hesitation in Duncan's voice, could hear how hard this decision was for him. "When I was working for *The Communiqué*, I wasn't chained to a desk, but now...."

"We could hire a dog walker," Barkley offered, trying to keep his tone casual.

"I guess," Duncan said with a small shrug. "But you've already done so much for me. I don't—"

"And you've done nothing to help me?" Barkley asked as he brought his hand up to Duncan's neck. "Either we're a couple or we're not." Duncan looked over at Barkley, his eyes uncertain. "I've subjected you to Lori, feeding kittens at all hours of the day and night, forced you into sharing our bed with all sorts of crazy, neurotic animals, and you still keep coming back to us."

"Well," Duncan said with a smile. "To be fair, some of those crazy, neurotic animals came with me."

"Just Zeus and Neptune. Lumi and Rainbow came after meeting me."

"Okay, I give," Duncan said with a chuckle, holding up his hands in surrender.

"Speaking of which," Barkley said, his voice husky as he leaned in closer to Duncan. "Do you have a lot of work to get to, or do we have time to fool around?"

"I'll make time," Duncan answered, his voice a mere whisper against Barkley's lips.

THEY WERE safely in the bedroom, the entire brood of animals in various other rooms of the condo. Duncan was on his back on the bed with Barkley trying to kiss him and remove his clothes at the same time. "Slow down, Barkley, or you're likely to strangle us both," Duncan said with a laugh.

"Need you," Barkley whispered, his lips against Duncan's ear, while he began to pull at Duncan's white dress shirt. "Here," he said finally as he stood up and pulled Duncan with him. He had Duncan undressed in a matter of seconds, then stripped himself out of his own clothes. He pushed Duncan back on the bed and squatted down between the muscular thighs, placing his hands at the backs of the reporter's knees. He pushed until Duncan's hole was exposed, his lips and tongue making immediate contact. "God, I love the smell of you," Barkley grunted as his tongue set to work preparing Duncan. "Can't wait to feel you around my dick."

"Jesus," Duncan said, panting, as his hands covered Barkley's. "Fuck, yeah. Thank God."

"What?" Barkley asked, taking his tongue away for a moment and pushing a finger inside of his lover.

"I thought maybe you were just a bottom," Duncan said, lifting his head to look at Barkley's confused face. "Oh fuck, again," he moaned when Barkley's finger made contact with his prostate.

"Definitely not just a bottom," Barkley said as he slid two fingers inside, crooking each of his fingers in turn as his mouth found Duncan's sensitive balls. He sucked and nuzzled, Duncan spurring him on with a continuous litany of groans and dirty talk. "And definitely not around an ass this perfect." Barkley smiled as Duncan arched his back. "And tight…. And hot."

"Ah yeah, fuck, yeah," Duncan moaned as he felt Barkley's fingers continue to tap against his prostate.

"Condom," Barkley ordered and Duncan fumbled on the bed behind his head, trying to remember where he'd put them just moments before. As he continued to search, he felt Barkley pull his fingers out slowly and then felt the soft, insistent kisses all along his body as Barkley made his way north. Finally, Duncan found the condom and tore open the package. When he looked back down, he saw Barkley's impressive erection in front of his face and brought his mouth to it, taking it hungrily all the way to the base. "Oh yeah, baby," Barkley moaned. Duncan moaned himself, his erection being stroked and massaged as Barkley reached behind his own body. "Won't last much longer, baby," Barkley warned.

Duncan removed his mouth quickly and rolled the condom over Barkley's throbbing cock. "Here," he said as he reached behind his head again and retrieved the lube. He squirted some all over the condom, feeling some of the cool lubricant trickle down onto his chest.

"You're giving me ideas," Barkley said, holding out his hand. Duncan squirted some slick onto his lover's hand and then Barkley was back between his thighs, his hands pushing his knees up again. "Jesus," Barkley groaned as he pushed the head of his erection against the pink hole. "So fucking pretty."

"Please," Duncan whispered. "Fuck me, baby."

Barkley looked at Duncan's face, studying it as he pushed in. Duncan usually found himself topping, not only because he had an impressive endowment, but also because he was bigger and more muscular than most men, and of course, it was the common misconception in the gay world—and world in general—that the big, muscular hairy man must be the "man" when it came to sex. But there was nothing that Duncan loved more than giving himself over to a man who wanted him like Barkley did. And Barkley was showing a side of himself right now that had Duncan so completely turned on he felt like he could come just from listening to the sounds of Barkley fucking him.

Barkley slowed to a consistent rhythm of thrusting balls deep and then pulling out to tease Duncan's hole with his big mushroom head while he used his hands to pinch Duncan's nipples and used his mouth to nip at the skin of Duncan's calves and knees. Duncan felt like his head was about to explode because of all the sensations that were assaulting him. But when Barkley finally leaned forward, buried deep inside of him, his only movements being small, repeated thrusts across his prostate, and took his mouth, Duncan knew he would be coming harder than he'd ever come before. And when Barkley's hand wrapped around his straining erection, pumping gently but firmly, Duncan arched his back, tossing his head from side to side, and surrendered himself to the most intense orgasm he'd ever had.

"Breathe, baby," Barkley whispered, his lips and tongue making their way from Duncan's mouth to his ear. "You're so fucking beautiful spread out like this for me." Duncan tried to calm his breathing while every nerve ending in his body screamed out for more of whatever Barkley had to offer. His hands were suddenly out at his side, Barkley's hands on top of his own, their fingers interlaced and holding on. "I'm gonna come, baby."

Duncan pulled his knees up slightly and pressed them against Barkley's sides, preventing Barkley from going anywhere. He wanted to feel this man on top of him when he finally rode out his own orgasm. Duncan squeezed the muscles that surrounded Barkley's dick, and he looked into his lover's eyes, delighting in the look of pure pleasure. "Come, baby," Duncan growled, straining his neck so that he could lick Barkley's lips. He moaned when Barkley's tongue came out and flicked against his.

"Oh fuck," Barkley yelled after a few more thrusts, his head coming to rest on Duncan's shoulder as he emptied himself into the condom. Duncan felt the throbbing of Barkley's cock, the sensation making him hard again almost instantly. He disentangled his hands and brought them to soothe over Barkley's sweat-soaked back, letting one travel north so that it was squeezing and caressing his lover's neck. "God dammit," Barkley sighed as he lifted his head to look at Duncan. "You're amazing." Barkley reached down between them and grasped Duncan's cock again. "Come here," Barkley said, his smile growing as he withdrew slowly, removed the condom, threw it in the garbage, and positioned their bodies for a sixty-nine.

"Jesus, you're hard again too," Duncan said just before taking Barkley into his mouth.

There was nearly ten minutes of hands and tongues and probing fingers until both men cried out at almost the same moment. Duncan pumped Barkley's cock and nuzzled and licked his balls while the singer rode out his second orgasm. And after Barkley's tongue teased the slit of his cock, Duncan felt himself going over the edge once more; he abandoned his sense of self-control and closed his eyes, imagining the day when there would be no more condoms and no need for self-restraint. Just thinking of finishing inside Barkley's magnificent ass was enough to push Duncan over the edge. He rode out his climax, releasing his grip on Barkley's hips and then caressing the exact same spot over and over.

"Absolutely fucking perfect," Duncan said as he rolled onto his back.

"I agree," Barkley said as he brought his body up to rest alongside Duncan's, kissing first his lips and then his collarbone before resting his head on the muscled shoulder. "And I thought I was pretty good too."

Duncan laughed and kissed the top of his lover's head. "If that's you being pretty good, I'm gonna have to start working out again." Duncan rolled over and straddled Barkley's hips, leaning over to look at Barkley's sated, playful expression. "Because if you get any better, you're liable to kill me."

"Don't worry," Barkley said as he brought a hand to the back of Duncan's neck. "You'll get plenty of exercise out on the farm. Come on. We'll shower and then go feed the kittens." Duncan didn't want to leave this particular moment, but knew that they had animals to look after.

"I hope we didn't scare any of them," Duncan said as he pushed himself to his feet and held out his hand for Barkley. "I never knew I could be that noisy."

"I liked that part the best," Barkley said as he wrapped his arms around his lover's neck. "Well," he said after he let one hand drop to slap Duncan's ass. "Maybe second best."

Duncan laughed and just shook his head. "I've created an insatiable monster."

Barkley's only answer was to kiss him passionately and deeply before taking his hand again and leading him to the shower.

"YOU HAVE a grey hair," Barkley said without really thinking about it. He'd been toweling Duncan's hair dry and noticed it behind his right ear.

"I'm surprised I don't have more," Duncan said.

"I'm sorry," Barkley said, realizing what Duncan meant by the comment. "I'm sorry you had to go through that."

"Hey, you've already said that," Duncan said with a smile and a kiss to Barkley's full lips. "And don't ever feel sorry for me. I haven't always had a perfect life, but if the good and the bad led me to you, it's a price I'd pay willingly, over and over again."

Barkley tilted his head to one side and smiled, pushing himself against Duncan's clean and naked body. "I know it's only been a week, Duncan, but I've never wanted anything as much as I want you."

Duncan brought his forehead to rest against Barkley's, his eyes closed, his hands resting on the smooth, warm skin of Barkley's shoulders. "You make me so happy, Barkley." He squeezed the solid trapezius muscles before skimming his hands along to the back of

Barkley's neck. "I want to help you on the farm. I want to help you save all of these beautiful, forgotten animals. I want to wake up with you beside me. I want to spend the rest of my life trying to thank you for being my very own angel."

Barkley wrapped his arms around the broad back, and he pulled their bodies together. Neither man spoke for a few minutes, each of them content to stand there holding the other. Barkley didn't know what was going through Duncan's mind, but Barkley wondered if any those wants would change if he ever learned everything about Barkley Reinhardt.

Chapter 20

BARKLEY MADE his way out of the cemetery, all seven dogs in tow, each of the leads threatening to trip him as the dogs jockeyed for a better view of the street and whatever loud noise happened to catch their attention. It had taken him almost fifteen minutes to coax Honey and Liberty to venture outside of the condo and then another twenty minutes before they felt acclimated enough to walk down the street. Barkley had begun to wonder if he shouldn't consider going back to school to become some sort of animal psychologist. On the way to the cemetery, Barkley had resigned himself to his true role with these animals: foster parent.

He'd now spent enough time with enough animals to realize that each of the animals—just like every human—had a unique personality. There were animals like Mozart who wanted nothing more than a sunny spot where they could nap in the afternoon, and there were animals like Shy Bunny who seemed content to stay in the same room all day long and only venture out for food and water. In any case, it didn't matter to Barkley whether every animal would respond to him like Tinkerbell and Honey; he would be more than happy to know that each and every animal he saved would find whatever they needed, either in his home or someone else's.

Even after speaking to Lori on the phone, just after Duncan hurried off to work this morning, Barkley still couldn't believe he had property in the country now, that he would be able to foster even more animals. He and Lori had discussed the ever-growing list of things that needed to get done, and yet, there were several moments during the conversation when Barkley still had to remind himself that he was discussing his very own farm. The most sobering realization had come, however, when he found himself approaching the cemetery; it hadn't been until that moment that he'd come to realize that he would not be able to visit his parents every week. And despite the fact that he'd not always been able to do so when he was touring and traveling the world, this move that would take him much farther away from them had been a conscious decision on his part. And his parents had not factored into the decision at all.

Barkley had sat in between the two graves, as he'd always done, and was somewhat relieved when he imagined that his parents would probably be happy that he was moving on. Not only would they be happy that he'd found someone, they would also be happy that he'd found something meaningful to replace a career that had, for some years now, left him feeling cold and alone.

He'd spent some time telling his parents about Duncan, whispering to them about how he was kind and caring and generous. Barkley wasn't naïve enough to think that they would never have arguments or disagreements or that the hour-long drive between the condo and the farm would not represent some frustration from time to time, but both men had agreed it was worth it so Barkley could continue his work with the animals. "Hey," Duncan had said late last night, "maybe I'll finally get around to writing that bestseller, and I can become one of those cranky writers who wears a sweater with patches on the elbows and smokes an empty pipe."

Barkley finally arrived back at the condo and hurried back inside so he could give the pups some water and then check on the kittens. He also decided that he should most definitely get out the Miele and do some serious vacuuming, especially in the spare bedroom where the kittens were. He hadn't realized how much hair there was in there until this morning when Duncan had sneaked up behind him. After sitting on the area rug in the spare bedroom to feed the kittens, Barkley was washing some bottles in the kitchen sink and Duncan had come to do some cuddling before leaving for work, only to come away with a ridiculous amount of cat hair on the front of his trousers. Barkley had tried to clean the trousers with a lint roller, but Duncan had finally abandoned the idea in favor of putting on a different pair altogether.

Barkley shook his head at the memory, setting out some clear, cold water for the dogs before heading to the spare bedroom. Duncan had not been too upset, however, and had even laughed when Barkley had made the amusing observation that Duncan should be glad Barkley's ass was not naturally that hairy. Whether Duncan had laughed to relieve some frustration at the situation or because he found it amusing, Barkley wasn't really sure. Duncan had probably been able to make up the time with a few quick sprints from the subway to his office, but Barkley had promised to ensure that there would be less hair by the time Duncan arrived home that evening. Barkley was also making a few other plans for when Duncan arrived home that evening.

After moving the kittens, who were still sleeping, out to the living room with Lumi, Rainbow, and Shy Bunny, he made quick work of the area rug and then headed back out to the give the kittens their bottles. As had been the case during every feeding, Barkley found his mind wandering in all sorts of directions. He thought about the farm, about what it would be like working so closely with Lori and John, and about all the tasks at hand for operating his new sanctuary.

He'd already decided to call Scott Alan and commission an original piece of music that he could have playing when the website was up and running. Nothing terribly annoying or intrusive, just something classical in nature that would also have a contemporary feel to it. He hadn't spoken to Scott since his long-time friend had fallen in love and moved back to British Columbia, but there had been the occasional e-mail over the past four years. And of course, Scott did owe him a few favors. It had been Barkley that had recommended a talented jazz singer by the name of Rankin to be a part-time replacement for Scott when he'd found himself wanting more time to compose.

Barkley would also have to make an appointment very soon with Lori and John's vet. They'd highly recommended her on several different occasions. Dr. Tara Flett had grown up around animals in Alberta before moving to Ontario to study veterinary medicine. Barkley had only ever met her once, but he'd been impressed by the strikingly beautiful, young doctor who did her job and did it very well, according to Lori and John.

And then there would be the move itself. Barkley still wasn't sure whether he would just purchase sturdy yet serviceable furniture or if he should take some of his parents' prized pieces from his condo. He was sure there would be animals in the house—probably on a daily basis—and he didn't want to take the chance that some of these beautiful pieces would be damaged in any way. He would miss them, of course, but he was sure that he could eventually figure something out that would help him keep the most treasured pieces safe at the new farm. *And besides,* he said as he deposited two kittens on the blanket so that Lumi could bathe them after their feeding and picked up two more, *Duncan will need some furniture if he's going to stay here during the week.*

Duncan. Just thinking of his name brought a smile to Barkley's lips. He still wasn't sure what it was about the man that made him weak in the knees, made him feel this overwhelming urge to protect and help him, but Barkley reminded himself he wasn't going to question it too much. He'd not always had much luck in love when he'd overanalyzed things and had had even less when he'd decided to be impetuous. Too many nights on the road traveling to parts unknown had led his loneliness to make some very poor decisions for him. And while he wasn't sure whether it was his head or his heart leading him with this man, he did know one thing at least: Duncan Spencer was hiding some deep wounds of his very own. *Perhaps we can help each other.*

DUNCAN OPENED his messenger bag for the umpteenth time. His laptop was not there when he checked it fifteen minutes ago, nor was it there when he checked it five seconds ago. "Fuck," he muttered to himself. *Dammit all to hell.* He knew he only had ten minutes to get that file printed out, or he was going to have to do some very quick digging to get himself out of the hole he would find himself in.

He picked up the phone, praying and hoping that Barkley would be home. *Home,* he thought as the panic gave way to a warm sensation that had nothing to do with the nervous dread he'd been feeling a moment ago. Duncan listened to the third ring and was just about to hang up when he heard that sweet voice.

"Hi, Duncan," Barkley said, his voice as seductive as ever.

"Barkley, I'm so sorry to bother you, but I think I left my laptop at home this morning, and there's a file I need within the next ten minutes or I'm dead."

"Okay. No problem. Do you need me to run it down to you, or—"

"No time. Can you just e-mail it to me and then I can print it off?"

"Sure," Barkley said. "By the way, you'll be happy to know that I just vacuumed, and you won't have to worry about getting fuzzy crotch ever again."

Duncan found himself laughing, wiping away the tiny beads of moisture that had accumulated over his top lip. "I told you I'd help you."

"I know, but I've been rather remiss in my cleaning duties, and I felt awful about it, so…."

"Well, then I will be sure to thank you properly when I get home tonight."

"Okay," Barkley said, and Duncan could hear some noises. He assumed that Barkley was now in the office and trying to locate the laptop. "Here it is. Do I need a password or something?"

"No, just open it up and it should be right on the desktop. A folder named *BrewsterBPD.*"

"Got it. Okay, now what's your e-mail address?"

Duncan recited it and fell into his chair, relief washing over him. "Told you," he said softly. "My very own angel. Thank you very much."

"My pleasure."

Duncan waited a few seconds, prepared to say *Goodbye* and open his e-mail so he could get that file printed. He leaned forward in his chair, placing one hand over his mouth. "I'll see if I can get away a little early tonight so I can meet you in the shower."

"Definitely my pleasure then too."

Duncan laughed again and looked around his cubicle. "Thanks again, Barkley."

"See you soon… hopefully."

"Absolutely. Bye." Duncan heard the line disconnect and reluctantly put the receiver back in its cradle. He moved to the computer keyboard and looked up at the screen, noticing the e-mail from himself with the file he needed. He opened it quickly, hit the print button, and made his way to the printer a few cubicles down. He was almost at the printer when he realized that there was another file folder beside *BrewsterBPD* on his desktop, a file folder that could end any happiness he might have found with Barkley. He only hoped that Barkley didn't find it before he got home.

BARKLEY SAT staring at Duncan's desktop for a moment. It was a picture of the Earth. A stunningly beautiful photo that had probably been taken from one of the many spaceships that had traveled to the moon during the last forty years. He wondered, briefly, before he heard the commotion in the living room, whether Duncan had an interest in astronomy.

Making his way very quickly to the living room, he wondered what the hissing was all about. He wasn't surprised to find that six of the dogs had decided to find a spot in the sunshine by the closed patio door. Nor was he surprised to find Zeus—curious, adorable Zeus—lying a little too close to the kittens for Lumi's liking. She was doing her best to move Zeus back a few feet, but for his part, Zeus only looked up at Barkley as if to ask, *What's her problem?* Barkley couldn't be sure, but if he had to guess what had caused Lumi to be in such a snit, it would probably be Zeus's overly curious nature. Up until now, Duncan and Barkley had done a pretty good job of making sure that Zeus didn't get too close, but with the unexpected phone call, Barkley had not even had a moment to realize that he was leaving all of the animals in the same room.

He wedged himself in between the kittens and Zeus, not sure whether to calm Zeus or Lumi first. The kittens did not really seem too bothered by the big dog. In fact, five of them were sleeping and two of them were making their way to the edge of the baffle. Zeus had found two kindred, curious spirits and was probably just introducing himself. And when Barkley managed to get the two wayward kittens turned around, and they both headed back to Lumi, everything returned to normal. Barkley had never had brothers and sisters and had spent most of his free time with piano or singing lessons, so he found himself wondering if having children would be a similar experience. Peace one moment, then all-out war the next.

Zeus rolled over, exposing his belly, and Barkley set to work rubbing and petting. He found himself wondering if Duncan wanted children. Barkley had never given it much thought while he was performing, but now that he would be on his own farm with plenty of time and love to give, he found himself reflecting more and more on the whole idea. One thing he was certain of was that he would definitely want to raise more than one. And he was sure that Duncan would agree. The loneliness of being an only child was almost unbearable at times.

Barkley gave Zeus's belly a final pat and then, under the watchful eye of Lumi, began to move the kittens back into the spare bedroom. With all of the kittens, Lumi, Rainbow, and Shy Bunny back among familiar surroundings, Barkley stood up to leave them to their midmorning nap, noticing that he had not powered off Duncan's laptop. He moved over to it and sat on the edge of the chair, taking one last look at the bright blue planet. He moved his finger over the trackpad and looked back at the screen to find the cursor, seeing a file highlighted in yellow.

BRBIO

He took a moment to look at the other file names, trying to decipher Duncan's system for naming files. It was one of those things that Barkley had always wondered about ever since he'd been in school. He was sure that there could be books written about the relationship between someone's psyche and what they choose to name a file. For simple clarity, Barkley had always chosen to name his files with complete words and sentences. Just like Duncan had done for all of his files except this one.

He knew he shouldn't, but curiosity about Duncan's past had gotten the better of Barkley on more than one occasion. He'd not tried to pester Duncan with questions, sensing that he didn't much want to elaborate on a childhood spent with a mother who didn't care about him, but Barkley was still human after all. He closed his eyes and clicked the icon for *BRBIO.*

DUNCAN ARRIVED at the condo, on edge and wondering what he would do if Barkley had noticed that file on his desktop. Of course, there would be an apology, and if Barkley was feeling generous, perhaps he would allow an explanation. Duncan had been debating with himself most of the day; he knew that Barkley was not the kind of person to snoop—he'd never asked too many questions about Duncan's past—but on the other hand, Barkley was also a human being. And human beings were curious by nature.

He closed the door behind him and greeted his welcoming party. He petted all of the dogs and squatted down, depositing his bag in the usual place, and waited for Tinkerbell to run from somewhere to greet him.

"There you are," he said with a smile and chortled when he saw Tinkerbell gallop up to him; she was still licking her chops when he scooped her up and nuzzled her neck. "And how was your day?"

He stayed squatted in that one spot until he'd greeted each of the animals. Duncan wasn't really sure if he was doing so because he loved and missed them or if he was doing it to avoid finding out just how badly he'd screwed things up. It wasn't until he was making his way to the spare bedroom that he realized that Barkley had not greeted him yet. Barkley had not even called out to him.

Duncan rounded the corner to the spare bedroom and saw Barkley sitting cross-legged on the floor, two kittens on his lap, each sucking eagerly from a bottle. Barkley didn't look up when Duncan said hello. It didn't take him long to realize that his laptop was still on the desk, open but in screensaver mode. A million and one thoughts ran through his mind as he tried to figure out how to broach this particular topic. Duncan always told the truth, and he would this time as well, but the only thing that he wasn't certain of was how to begin the actual discussion.

He walked over to the laptop and closed it. From the silence, Duncan knew that Barkley had done what most people would have done: he'd opened the file. And he'd probably read enough to realize that Duncan had been, in fact, lying when he'd assured Barkley that he'd not even written one word of the biography that had raised such vehement objections from the singer.

"I owe you an apology."

Duncan turned at the words, fully facing Barkley, his eyebrows knitted. "For what?"

"I got exactly what I deserved."

"Barkley," Duncan said as he sat down on the floor across from Barkley, welcoming Lumi into the hollow created by his crossed legs. "You have every right to be angry, and I swear it's the truth when I tell you that I was going to delete the file—" Barkley finally looked up and Duncan could see the red eyes, as if he'd been crying. "Please don't—"

"I'm not angry with you, Duncan," Barkley said as he added the last two bottles to the other empty ones at his side. "I'm disappointed but not angry. I am angry with myself, though."

"I'm sorry I disappointed you, Barkley. That's the last thing I ever wanted to do to the man who's done so much for me."

"I'm angry with myself," Barkley said with a sigh, continuing on as if Duncan had said nothing. "I kept telling myself that I could change, that I *would* change."

"Will you let me explain?"

"There's nothing to explain, Duncan."

Duncan looked down at Lumi still in his lap, and wondered if there was anything he could say to take that betrayed look away from Barkley's eyes. "Tell me what I can do."

Barkley sighed heavily and moved to stand, but Duncan placed his hand on the singer's knee. "I would like to be alone tonight. Please go."

Duncan looked up quickly and into the sad amber eyes. "Okay," he whispered softly. "I'll do that, but please don't tell me we're over."

"I don't know what to think," Barkley said, pushing away Duncan's hand and raising himself to his feet. Barkley started walking toward the door and then stopped. "Could you leave Lumi and Rainbow here… for the kittens? I'll be sure to get them back to you as soon as I can."

"That's very thoughtful of you," Duncan said, rising to stand as near to Barkley as he could.

"I apologize for opening that file," Barkley said again and then turned and left the room. A few moments later, Duncan heard a door close. He moved quickly to the hallway and noticed that Barkley was in the bathroom, probably so that Duncan could collect whatever belongings of his own that were in the master bedroom.

Chapter 21

"How LONG has it been? Six days?"

Barkley looked over the wall that separated the goats from Mr. Dill Piggle, the very large Arapawa Island pig that Lori had saved when he was just a piglet. She'd named him Mr. Dill Piggle because he'd had some sort of skin condition that made him look like a dill pickle. Barkley sighed, keeping his seat on the straw, one kid on his lap feeding from a bottle.

"Barkley?"

"Sorry," Barkley asked when he noticed Lori waving exaggeratedly.

"How long are you going to let him suffer?"

"I don't want to talk about it."

"I'm not a psychiatrist nor am I running some sort of halfway house for heartbroken homos who are only heartbroken because they're too afraid to face... whatever." Lori finished cutting the string on the last bale, quickly and efficiently scattering the straw throughout the goat pens. "And by the way, you know that kind of crap doesn't work on me. I don't give two shits if you don't want to talk about it. Now, I asked you a question. How long are you going to let him suffer?"

"I don't know, okay?"

"For fuck's sake, Barkley," Lori responded, her voice loud and clear in the spacious barn.

"He deserves better!" Barkley bellowed, wondering why Lori wasn't outraged by all of this. He'd explained it to her already, and he was pretty sure he'd already included this important line.

"I know. So why don't you go and tell him whatever's got you so twisted?"

Barkley stopped what he was doing for a moment and looked up at Lori, at her confused expression. "It's complicated."

"Yeah," Lori said loudly, her hands on her hips as she came over to tower above Barkley. "What isn't with you? Even the way you're talking about this has me confused, so I can't imagine how he's coping. I mean, you make it sound as if you've done something wrong, but then in the next breath, it sounds—"

"You know," Barkley spat, his eyes mere slits as he glared at Lori. "I wanted to come out here to help you and to visit my farm so I could start making plans for it."

"Christ, Barkley! You know you're welcome here any time you want. But can this shit about coming out here to help me. You came out here because you wanted someone to talk to." Lori pulled her gloves off and moved to the other side of the goat pen, reaching out to stroke Ro, the doe, who Lori had discovered to be pregnant, despite being in the female-only pen. "I hate to break it to you, but you're not holding up your end of the conversation!"

"I know," Barkley said petulantly.

"What is it with men?" Lori was palpating Ro's belly. "I thought you fags were supposed to be like women, except with a penis."

Barkley tried not to laugh. He had to admit to himself that she had him on that point, but he wasn't ready to listen to reason yet. "I'm sorry, but… I just can't talk about it right now."

"Jesus H. Christ," Lori groaned as she put her hands on her knees and pushed up to a standing position. "You know, you are so full of shit, I'm surprised you're not covered in flies."

Barkley laughed in spite of himself, letting the little goat he'd been feeding wander over to her two sisters. "Come on, I'll help you move Ro."

"She doesn't need any help," Lori said, bending over to pick up the two sisters. "We'll move these three to that last pen. I changed my mind. I'm going to leave Ro here."

"Why? What's wrong?" Barkley scooped up the remaining sister, the one he'd just been feeding, and nuzzled her neck.

"I don't know," Lori said, shrugging her shoulders. It was her attempt at playing it cool, trying to ignore that there might be something wrong. Ro had not been acting like herself for a few days now, and even Barkley had figured that there might be something amiss. "Tara will be coming out tomorrow to take a look at her."

"And I'm the one full of shit?"

"About Duncan? Yes, you are full of shit." Lori waved him out of the pen. He went without further comment and moved to the last pen on the north side of the barn, lifting the latch on the door. He and Lori put the kids down on the fresh straw that Lori had laid out that morning and then headed to the house for lunch.

"When will you be in your new place?" John asked as they sat at the long harvest table in the kitchen that also served as the makeshift hospital for injured animals, changing table for any of the little babies whom Lori insisted should wear diapers, and accounting central for paying bills and fulfilling online orders for calendars that Lori and John sold through their website.

Barkley shrugged, picking at his food. He sighed heavily and shrugged again. "I guess by the end of the week." Barkley leaned back in his chair and gave up trying to eat anything. He'd not had much of an appetite since he'd come to the decision that Duncan deserved better than anything he had to offer.

"Hopefully, you and Duncan will have worked everything out by then, as well."

Barkley looked up and smiled at John. He was a very quiet and very stoic man; of course, he'd have to be to marry someone like Lori. And Barkley didn't like keeping secrets from these two, but nothing good would ever come from him admitting the truth, to them or Duncan. This was the kind of secret that was better kept very close to the heart.

"He's a good man," John offered as he filled Barkley's glass with more lemonade.

"Yes, he is," Barkley said in agreement.

"Oh, for fuck's sake," Lori muttered, gathering up the dishes and heading for the sink. "Maybe Duncan's better off, now that I think about it."

"Hey!" John said, his brow furrowed, looking over at his wife.

"It's okay," Barkley said, taking another big gulp of his lemonade. "I wish I could tell you. I really do, but she's right. No use yelling at her."

"Barkley," John said, his voice soft and comforting. "We've known each other for so many years now, and if it hadn't been for you, we might not have been able to do this work that we love so much. Please, tell us what happened and maybe we can help."

"I'm sorry," Barkley said, standing up and shoving his hands in the pockets of his shorts. "I just can't." Barkley moved to the door and turned back to look at Lori and John. "I'd like to come back tomorrow."

"Of course—" John started to answer, but Lori cut him off.

"You're welcome here any time you like, Barkley." She stopped what she was doing and looked at Barkley when she said it, then resumed rinsing the dishes. "You moron."

John just shrugged his shoulders and walked over to the door where Barkley stood. "At least she didn't call you a *fucking* moron." The two men smiled at each other, and John reached out for the door handle. "Come on, I'll walk you out."

DUNCAN WAS on his own sagging double bed in his own tiny furnace of an apartment wondering, as he'd done all day long, what Barkley was doing. And when he wasn't wondering what Barkley was doing, he was wondering if he should grab the bull by the horns and go to Barkley, force him to listen. And in those moments when neither thought crossed his mind, he would find himself thinking about Tinkerbell, and he would try not to miss the little escape artist so much.

Even Zeus and Neptune seemed to be pissed at him for costing them a huge condo with a king-size bed and air conditioning. He rolled onto his side and looked over at the two dogs, fast asleep in their own beds. *Yeah,* he sighed, realizing he wasn't going to get any sleep tonight, *you sure fucked up the best thing that ever happened to you, Duncan.*

It was just past four in the morning, and in another fourteen hours, he would have been without Barkley for exactly seven days. Seven days. Almost as long as they'd been together. Duncan shook his head as he made his way to the kitchen, dressed only in his boxers, to get the coffee ready. He would have another busy day at the studio, and if he wasn't going to get any sleep, he might as well get as much caffeine as possible into his system.

His mind could not seem to stop playing those words over and over again. Barkley had apologized for reading the file. Duncan had not realized it until later, but Barkley had almost acted as if he'd committed the greater sin. But what could Barkley possibly have to feel guilty about? What was the connection between Duncan writing a first chapter of a biography, and Barkley acting like the guiltier party?

Duncan poured the water into the machine and sat down at the table, hearing the click of toenails on the worn parquet flooring. He saw Zeus's mug peek around the corner. He smiled at him and pushed himself off the chair to sit on the floor. Zeus came over almost immediately.

"Did I wake you?" Duncan pushed his hands over Zeus's head, playing with his ears and scratching lightly, just the way Zeus liked. Zeus responded the way he always did, by licking at Duncan's face. "I love you too, baby." Zeus closed his eyes when Duncan began to rub under his chin. "I'll figure this out," he said, wondering if the two dogs were as confused as he was.

As the water dripped into the carafe, the tiny apartment filling with the smell of cheap, no-name coffee, Zeus rolled onto his back and Duncan rubbed his belly.

"DUNCAN SPENCER." Duncan wedged the phone between his ear and his shoulder, trying to find that piece of paper he'd had in his hand not three seconds ago.

"Duncan? It's Lori. From the animal sanctuary?"

Duncan dropped everything in his hands, his blood running cold. His imagination, fueled by lack of sleep and too much caffeine, automatically assumed the worst. "Is it Barkley? What happened? Is he all right?"

"Oh my God, yes," Lori said, her voice rising an octave. "I'm so sorry. Barkley is fine."

Duncan let out the air that was trapped in his lungs and then took a deep breath. He leaned back in his chair, quickly glancing at the clock. It was just past three. He hadn't even stopped for lunch yet.

"I'm sorry, Duncan. I didn't mean to frighten you."

"It's okay, Lori. What.... Is there something you need help with?"

"Listen, I'm just outside your office building. I had to drive in for some supplies and to pick up a rescue, and I was hoping I could talk to you." Lori seemed nervous and Duncan couldn't help but wonder why one of Barkley's best friends would be calling him. Surely Barkley had told her what had happened. "I promise I won't take up too much of your time. Please?"

"Uh, okay, sure. I'll be right out." Duncan made his way to the lobby of the building, absentmindedly checking that his security pass was still clipped to his belt. He noticed Lori right away through the floor-to-ceiling glass of the front lobby, squatting down off to the left of the revolving door. She was pulling out a plastic bag from her back pocket and bending over to scoop up whatever the little poodle had deposited on the pavement. "You could have just asked to come in and use the bathroom."

"Funny," Lori said as she put the plastic bag inside of another and took a few steps to toss it into the nearest garbage can. "Thank you," she said as she returned to stand in front of Duncan.

"Who's this little guy? Gal?"

"This is Gizmo."

Duncan squatted down and held out his right hand, allowing the dog to sniff him. "Hello, Gizmo. You don't know it yet, but you are one very lucky little fella." Duncan looked up at Lori. "How is he?"

"Oh, he's fine," Lori said, shrugging her shoulders. "There's nothing wrong with him, per se, but the shelter called me and explained that he was showing some signs of aggression—"

"I meant Barkley," Duncan said, laughing and rubbing behind Gizmo's ears.

"Oh, sorry, of course."

"Do you want to take a walk? There's a little park just around the corner there."

Lori nodded and Duncan couldn't help but wonder what she had to say. This brazen and hilarious woman had seemed absolutely indestructible the one—and only—time Duncan had met her. He was very curious to see what had her so befuddled.

BARKLEY SAT on the grass just outside of his condo complex, waiting for Mozart to bring the bright yellow ball back. They had another twenty minutes of fetch before the kittens' next feeding.

"Come on, boy," Barkley said, encouraging Mozart as he headed back with the ball in his mouth. "That's a good boy." Mozart was only a few feet from him when he suddenly dropped the ball from his mouth and stopped, looking at something over Barkley's shoulder. As Barkley turned to see what had become more fascinating than a game of fetch, he heard the barking before he saw two dogs running toward them.

Barkley immediately stood when it appeared that the dogs were not about to stop, and went to stand beside Mozart. He reached a hand into his pocket so that he could get Mozart on his lead and whisk him back into the building at the first sign of trouble. But as the dogs approached, Barkley recognized first Zeus and then Neptune. He'd spent more than enough time with the two beautiful dogs to recognize those amazing coats and the unique coloring.

Of course, if Zeus and Neptune were here, that could only mean that Duncan was nearby. And sure enough, when Barkley squatted down to welcome the two dogs, he saw the tall, handsome man who had never been far from his thoughts over the past seven days.

"Hey, boys," Barkley said to Zeus and Neptune as they licked his face and hands. "I've missed you so much." Mozart barked once, as if he was insulted that Zeus and Neptune wouldn't come first to one of their own kind, and then Zeus and Neptune were off to greet their canine friend. Barkley stood up again and couldn't help but smile as Duncan finally reached him.

"Hi," Barkley said, feeling stupid and lost. He looked over at the happy reunion, the dogs wasting no time in nipping and playing, as if no time had passed at all. "He's been kinda lonely since we dropped off Honey and Liberty and the beagles."

"They sure missed all of you."

Duncan was now standing a foot away from him, and Barkley put his hands inside of his pockets so that he wouldn't embarrass himself by reaching out and touching him. He inhaled deeply, the familiar scent of this man's musk and his cologne calming his troubled mind like music used to do.

"Don't be angry," Duncan said, stepping a little closer, his voice hushed. "But I had a visitor today at my office." Duncan's smile was tentative and shy. "Lori," he said in answer to the question Barkley didn't think he had a right to ask.

"Oh," Barkley said with a sigh. "Sorry about that."

"No," Duncan said, reaching out his hand, almost making contact. Barkley's heart skipped a beat when he thought he would actually feel Duncan's hand on his skin again. "Don't be. We had a good talk, and that's why I'm here right now."

"What did she say?"

"She seems to have this crazy idea that you think I deserve someone better than you."

"Oh," Barkley said, his voice soft, as he looked down at his feet.

"Of course, I told her she was nuts, 'cause I'd never find anyone as wonderful and generous and unselfish as you."

"Duncan, look—"

"No," Duncan said, and Barkley looked up, taken aback at this reaction. "I don't know what's going on inside your head, and the only way I will is if you decide to talk to me. And I'll go away again, for good this time, if that's what you want. But I want to hear you say it. I want to hear you say that you don't deserve what I have to offer, that you don't deserve what you've given me." When Barkley didn't answer right away, Duncan tried one more time. "Look, I know there's been something on your mind. I'm perceptive enough to know that you abandoned singing and music and want to spend the rest of your life helping abused and forgotten animals because there was some sort of catalyzing event, but... I don't know how to tell you it doesn't bother me—and never will—unless you tell me what it is. Unless you trust me." Duncan reached out and took ahold of Barkley's hand. "Why did you apologize for reading that biography?"

Barkley looked down, closing his eyes so that Duncan would not see the shame in them.

"Baby, please."

"It was beautiful. What you wrote about me." Barkley glanced up for a moment and saw the look on Duncan's handsome face. Just as quickly, he looked back down at his own feet.

"Please, tell me."

Barkley shook his head and glanced over to see how much fun the three dogs were having while being together again. He looked back one more time and looked into Duncan's eyes. "I can't."

"Okay," Duncan said, letting go of Barkley's hand. "I'm sorry you don't trust me, Barkley. I'm sorry that you won't let me give you a second chance like you gave me by calling Edward and arranging the interview. And I'm sorry that you won't give me a chance to show you that nothing you'll ever do could possibly make me feel any different about you." Duncan whistled for his dogs, both of whom obeyed immediately, despite how much fun they seemed to be having. "I'll make arrangements to have Lumi and Rainbow picked up whenever you think is best. Goodbye, Barkley."

Barkley had tried to be stoic, but at the sound of *goodbye*, his face fell in on itself and the tears seemed to come from nowhere. "Please," Barkley said, a mere whisper in the cool night air. He watched as Duncan stopped and turned. "Please," he repeated. "I'm sorry, but...." He hiccuped and brought his hands up to wipe at his eyes.

Duncan walked back to him, his arms enfolding him almost immediately. "It's okay," he said, his voice soothing. It was this Barkley missed the most: these tender words that were meant only for him. The way Duncan was when it was just the two of them. Duncan pressed his lips to Barkley's temple, a small kiss against the heated skin.

"You think I'm generous and unselfish," Barkley said finally. "But I'm not."

Duncan pulled back, his arms still around Barkley, his face a study in confusion. "You're gonna need to explain that one to me."

"What if you hate me?"

"Okay," Duncan said, his hands coming to rest on Barkley's shoulders. "I don't know how many different ways to say this, but there is nothing, and I do mean nothing, you could ever say that would make me think you are anything but kind and generous and giving and my very own angel. We all have baggage, Barkley. Do you remember me telling you that?"

Barkley wiped at his eyes, his breathing returning to normal.

"How about this?" Duncan wrapped his arms around Barkley again. "Evidently, I haven't earned your trust yet." Duncan held up a hand when he saw Barkley open his mouth. "And maybe that's my fault. Maybe I should have come by and thanked you with a handshake and asked you out on a proper date. So, how about I call you tomorrow and we can go for a walk or I'll buy you an ice cream cone or something."

"I do trust you," Barkley said, interrupting.

"Obviously, you don't," Duncan said. "But I don't mind taking it more slowly, you know, so I can prove to you that you can trust me."

Barkley disentangled himself from Duncan's arms, missing the contact almost immediately. "Will you come back inside with me?"

"I don't think—"

"Please? Please don't make me tell you out here."

"Okay," Duncan said, then whistled for Zeus and Neptune, who'd gone back to playing with Mozart.

Once back inside the condo, Barkley put out some food and water for the dogs, not surprised to find Tinkerbell lying on Duncan's lap. "She missed you. She's been very angry with me."

Barkley heard the mewing from the spare bedroom and went back into the kitchen to fetch the bottles. "Would you like to help?"

Duncan picked up Tinkerbell and nuzzled her neck. He stood and followed Barkley into the spare bedroom.

They set to work, each feeding two kittens at a time. Finally, Barkley took a deep breath and began to talk.

"After I read all of the wonderful things you'd written about me, I was sitting here, like we are now, feeding the kittens, and I couldn't help feeling like I'd lied to you." Barkley waited for Duncan to interrupt or to ask a question, but he remained silent. He continued feeding the two kittens in his lap. "I started crying and couldn't stop myself. You wrote about what great people my parents must have been to raise someone who was so dedicated to making a difference in the world. But that's who I am now. At least that's who I thought I was."

Within moments of each other, each of his two kittens finished feeding and he lifted them off his lap and put them back into their makeshift bed, Lumi going to them almost immediately and cleaning them.

Barkley watched as Duncan did the same with his two. Barkley took two more, leaving Duncan to take the last kitten. Barkley found it a little easier to confess his sins when he had something else to focus on. "When my father died, I was performing at La Scala and I remember being really angry at how inconvenient it all seemed."

"But that's normal—"

"Not because of the performances I'd miss, but because I was seeing someone and my father's funeral would be during the time I'd wanted to spend with him." Barkley didn't look up, not really wanting to know what Duncan thought about this admission. "And when my mother died...."

"Barkley, they knew you loved them. They knew—"

"She was lying in the hospital bed, asking for me. I was only an hour away by plane, in Montreal, and I never picked up the phone because—" Barkley took a deep breath and continued. "The other guy was history, but then I'd been introduced to Marc Desrochers, the real estate developer from that television show." Barkley felt sick to his stomach, but he took another deep breath. "The phone was ringing in the hotel room. I didn't know it was to tell me my dying mother was asking for me. I was too busy...." Barkley remembered that night, receiving the news only after he'd satisfied his lust for the television star.

Duncan finished feeding his kitten and reached out a hand and placed it on Barkley's knee. "Barkley, look at me."

Barkley did, trying to blink away the heat from behind his eyes.

"None of that changes what I wrote in that first chapter." Duncan's thumb was rubbing soothingly over the skin of Barkley's knee. "You had no idea what that phone call was about. Hell, I knew my mother was dying, and I still stayed away. Didn't even go to her funeral. I don't even know where she's buried." He moved his hand so that it was cupping Barkley's jaw, his thumb caressing his cheek. "Nothing you've told me makes me feel any differently about you or about us. It just tells me you're human. And it doesn't change what you're doing for Lori and John or for these animals. These animals don't care why they're getting a second chance, why they're getting a safe place to live out the rest of their lives. It seems that the only one who's judging you right now is you."

Barkley felt a small smile transform his face as he moved his head and kissed Duncan's palm. "There were all sorts of crazy thoughts in my head when I read that first chapter. I thought about the promise I'd made myself that I wasn't going to let myself get swept away in another romance that would only end up making me hate myself. If only I'd been able to control myself. I read all those things you'd written, and I just knew I'd let myself move too quickly again. But this time, I would end it before you learned the truth... before I could hurt you any more. And then when I had that run-in at the shelter with that asshole, I couldn't help but feel guilty that I'd be dragging you into the limelight again and then each time—"

"Okay, so that settles that." Duncan nodded his head, obviously pleased with the decision he'd made. "The pups and I will be going home tonight and I will call you tomorrow and we'll have a proper date. We'll take the pups for a walk or stay in to watch a movie, and then I'll go home with Zeus and Neptune and we'll do it all over again the next night, and the next, and the next...." Duncan smiled and Barkley felt, for the first time in almost a week, as if he wasn't completely alone. "And when you're sure, I'll still help you with the farm, I'll be right beside you when you wake up every morning. And you'll still be my very own angel." Duncan leaned over and kissed Barkley on the lips. "And as for the limelight, the only person's opinion I care about is yours. And you like me."

"I do, very much."

Duncan said nothing, only leaned over for another kiss.

Epilogue

THE SNOWFLAKES had been falling off and on for the better part of three days, blanketing the trees and buildings that made up the Peaceful Coda Animal Sanctuary. Barkley had tossed around so many ideas for naming the sanctuary, not really able to settle on any one in particular until one fateful afternoon, when he was preparing for one of his penultimate performances. He would be singing Mendelssohn's *Elijah* again in October and had noticed the coda in one of the arias. And it had hit him from out of the blue: *coda* was Italian for tail, which seemed fitting by itself. Additionally, however, a coda was the musical symbol that would signal the end of a movement or a section of music. So, why not call the Sanctuary something with the word *coda* in it? Many of the animals would not only have a tail, but each animal was at their final, loving home; some of them in their final moments. And even though the mere thought was not a pleasant one, the symbol for the coda would make a very nice marker for those animals who would eventually leave the sanctuary for the Rainbow Bridge. Names of the animals, and perhaps dates as well, could be engraved or stamped on the metallic markers. The coda would serve as a reminder to treasure these final moments, to continue the work that gave Barkley's life more meaning than singing ever had.

As he lay there, Duncan snoring softly beside him, Barkley realized that he was finally happier than he could ever remember being. It was because of the man who had fulfilled his promises to help him on the farm and to wake up with him every morning—or as many mornings as he was able. And it was because of this man who lay beside him that Barkley was finally able to recognize why he had been behaving so badly while he was off the stage. Of course, on some level, Barkley had been cognizant enough to deduce that he was self-destructive because he resented his life and the intrusions that came with being an internationally renowned singer, but had never been astute enough to figure out how to walk away from it all.

Rolling over, Barkley placed a quick kiss on Duncan's cheek and then shivered as he threw the covers off himself. He wondered if the furnace was acting up again. The repairman had been out so often during the autumn months that Duncan had joked that they should be getting him a present for Christmas. Of course, the furnace was only months old now, so it was more likely that Barkley would have to call in some contractors to assess the state of the insulation. He made a mental note to call around after Christmas holidays.

Christmas, Barkley thought as he looked over at the sleeping figure beside him. *First Christmas with Duncan.* They'd been together now for six months, six incredibly happy and exhausting months. Setting up the farm, even with John and Lori to guide them, had proved much more work than either man had anticipated. Barkley had missed three days in October, but his contractual obligations were down to only three more performances next April and then he would be a full-time farmer. *Poor Duncan. My beautiful Duncan*, Barkley thought as he pulled on a sweater to go over his pajama shirt. *He never complains about working all day at the station only to come home and work until midnight making sure all the animals are fed and cared for and the barns are cleaned and the food is sorted and stored.* Barkley thought about all the work they'd done and began to feel exhausted, fighting the urge to fall back into bed.

As he'd done almost every morning, he awoke before first light to go out and feed the animals. He would put his boots on, load up the white buckets with bagels and baguettes and bread rolls and whatever other kinds of treats the animals loved to eat and then make his way through the gauntlet of llamas, donkeys, horses, sheep, goats, dogs, cats, raccoons, and one very cranky, ornery bull. Some of the animals were transplants from John and Lori's sanctuary, and some were brought specifically on the recommendation of Dr. Tara Flett.

Barkley and Duncan had been fortunate in finding her. Of course, Dr. Flett had come highly recommended by John and Lori, but Barkley felt sometimes that they'd found a friend and not just a vet. They'd even had Tara, her husband Cory, and Cory's brother William over for a couple of barbecues. William was studying to be a vet in Guelph, as well, and Tara had hired him as her own veterinary assistant.

Barkley made his way to the back door, where he would find his boots, the ones that had recently split up the back and that Barkley never seemed to have enough time to go out and replace, and his parka. He stopped short when he reached the landing, looking around for a moment and wondering where he'd put his boots.

"Merry Christmas."

Barkley turned to see Duncan standing behind him, both of his arms extended, a brand-new insulated winter boot in each hand. Barkley laughed and pushed his way between the boots, intent on kissing the man. "God, I love you."

"Love you too."

Barkley felt the boots hit him in the ass as Duncan's arms came around him, pulling him close. "You know Christmas is two days away, right?"

"I know, but I thought you could use them right now."

"When you're right, you're right." Barkley took the boots and, putting one hand on Duncan's shoulder for balance, slipped first his right foot into one boot and then his left into the other. "Oh yes, yes," Barkley moaned when he felt the plush interior.

"Stop it, or I'm gonna drag you back to bed."

"Speaking of which," Barkley said as he moved to the back door and pulled his parka and snow pants off the hook. "Go back to bed and get some sleep. I'll be back soon, I'll get breakfast going, and then maybe I'll let you have your way with me."

"Maybe?"

"You are not that irresistible, Mr. Spencer."

"I seem to remember you moaning a different tune last night."

Barkley zipped up his snow pants and made a show of rearranging himself. "I don't know what you're talking about."

Duncan laughed and Barkley smiled, never tiring of making this man laugh. Duncan had given up quite a bit to keep his promise of helping out on the farm. And Barkley would make sure that he never regretted making that promise.

DUNCAN WAITED patiently while Barkley exited the house. Once the door was closed, Duncan set to work. First, he had to find Stinkerbell.

"Stinkerbell!"

She had not been on his pillow this morning. She wasn't really a kitten anymore, and Duncan knew that on some level she would not always behave like she had six months ago, but it didn't quell the disappointment when he found she wasn't beside him some mornings.

He made his way through the house, hearing the baby goats stomping in their pen. Barkley had decided to keep them in the house instead of the barn because they still seemed frail to him. They had been brought to John and Lori's sanctuary as one-week-old babies, and no one really expected them to survive, but with round-the-clock care and all the love and warmth that two grown men and a house full of cats and dogs could lavish on them, they'd become two thriving miracles.

Duncan called out for Stinkerbell one more time before releasing the kids, Dolly and Parton, from their pen. It had been Duncan's idea to name them Dolly and Parton. He'd thought it would sound funny when anyone called them by name. Of course, no one else thought it was funny, but Duncan just figured that showed a lack of imagination.

The two kids started racing around, jumping and stomping, while Duncan got out the box of diapers. He called them over, laughing at the names again, and wasn't surprised when they came right over. He put a diaper on Dolly first and then patted her on the bum, telling her to go wait for her bottle in the living room. Parton was always a little less cooperative when it came to the diaper. But within a few minutes, Dolly's brother had a diaper as well and was racing Duncan to the living room.

Duncan made a quick stop in the kitchen to heat up the bottles and then parked himself on the sofa, Dolly and Parton coming over as soon as they saw the bottles.

"You know what this means, don't you, Dolly Parton?" Duncan held the bottles while the two kids each got the right amount of suction. He closed his eyes for a moment and heard a little mew coming from behind him. "Is that you Stinkers? I've been looking for you." He tried to turn around, but couldn't quite make out which cat was behind him. After a few moments, a familiar face appeared on his right. Tinkerbell perched herself on the arm of the sofa and waited patiently. Duncan leaned over, careful not to break the suction on the bottles, and nuzzled Tinkerbell's neck. "Are you ready to give Barkley his surprise?"

Tinkerbell mewed softly and jumped off the arm of the sofa onto Duncan's lap, seeming to settle in for a nap while she waited for Dolly and Parton to finish with their bottles. Tinkerbell was purring, the kids were feeding, and the house was starting to come to life. Zeus, Neptune, and Mozart entered the living room one by one, and Duncan greeted them, promising that their bowls would be filled very soon. And then Lumi and Rainbow came around, followed by the seven grey kittens. They weren't really kittens anymore, but Duncan would always think of them as those little balls of toothless fur that had been the beginning of his sleep deprivation.

"Morning, beauties," he said through a yawn. "How is everyone this morning?" He smiled as each of the cats wandered into the kitchen and sniffed their bowls. Dolly and Parton finished their bottles within moments of each other and then bounced happily away, going from one canine sibling to the other looking for someone to play with. When the dogs only appeared interested in licking them, the two kids pranced amongst their feline siblings, much happier when the cats seemed more interested in playing.

Duncan picked up Tinkerbell and made his way over to the kitchen and filled each of the bowls, being sure to put the exact same amount in each. He didn't want any fighting this morning; he had a few things to arrange for Barkley's return from the barn, and he didn't want any distractions arising from the cats thinking their siblings had gotten more than the rest.

With the food bowls filled and the water bowls almost finished, he reached into the pocket of his pajama bottoms and pulled out the dark-blue box. He opened it and pulled out the ring and the blue satin ribbon he'd stuffed in there last night. Once he'd threaded the ribbon through the ring, he squatted on the floor and tied it around Tinkerbell's neck. Duncan was quite certain Barkley would notice that Tinkerbell's collar had suddenly changed color. Duncan felt a slight pang of guilt as he watched Tinkerbell paw at the ribbon almost immediately. "Hopefully, he'll notice right away, Stinkers."

Satisfied that his plan would work without a hitch, he set to making coffee and breakfast. If all went according to plan, he and Barkley would be back in bed as soon as breakfast was over. And with any luck, there might even be an hour or two for a nap before they headed back out for the noon feeding and to finish a few chores around the farm.

"Holy Dinah," Barkley said as he came back into the house. "The sun is shining, but that wind is relentless."

Duncan scooped out the scrambled egg substitute onto two plates and threw in a dozen slices of tofu bacon before putting the homemade bread in the toaster. "Breakfast in five."

"Time for me to make some more bread, I guess." Duncan watched as Barkley did a quick survey of the food. He checked the breadbasket on the counter, then moved over to the fridge, opening it and pulling out the orange juice before studying the rest of the contents. "I'll do some grocery shopping tomorrow early in the morning," Barkley said as he deposited the juice on the table. "With any luck, we won't have to drive anywhere until after New Year's."

Duncan was just setting everything else on their plates when he heard Tinkerbell start to mew, loudly. He said nothing and tried not to grin. He watched as Barkley abandoned his inventory and made his way over to the cat.

"What's wrong, Stinkers?" Barkley picked up the cat, a perplexed look on his face.

"Breakfast is served," Duncan said as he deposited the plates on the table. When he turned back to face Barkley, he saw the singer moving toward him, the blue ribbon—with the ring still attached—in his open palm. "How were the performances?"

"You didn't read the reviews?"

"No, too busy with work and chores," Duncan said as he sat down at the table, following Barkley's lead. Duncan wasn't about to give anything away; he noticed Barkley toying with the ring, but said nothing about it. "It was hard having you gone for almost the entire week."

"I'm sorry," Barkley said, still playing with the ring. "I'll work extra hard this week if you want to take some time off."

Duncan took a sip of his coffee and reached over to take the ring from Barkley. "Not what I meant." Duncan, the ring still in his hand, took Barkley's hand and pulled him over until the singer was sitting on his lap. "There was almost an entire month of you rehearsing and playing the piano, filling the house with that wonderful music." Duncan kissed Barkley's chin, his free hand traveling up to try to tame the wild runaway tufts of hair. "But last week, it was quiet without you here. Too much silence."

Barkley put his arms around Duncan's neck, smiling. "There's only one more contract I have to fulfill and then you'll never be rid of me again."

"Is that a promise?"

"Absolutely," Barkley said, taking the ring from Duncan's hand. "I promise to be around to paint pictures on the silence anytime you want."

"I love you, Barkley."

"And I love you, more than you'll ever know." Barkley held up the ring and smiled. "I'm ready to make one other promise too."

"Oh yeah," Duncan replied. "And what promise would that be?"

Barkley put the ring back into Duncan's hand and smiled before leaning down to kiss Duncan's beaming face. He sat back and winked. "You'll find out once you ask the question."

When D.W. MARCHWELL is not teaching future generations the wonders of science, he can usually be found hiking, writing, riding horses, trying new recipes, or searching for and lovingly restoring discarded antique furniture. A goofy and incurable romantic, D.W. admits that his stories are inspired by actual events and that he has a soft spot for those where boy not only meets boy but also turns out to be boy's soul mate. After almost fifteen years of working his way across Canada, D.W. has finally found the perfect place to live at the foot of the Canadian Rockies. He still can't believe how lucky he is, and, as his grandmother taught him, counts his blessings every day.

Visit his web site at http://www.marchwellbooks.ca/.

You can contact him at dwmarchwell@hotmail.com.

The Good to Know Series by D.W. MARCHWELL

http://www.dreamspinnerpress.com

Also from D.W. M<small>ARCHWELL</small>

Also from D.W. MARCHWELL

D. W. MARCHWELL

A Still, Small Voice

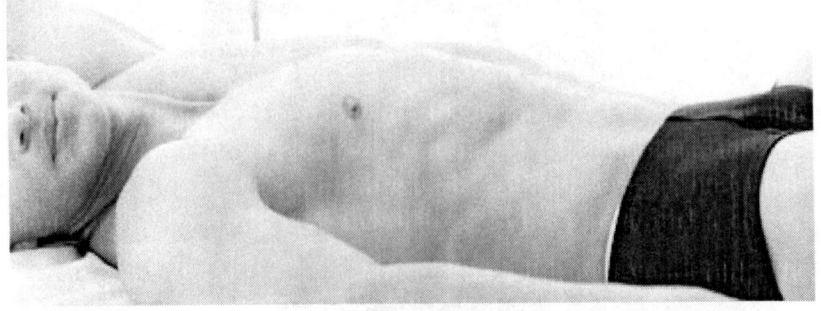

http://www.dreamspinnerpress.com

Also from D.W. MARCHWELL

WHEN
MEMORY
FAILS

D.W. MARCHWELL

Translated Titles from D.W. MARCHWELL

http://www.dreamspinnerpress.com

CPSIA information can be obtained at www.ICGtesting.com
Printed in the USA
BVOW04s1712250914

368139BV00009B/522/P